J. Lad

CAR
TROUBLE

outskirts
press

Car Trouble
All Rights Reserved.
Copyright © 2018 J. Ladd Zorn Jr.
v1.0

This is a work of fiction. The events and characters described herein are imaginary and are not intended to refer to specific places or living persons. The opinions expressed in this manuscript are solely the opinions of the author and do not represent the opinions or thoughts of the publisher. The author has represented and warranted full ownership and/or legal right to publish all the materials in this book.

This book may not be reproduced, transmitted, or stored in whole or in part by any means, including graphic, electronic, or mechanical without the express written consent of the publisher except in the case of brief quotations embodied in critical articles and reviews.

Outskirts Press, Inc.
http://www.outskirtspress.com

ISBN: 978-1-4787-9370-0

Cover Photo © 2018 thinkstockphotos.com. All rights reserved - used with permission.

Library of Congress Control Number: 2018900503

Outskirts Press and the "OP" logo are trademarks belonging to Outskirts Press, Inc.

PRINTED IN THE UNITED STATES OF AMERICA

PRELUDE

"Ashes to ashes," he chortled. "Dust to dust." Whirling devils of it seemed to follow him, engulfing and choking as he trudged through the sage. Even now, he thought he could hear the distant pop of bullets echoing off the rocky hills. Mostly, he kept taking steps. The singing had stopped, but he didn't do much thinking. When he did think, he wondered how he had gone from working as Disneyland Goofy two days earlier to walking away from a smoldering car full of assault weapons the middle of the Nevada desert. He pictured Ben with the pile of hundreds on the table back in Anaheim, and even now, he couldn't imagine doing anything differently. He knew, though, that everything had been set in motion long before that. Maybe if he had taken all those guns to a pawn shop he might have had a more desirable outcome—he laughed and coughed at this thought, and realized he was very thirsty—but then God knew how many people, maybe even good people, would not be killed now thanks to Jim. He licked his dry lips with his sandy tongue and thought, I'm a hero. *I am a God-damned hero.*

PART 1

INTERNAL COMBUSTION

"*Oh, give me a home,*" Jim Crack sang despite the ache of a blow to the hinge of his jaw, back in the olden days before cell phones. He trudged down the sidewalk on the soles of his shadow's shoes, eyes stinging from exhaust and whatnot. When everything in the world was already owned, and for over a hundred years there had been no West to go for a young man, then your own Little House on the Prairie might be a wonderful little dream to sing about to distract you from the murderous feelings plaguing you on the way to your stupid job, especially after this latest development.

Half an hour earlier, Jim had been screaming obscenities on the shoulder of the Santa Ana Freeway as smoke billowed out the back of the twenty-one-year-old 1973 Volkswagen Squareback, a car as old as he was, which his one-time stepfather, Josh Wesley, had bought for $999 after the engine in the old Buick Jim's father had given him had seized up on the way to that same father's fourth wedding. The car hadn't lasted six weeks, the marriage even less.

"Get a new rear-view mirror. It'll be a good little car, easy to work on," said Josh.

The mirror had fallen off the windshield and was fractured by four straight vertical cracks. Rather than get a new one, Jim had reattached it, which made for unsettling lane changes, and it was not lost on him that the mirror kind of reflected his own past. If only he'd gotten a new one, maybe it wouldn't have been so hard to get over when he smelled the smoke. It was at once incredible and expectable. After all, "Car Trouble" was his middle name, some said. "Jim 'Car Trouble' Crack," he'd said to Tink when he'd first met her. "That's what they call me."

CAR TROUBLE

She crinkled her nose. "Crack?"

"They changed it at Ellis Island. It was something like Krazcyckz." He spelled it for her. "At a family reunion once in New Jersey they told me it means anger." He didn't have any idea what it meant and had never been to New Jersey, let alone out of California but one time, and then only barely, but sometimes he didn't know what to say, and would make things up, especially if it might prolong a conversation with a beauty like Tink.

"In what language?" she asked.

He shrugged.

"It sounds Polish," she said.

"Maybe. I don't know. My grandfather came here from Yugoslavia after the first World War..."

"...*where the buffalo roam*..." Thirst rasped his voice, but he sang to stem the torrent of hatred in his throat for anything manmade. Just driving to work and the sonofabitch started smoking. He had been having trouble with his starter. Tried to fix it himself, probably wired it wrong. Even with the smoke filling the inside of the car, he kept driving, hoping he could get to work and have a look at it after his shift, but the engine cut out on him. The whooshing of the freeway over the radio sounded like silence when the thrum of the motor ceased. He stepped on the gas but got no acceleration. In the fast lane, coasting slower and slower, signaling right, his ticker palpitated unevenly, horns honked, and a Benz bore down on the gap that would have gotten him over. He searched the pieces of the broken mirror for an opening. There were sixteen lanes in it. They were all full of cars. He steered into the emergency lane and braked to a halt.

Cars whizzed by, as he hopped out, went around back, and popped the latch on the hatchback. "Gonna fucking be fucking late, again," he muttered, yanking the rug off the floor and pulling the pins to lift the lid over the engine where a little flame danced, divided in two, and

PART 1: INTERNAL COMBUSTION

stuck out its tongue.

Jim blew on it.

The flame danced faster and divided again.

"Fukfukfukfukfukfukfuk..." Jim said.

He blew and blew, like at prank candles on a birthday cake, but the fire kept coming back. He threw the rug over the flames, trying to smother them, but soon the rug was on fire, too. "Hell," he said, tossing the rug to the cement.

Four lanes of speeding traffic stood between him and the freeway call boxes. "Ford's Fury," his stepfather, who had been a tanker driver for Shell, and who was fond of scribbling out the S's on any document with the corporation's name, had called the mayhem of cars that had overtaken the country. Normally at this hour, the Five freeway through Orange County would be clogged, but today, the traffic cruised smoothly, marooning him on an island of concrete twenty feet wide and a thousand miles long. Jim looked to the north. The concrete stretched under an overpass and out of sight. How long did it go on like that? To Canada? He turned around. He was astounded to see a palm frond growing out of the dust in a crack in the asphalt. *Probably at the Mexican border I could get across*, he thought. He started in that direction. What was it, like a hundred miles? Two days of walking? Surely before then the traffic would thicken to the point where he could just walk over the hoods of all the cars to get to the other side, to get food and water and such things as humans need to survive.

"Fuk, fuk, fuk..." He had taken his pills that morning, but he ground his teeth trying to keep all the motherfuckers and cocksuckers from escaping. Even still the steady, "Fukfukfuk," slipped through his lips. He turned and walked backward, waving for assistance, as if anyone in the Southern California hurry would do anything more than slow down for a look. ZZZimZoomzoom. The freeway created its own weather; the wind mussed his hair. He turned back around and walked in the hazard lane, his thoughts becoming black-and-white static. A quarter mile farther he heard the rumble of a diesel grow suddenly behind him. He turned. In a rickety landscaping truck with a slatted wood fence running around its bed, piled high with lawnmowers and the jiggling severed limbs and rooted stumps of a dozen trees, a crew of leathery-skinned Latinos jabbered, Jawa-like, to Jim; they reached out their hands and pulled him in.

A silver-toothed old Mexican smiled wryly. "Jew ca is on de fier," he said.

"Goddamotherfucking piece of shit," said Jim.

The man nodded knowingly. "Jew having to chang de hose in de Volkswagen. Es no good. Da hose de la gasolina, de rubber es bad in Volkswagen." He shrugged. "Jew needing de neoprene, pero es too late now."

The old truck had managed to merge back into the traffic, creak across the freeway, and stop at a call box. Jim climbed over the wooden slats back onto the asphalt. The landscaping crew wished him luck, but he didn't know. He thanked them hoarsely, and the truck groaned a moment and lumbered back into the river of traffic.

Jim picked up the phone.

"Roadside Assistance." She sounded pretty. "Do you have an emergency?"

"An emergency?" *What constitutes an emergency?* he wondered. No one's life was at stake. "Uh, not exactly. My-"

"Name, please."

"Jim Crack ,c-r-a-c-k, Crack. My car—"

"Do you require roadside assistance?"

"Yes! My car—"

"Read the call box number at the bottom of the sign."

"Five six six seven."

"License plate number?"

"Uh…you know, I don't know. I've only had it a few weeks."

"What's the make and model of the vehicle?"

PART 1: INTERNAL COMBUSTION

"It's a '73 Volkswagen Squareback."

"Color?"

"Yellow." Jim turned around. A quarter mile behind, a pyre had engulfed his car. "With orange, red, and bluish flames and black smoke pouring out the fucking back."

"Sir?"

"It's on fire. My car is burning on the 5 southbound, north of Harbor Boulevard." He slammed the phone into its cradle. Then he picked it up and slammed it again. And again, and the mouthpiece shattered, and the speaker spilled out and hung from its wires, and Jim staggered back a few yards and fell against a slope of ice plant. He closed his eyes against the sting of the sun. What did this mean? He folded his arms on his knees, rested his head on his arms, and felt dull and senseless for a while, until he noticed in the roar of the freeway the pat pat pat of blood drops drumming the toe of his sneaker. A piece of the shattered phone had left a gash in the flesh of the web of the thumb on his phone-slamming hand. He pulled off his shirt and wrapped it around the wound. He thought he heard distant sirens and guessed he better try to get back to his car. The phone swung and swayed slightly, like a man on the end of a noose, and Jim walked to it and placed its remains gently back in its box.

By now enough smoke belched out the back of the VW that the traffic had become that maddening stop-and-go in which whenever Jim was stuck, he would curse to Hell whoever was the cause. Now he could cross the glacier of steel and glass with nothing more challenging than an irritated honk and one "Get off the road, asshole!" Someone else hasn't taken their pills, he thought as he jogged toward this car. When he was about fifty feet away he stopped short. Would the car explode? Or had he seen too many episodes of *CHiPs*?

"Fuck it," he muttered. It was something he muttered often, and usually it preceded a period of minutes when all planning ceased. Jim went into a state of pure action and reaction. He bolted into the creeping traffic again, dodging between cars, and was nearly across when an orange Pinto swung out from behind a mini-van and with a screech of rubber on pavement, it was rammed from behind by a big Ford pickup, and the Pinto slammed thigh-high into Jim. He jumped as he was struck, was flipped over the hood, and came down in such a way that for a second his lips slid across the windshield like a suckerfish before he was tossed to the road, scraping the heels of his hands and tearing holes in the knees of his jeans.

He rolled onto his back with a groan. The sun stared into his eyes and he shut them. "Oh, my God! Are you okay?" said a woman's voice. He opened his eyes again and looked into a silhouetted head with a halo glowing around it.

"Am I dead?" he joked.

"Chris, go to that freeway phone and call an ambulance."

"It's broken," Jim said.

"Oh, my God! What is? Your leg? Your back? Don't worry. We're calling 9-1-1."

"What year is this?" he joked again.

"Oh, my God. It's 1992. You must have amnesia. Just lie down."

That would be fun, he thought. He sat up. "That phone is broken." When he talked, he could feel that his lip was numb and fat.

"You're delirious. Lie back down. You shouldn't move."

"What the fuck! Look at my truck," said the guy who got out of the pickup that had rear-ended the Pinto. "What the hell were you thinking, cutting in front of me like that?" He spat a stream of tobacco juice.

"Excuse me. There's a young man hurt right here. I think that's a little more important right now."

Chris came back. "That phone is broken."

"Oh, my God. We've got to try one of those farther ones. One of you go that way, and one of you go that way. I'll stay here with him."

"He's fine. Look at my truck. You got insurance?"

Jim got slowly to his feet. Their backs were turned to him, and he

PART 1: INTERNAL COMBUSTION

began to sidle away. He was sure he could hear sirens. Cops and firemen and ambulances. Paperwork and questions of responsibility. He could see the Harbor Boulevard off-ramp. He edged toward it. "Oh, my God. You shouldn't be moving!"

Jim took off, sprinting as fast as his sore legs allowed, determined to leave all thoughts of that car behind, already forgetting it.

By the time he reached surface streets, his lungs were doing the Big Bad Wolf and his sneakers were floppy-stomping over gravel and broken glass, crushing ants, and he remembered one day his step mom called him Mister Peanut-Butter-Leaver-Outer and told him to put the jar away.

"It's empty."

"Then throw it in the trash."

A trail of ants ran up the side of the trashcan. "There's a bunch of ants here."

"Spray them."

Jim opened the cabinet under the sink and took out a can of Raid. He stood up again and watched his step-mom a few seconds, who was watching a man and woman rolling around under the covers of a bed. He stepped to the drawer with the matches, slid it open, removed a book, slid it closed, and slipped the matches into his pocket. She didn't notice.

He followed the ants across the fake-brick linoleum floor, up the corner of a cabinet, across the countertop to the windowsill, spraying them with poison. Outside, he picked up the trail again, dropping spit bombs on their little ant highways, and he wondered as they struggled in his sticky, Kool-Aid-red saliva, if there were little ant families in their little ant living rooms wondering why daddy wasn't coming home. Along the edge of the house he traced the path of the ants, raining Raid. The line of ants moved over the driveway, some coming and some going, bump head, move on, bump head, move on. Through fractures in quake-cracked concrete, they commuted to holes in the earth on the edge of the lawn where Jimmy delighted in stomping the ground to see their tunnels collapse before he took the matches from his pocket, squatted, and watched with scientific fascination how their little bodies curled up under the flamethrower he'd made, until he spotted his father's car coming down the street. Jim stuck the matches in a squirrel hole and stood up as his father pulled into the driveway. Jim's dad got out of the car with his tongue between his teeth, eyes burning ice-blue.

"What were you doing?"

"Mom told me to kill the ants." Not my mom.

"You playing with matches?"

Jim looked down.

"Come here. Right here." Jim's father clamped his hand around the back of Jim's neck, his thumb and fingers pressing hard against both jugulars. The constriction of the blood flow to and from his brain felt like the strain of heavy lifting, or like trying to force along a stubborn bowel movement. He was used to it. His dad steered him into the house. It was much darker in there now.

"What happened?" Jim's stepmother asked.

His father pushed him along into Jim's bedroom and closed the door before he let go of Jim's neck. "You still don't know any better? How can you be so stupid?"

Jim felt light-headed, felt far away. "I don't know."

His father unbuckled his belt and pulled it slithering off. By now Jim was gone. Ha ha. He'd learned a neat trick. He could crumple up his soul inside himself, roll up like a rollie-pollie pill bug. He felt little, until later in bed, in the dark, when he refilled his body, and his skin crawled with ants that weren't there.

More of a stuttering stomp was Jim's stride now as with each step a pain shot up from the bottom of his sole, where a sharp bit of gravel

PART 1: INTERNAL COMBUSTION

had pierced the worn-thin rubber. He tried to ignore it by playing the old "step on a crack, break your mother's back" game. As he did, his shirt—polyester, maroon, with gray polka dots and an oversized '70s collar—jerked along as it dangled from where it was wrapped around the hole in his hand. It had been his father's. Jim wore it because it was outlandishly out of fashion, and, on some level, he must have realized that it pissed off the old man to be reminded that he had once dressed in such a way. Jim remembered playing the game on the way home from school when he was young, jumping on each crack, trying to get home as slowly as possible.

The shadow of the monorail unshriveled his squint as it came by, touching his thoughts off in another direction. Why couldn't it all be monorails? Monorails and horses. Jim rounded the corner of the razor-wired backside of the park onto the street with the big HAPPIEST PLACE ON EARTH sign. The monorail passed, and the sun reappeared in the colorless sky, pinkening Jim's shoulders beneath its glare. Bits of glass twinkled on the concrete, and the sun dazzled where it glinted off the traffic, all chrome and mirrors and windows, metallic, mechanical, rushing and halting at the red and green lights. Jim wondered what time it was, and he kicked something that clattered into the gutter.

He stopped and stooped. An old Zippo lighter had somehow found itself abandoned to the sidewalk. He picked it up and opened it, the metal hot in in his hand. His clean-cut reflection grimaced back at him, flecks of rust mingling with the freckles on his face. Balancing and hopping on one foot, he turned the other foot up and used the open edge of the Zippo top to dig out the pebble that had been wedged in the bottom of his shoe. He closed the lighter, put it in his pocket, and resumed walking, but his stride felt no less off-kilter, as if the phantom of the pebble remained lodged in his sole, subtly hobbling his progress.

A high hedge of oleander masked the barbed wire around the park. Specks of pollen and dust, like little galaxies, floated in the sunbeams that fell through leaves. A tickle of cough seized Jim's respiratory system and he hacked up a glob of mucous and spat it arching end over end where it splattered against a NO PARKING sign and hung bulbously toward the curb. Threads of blood in it, he noticed as he passed, and he worked his hand into the pocket of his jeans and extracted his inhaler. He shook it up, took a big hit, and tried to hold his breath as long as he could. At an intersection, a man in a turban and a woman with a red dot on her forehead and two children with Mouseketeer ears waited for the light to turn. The children's eyes widened and bulged, and they grew closer to their parents' thighs as Jim approached.

"Howdy, Swami," Jim exhaled. A memory flickered of Steve Brody addressing Bugs Bunny in a turban with the same greeting, just before Brody jumped off the Brooklyn Bridge. The man's watch glittered around his wrist. Jim eyeballed it and shoved his fists in his pockets to where his pants rode low on his hips and orange hairs kinked out above the waist band of his boxers, he rocked back on his heels and smiled his one-sided smile with its dead-center gap, pointed to the back of his wrist and asked, "Have you got the time?"

The man's eyebrows arched into worried question marks as the electric red hand turned into the white pedestrian, and he gathered his family and shooed them ahead of him across the street.

"What's the matter?" Jim called, hoarse voice cracking. "Does my shirtlessness offend you? Aren't you from India? Fucking Mowgli didn't wear no shirt! See what kinda Karma this gets ya!"

Then it went internal: *Anybody wearing a watch would know what I was wondering; why's the guy gotta shun me? Do I look bad? Do I scare people?* He shrugged and muttered, "Fuck it," and laughed finally, knowing he was late anyway.

When the light turned green, Jim crossed the street again. The sidewalks became more crowded, he had to turn his shoulders at right angles to maneuver through the clumps of women pushing baby strollers, men with tots on their backs, and children bouncing like Tiggers.

PART 1: INTERNAL COMBUSTION

He came to another corner and almost went around it but did a tango-like turn around swivel on his heel and paused. It had become a habit to stop at Adam and Pete's before work. He didn't have any time now, but he was already late anyway. He held the inside of his wrist to his heart, and with his index finger, he pointed like a metronome, left then right, at each of the two ways he might go, while silently he incanted, "Eenie meenie miney mo, catch at Tigger by the toe, my mother said to pick the very best way, and you are it." His finger pointed down Harbor Boulevard, not the right turn to the employee entrance, but the way to Adam and Pete's. It probably wasn't the right thing to do, but he had already done the eenie meenie, and it would have been bad luck to go against it now. Being Goofy would have to wait.

His father, head of security, had gotten Jim the job. He had at first been assigned to sweep Tomorrowland, spilled popcorn mostly, and the stray frozen-chocolate-covered-banana wrappers that didn't quite make it to a trashcan in Fantasyland, but he was the right height for Goofy, and the pay was thirty cents more an hour. So, the operators of the Magic Kingdom paid Jim to roam the park as the real-life, flesh-and-blood, fabric-and-plastic version of their animated, ink-on-celluloid, enormously buck-toothed, dimwitted, talking humanoid dog (except Jim wasn't allowed to talk). He had come to love being in the suit. People were happy to see him. Little kids—well, not the littlest ones, who got scared, but kindergartners—would shriek with joy when they spotted him, and would laugh their holy laughs if Jim jigged a little or played peek-a-boo. Even grown women, beautiful ones, would hug him; one even fondled him one time. He got to be in all the pictures, and everybody smiled. Out of the costume, no one noticed him. People wouldn't even give him the time of day.

He crossed Katella and proceeded past the family restaurants and motels, his reflection warped in the windows, gangly, elbows and knees pointy, nose sharp and pointy; the corners of his mouth were just that. "GODDAMN MOTHERFUCKING CARS!" he saw his reflection blurt through his twisted face. A hotel maid coming the other way went wide around him. "Aren't cars man's most evil invention?" he asked her. "Polluting the air, sucking up oil, putting villains in power, covering the world in concrete, killing and maiming every day." He walked backward to keep talking to her. "And you gotta have one! You gotta have a car to have food! They won't let you have any food if you don't have a car! Gotta have a car to go to work, and gotta work to pay for the car."

He was mumbling now. He turned and walked forward again. He had tried riding the bus to work once. He'd walked a mile to the bus stop and waited. Rode the bus, stopping every half mile to pick people up and let people off, vacant-eyed, dreary, silent people, hopelessness etched in their faces, exuding from their pores a stale soapy-sweaty odor. He got off the bus and waited for another bus. Rode it to another stop and waited for another bus. Got off and walked to work. Did the same home. It took longer than sitting in traffic.

"And just try to get a date without one!" Jim walked past a man sitting in an idling Jeep Cherokee. "You know your car is named after a slaughtered people?"

The man rolled up the window, and Jim walked away as a waitress opened the door to a dented up ten-year-old Escort with a mismatched door. She drove off in a cloud of bluish smoke, and Jim fell into a trance staring at the rainbow-streaked puddle of oil left behind.

Another car pulled into the space, and Jim slapped himself, shook his head, and moved on. The motels and diners dwindled the farther he got from the park, the people vanished, and soon there were only cars driving by. Weeds struggled up through slabs in the concrete where Jim turned the corner onto a residential street. Jacaranda roots buckled the sidewalk, and only the sound of a far-off gas-powered leaf blower broke the silence. He crossed the street. It was the first time all day he hadn't had to wait to cross a street. The sidewalk ended, and he walked down the road, asphalt crumbling against variously maintained

PART 1: INTERNAL COMBUSTION

lawns. A willow wept over an old Lincoln on blocks in the yard of a two-story house peeling white paint. Jim strode across overgrown crabgrass, kicking up dandelion paratroopers, to where a wooden staircase ran up the side of the place, and he ascended to a door there. He tried the doorknob and knocked. No one answered. He returned to the ground and studied the house.

In a floor-length window upstairs, curtains undulated ghost-like in the breeze. Jim went around back of the house and returned pushing a wheelbarrow with a screeching tire, and he leaned it against the house under the window. He took a few steps back, humming the Spiderman jingle, and bolted forward up onto the upturned wheelbarrow; he vaulted upward and caught the ledge of the windowsill. He pulled his chin up, his wounded, shirt-wrapped grip struggling to hold, feet scrabbling against the side of the house; he got in up to his waist, ass hanging out, legs kicking to swim in, his upper half tilted forward, and he fell into the gloom.

A room merged with his dilating pupils: a coffee table cluttered with bottles and cans, a couch of indeterminate colors, a pizza box and newspapers on the wooden floor. He stood up, and with his first step, kicked over a bottle that went rolling under the couch. In the kitchen, past a sink stacked with crusted dishes, he opened the refrigerator where there was a small collection of mold-filled Tupperware. He closed the door and cleared enough space off the top of the pile of dishes in the sink to cup water in his hand from the faucet to his mouth. A dozen slurps later he turned off the water off, went to the couch, and plopped down.

The coffee table was nicked and carved into with initials and dates. Among the cigarette butts and other debris, a naked woman squatted over the carrot nose of a reclining snowman on the cover of a magazine with blurbs boasting "CUM HUNGRY SLUTS." A tall blue bong towered over everything else. Jim picked it up and examined crumbs of black and white char in its bowl. He held up the bong to the light from the window and peered into the black water through the clear blue plastic. He thought about pouring the water through a coffee filter, or even a paper towel, and nuking the dregs in the microwave until they were dry, and smoking it. Or he could have scraped the tar out of the stem and smoked that. He spotted a pair or roaches in a bottle cap, though, and picked them up and pressed them into the bowl of the bong. A matchbook lay among the table's detritus, but it was empty, the burnt, ripped-out matches strewn about its carcass. He reached into his pocket and pulled out the Zippo he'd found on the sidewalk. He flicked it, and it sparked but did not flame. He pulled an imitation brass ring on a door in the side of the coffee table. Magazines spilled out glossy and pink, and so did a can of lighter fluid he wished would be there and miraculously was.

He soaked the fibers in the bottom of the Zippo with fluid, inhaling deeply as he did. A few flicks of the lighter later, he had flame, and he put the bong to his lips, his thumb to the carb, touched the fire to the roaches and sucked smoke through the gurgling water. He sucked and sucked and sucked. "I suck," he thought. "I suck; therefore I am," he thought and giggled, struggling to hold the smoke in while he did. He regained his composure, kept sucking, and when he could hold his breath no longer, he sucked a little more, took his thumb off the carb, and cleared the chamber with one final spasm of inhalation. He held his breath as long as he could, allowing as much time as possible for the molecules to enter his bloodstream, counting Mississippis, until, like one of those free divers who go as far down as they can with no oxygen, he turned back for air and broke the surface gasping. His blood thump-thump-thumped in his head. A helicopter flew low over the house with an X-ray camera adding this to his list of crimes. Jim took a deep breath and his jaw unclenched and something inside him unclenched, and his shoulders sagged and his eyelids drooped.

He picked up the phone and dialed carefully. A tube of Krazy Glue lay on the end table. He picked it up and played with it nervously as

PART 1: INTERNAL COMBUSTION

the phone rang on the other end; he uncapped it, took a sniff, wondered if he could use it seal the gash in his hand.

"Disneyland Personnel. How may I direct your call?" she chirped like an animatron.

A gluey saliva bound Jim's tongue and palate. When he'd succeeded in parting them, he said, "Extension one zero one."

"One moment." Children sang about a world of laughter, a world of fears, a world hope, a world of tears.

"Mr. Fleming's office."

His heart pounded. He cleared his throat. "This is Jim Crack. Mr. Fleming told me I needed to speak to him personally the next time I was going to be late for any reason."

"Just a moment." The children sang that it was time we're aware.

"Hello." Impatient.

His head pounded. Wombwombwomb, it went. "Mr. Fleming," Jim's voice regressed several years, the voice of a boy; the pitch went up. "It's Jim Crack." Silence on the other end. "My car caught on fire." Preposterous. "I know I said I wouldn't be late again. I'm going to be a little late. I'm waiting on tow truck right now, and then I've got to see about getting a ride. I don't know how long it will take, but I'll try to get there in time for the parade."

"I'm sorry to hear that," he said cheerfully. "Your role will be covered. However, as you know from our last meeting after your suspension, this means the termination of your employment here." A silence followed. Then, "Good luck in your future endeavors." Click.

Jim sat. It was strange not to be moving. Nothing was moving. The curtains did not flutter. The ceiling fan was not whirling. The VCR glimmered 12:00 interminably. Jim looked at his hand on the couch and thought to move it, to assure himself that time had not stopped. He thought to give the command, to send the impulse down his arm, but it didn't happen. High was not the word to describe him. Low was. Had some severity of gravity pinned him to that couch? He remembered how the smoke used to lift him and send him off like a dog escaped from the backyard, trotting away from his owner, sniffing along down the street through a happy world of new sensations—until the owner drags you back by the collar. It used to be fun. But now he was stuck. Like a quadriplegic, he tried to rise, but the pattern in the couch was jamming his neurotransmitters or something. His feet were on the floor, but his weight was on his ass, and it was physically, scientifically impossible for his ass to lift his body. Had he forgotten how to get up? Maybe if he leaned forward, transferred more of his mass over his legs, pushed off with his arms—but his arms seemed to just sink into the cushions as if he were sitting on a tar pit, or some black hole had formed beneath his butt. He struggled to find a thought, an idea, something, anything he cared about. His eyes searched the room and fell upon the remote control on the coffee table. Television! Television would save him. If only he could reach the remote. He strained to raise his arm out from under the nothingness that engulfed him, extending outward; his fingers yearned for the remote, like Luke Skywalker using the Force to telekinetically summon his light saber. A bead of sweat rolled out of his hair and down to the point of his nose and hung a moment before falling into the abyss. The remote jiggled ever so slightly; the toe of his sneaker had jarred the table when, with a supreme exertion of will, he leaned forward enough to snatch up the remote control.

Jim pressed the POWER button and the TV clicked on, but the screen was a cartoon blue. He tried to change the channel, but the screen stayed blue. He pressed PLAY. A naked woman appeared, palms and soles flat on the thrashing bed, arched backward, joints locking and unlocking, supported by the hands of a man on her ass, the shot staring into her open legs, his turgid penis plunging in and out of her. It was fascinating, the innocence and wisdom of their act. Wasn't it one of life's rare natural pleasures? The lucky bastard. Jim wished he was the guy. His hand roamed to his zipper and clenched into a fist.

PART 1: INTERNAL COMBUSTION

Weren't they Hell-bound fornicators? Ugh. How had sex become linked with evil? Men thousands of years ago wanted to make sure they controlled who women fuck, so they made up all kinds of rules about it. The people on the screen were like animals now, rutting without humanity. Or were they more human? Weren't they sharing themselves with each other and anyone who cared to join in through the camera? Jim couldn't decide if they should be commended or condemned. The contradictions sixty-nined each other; he grew disgusted and turned it off. But it was too late. Not again, he thought. He turned it on again. He'd been doing it a lot lately, even on his break, slipping into the bathroom and unzipping the Goofy suit, the big shoes showing under the stall. Sometimes a fraction of a woman's form spotted for a millisecond through the crowd fifty yards away would overwhelm his thought process, and the idea would have to be dealt with, or it would never go away.

He'd never forgotten his first orgasm, years earlier, before he even knew what one was, before anything even came out, without even touching himself, looking at photos of simulated sex acts in a review of a nude stage show in a *Playboy* from the short stack his dad kept on the back-bathroom toilet tank. Mysterious shudder of body and mind. Before long he'd had the idea to repeat the feat by humping the couch while his stepmother was out, and then there was a rumbling on the steps and a tinkling at the door.

It was Adam. Jim dropped his penis and stood up, pants around his ankles, semen webbed between his fingers. He flung it off, pulled up his pants, switched off the porno, and was wiping his hand behind his knee when Adam stepped in after a day of working as a Campbell's Soup rep.

"What's up?" asked Adam.

"Uh," Jim zipped real quick. "Nothing."

"Haven't seen *you* for a long time. Where you been?" He walked to the refrigerator, untucking his shirt, and opened it. "No beer." He picked up one of the glasses off the table and wiped the rim with the tail of his shirt. "I don't even know why I want it. We partied on the peninsula last night, and I was hurting at work all day and swore I'd never drink again. I swear to God, I think I need to just get out of this shit." He walked around the house picking up near-empty bottles and poured the remains into the glass. He looked around the place and shook his head. "And I'm not going to be the only one to clean this place anymore, either." He spotted the bottle Jim had kicked when he came through the window sticking out from under the couch and picked it up. "Aha." It was a half-full bottle of Herradura. "I got paid today, but I'm not going to spend a penny of it. On Monday, I'll take it straight to the bank and deposit all but fifty bucks that I'll live off until next month. I can eat soup. I gotta quit drinking, man. I'm thinking of heading back to Utah…."

Adam was, in his own words, a jack Mormon, who had mostly abandoned the church's precepts forbidding drugs and sex. The indelible image Jim had of him was from Fourth of July a year earlier, the both of them shrooming at a house on the beach. Adam was wrapped in a toga of the American flag, leaning against a wall in a hall down which the light reflected off the Pacific, mumbling repeatedly, "How do they know? How could anybody possibly know?"

Jim had first met Adam over the course of that booze-soaked Independence Day weekend. He had gone down to Newport Beach the night before the Fourth, and Adam was among the friends of the friends of the people with whom Jim had found himself when he woke up the next morning on the concrete strip between the house and sidewalk that was the porch of whoever's house it was.

"Better get up and start drinking before our hangovers kick in," Adam said.

Jim opened his eyes, staring up from where he was lying on his back on the concrete. Adam's head floated in the corona of the sun between the wispy clouds. Jim sat up wincing, and Adam handed him

PART 1: INTERNAL COMBUSTION

a can of beer.

"Wish we had some weed," Jim said.

"I wish we had some mushrooms," said Adam. He was balancing like a tightrope walker on a two-brick-high wall that separated the porch from the sidewalk. Practically moments later, a long-haired guy with blue-flame tattoos down his forearms walked by, pushing a baby carriage. "Got any 'shrooms?" Adam asked.

It was the weirdest thing. He did. As if by divine order, he met them in the alley behind the houses. He gave them a cap and a stem each and told them if they wanted any more, he'd be out on the beach. They ended up buying all he had. It was an amazing day. Jim saw exactly what was real and exactly what was bullshit. He saw that man had become a perversion of his true nature, stuck in offices and traffic all day, saw that cars, and VCRs, and lawnmowers had nothing to do with life. He believed he would renounce consumerism and practice peace. All that was necessary was food when you were hungry and warmth enough against the cold. Saw that the world would be provident if people would share, would just quit hoarding it all, fencing it off, and paving it over.

A year later, though, sitting there in Adam's place, Jim felt low and hopeless. He hadn't followed through on any of it, thwarted by habit, by the impermanence of love, by carnivorism, and the fear of no health care. Without his medicine, he'd be dead. If he wanted to live, he had to go to his job. It felt wrong. He felt like a slave. Freedom was a hoax. Wrong. It was all wrong. How to feel right? He seemed to remember feeling right before, babbling joyously, full of animation, people listening, laughing. What happened? He hardly talked anymore. He didn't want to open his mouth and have people learn how wrong everything was. He couldn't figure out precisely what it was that was so wrong, but it seemed something hugely prevalent that should have been obvious, something right in front of him, in his head. He was surrounded by lies, but the origin of their construct was too rife with possibilities to be brought into focus, and his wrong feeling remained intact, indistinct.

Sure, the car going up in flames explained some of what was wrong, and he knew it was going to be a hassle beyond even what he could conceive, but everything had been all wrong long before that. It seemed to go back as far as he could remember, which may have been the day when he was six, and his parents argued over whether or not he had to finish his cold, dry meatloaf, and they finally told him they would divorce. Everything before that was blank. They'd hated each other, and of that, he was made. If that was what made him all wrong, why couldn't he just get over it? People dealt with worse burdens. He felt aborted after the fact. *I just need to get away from myself. Do all the children of divorce grow up to feel as wrong as I do? No, that's just an excuse to deny myself any responsibility for being wrong. It's my mommy and daddy's fault I'm like this. Knock it off, you little self-sorry pussy. I need to make changes. Get into the here and now. Get into the here and now somewhere else. There's got to be a way.* He began to pray silently to feel right again, and the phone rang.

Adam, Jim noticed now, had been talking the whole time and stopped to answer the phone. "Hey, girl!"

Jim's ears perked up. Adam's tone was the one you used with girls you wanted to screw, and if anything might save him from despair, it might be a pretty girl who might want to screw. It had to be Tink.

"Who is it?"

"Pamela. Shut up."

"Dick, let me talk to her."

"Uh-huh," Adam said into the phone and gave Jim his best "Yeah, right" face, pursing his lips and squinching his eyes, and then he opened his mouth into a wide smile, and let his tongue wag out, and did a little dance, and flipped Jim off. Jim grabbed for the phone, they tussled a few seconds, and he succeeded in wresting the phone from Adam's grip. "Pam-mala! I couldn't stand for you to have to listen to that dork

PART 1: INTERNAL COMBUSTION

when the whole time the better man was right here in the room."

She laughed for him. "Are you going to come party with us? Some of my girlfriends are here from out of town. We want you guys to come entertain us. We might go dancing. You've got to come."

"You are my savior. You don't know how bad I need to have fun tonight. I promise you an all-out, knock-down, drag-out, party, high, fun and games up the yin-yang night to remember for all time!"

"Yeah. That's what I'm talking about. Good, then. Get your asses over here. But I better not hear you calling me Tink. Bye."

Jim put the phone in its cradle. He heard the shower running and Adam singing. He went into a trance, examining the holes in his pants and the fraying canvas of his shoes. Adam soon dripped out of the bathroom with a towel around his waist and went into his room.

Jim went into the bathroom and wondered what he looked like beyond the shroud of steam that clung to the mirror. He often had trouble recalling his own face; it seemed the product of infinite variables of light, time, and place, and what was going on in front of it, and behind it, rather than the composition of any set structural features. He rubbed a circle of steam off the mirror, baffled by what he might find. The end of his nose was the first thing about him. It was somewhere between an aquiline nose and Woody Woodpecker's beak, except at the end where Jim was convinced his septum deviated wildly, the cartilage in one side sliding south of the other with tectonic implacability. From there, the bridge angled straight up to his forehead as if drawn with a protractor, where two vertical lines of —concern?— were etched between his eyebrows. He leaned forward, peering into his pores, and pinched his skin between his fingernails, fascinated with revulsion at the white squiggles that wormed out, and he got a corner-of-the-eye close-up of the gash in his hand. He looked in drawers and was amazed to find Band-Aids and gauze and white tape. He tore the tape with his teeth and stuck a patch of gauze over the wound. He threw his bloody shirt toward the trashcan in the corner, already overflowing with toilet paper rolls, and he went into Adam's room.

"Lemme borrow a shirt."

"No. You'll rip it or lose it or get shit all over it. You got come stains all over the last one."

"That was snot. I got allergies, man. Gimme a break; it'll wash out."

"Yeah, right. What do you know about doing laundry?"

"How about this one?"

"No way. Pamela gave me that one."

He put it on.

"I said no."

"What are you gonna do? Are these Pete's shoes? They fit all right. I'll wait for you out front."

The car Campbell's Soup had given Adam to drive, a beige, FBI-looking sedan of inconspicuous make and model, clicked and ticked as it cooled in the driveway. The door was locked. Unassembled cardboard soup displays littered the back seat, and Jim spotted his skateboard among them. He'd been looking for that. He thought it had been stolen by a surf punk with dyed red hair who had been lurking around the party where Jim had last remembered having his skateboard, and Jim was going to kick his ass if he ever saw him again. He must've left it in Adam's car, though, drunk.

He bent down to the side view mirror and gave a big cheese to inspect his teeth wherein resided The Gap in his top incisors. "Gives me character," he would say to anyone who brought it up. He nearly murmured it to the face in the glass, and the glistening, pinkish-red plastic mold of the roof of his mouth flashed behind his eyes: the metal wire retainer that he was supposed to wear to keep in check the chaotic drift of his teeth, teeth that had been stacked one behind the other, and turned sideways, either because they were too big and too many, or, as one orthodontist said, his mouth was too small. He'd had eight teeth pulled, all during the same procedure, before his braces had been put

PART 1: INTERNAL COMBUSTION

on, including four impacted wisdom teeth, ripped from his jaw the day before eighth grade graduation. His cheeks had swelled up like a chipmunk's full of nuts. Jim hadn't wanted to go to the ceremony, but his stepmother that year insisted he go, backed by his father's impassive stare. He heard every variation of junior high cracks about having nuts in his mouth, mainly the testicular kind, so by the time he stepped up to receive that highly self-esteem-affirming eighth-grade diploma, some of his classmates were chanting, "Nuuuuuutface! Nuuuuutface!" as he walked across the stage. The pain perplexed him. It wasn't the kind he was used to; it couldn't be outlasted. The one good that came of it was that his father had said he was proud of Jim for going to baseball practice later that day after the nitrous had worn off. Jim had wanted to go, and his father told him he was tough. But that little tidbit had become lost in The Gap—The Gap that was still in his smile after thousands of dollars in orthodontics, because he kept losing his retainer after the braces had come off, lost it in the sawdust on the gym floor at homecoming, threw it away in the paper bag his lunch came in, and because he ground his teeth at night—

"Nice do."

Jim straightened up and turned around as Adam was turning the key in the deadbolt at the top of the stairs.

"Never come the day any pussy-ass mousse touches these locks," Jim tugged a clump of his old-penny hair. "At least I don't spend chick time in the bathroom like some homos I could name."

"Why don't you hawk up some of that Crack mucous? That would probably hold down that Alfalfa cowlick you've got sticking up out of the top of your head."

"I'm stupefied. That's the first time any of your smack has ever been even remotely funny."

Adam came down redolent of perfume or aftershave or whatever; Jim didn't know the difference. "I hope you know you're driving," Adam said.

"Wrong."
"Where's your car?"
"In car Hell."
Adam looked at him. "I'm not driving."
"Give me your keys."
"You can't drive my car."
"You drive, then."
"I can't risk another DUI."
"So, don't drink." Jim hissed a laugh.

"Just be careful, please." Adam handed over the keys, and they got into the car. Jim put the key in the ignition and tried to turn it, but it wouldn't budge. "Sometimes it gets stuck," Adam said. "Turn the wheel back and forth. It's in park, isn't it? And push the brake down. Take off the parking brake, too. You want to kind of push it in and pull it out at the same time while you're turning it, and jiggle it a little."

"Push it in and pull it out at the same time?"

"Yeah, and jiggle it and turn it on."

"I love it when you talk dirty," said Jim, but six minutes later the car still hadn't started.

"GODDAMN MUTHERFUCKING COCKSUCKING PIECE OF SHIT!" An intensely guttural rush of frustrated anger burst from Jim, and he hit the roof hard three, four, five, six times, and tried it again. It started. Adam looked out the window. "Fuck," said Jim and pulled out of the driveway and onto the road.

"We need beer. Let's pull in here." A red neon arrow curved down through the approaching dusk into the flashing word LIQUOR. They parked and walked in and stood in front of the hum of the beer aisle. "What should we get?" asked Adam.

Jim's teeth hastened their decay. "Whatever. As long as it'll get us buzzed."

"Lucky Lager? Or will the girls think we're too cheap?"

PART 1: INTERNAL COMBUSTION

Jim smirked.

"How much have you got?"

Realization plowed Jim's brow as he felt his back pocket. "My wallet was on the front seat."

"You don't have any money again?"

"A fiery hand reached into the world from the engine of my car and stole my means and identity."

Adam looked at him quizzically. Jim could almost feel the heat of the fire again, and he pressed his face against the cool glass in the beer aisle. "Please tell me you have some money," Adam said.

Jim straightened up and opened the glass door. "If you're worried about looking frugal in front of the girls—then, here." He handed Adam a six-pack of Heineken, and one of Amstel Light. He put a six-pack of Sam Adams under his arm, opened another door and grabbed a couple of four-packs of wine coolers. He walked to the cashier, snagging a bottle of Bacardi in two unoccupied fingers, and laid it all on the counter.

"ID," said the Vietnamese-looking clerk, who gave Jim a look that wondered if he would have to kill Jim.

"I'm not paying for all of this," said Adam.

Jim looked at himself in the convex mirror in a corner of the store. His deformed head curved long down into the shirt on his shrunken body. A video camera mounted above the counter showed them in a monitor nestled among the fifths of Jim Beam. He wiggled his fingers, and the Jim on the screen wiggled his fingers. He looked directly into the camera and tried to see himself looking directly out of the TV, to look himself in the eyes, but the angles were all wrong; to look at the screen he had to look away from the camera, so he only saw his profile. He tried to look obliquely at himself and for a split second he separated enough to see himself dead on. Whoa.

"ID," said the clerk.

"Did you hear me?" asked Adam.

Jim leaned against a magazine rack, selected a *Swank* magazine, and casually leafed through it.

"Dude—"

"I get paid tomorrow. I'll pay you back tomorrow." He didn't look up from the magazine.

"No ID, no liquo," said the clerk.

"The police took mine," said Adam. "Show him yours."

Jim jammed the magazine back in the rack. "If I had my ID, I'd have my wallet, and if I had my wallet, we wouldn't be having this pussy-ass conversation. I'd buy the beer, and we'd be on our way, but you want to be a little nickel-and-dime-counting bitch. Why don't you just do the combination for your little safe, and let's get the fuck out of here."

"I don't have my ID."

"Just reach into your pocket and put the money on the counter. The only ID this guy wants to see," Jim did a backhand thumb jab at the clerk, "is Andrew Jackson."

"I don't have enough."

A tic kicked in. Jim frowned it away. "Use your credit card."

"My dad cancelled it."

"Your dad—aren't you a grown man?"

"Look who's talking."

"You don't have twenty bucks?"

"That's all I've got, and I need some for the girls tonight."

"You gotta be—" A rack of cheap toys cut him off. He picked up a paddle ball, the ball tethered to an umbilical strand of rubber stapled to the splintery wood. The clerk muttered in another mother tongue and began to remove the booze from the counter. "Let's get out of here," said Jim. "There's an ATM at the BofA down the street." He walked out the door as if hypnotized. Adam followed him to the car.

"What's up with those stupid paddle ball toys?" Jim asked. "They never work. You hit the ball once and they just flail on you. What a dumb fucking toy. You'd have to be one lonely kid to have any fun with

PART 1: INTERNAL COMBUSTION

one of those. Just plunk down an extra buck to fake out your dumb-ass kid. 'Here you go, son. I got you a present. I sure do love you,'" Jim said in a false voice.

They got in the car and pulled out onto the boulevard where the sun was a red blob of fumes between telephone wires. At the bank, the word CLOSED blinked on and off in red letters on the ATM.

"What's the point of having an automated teller if it's not open twenty-four hours?"

"I heard they were closing them at sundown or eight o'clock or something to reduce crime. It's to keep people safe."

"It's retarded," Jim rejoined, wrenching into reverse. "Why don't they put us all under arrest for our own safety. There's another bank up here, a Nippon Lippo Sanwa or something, but the way things are going, it'll all be in Chinese, and it'll eat our card."

The sun sank into the asphalt dead ahead.

"*Our* card?"

"ATM's, ATM's," Jim muttered. "There was this friend of my mom's who told me that ATM's were a sign of the end of the world, that someday there would be no money, it would all be done by computers, and everybody would have like a scannable account number tattooed on their skin, and that number would be the Number of the Beast or some shit, and only those without numbers would be saved at the Rapture or the Apocalypse or whatever the fuck."

"How can they know?" Adam said. "How can anyone *know* that stuff. Religion, man, I don't know. It seems like a bunch of crap to me."

"Oooh, you're going to Hell now. Here it is." They pulled into the parking lot of the bank. They sat there. The engine idled. "Well?"

"Well, what?"

"Well, what the fuck are we doing here?"

"I don't know."

Flabbergasted-ness overtook Jim. He clawed at his face with his fingertips as if he had just walked through a spider web. "We're getting money, dumb-ass."

"I already told you, I'm only spending twenty dollars."

"Twenty bucks? Dude, I know you. You're going to drink twenty bucks' worth of alcohol, and get all drunk, and want more, and go to the ATM. Let's just cut to the chase. Do it now while you're sober. Or if you want we can just go back to the house and make popcorn and cuddle and watch *Beverly Hills, 902fuck0*. And if you say yes to that, I'm going to beat your sorry ass and take your wallet and leave you lying bloody here in the parking lot, and then they'll close this ATM, too, and little old Chinese ladies won't be able to get money anymore, and they'll go hungry because of you."

"Why do I even hang out with you?"

"Because I'm cool, and you're a dork, and the only chance you'll ever have of being cool is through me."

"Yeah, that's it. You are funny, I'll give you that."

"We are bound by common loves, my friend."

Jim unzipped his pants and pulled out a fifth of Jim Beam.

"Where did you get that?"

"Magic fingers. I wiggled 'em and made it happen." He unscrewed the bourbon and took a swig. "I wish it always worked." He stuck the bottle in Adam's face. "The women are waiting."

Adam visibly caved in and took the bottle. He sniffed it and shivered before taking a drink that gave him the face of a man who had just hit his thumb with a hammer. Giving the bottle back to Jim, he smiled fiercely, nostrils flared. "Okay." His voice had the slow basso of a movie demon.

They got out and walked to the ATM. Jim watched over Adam's shoulder. "Please Take Your Cash," Jim read the screen. "That's a laugh."

On Harbor Boulevard again, they waited at a red light for what seemed like eons. The signals on the cars waiting in the left-hand turn lane blinked at slightly different intervals, and as Jim stared at them, his eyes began to cross, his vision doubled, the images pulled in

PART 1: INTERNAL COMBUSTION

opposite directions, the world tore apart, and there was Mary, glowing pure and beautiful in the cool, clean air. How had he fallen for her? It was she who led him into the hills beyond her backyard, where a bulldozer-resistant brotherhood of canyons and oaks held out against the ever-encroaching onslaught of suburbs, a place where deer still roamed, and coyotes could be heard cackling at night. She and Jim climbed the path past the rusted junk and dead appliances of earlier eras, door-less fridges, busted stoves, Whirlpool washers that didn't whirl or wash anymore, all dumped surreptitiously in the high grass. They passed rusted tin cans, squashed beer cans, broken bottles, and torn condom wrappers, until, farther up, they left behind the debris of civilization and the brown hills seemed to be turning green before their eyes; the grass sparkled in after-shower finery; it had just rained. Droplets of water hung like jewelry from budding sycamore twigs, rivulets ran giggling into thirsty creek beds. She was telling him as they hiked that she and her family had been awakened during the storm the night before by the breaking of glass and a terrible thrashing in the living room. Her father tiptoed down the stairs to find a stag had jumped through the bay window and was bucking around the house, smearing blood on the walls and breaking lamps and pictures before it leaped back out the window and sprang zigzagging down the street.

How could he not have fallen for her? They had geometry together, but he often helped her with her American Lit class, dictating for her essays to turn in about *The Catcher in the Rye,* and *The Scarlet Letter*, and *Huckleberry Finn.* It was the last day of school before Spring Break, Good Friday. "I probably won't see you all week. Why don't you walk me home?" His mind raced, wondering if she cared about him. Jim wasn't sure what love was, except something he lacked and desperately desired, to touch and be touched, to feel wanted, but love had always been unattainable, abstract, a picture on a wall, something people on TV had, something that occurred in worlds other than his. Up in the hills, birds sang choir; his actions felt divinely orchestrated.

He reached for her hand without thinking as they came to an ephemeral stream of clean water. They watched a minute in silence. An overwhelming temporality rushed over Jim; in the blink of an eye, the water would be gone, and so would he, and so would she.

"It sure is rare to see running water anywhere around here other than from faucets and in gutters."

"It's pretty. I love the sound of it," she said.

"Let's step across on those stones."

"I can't. I'm wearing brand-new white shoes. My mom will kill me if I get them dirty."

"We've already come this far. They're going to get dirty sooner or later." He stepped down from the bank into the gully, and his foot sank in mud up to his ankle. He tried to lift it out, but the mud sloorped off his shoe with a contented farting sound. Jim laughed and fell back onto the bank and pulled off his other shoe and his socks and planted his feet in the cold mud and wiggled his toes. Exquisite. "Come on."

"Nooo," she said in a singsong voice that already seemed to be heading back down the trail. "I'm supposed to go to church in a little while."

"How about we strip down like Adam and Eve and look for fruit instead." Surprised to hear himself speak so boldly.

"I'll be in trouble if I'm late."

He felt pulled in two directions, felt stretching in his abdomen. He wanted her to tempt him. What if Eve hadn't offered the fruit to Adam or Adam not accepted? None of us would be here. In his dentist's waiting room were Illustrated Children's Bibles, from which came most of Jim's religious imagery. The inside cover of them said, *The Beginning of Knowledge is the Fear of God*. Jim had puzzled over those words for years. *Why does God want us to be afraid of Him?* he would lie in bed wondering. Then one night it hit him like a revelation: it might mean that God was afraid of man's knowledge. Knowledge is God's fear. He doesn't want us to know anything; He's afraid of what we'll find out.

PART 1: INTERNAL COMBUSTION

"Why do you think God forbade Adam and Eve from eating from the fruit of the Tree of Knowledge of Good and Evil?" Jim asked Mary.

"I don't know. I guess he didn't want us to learn how to sin."

"So, God would have preferred we didn't know the difference between good and evil? That doesn't make sense."

"Ignorance is bliss," she said. "My dad says God just wants us to be obedient."

Jim stared up at the sky through the branches of the trees. "It's Free Will." The words came murmuring out of his mouth almost as they occurred to him. "It's so we have a choice."

"Dude, the light's green."

"Do you think they knew how to have sex before the serpent got them to eat from the tree?" he practically blurted.

"I don't know." Her voice fluttered. "I have to get going."

"Dude."

They'd made arrangements to go to a movie together, just the two of them, a date. When the credits rolled at the end, she took his head in her hands and licked her tongue along inside his lips. He walked up the aisle on wobbly legs, and that night in bed, he didn't even masturbate, but stared at the ceiling in the dark with his fingers interlocked behind his head, enjoying a glow in his body he had never felt before.

A horn honked. Jim shook his head and stepped on the accelerator. He and Adam pulled onto the freeway, heading south. The sky looked soft. Like the unimaginable confirmation of soft flesh under her shirt the next night, kissing on the couch across from the semi-strobe of Johnny Carson's monologue. Eventually, near the end of the following summer, he had worked his caress down to where she normally guided it away, but this time she didn't. He slid down under the waistband of her panties and back out and down again, and was thrilled to feel the soft fuzz and then the moist warmth, and her breath quickened, and he ground against her and pulled her shirt over her head, and—

"What's going on out here?"

Jim rolled off her and froze. Her father stood in the middle of the flickering room in his pajamas.

"Dad!" She sounded embarrassed and scolding.

"Oh, sorry." He retreated into the darkness of the hall, but that was that.

"Oh my God," she sobbed. "You have to leave now."

He walked out mystified by the lingering impression of damp warmth on his fingertips, and felt awe and joy. But that was that. On the phone the next day, she told him she wasn't allowed to be alone with him anymore, and a few days later, she left for Pitzer. Neither of them had a car. They stayed in touch over the phone at first. She joined a sorority, and the calls became less frequent. One day over Christmas break she called him over to her house. No one was home, and she invited him into her bedroom. She sat on the bed and patted the spot next to her. His heart raced. "Will you sit down, please?" She took his hand. "I have to tell you something."

And so, it went. When she was done, he could only think to ask, "What's his name?"

"Pietro," she said, and that seemed to bother him as much as anything, not just that she was dumping him, but for a guy named Pietro. That, and in all the time they had been together, kissing and touching, her hand had never so much as brushed against his zipper, but Jim knew, he knew, he knew from the flush in her cheeks and the twitter in her voice when she said, "Pietro," that Pietro's dick had entered her world.

"What are you tripping on?"

Jim blinked and looked at Adam. "Your mom."

"Do you believe in destiny?" Adam asked out of the blue-purple.

Jim looked at him as if he had just farted.

"Like when I do the stupid stuff I do, I know it's stupid beforehand, and I do it anyway. Is that fate? Or did I have a choice."

"That ain't fate. That's dumbfuckedness."

PART 1: INTERNAL COMBUSTION

"What about you? When you get all drunk and start breaking windows and pissing on police cars, what makes you do that? Are you choosing to do those things, or does it happen because it's your destiny? Could you not bust stuff up if you didn't want to, or can you not help it?"

"Are you trying to philosophize so you can have butt love with Greek boys there, Plato?"

"You're the one that pulled the A out of your ass in Criticism. I just wondered if you think we're doomed from the start, or do we do it to ourselves?"

"Who gives a fuck? It doesn't matter either way. Do what you want and enjoy it while you can."

"See? I like that. I'm glad I asked." Adam stuck his head out the rolled-down window and screamed at the cars they passed, "Who gives a fuck! It doesn't matter! Enjoy it while it lasts!"

Adam had perfect thick dark hair that stayed impeccably combed. Jim had never seen a hair out of place, even as Adam pulled his head back in from the eighty-mile per-hour wind of the freeway. Jim wondered if that was what girls liked about him, his neatness, his dress, his grooming. He'd seen Tink rub her hands through that hair, and with each pass, it sprang back. Jim examined in the rearview the rollercoaster that was his own hair. The Disney Employee Handbook forbade hair past the neck. Still, Jim's jutted out at the sides like little wings over each ear, and on the top, each strand seemed to strive for its own direction. It was light red when clean, but now it was dark with dried sweat. "Ugh."

"What?"

"Nothing." Then a few seconds later. "Tell me about the first pussy you ever touched."

Adam snorted a strange sound. "Above or below the clothes?"

Jim shrugged. "Above, first." He stole a look at Adam. Adam was smiling, but then his face went blank, and he sucked in a breath and blew his cheeks out like Louis Armstrong. Jim thought he heard Adam sigh something rueful that blew out the window. Adam groaned.

"Come on. Who was she?"

"She was a girl from our church named Melanie Smith who used to babysit me."

"You finger-banged your babysitter?"

Adam's head started slowly to nod.

"Same last name as you?"

"Yeah, but we weren't related."

"How do you know?"

Adam shrugged.

"Sounds a little freaky."

"Whatever."

"How old were you?"

"Like eleven, I guess."

"Eleven! How old was she?"

"Mmmbout fifteen, I think."

"Hot chick? Did she have tits?"

Adam pulled a pack of Marlboros from the ashtray, shook out a cigarette, placed it between his lips, and pushed in the dashboard lighter. "Beautiful. She had been my babysitter for as long as I could remember. I used to try to see under the bathroom door when she went in there. One time she caught me and sent me to bed early, but I snuck out and was spying on her. She was reading a *Cosmo* magazine or something on the couch with her dress up and her hand in her panties, diddling herself. I was peeking around the corner and she really started going at it. I'll never forget it. I carry it around in my head like a picture in my wallet. I didn't know what she was doing exactly, but it made my weenie hard and my heart beat fast." The lighter popped out and he lit the smoke, inhaling a long drag, and held it a few seconds before sighing it all out, roiling off the windshield.

"She must have been about to have an orgasm. It looked like she was about to cry. Her eyes were closed, and she was whimpering, and I must have made a noise myself, because all the sudden she opened her eyes and looked right at me. I took off running to my room and dived under the covers, and she came in behind me, begging me not to tell on her. She sat on the bed and was going, 'Oh, Adam, please don't tell. I'm so sorry,' and she was like stroking my hair and kissing me on the head, and I'm thinking *I* was the one who was supposed to be sorry, but when I heard her say that, I start thinking, okay, let's hear what she's sorry about, and I go, 'What were you doing?' Well, then she gets all mad and her voice got all mean, and she's all, 'None of your business! You just go to sleep and forget all about it, and don't tell anybody, or you'll be sorry.' And I go, 'Why?' and she grabs my nuts and squeezes really hard and goes, 'That's why.' And like, it hurt, but it was, you know, kind of cool, too. I still had a little chub left and pretty soon the nut squeeze turns into a little exploratory feel-up, and the next thing I know, she's under the covers with me, and she grabs my hand, and's using it to rub her puss through her underwear, and that was the first time I ever felt a girl's pussy above the clothes."

"Shit, dude! What happened?"

"We heard the car drive up and the garage door open, and she said, 'Better not tell,' and she went out and collected her money and left."

"Dang. How come I never got a babysitter like that? Fat old Mrs. Martino. She probably didn't even have a pussy. It probably just dried up from lack of use. So, what about below the clothes, the actual pussy, no barrier."

"Agh. Well, a few weeks later I come home from playing guns with some other kids after school, right, we used to play this game kind of like hide-and-seek, but we all had toy guns, and one team counted and the other team hid, and we'd take turns having these shootout ambushes, making the sound of the gunshots with our mouths, you know, and like one guy might be a soldier in camouflage with a machine gun, and another guy might be a cowboy with a pistol, and we'd shoot the shit out of each other and then argue over who was hit, right? 'You're dead.' 'No, I'm not. I shot you first. You're dead.' So, I come home with my little holster and my little pistol, and Melanie's sitting at the table with my mom, and I drop my lunchbox on the floor thinking she has confessed that I felt her up, and I'm in trouble. But my mom goes, 'Adam, honey, where have you been? I didn't want to leave without telling you. Your Aunt Edna is in the hospital. She had a stroke. I'm going up to Salt Lake to stay with her for a while.' And I'm like, 'Aunt who?' My mom had fourteen brothers and sisters. 'Your dad will be home later. Until then Melanie is going to keep you company, okay dear?' And Melanie goes, 'Yeah, Adam. Amber's coming and we're going to bake cookies for you.'

"Dude, I about shot my pistol. Amber was the only girl at our church in Ogden even hotter than Melanie. My mom kissed me and left. Melanie was acting like nothing had ever happened, cracking eggs and pre-heating the oven, and all that when the doorbell rang. I ran to open it and Boom! There's freaking Amber in this short, sleeveless like toga or something, and she's wearing these like Roman sandals with leather cords that crisscrossed up her calves. She saw me staring and she's all, 'Like my dress? I borrowed it from Heather Struthers. I brought Twister.' Then Melanie called her from the kitchen, "Am, come in here!' They called each other Mel and Am, right? I followed Amber into the kitchen. Melanie was dabbing lumps of cookie dough onto a baking sheet and putting her fingers in her mouth and kissing the dough off her knuckles. 'Wanna lick it?' she says and hands me the spoon. I licked, and they talked about Amber's dress and some other crap, and there was some whispering, and when the cookies were in the oven, they were like, 'Let's play Twister.' So, they set it up on the floor in the family room, and Melanie volunteers to be the spinner. So, Amber and I play the first game, and she's fucking working it, like she's got her boobies in my face on her first spin, and her ass on my crotch on her second spin, and at one point she's about humping my leg. She

PART 1: INTERNAL COMBUSTION

smelled like sweat, and bath gel, and cookies and puss, and I was fucking slobbering from it, dude; I drooled right onto the Twister mat, and she goes, 'Look at the little baby dribble,' and she bumps me with her ass so I fall and says, 'I win.'

"So now I spun while Melanie and Amber played. I swear my dick grew about six inches that day. Melanie got herself in like a limbo position and Amber was bent over her the other way, and I could see a big wet spot on her panties and hair sticking out. I started feeling weird, man, like I didn't know what to do, or I did know what to do, but I didn't know how, or I knew I shouldn't be doing anything like what we were doing, I don't know. I was feeling like a geeky little kid, and I wanted to be bigger and older with the chicks there, right, but I'm in my stupid little cowboy costume. So, I go to my room to change, but the buckle was stuck, like the hasp, or whatever you call it, was stuck in the belt hole, like I'd put it on too tight, and then eaten that day, and couldn't pull it tight enough to get the hole off the hasp thing that sticks out? I go back out there to tell Melanie, and fucking Amber starts making fun of me, 'Oh, is you widdle zipper-wipper stuck?' and I'm like, 'No, it's my belt,' and Amber goes, "I'll get you widdle zipper-wipper down for you.' And she's tugging me around by my belt, and Melanie's laughing at me, and Amber goes, "Ooh, a gun," and she snatches the gun from my holster, and she's like, 'Alright, don't move.' And I laughed a little because she was being kind of funny, and she screams, 'I said don't move!' and I was like, 'Ok,' and she goes, 'Sit in that chair!' and I'm like whatever, and I sit down. Well, she gives the gun to Melanie, and she goes, 'If he moves, kill him.'

"The toy gun?"

"Right. And I'm sitting in the chair and fucking Amber takes the cords out of her Roman sandals and ties me to the chair, tight. And like at first it was just playing around, but when she was done, I seriously couldn't get out. So, she takes the belt and pulls it super tight, and at great pain to me, she gets it undone, and pulls my pants and underwear down to my ankles. Now, I'm embarrassed and struggling, and telling her to stop it, but I don't know what I wanted. She was scaring me, you know, but part of me wanted to see where it was all gonna go. I don't know how hard I tried to get loose. Well, they put on some music, and they're all dancing around me and laughing their asses off, and fucking Amber's flashing me her boobs, and her bush, and she's saying, 'Melanie told me about you.' The next thing I know, she drops her panties to the floor and kicks 'em up onto my head and turns around and hikes up her skirt and bends over and puts her puss right in my face and looks at me upside down from between her thighs, and she's all, 'Kiss it, Adam. Kiss me,' and she's rubbing her puss all over my face. And that was the first time I touched a girl's pussy below the clothes."

"What the fuck! What happened?"

Adam stubbed out his cigarette butt in the ashtray. "I'm not supposed to smoke in this car," he said. "I was like, 'Nyaaah,' I had my lips pressed together, and I was turning my face away, and she like slid down onto my lap and was sliding around and playing with me and playing with herself, and I don't know if I was in for sure or not, and like, I thought I was going to pee back then, but now I think I might have been about to come, when Melanie starts screaming because the house is filling with smoke, and she ran into the kitchen and opened the oven and the house flooded with smoke, and the smoke alarm starts wailing, and that's when my father walked in."

"Holy shit," was all Jim could say.

"Holy shit," Adam concurred.

"Man, I was just expecting an old-fashioned backseat finger-bang story."

"Yeah. I was hardly allowed out of the house after that—shit, hardly allowed out of my mother's sight. I had to go to counseling twice a week for a few years. Melanie's family moved away somewhere. Amber fucking ran away from home, and was never heard from again

PART 1: INTERNAL COMBUSTION

as far as I know, which makes me really sad." Adam shook his head. "My mom kept saying, 'They ruined our little baby, my little baby,' but my mom was the one that was ruined by it. She was always talking about whoredom and Satan and shit after that. I mostly got over it pretty quick. It doesn't seem that bad to me. They said I was sexually abused, but you know what? Sometimes it seems kind of cool to me. They were hot chicks....Maybe my mom was so distraught because I was her only child. She couldn't have kids after me. She's from this huge Mormon family, I'm her only kid, and this happened. Shit. I don't know how much of it was my fault. I really don't know if I could have gotten away or if I was participating. I don't know if Amber was cruel or just curious or what. She and her mom were like refugees from one of those southern sects."

Jim didn't know what to think either. He felt lost, like he didn't know where he was heading, but he couldn't wait to get there when Thump thump Thump thuMp, Thump thump thump thump thump "Do you hear that?" thump thump Thumpt thump thuwup thwump thumbp whump Fump Fwump thumpa dump

Thump "Yeah, what is that?" THump Thump thump Bump wump thump a bump bump thump thump thump The car was shuddering. "Don't tell me we got a blowout." Jim slowed to the side of the road. Thumpthump thump thump thump thumthum thu mpth

The came to a stop on the dirt entryway to a freeway construction site where bulldozers dozed. They got out of the car. Phantoms of dust wafted through the beams of the headlights. Sure enough, the back, right tire was flat. The tread had shredded where a nail was stuck up to the head in the rubber.

"You got a spare?"

Adam frowned as if Jim had just asked him the capital of Uzbekistan.

"Pop the trunk then, ya idget."

"Holy crap," the open trunk elicited from Jim. Two dozen plastic-wrapped cases of soup cans, twenty-four cans per case, filled the trunk, along with another hundred or so stray cans. "What the fuck? You got a can opener?"

"What for?"

"I don't know. Just in case, I guess."

"In case what?"

"For shit's sake, man! In case the big one hits, and it's Armageddon, and you're trapped on the wrong side of some crumbled overpass, you could eat soup to survive, but not if you didn't have a can opener."

"Right. Now I see."

"You think you got a spare tire under all this chicken shit noodle soup. Ya got a jack, chowder head?"

They stacked the cases of soup on the ground. Jim tried to see how high a tower he could build with the loose cans. "Look, I'm building a tower to God." The tower collapsed.

"Good job. Here's the jack. Get busy and I'll get the spare out."

Jim took the jack. It was not one of those easy ones with a lever, but one you had to crank around. Jim positioned it and started cranking. "Don't we have to loosen the lug nuts before we jack her up?"

"That's what I'm looking for. The lug wrench."

Jim came back to the trunk where Adam was sifting through soup cans. Jim pulled out a newspaper with Gulf War headlines. Adam pulled out a set of rusty jumper cables. Jim found an unopened can of Brew 102. "They stopped making this stuff. Check it out. It's got an old pull tab." He pulled the tab, and foam fizzled over his fingers. He put the can to his lips and slurped. "Yck," he said, before glugging down most of it, crumpling the can, and tossing it to the ground with a little belch that had a little Jim Beam vomit in it that gave him a shiver. Adam pulled out an old black and yellow California license plate. Jim found a baseball. "Dude, it's like we slit open the shark from Jaws." Jim leaned against the car. "He musta spit out the lug wrench."

"There's an auto parts store down the road. We can walk there in like twenty minutes."

PART 1: INTERNAL COMBUSTION

Jim took the keys from the ignition and locked the door. They crossed the construction area and came out onto Newport Boulevard, walking in silence from one cone of street light to the next. Their shadows walked up under them as they passed each light, then stretched ahead where they'd fade in the glow of each new light Jim and Adam came to, and a new set of shadows would strive forward again, only to meet the same fate. Jim searched himself and felt no frustration born from this latest mechanical malfunction. He felt an ironical satisfaction, a verification of his existence, an uncanny tinge of pride in the way fate so often thwarted his aims. It lent him a sense that he had a destiny man's inventions couldn't resist, and he would take anything fate could dish out. The music of the Friday night traffic heading toward the beach had the summery feel of potential. He let out a whoop, and his whoop was answered over the booming bass of a car full of girls who slowed down to scream at Adam and Jim.

"Hey," Adam called. "Give us a ride." The car slowed and stopped. A new blue Nissan. It throbbed. Might fate be an accomplice for a change? As he and Adam approached the window, Jim expected to be pelted with eggs before the girls drove off, laughing. A head popped out of the window. Glow-in-the-dark yellow hair spilled down the door.

"Where ya guys going?" She had the voice of a mockingbird. Her face was about seventeen or so, but her cleavage was in its mid-twenties.

"We had a little car trouble. Can you give us a ride to the auto parts store down here?" Jim felt like his eyes were bugging out like a Tex Avery cartoon wolf. A fire truck drove by, howling and honking.

"Get in." She threw open the door.

Jim was paralyzed with what-the-fuck. Was something good happening? Its alien-ness filled him with suspicion. He was baffled that anyone would help, let alone someone with great cleavage. He peered into the car. Two other girls sat there. "How do we know you're not psycho-hitchhiker-killers? You might perform all kinds of perverse tortures upon us." Jim said.

"You don't," she said. "We might."

Adam jumped in the backseat and Jim squeezed in next to the girl in front. The music vibrated Jim's intestines. The girl next to him danced around on her ass. She smelled of flowery body lotion. She kept whooping. A strange mix of elation and apprehension filled the car. *Gotta say something. Can't just not say anything. Mouth dry. Want to uncap the Jim. Beam, that is. Then I'll be able to talk.* He wanted to establish himself as dangerously manly. Say something. Now or never.

"Sure is nice of you guys to help us," he said, yelling to be heard over the techno throb. "Or, well, of course, you're not guys. I guess I should say girls. Or ladies, maybe, is better. Or I guess you guys are women. I never know what to say—" Just then the driver turned down the stereo so that "I never know what to say" came out much more loudly than needed. A moment of silence ensued in which Jim was mortified. Girls this age will decide you're a dork in heartbeat, over just such a thing, but then the girl next to him snorted a giggle, and Jim smelled the air sweeten like cherry Chapstick. "What're your names?" he asked.

"I'm Lainey." Her hair writhed in the moon roof. "And this is Lisa," Lainey said, giving the driver a little tickle-pinch, which caused her to flinch and swerve a little with a look of irritation that became slightly amused. She looked at Jim and they made eye contact for an instant before shadows passed over her face as the headlights of an oncoming car passed. They were big and green, and he felt like she had searched for his soul before she looked back at the road.

"And that's Tamara in the back seat," Lainey said, Tuh-MAH-ra, adjusting the mirror to study the glossy pucker of her lips.

Jim craned his neck to see Tamara behind him, but he was wedged so tightly between Lainey and the door, that he was able to see little more than the sparkle of her braces on the periphery of his vision.

"I'm Jim and that's Adam."

PART 1: INTERNAL COMBUSTION

Lainey pushed the mirror back at an angle by which Jim could see a diagonal band of Lisa's face, high round cheekbones, a nose with a ski jump slope and squarish end, lines —of concern?— etched into her forehead that made Jim wonder if she was worried about picking up two strange boys. She adjusted the mirror and looked again at Jim, and he noticed two sly dimples around a hint of smile that made him wonder if she was thrilled about picking up two strange boys. Men, he reminded himself, two strange men. She looked back at the road and her profile was nothing but long straight hair with a tip of nose sticking out.

An awkward silence fell over them. Jim Beam whispered in Jim's ear. He didn't think the girls would care if he took a swig; they might even be impressed, but a pang of conscience held him up. Maybe if they had all been the same age, it wouldn't have bothered him to involve them in such criminal activity as drinking and driving, but they reminded him of Lauren. She had been his stepsister for a few years during his father's second marriage. She was an only child, too. When their parents married, she was four and he eight, but they had had an almost instant empathy for one another. Jim remembered crawling after her on all fours; he was a lion, and she escaped between the legs of the table and shrieked happily when he swiped at her with his paw. He let her escape again, and she hid behind the curtains giggling. The couch was a mountain; he rolled off the ledge, buried under an avalanche of cushions, dead. She pulled open his eyelids, and he grabbed her and tickled her. He sneaked money out or her mom's purse when the ice cream truck came, and when the street bully tried to take her Fudgsicle, Jim grabbed the long metal handle to turn on the sprinklers and threatened to smash in the big boy's brains if he didn't give the ice cream back. He did.

When it was clear that Lauren and her mom were moving away, Jim took her play teapot, and a stuffed bear of hers, and hid them under his bed. He wanted to be able to find them in a few days, so he could ask his dad if he could bring Lauren her missing toys, but his dad said no. For many months afterward, Jim would sneak the bear out from under his bed at night and use it for a pillow.

She was lost to him now, though. She'd be about the same age as these girls.

"So." Lainey slapped his thigh. "What's something you've always wanted to do but haven't done yet?'

Whoa. Wasn't this some invitation to say that the thing he wanted to do but hadn't was her? "Is this a survey you saw in a *Cosmo* magazine or something?"

"It's what we were talking about before we picked you guys up. So, what do you want to do that you've never done?"

Do you. Right between those—what if some twenty-one-year-old creep was working on Laurie like this? "Fly to the moon. Navigate the Amazon. Scale Everest. Bone a Tahitian babe on a beach." Oops.

Lainey squealed. "Tamara's Tahitian!"

"I'm Fijian," said Tamara.

"You should work for *National Geographic*," said Lisa.

"I'd probably have to finish college first."

"Oh, you're in college."

"He'll finish," Jim heard Adam.

"I'm in college," said Lainey.

Lisa said, "Shyeah."

"Freshman year was so easy it ruined me," said Jim. I had a bunch of units going in from taking Advanced Placement courses in high school. Your school schedule is all different in college, and I was working at my job, and my old man couldn't keep track of me. I started having so much fun, I never studied, but I was still getting all A's and pretty soon, I stopped going to class altogether—"

"All together," said Lainey.

"Sophomore year, I would just show up to take tests, or I'd find out when a paper was due and write it that day, and I was still getting A's

PART 1: INTERNAL COMBUSTION

and B's. I started using my book money to buy beer and was partying every single night, but by the time I started junior year and had to take upper division classes, being drunk all the time wasn't getting me anything but B's and C's. Then I came down with pneumonia and had to withdraw from a bunch of classes. When I got better, I got kicked out for—" he made quotes with his fingers "—'assaulting' some university meter maid dude."

"He didn't get kicked out. He's just suspended."

"Whatever. I don't even care anymore. So what if I graduate? What am I going to do with a degree in English? Hey, yeah, wow, I speak fluent English. I can work in a cubicle forty hours a week! Or I can become a sorry-ass, sad sack, fucking teacher and be stuck in a room everyday brainwashing to be slaves a bunch of kids who all hate me and would rather be somewhere else just like me—"

"Amen!" shouted Lainey.

"I could major in business or something, become a greedhead, but—I'm sorry. I just want to be free. Yeah, free. The big lie. The big F-word. Freedom, my ass. You can't smoke pot. You can't just go live by a creek in the woods and eat nuts and berries. The land ain't free. I swear, I'm going to find some cave in the desert, and wake up when I want, and sleep when I want, and no one will tell me what to do, or what to wear, or how to cut my hair, or what I can and can't smoke, or anything else, and if I starve to death, so be it."

"Uh, the auto parts store is right up here," said Adam.

They pulled into a driveway of a strip mall and parked in front of an auto parts store tucked between a 7-Eleven and a Kentucky Fried Chicken.

"We're going to a party on Thirty-Third," Lainey said, "and Tamara's cousin works at this cool bar he lets us in. Why don't you guys come with us?" She gave Jim's thigh a squeeze.

"That's a capitol idea," said Jim. "Or is it capital?"

"Why don't we meet them there?" Adam said.

47

"Where on Thirty-Third?"

"At Oceanside, on the corner. You can't miss it. Just follow the music."

"Dude, come on. I think they're about to close." Adam got out of the car.

"I'm coming." Jim turned to Lainey. "So, what was it *you* wanted to do but have never done?"

She wrapped her arms around his neck and pulled his ear to her wet lips. Her breath was hot. "That's for me to know and you to find out."

Jim got out of the car. He looked at Lisa, who was smiling even more thinly than before. "Thanks. So, we'll see you guy- ah, gir—ah, ladies later." He closed the door.

The music went back up. The girls pulled back onto the boulevard and were gone.

"Fuck," said Jim. "Brzzt grrtz," said Jim. "She was coming on to me."

"She was teasing you."

"Cocksucker," said Jim.

Adam's eyes narrowed. "Did you take your medicine today?"

"Fuck," said Jim and pulled the see-through brown container from his pocket and unscrewed the childproof lid. He popped one of the pills into his mouth, took the bottle of bourbon from his pants, unscrewed it, tipped it to his lips, swallowed. "Shit! Why didn't we ask for a ride back?"

"Too late now. Come on."

They walked up to the glass door of the auto parts store just as the clerk was turning around the OPEN sign to CLOSED. He saw Jim and Adam coming and quickly locked the door.

"Oh, hey, man, wait a minute," called Adam, knocking on the glass. "We've got a flat. We just need a lug wrench. It won't take a minute." Right through the door at the end of the first aisle, lug wrenches were on sale.

PART 1: INTERNAL COMBUSTION

"Sorry, sir," the clerk said through the glass. "We're closed."

Adam looked at his watch. "Come on, dude. It says here on the door you don't close until nine. It's only eight fifty-three." He showed the clerk the face of his watch.

"Not according to my watch." He smiled like a toad. A short, fat, bald toad man with a round belly and a round head and fat toad lips and two nostrils stuck in his face. Jim sensed that this was the only place in life where the toad man had the novel pleasure of control, and he was going to exercise that pleasure.

"It's an emergency. I swear it will only take a minute. We'll grab the wrench and leave the money on the counter. You can keep the change."

"Sorry."

If the toad man would have just turned away right then, Jim might not have done what he did next, because in the ten seconds the toad stood doing nothing but look at them, they could have paid for the wrench and left. "Don't make me angry," Jim said. He felt his shoes crimping his feet. "You wouldn't like me when I'm angry." His shirt tightened across his back. The toad man did not move and Jim roared, "You fucking PRICK!" The gash in his hand began to throb, his muscles jittered. "OPEN THE GODAMN DOOR!" There it went. His mouth was going on its own again. He listened to hear what he would say next. "YOU SUCK SHIT, SHITFUCKER!" In the reflection of the windows Jim watched himself squat and hug a heavy stone and metal trash receptacle. He stood up with it, and—seemingly in slow motion under the strobe-like flicker of strip mall lights—heaved it through the window. Like McMurphy, thought Jim of the Jim in the window, before the latter shattered in a blast of glass. Jim surged for the jagged hole, intent on bludgeoning the toad with a tire iron, but he felt himself pulled back by Adam's grasp on the back of his shirt as a plate of glass guillotined down, hit the ground and exploded.

"—get out of here! Come on!" Adam was yelling in Jim's ear. He pushed Jim out toward the street and then ran ahead. An alarm was ringing. The toad was gone. A couple of guys at the 7-Eleven looked at him and sucked their Slurpees. Jim took off running after Adam.

Jim had always hated running. As soon as he ever started running, all he wanted was to stop. But he would push on to spite his asthma and to spite his father, determined to prove everybody wrong, to prove his father wrong for not letting him play football, to prove God wrong for giving him such a shitty pair of lungs. Jim had been the captain of his track team in high school. He hated track. He wanted to play baseball. His dad let him try out for the team. "Baseball's not as tough as football." Jim practiced constantly. He threw tennis balls against the garage door to practice fielding grounders; he hung a ball with twine from the branch of a tree in the yard and would whack at it with a bat until his hands were calloused. He had desire. He had determination. He had no talent. Plus, Coach Godino disliked Jim because he wore his grandma's green pants to tryouts one time. She had died that spring. The pants were pretty short in the ankle, but they had an elastic waistband. He knew it was silly, but he didn't care. He got cut, that year and every other year. And then he'd go over to the track team to run headlong against an entire universe of opposition, as if by building speed he could penetrate it, and it would collapse like a punctured balloon, and he would be free. That was before he started smoking, though.

Adam's silhouette darted around a corner, and Jim closed with him feeling strong, proud, giddy, and alive. Breaking the window was the first right thing he'd done in months or more. He'd struck a blow against evil. He was not just helpless, not just a cog. He was a freedom fighter. *Yeah, I'm a freedom fighter.* He let out a whoop, savoring the cinematic, Technicolor sky; it reminded him of the bayou night painted on the ceiling at the beginning of the Pirates of the Caribbean ride. The tears that streamed down his face were as much from joy as from the rush of cool air against his eyeballs. Adam and Jim dashed across a busy

PART 1: INTERNAL COMBUSTION

street and into a residential area where Jim could just begin to hear the insane old woman laughing in his chest. They slowed to a jog as they came out onto another boulevard. Now the Phantom of the Opera was banging on the organ of Jim's lungs. By the time they stopped in the parking lot of whatever shopping center they were at, bent at the waist, hands on knees, panting, the boa constrictor behind Jim's ribs had tightened its coils around his bronchi, and he collapsed in the parking lot, gasping for oxygen. He stuffed his fingers into his pocket and fumbled out his inhaler, put it to his lips, and blasted away. One, two, three puffs. The mist needed to be held in the lungs for at least ten seconds, but in his gasping for air, he exhaled the medicine without it doing any good. His heart thumped, his blood pounded in his head, and his tongue lolled out. He tried to focus the energy to sit up. His abs failed him, and he fell back. He rolled onto his side, pushed himself to a sitting position, shook his inhaler, and tried again. One, two, three puffs. This time he was able to hold his breath about three seconds.

Adam squatted next to him. "Dude, are you all right?" he asked.

Jim coughed up a tablespoon of modeling glue, spat, and fell back to the pavement.

"Come on, Jim, dude. You've got to take deep breaths."

Jim tried to say, "No shit, Sherlock," but couldn't. He tried to calm himself, tried to consciously slow his exhalations. Adam helped him sit up again. Jim shook and blasted the inhaler again. He held his breath and counted one calm two like a meditating monk three self-discipline four like those Indian yogis that five lower their heartbeats six and are found alive in mud seven like frogs after the rainy season eight. Peace washed over him. The serenity of which the near-drowned speak. He fell back to the asphalt. Pussycats sat on his face, put their tails down his throat. His breathing stopped. His heart hammered in his eardrums.

"Dude, are you going to be okay? Should I go get help or something?"

Jim rolled onto his knees and coughed up a hairball. He nodded. "Yeah." Short shallow pants of breath returned. The pussycats scattered into nearby shadows. He could still hear purring. His lungs. "When I was a kid," he said between labored breaths, "I used to take all these pills and whenever I had an asthma attack (gasp), I had to go the E-room (wheeze). Now all I need is this baby." He shook up his inhaler and sucked three more blasts. "God, what a lot of pills I had to take," he said, holding his breath. "When you had asthma in the seventies, they kept you all sped up on epinephrine and shit. (Wheeze) I was such shaky little bastard. My hands (gasp) shook like an alkie in detox. My teachers used to bust me (sputter) cuz my writing was illegible cuz I was all hepped up all the time. Every weekend when I used to stay with my mom, I'd have to go to the hospital in the middle of the night to get these crazy shots (cough). Adrenaline. Epinehprine, Susfrin. I remember the doctor telling me the first shot would make me feel like Mighty Mouse, the second would make me feel like (wheeze) Superman, and the third like a Super Giant. They made me puke, and then everything would become crystal clear. They'd hook me up to this breathing machine. Dude, I sounded like Darth (gasp) Vader, and the same old nurse was always there, and she would call me sweetie and baby and honey and all that. And after, when I could breathe again, it was like all worth it. My mom would take me to Winchell's and get me a donut, and it seemed kind of magical to be out and up late with my mom, you know cuz like three in the morning was some privileged time most kids never saw. The donuts were super fresh that early. I felt like I had the whole world to myself." A big sigh that crackled like the end of a long peal of thunder blew out of Jim. "One time it was super foggy. We were on the freeway, and my mom couldn't see, and there was some construction, and the lines on the freeway vanished, and we were all of a sudden just rolling through dirt and fog at sixty miles per hour. It was a trip, dude. My mom was getting all panicky, but I was pumped full of adrenaline in this super-heightened state of alertness, and I felt like I like got her through it—I guess it's not any big story, but I've always remembered it."

PART 1: INTERNAL COMBUSTION

Adam stood up. "Let's go."

"But you know what was funny? We found out that I was allergic to the cat, and that was what was triggering the attacks. But my stepsister loved that cat. She was already an emotional wreck from her parents' divorce, and she used to carry on about coming to see her dad and would scream bloody murder that she wanted to go to her mom. Until they got the cat. The kid loved the cat. She would stay peacefully at my mom's and step dad's once they got the damn cat. My mom and her husband were just as afraid of sending her back over the edge as they were of me suffocating in the night. They tried shampooing the floors and keeping the cat outside, but I still had to go to the ER every night I stayed there. One day the cat got run over, but my stepsister freaked, and they got another one! They said it would stay outside, but it didn't. It ran away, and they got another one! Dude, it—"

"This is a pretty long story for a guy who couldn't breathe two minutes ago."

"You're right. Who gives a shit? You think that Kmart is open? They might have lug wrenches." The doors swung open as a woman and her three children went into the store.

Adam helped Jim up and brushed off the back of Jim's shirt. "I knew you'd get crap all over my shirt."

As they neared the store, Jim half expected the doors would not swing open for them, but they did, and he felt as if he had stepped into a UFO, the light seemed so unnatural.

"We close in fifteen minutes," a security guard informed them.

"Why, thank you, kind sir," said Jim.

He and Adam located the automotive section and selected a four-pronged lug wrench. "Hey, why didn't we ask those girls if we could use their lug wrench," Adam said, slapping his forehead as if he could have had a V-8.

Jim shrugged. "I was too busy staring at that Lainey's tits. How old do you think she is?"

53

"Sixteen, seventeen."

"One more."

"I don't think so."

At the checkout stands, two cashiers were still working. Each was helping one customer. Jim and Adam got in line behind one of the customers, a woman buying rubber sheets. The man in the other line paid with cash and left, and the cashier put up a Sorry Next Register sign while the woman in front of Jim and Adam wrote a check for her rubber sheets. Three kids came running up. "Mom! Mom! Can we get these?" One of them begged, shoving a pack of pogs in the woman's face.

"I don't think you need those."

"Come on, Mom, please," the girl moaned. The cashier drummed her fingers on the counter.

"Well, I'm not paying for them. If you girls want those things, you're going to have to use your allowances."

The girls jumped up and down in celebratory ecstasy, and the woman finished writing her check. The cashier asked to see ID. After a minute of searching, she found it in her purse. The cashier bagged the sheets. One at a time, each girl stepped up to the cashier to pay for pogs with nickels and dimes. "I'm trying to teach them about money." The mom smiled apologetically at Jim and Adam. Jim tried to burn her with his heat vision, but it only seemed to discomfort her slightly. When the third girl stepped up to pay for her pogs, Jim noticed she was actually a teenaged midget with Down's Syndrome. She pulled a handful of coins from her pocket, most of which spilled to the floor and rolled in different directions with the girls scurrying after them. Someone somewhere had a voodoo doll of Jim that they were spit-roasting over hot coals. He was about to scream out in pain when he felt the coolness of Adam's hand on his forearm.

"Dude, stay cool."

Jim turned to the woman while the cashier helped the midget

PART 1: INTERNAL COMBUSTION

count her coins. "You know what just occurred to me? Irony is proof that God exists, don't you think?"

"I don't know what you mean," she said, getting a firmer grasp on her purse.

"Oh, well. Never mind, then. But let me ask you this: Have you ever read *Moby-Dick*?"

"Come on, girls. Let's get going." The lady's voice fluttered.

Adam laughed. "Dude, what are you talking about?"

"I was just thinking Ahab's problem was that he couldn't accept that bad luck is just bad luck. He thought the white whale fucked with him on purpose, or like even that God was fucking with him on purpose through the white whale. But a whale is just a random force of nature, right? It's like the Law of Probability. If you flipped coins long enough, eventually you're going to guess wrong ten or twenty or maybe even a hundred times in a row. You take all the whales that ever existed, and eventually one might come up with the seemingly malevolent intelligence of Moby-Dick. But a whale is just an animal looking for its next meal; it doesn't plan; it's just a force of nature. It wasn't the whale that ruined Ahab, it was Ahab's reaction to the whale. Only in life, today, there aren't any white whales—we have lost car keys and uncanny strings of red lights, or a train crossing when you're late. Or this," he indicated with his chin the delay at the checkout stand. "Is this some cosmic conspiracy designed to personally fuck us, or is it just the Law of Probability? Is it that God has chosen me to mess with, or is it just that I'm the hundred times wrong in a row that was going to inevitably, eventually happen? All I know is that some invisible force always seems to prevent me from getting what I want, which, usually, is to be drunk and surrounded by hot chicks."

The woman made a disgusted sound. The cashier completed the transaction. "Bye," said the midget with Down's Syndrome. Jim felt a wave of regret.

"I had a class where we explored the idea of the whale as a father figure," said the cashier.

Jim stared at her slack-jawed.

"Psychoanalytical Symbolism in Literature," she said.

Jim turned to Adam. "Gilligan, li'l buddy! Look, it's the Perfessor!"

He turned back to the cashier. Her nameplate said LARISA. "You've read *Moby-Dick?*"

"I have."

"And you guys tore up *Moby-Dick* with a lot of psych-babble?"

"I was a psych major with a minor in Comparative Lit at UCI."

"You didn't major in cashiering at U of K mart?

"You're sweet. No, jerk. I teach high school English during the day, and I'm doing this at night to save up some money to go back to school and get my doctorate in psych."

"Psych! Psychology is the biggest fraud perpetrated on mankind in the twentieth century. 'Oh, I'm all screwed up because my dad was mean to me and I want to fuck my mom.' What a lot of crap. They just made up a bunch of new terms to try to explain life in a way your average joe would think sounded scientific, and would pay through the nose for, when what average joe ought to be doing is turning to art and nature and literature and friendship for models of behavior, not a lot of clinical babble."

"Sounds like you could use a therapist."

"And to think I was going to ask you to marry me because you've read *Moby-Dick*. Now that I know you're one of those psych trippers, I'm not sure I'm going to even ask you what time you get off."

"And to think I saw inside of thirty seconds that you've got about nine classic disorders. Nine-fifteen," she said.

"Is that what time you get off?"

"That's how much the tire wrench costs."

Jim turned to Adam. "Pay the lady." She was about thirty, with high cheekbones, a quick, mischievous smile, an impish arch to her eyebrows, and freckles on her nose that won Jim over.

PART 1: INTERNAL COMBUSTION

"Please, forgive my friend, Miss," said Adam. "They don't let him out of the hospital but once a month, and he gets a little over-excited sometimes." He handed her a twenty. "I know this seems forward, but what time DO you get off? I wonder if you might be able to help us out."

"ATTENTION KMART SHOPPERS: KMART IS NOW CLOSED. PLEASE MAKE YOUR PURCHASES AT THE CHECKOUT STAND AT THIS TIME."

"How?"

"We got a flat tire a few miles back and we're running late. I don't suppose there's any chance you might consider giving us a ride back."

"I'd have to ask my boyfriend. He drives us here."

"Let me guess," said Jim. "Assistant manager?"

"Sporting Goods. But he's really a novelist."

Jim sputtered and waved at his face as if wasps were flying around.

"We can leave this guy behind," said Adam.

"Wait out front," she said. "I'll talk to Jeffrey, but I can't make any promises. He doesn't have my good sense of humor." She pressed a button on the register, and receipt tape came rising out of it like a snake out of a charmer's basket.

"Wow. Okay. Great. Yeah. If you could just see what he says. Thanks. We'll wait out front."

"Night," said Jim to the guard as they walked out. Once out front he took the bottle from his pants and took a sip. "Uhmsum?" He offered it to Adam.

"No, dude, and don't let them see you with that shit, okay?"

"Okay, Mom." He put the bottle back in his underwear. "I could go for a cigarette right now."

"Let's just wait."

"Okay, Dad."

Neither of them said anything for a minute, until Adam said, "What was that bit about God and irony you were talking about in there?"

"Just that shit happens that's so contrary to what you're trying to do that there seems to be some cosmic jester behind it. When bad luck seems designed. It seems like there's some intelligent, unseen force that affects outcomes. Like God or something."

"Or the Devil," said Adam.

Something convulsed Jim's shoulder. The Devil? His stock answer had always been that he didn't believe in the Devil. But couldn't the cosmic, unseen force be—

"Here they come."

"Oh, my shit," said Jim as Larisa walked out holding hands with a slight fellow from whom sprung corkscrews of hair, and whose pale, pasty skin, glowed purple under the red and blue Kmart sign. He had whisky bottle bottoms for eyeglasses, and Jim wondered how the hell he was ever going to keep from making fun of the guy until after they had gotten a ride back to the car. "How the hell am I—"

Adam elbowed him. "Don't blow it," he hissed.

"Guys, this is Jeffrey."

Jeffrey's posture indicated to Jim that he and Adam were about to be shut down. The guy's head lolled around on what neck he had like a newborn's. He had no shoulders; his arms just stuck out of his ribcage. As he neared them Jim saw magnified by eyeglasses the soft pillowiness of the guy's lower eyelids, and that he had an extremely wet mouth. And then a thought stupefied Jim: *He bones her.*

"I'm Adam." Adam offered his hand. "And this is Jim."

Adam elbowed Jim in the liver and Jim took the wet rag that was Jeffrey's hand.

"It sure is nice of you to help us out," Adam said.

"I didn't say we would yet." Jeffrey's voice sounded like he was talking through a tin can.

"I don't blame you," said Adam. "No one picks up strangers anymore. It's really too risky these days. I was surprised we got a ride this far. From some teenage girls. You wanted to ground them for two

PART 1: INTERNAL COMBUSTION

weeks. That's one of the first things they teach you, isn't it? Don't talk to strangers. Really, it was too much to believe that we'd get helped out on this two times in a row. It's cool. We'll—"

"Okay, you can stop now. We'll give you a ride."

"Oh, you guys are the best. Thank you, so much."

"The car's this way."

Larisa and Jeffrey led Jim and Adam to a ten-year-old Datsun, and Jim hoped it would withstand his curse until he and Adam were safely deposited back at their car.

"Why doesn't one of you tall guys sit up front?"

"I think you're a little taller, Jim," Adam said.

"That's okay, man. I'm like the Yogi Kudu. Member that guy on *That's Incredible!*? He was one of those Indian swami guys about seven feet tall, but only weighed about one-fifty, and he would fold himself into this little glass box, and they would submerge him underwater for a few days and then pull him out, and he'd be fine. I'm like that. I can fit in the backseat. Besides, you're going to need all the leg room you can get for the heels on those shoes."

Jeffrey opened the driver's side door and let Larisa into the back; then he got in and unlocked the passenger door. Adam opened the door and began jockeying with Jim to sit in back with Larisa, but Jim pushed him aside with a subtle, though vicious, hockey hip check and jumped in back. Jim had to slump down and scrunch his head into his shoulders and tilt it to one side with his knees in the vicinity of his chin before Adam could get in. Adam slammed the seat back against Jim's shins. Jim stifled a grunt and flicked Adam's ear. Jeffrey started the car and drove out onto the street, and Jim flicked Adam's ear again. "Our car's up Newport by where the freeway lets off near all that construction," Adam said.

"So, what will you be doing with the rest of your evening?" Jim asked Larisa.

"Jeffrey will be working on his novel tonight, and I'll probably make some tea and grade some papers."

Jim gagged for a moment and coughed. "We're going to a party on Thirty-Third Street; why don't you come?"

"A California beach party?" said Jeffrey. "With bunches of bleach-blond, boob-jobbed bimbos and vacant-eyed surfer boys? No, thanks."

"What! You mean their tits ain't real?" Jim said loudly and flicked Adam's ear. "So, where you from, Capote?"

Jeffrey sighed. "Originally, I'm from New York, but we moved out to California almost a year ago because Larisa wanted to."

"Isn't 'she wanted to' like dangling infinitive or something, dude? Don't you mean 'she wanted to do so'?"

"My meaning was clear."

"I don't know either, guy. I'm just bustin' your balls. Whudduhya got against California? What's with the stereotype?"

"It's an intellectual wasteland out here. Everybody is so image-conscious. The only thing people care about out here is their looks. You can't talk about anything but movies. Philosophy and literature don't exist out here. There's no literati to speak of. It's completely stifling."

"Don't you mean, 'of which to speak'?" Jim snorted. "People in New York don't care about their looks? Isn't that where they have all those fashion shows where the guys and girls all where the same queer-looking stuff? I thought it was some big fashion mecca out there."

"I'm not talking about fashion. See? I mean everybody out here is all-conscious of their bodies."

"So, clothes are more important than bodies?"

"Look, not one good writer has come from California. All the good writers in this country come from back east because that's where all the intelligentsia is."

"You ever hear of a fella named John Steinbeck. Won a Nobel Prize for literature?"

"That's Northern California. I'm talking about L.A."

"You ever read any Raymond Chandler?"

PART 1: INTERNAL COMBUSTION

"Pssssh. See? I'm trying to talk about literature and you bring up pulp fiction."

"Dude! Chandler was a great writer. He was the first to tackle the burgeoning urban immorality of the twentieth century. *The Big Sleep*, man, about a father's unconditional love for his daughter. Marlowe was all about honor. A noir knight errant. But without the satire of Cervantes. Chandler tackled pornography and violence and such issues as had never been done, but now it's imitated over and over. In a lot of ways, no one ever says this, but in a lot of ways he had the biggest influence on American culture of any writer of the period."

"I can't believe I'm debating the merits of detective fiction with you. All the best writers come from east of the Mississippi: Saul Bellow, Norman Mailer, Ralph Ellison, Truman Capote, Gore Vidal, Hemingway, Styron, Updike, Irving, Faulkner, Melville, Emerson, Thoreau, Dickinson, Frost…I could go on and on. The West may have been an inspiration for some in its frontier days, but there has never been a decent writer born of the West. Okay, except Steinbeck. The people who settled the West were uneducated miners, and laborers and merchants and farmers. Great ideas out here have never been valued unless they could turn a buck. Now everyone comes out here because they want to be in the movies or because they hate winter. Most people out here can't even speak English, like, dude. And I think Chandler was from England originally!" Drops of spit dotted the windshield.

"Why dontchya go back?"

"As soon as Larisa finishes her master's, we are."

Jim's stomach grumbled. Glowing golden arches glided to the window and stopped under a red glow.

"I know what you mean," said Adam. "I came out here from Utah, and it was like a whole nother language when I first got here. Every other word's like 'like', or 'dude,' or 'bail' or whatever."

Jim flicked his ear hard. "Cool it, dude," said Adam.

61

CAR TROUBLE

The glow turned green, the arches drifted away, and Jim remembered the fifth grade, when Mr. Webb sent him up for an IQ test to see if he was eligible for the Gifted Program. Jim scored a 139 and got into the program. Later he learned that an IQ of 140 was considered genius. Warning track power.

The lady who tested him said, "Raw intelligence doesn't make you smart, James. You've got to use it wisely. Intelligence is nothing without wisdom." And knowledge is the fear of God. "You know what factor MENSA considers most indicative of intelligence?"

Jim thought he'd heard this one before. "Sense of humor?"

She chuckled. "Very good guess, but that's not it. It's vocabulary. And you have a very good vocabulary for a boy your age. Very high. Your vocabulary scores are higher than the standard for high school graduates. You should be very proud of that, but don't forget you should always continue to develop your abilities."

After that, he rode the short bus to a different school twice a week. He hated it. The kids were all geeks. They did a lot of stupid stuff like slitting tennis balls to make mouths in them and gluing on googly eyes to make funny faces. Very creative. They made acrostics with their names. Profound. Jim didn't want to use his vocabulary. He wanted to be understood by the other kids. He wanted to cuss and use bad grammar like the cool kids.

"It's not the natives who make California seem shallow. It's all the people that come from somewhere else to be famous that give us the bad name. The people born here are just regular people," Jim said.

"Ptsh," Jeffrey began to say something when the car sputtered, putted, vroomed, putted again, and began to shudder. "Oh, shit. I forgot to get gas."

"Jeffrey! I reminded you this afternoon."

"I'm sorry. I forgot."

"Hey, Holmes, at least most Californians could tell you that E stands for EMPTY."

PART 1: INTERNAL COMBUSTION

"Maybe you'd rather walk, man."

"Looks like we're all gonna be walking. You better pull of the road, bro. Californians don't much appreciate guys clogging the road with their heads up their asses."

The engine coughed and died and the Datsun slowed to a halt along the side of the road.

"Shit," said Larisa.

"Damn," said Adam.

"Fuck!" yelled Jeffrey.

And they just sat there, Jeffrey with his forehead on the steering wheel, until Jim said, "So, I guess we'll just chill here until someone brings us some gas, huh?"

"No one's going to just bring us gas."

"That was sarcasm, Sherlock. Don't they have that out in Geniusland where you come from? Cripes. How about this? I got an idea. HOW ABOUT WE GET OUT OF THIS FUCKING CAR!" he shouted and shook back and forth and up and down.

"What the hell is your problem?"

"My problem is we're just sitting here doing nothing."

"He's right," said Larisa. "Jeffrey, let me out. I'll go to the pay phone back at that McDonald's and call the Auto Club. They'll bring us gas." They piled out of the car.

"I should go with you," said Jeffrey.

"What if the tow truck comes before I get back?"

"One of us could go with Larisa or stay with the car if you guys want," said Adam.

Mr. Goodfucking Samaritan, Jim thought. *It's the Mormon in him. No way I'm waiting around this car with that dickhead.* He said, "I'll go to McDonald's. I'm starving anyway. Maybe we should call Tink and tell her what's up. Dude, will you float me five bones, though?" His stomach rumbled.

Adam shook his head, but pulled out his wallet and handed Jim a five. "Why don't you just apply for welfare?"

"I will. Farewell."

Jim and Larisa walked toward the McDonald's. He felt a confused little thrill because he was attracted to her. Why are so many girls attractive? Is there any such thing as one true love? He'd already had crushes on a dozen girls. He could even remember as far back as kindergarten when girls wore those very short dresses with big plaid patterns and tights and shiny black buckle-shoes. A girl named Lisa who had very long brown hair used to chase Jim around. He was a loner weirdo even back then; he would limp around the playground by himself with one eye squinted up, pretending to be some great hero returning wounded from some commando battle, and Lisa, and her friend Elizabeth would stalk him and pin him against a wall and scold him and kiss him, and even back then, he got butterflies in his stomach and testes like you get in the big swing boat rides at amusement parks.

He remembered a girl in second grade named Angela who had really white skin and really red hair, like his mom's, and really red lips, and no one could beat him at tetherball, not even the third graders, but she could sometimes, and one time she pointed out that his shoe was untied, and she knelt and tied it for him, and he could feel himself rising because she was close to him, touching him, doing something nice for him; he might have risen right up to Heaven in the clouds where God was, except she had him tethered, tying his shoe; and on the last day of school he prayed fervently to God that she would be in his class the next year and have a seat right next to him.

But she wasn't in his class the next year. He didn't remember any loves that year or the year after that. What Jim remembered then was the day that summer his mother left. He could see it clearly, but it wasn't so much a memory through his own eyes, but one he saw like an audience member watching a movie, seeing himself on the screen. He could see the purple T-shirt and brown Toughskins he wore; could see how skinny he was. He helped her carry some boxes out to her

PART 1: INTERNAL COMBUSTION

purple Plymouth Duster. When it was time to go, she crouched down and held him tight, and he felt her tears on his cheeks before he was back in the audience watching himself watch the Duster go around the corner and disappear, leaving him sitting alone on the splintery woodpost fence.

Every night he would pray that he would wake up the next morning to find that it had all been a bad dream and his mom would be home again.

But the night before the first day of third grade, the very night before, a Sunday, his dad's girlfriend got Jim all dressed up. Jim thought maybe he was going to meet his new teacher. Soon his Grandma and Grandpa Crack arrived, and a couple of other old people who turned out to be his dad's girlfriend's parents. Jim asked his dad why they had to get all dressed up, and his dad said because they were going to church, and that was weird, because they never went to church, and when they got to church, Jim still hadn't figured it out until the ceremony had gotten under way. They were getting married.

Her name was Bonnie. The first time Jim had met her, earlier that summer, his dad had taken them all to Disneyland. The next thing Jim knew, she was in her robe making pancakes and doing the dishes at the house.

After the wedding, after coming home from the church, in the driveway, where the Plymouth had once been parked, his father stopped him going back into the house.

"Hold on a minute, buddy." His dad held his shoulder after the grandparents had gone inside. His dad put his hand on the back of Jim's neck. His dad's girlfriend stood in a woman's white business suit and skirt, holding a bouquet of flowers in her gloved hands. "Bonnie really loves us, and she really wants to be your mom, now. What do you think we should call her, Bonnie or Mom?"

"What are you thinking about so intently?" Larisa asked.

Inner panic. He stared at the cement. Stared at the driveway. He thought he knew what he had better say. "Mom," he croaked.

"Hello?" Larisa called.

From thereafter they referred to his real mother as his other mother.

"Are you okay?" Larisa asked.

Jim shook his head violently. "Yeah, I was just thinking."

"About what?"

"I don't know. You're the shrink. Isn't there some dormant stage in Freud's psychosexual stages of development or Piaget or one of those guys? I was thinking about all the girls I've loved before," he sang the last few words with a Julio Iglesias lilt, "and I started with kindergarten, but by the time I got to third grade, I didn't remember liking any girls again until about sixth or seventh grade."

"What happened then?"

"Christina Turina told me I was cute. And one day the teacher picked table captains and the table captains got to pick the people they wanted to sit at their tables. Christina was one of the table captains, and she picked me. All through the rest of elementary school, through like sixth, seventh, eighth grade, I had this crush on her. But I didn't really know what to do about it. I used to lie in bed kissing my pillow, imagining it was her. But then my dad got divorced AGAIN, and I ended up going to a different school. I had a girlfriend that summer before high school started, but I didn't really like her. She was nice and all, but I didn't think she was pretty. She *was* pretty, just not pretty like Christina. I was just her boyfriend because she wanted me to be. By the time I was a sophomore in high school there were dozens of girls who were so beautiful I could have loved any of them. But I ended up doing the same thing. Went out with a girl because she liked me, not because she was the one I wanted or even one of the ones I wanted. Stupid, huh?"

Larisa heaved a sigh. "I think I know what you mean. It's like Jeffrey and me. You know I have these like—I have these dreams that

PART 1: INTERNAL COMBUSTION

I'm sleeping next to a monster, and I wake up and I have to go sleep on the couch. We've been together nearly seven years, and I don't know why I'm telling you this, but I don't really love him anymore. Love is so fleeting. After a while, you end up having to decide to stay with a person even if you're not in love with him anymore, or else you would just go through an endless cycle of falling in and out of love until you were too old to attract anybody. I don't think I can stand that kind of pain. I guess I'd rather just be bored."

"Here we are." It was a McDonald's just like tens of thousands of others: square building with a red tile roof, wrapped by windows except in back where the kitchen was, kitchen separated from lines of customers by the cashiers' counter, redolent of the greasy sizzle of flesh, pickles, onions, buns pre-slathered with special sauce, Styrofoam containers eating away at the ozone layer, salty fries, carbonation, arched M's everywhere, lines of people pushing the words on the sign outside toward trillions and trillions served.

Children chased each other into McPlayland throwing chicken McNuggets at each other, as Jim and Larisa got in line behind a woman who must have outweighed the two of them together. She ordered a Mig Mac Meal, Super-sized, with a chocolate shake. "Are you going to get a burger or something?" Jim asked Larisa.

She made a face like she tasted bile. "I don't eat meat."

Probably don't swallow, either. "What are you, a veterinarian?"

"Ha ha. I think it's wrong to kill and eat other living creatures. It's also a healthy choice. I stay away from meat to avoid obesity and heart disease. But really also, I just don't like the taste of meat, especially the texture. It disgusts me."

"That's funny. Sometimes I justify smoking weed because I figure it's not as bad morally or health-wise as eating a cheeseburger. It's incredible that dealing organic high-ness is a crime, but butchery, heart disease, and diabetes are peddled on every street corner. I'm sure saturated fat has killed a lot more people than cannabis."

"Right on, bro," said the pimply-faced cashier.

Larisa laughed a little and asked for change for the pay phone. Jim ordered a double quarter-pounder with cheese, fries, and a Coke, to go.

"Half a pound of death," said Larisa. "I'm going to see if there's a pay phone by the bathrooms."

She walked away, and Jim's eyes followed the sway of her hips before she turned the corner. His breath hitched. It is not good that man should be alone. He longed for Tink, and then he missed Mary, and queasiness gripped his abdomen. He wished he had some weed. The cashier handed him his bag, and Jim shook his head as if to knock loose his longing. He went around the corner and found Larisa on the phone.

"How can it be expired? It says on the card that it doesn't expire until eight/ninety-four.... Well, why doesn't it say that on the card? I would have known to pay it.... This is absurd.... Yeah, great. Thanks a fucking lot." She hung up the phone with a little slam.

"Want me to hit it against the wall so hard that it breaks?"

"Do you have a credit card?

He made a snorting breath, blowing air along the spit inside his cheeks and fluttering his lips together, making a sound that meant "no" in a way that was more than no, extremely, ridiculously no.

"I have to go to the bathroom," she said. She walked through the door and left him standing there. He put his Coke on top of the pay phone and took his Styrofoam-encased cheeseburger from the bag, and held the bag against his side with his elbow while he removed the burger from the box. He put the box on top of the phone with his drink, took a bite of the burger, and pulled some change from his pocket. He dialed with a slippery finger, hoping Adam wouldn't wonder why Jim had her number memorized. Her machine picked up on the first ring. "Hi, this is Pam. I might be out, or I might just be waiting to hear who you are before I decide to pick up, so leave a message.

PART 1: INTERNAL COMBUSTION

Luvya." The inflection went up on every phrase. Beep.

"Hey, it's Jim. Surprise—we had car trouble. Long story. We should be there hopefully in about forty minutes. Bah."

Something about that made him feel even emptier. He took a bite of his burger. It did seem to partially fill the emptiness. The air sucked past him as Larisa pulled open the door and came out of the bathroom. "Maybe that Texaco station down the street has a gas can. How far do you think it is?"

What Texaco station? He wondered. "Less than a mile, I think," he said and took another bite of his burger. "I can eat this while we walk," he said pulling from his bag some shiny fries and cramming them into his mouth.

Back out on the street, a cool breeze blew. They walked without talking. Jim finished his burger and fries and wiped his mouth with the back of his wrist, dropping the bag in a trashcan they passed. "You know what? You're right about me," he said.

"What?"

"What you said back at the store. About me having disorders. I used to have to see doctors and psychologists when I was growing up. I take pills now, though."

"For what?"

"To try not to be so crazy. I cuss too much and make faces and junk if I don't take my pills."

"You have Tourette's Syndrome?"

"That's one of the things I've heard them say. Who knows for sure? You know how they say it's involuntary, though, all the cussing and noises and the faces? It's not exactly like that for me. It's not like these things just come out of my mouth without me knowing. It's more like I can feel them building up in me, in my mind, and like in my chest, too, and soon the pressure gets to be too much, and I have to let them out. It actually feels good. Like kind of a release, to just let the shit out. When I tried to control it, I was miserable and exhausted from the effort of trying to not say shit. It's weird. I'm a weirdo."

"When were you diagnosed?"

"I was a kid. About nine or ten maybe. I was always in the office for being wiggly and making noises. At first, they put me on Ritalin for Attention Deficit, but soon after that I came home from school, and I don't know why exactly, but I dropped all my books and papers in the driveway and climbed on top of my stepmother's car and pulled off my shirt and just started yelling every cussword I'd ever overheard in my life. Just standing up there screaming goddamnmotherfuckingcocksuckersonofabitchpieceofshitwhoreassdick poopoocacapeepee—whatever I could come up with. I guess the lady across the street called my step mom. Eventually I ended up at the City of Hope. I was like the first kid to try the Tourette's medicine."

"Does it work?"

"Fuck if I know. I guess I don't act quite as stupid as I used to with the weird noises and faces. Sometimes I don't feel like taking the pills. I feel like I'm not being the real me. Crazy. Like a lot of my friends liked me better when I cussed all the time. The profanity is still always in my head waiting to come out, but I can go to work and stuff and usually keep it inside when I take my pills. But it's weird, it's like there's always this foul-mouthed commentary running through my head that only I can hear."

"Are you hearing anything now?"

"No. When I'm with people I like, it pretty much goes away."

Her cheeks seemed to blush beneath the red lights of the Texaco sign. The lights over the pump islands cast shadows across the busy gas station in several directions at once. Adjacent to the center island stood a small kiosk in which resided a cashier with one eyebrow behind bullet-proof glass.

"No garage," Jim observed. "No bathroom. No squeegee. No paper towels. No air. No water. They probably got a sale on gas cans, though."

The cashier pulled a lever and shoved a drawer out at them as they

PART 1: INTERNAL COMBUSTION

approached the kiosk. "Do you sell gas cans?" Larisa asked.

The man did not take his eyes off the soccer game he was watching on a little TV. His brow furrowed. "Yes, we sell gas." He turned his palms out and shrugged. "We sell gas." He nodded.

"No, you don't understand. I need a gas *can*. Do you have a gas can?"

"We have oil. What kind oil you want?"

Jim felt a tap on his shoulder. He turned and faced a woman with lines around her smile just deep enough for her to have a decade or more on Jim. "Hi. Do you know where to put transmission fluid?"

That jerked his head a little. "Do I know where to put what kind of fluid now?" The top buttons of her shirt were undone and the valley there looked like a nice place to build a home. She was quickly ascending the list of his favorite females. She seemed to be emanating pheromones.

"Transmission fluid." She nodded her head then shook her head trying to elicit a yes or no answer from him, smiling all the while.

"If I look under your hood and poke around a little, I might be able to figure out where to put it."

Her smile got even bigger. "The car is right over here." She turned and walked, and Jim examined her back side. He thought she exaggerated the side-to-side bump of her hips, perhaps for his benefit, as she led him to a five-year-old Mustang. An orangutan sat in the passenger seat. Like the Clint Eastwood movie. Clint would say, "Right turn, Clyde," and the orangutan would stick his arm out the window and sock a highway patrolman. Jim wished he had an orangutan to sock highway patrolmen. But it wasn't an orangutan. It was a very old woman with very long hair dyed kind of orange. He shook his head and peered under the popped hood at the tossed salad of hoses, wires, and metal parts. He unscrewed a few caps. The first one clearly was where the oil went. Another was for windshield wiper fluid. Another one he was pretty sure was the master cylinder where the brake fluid went—or wait, he thought, wasn't the Master Cylinder Felix the Cat's archenemy? He found two more caps to unscrew, one of which was buried way down under a bunch of hoses and difficult to get at. He guessed one was for power steering fluid and one for transmission fluid, but which was which? The dipsticks on each came up with the same unchilled-cherry-jello-looking substance, but one was way lower. He unscrewed the quart of transmission fluid. It seemed to contain the same substance. He thought of asking the orangutan if the manual was in the glove box, but since the dipsticks showed one reservoir to be lower on unchilled-cherry-jello-looking shit than the other, he decided that was enough to go on. It was the one difficult to get at, natch.

"You don't have a long-stemmed funnel in your trunk, do you?"

"A what where?"

"Long-stemmed funnel in your trunk."

"No, I'm sorry. Should I ask the gas station attendant?"

"No. We'd all be better off if we just rode horses, don't you think?

She gave him a little giggle that tickled his Adam's apple. "I guess I'll just have to eyeball it, then." He glanced involuntarily at her crotch and swallowed. "I might end up spilling it all over, unless you want to wait until you get somewhere with a long-stemmed funnel."

"That's okay. Go for it."

"How do you even know you need transmission fluid?"

"When I'm driving, it takes a while for it to shift gears. A guy at work said it sounds like my transmission, and the first thing I should do is check the fluid level. He checked it for me and said it was low, but I didn't see where he checked."

"I see." Jim put his thumb over the mouth of the bottle and turned it upside down. Lowering it down through the hoses and belts and far as he could over where it looked like the fluid should go. He unthumbed the bottle and the fluid glugged out. He couldn't see if it was going in or not. A thin trickle began to bleed out from under the car.

"What's going on?" Larisa asked.

PART 1: INTERNAL COMBUSTION

"I'm spilling transmission fluid all up inside this engine. Whatcha got there?"

"Four quarts of oil. I had a brainstorm. We'll pour out the oil and fill the containers with gasoline. That'll give us a gallon which should be enough to get the car to the gas station."

"Ingenious. You're a real McGyver."

When the transmission fluid container was empty, Jim pulled the dipstick to check the oil, incensed that the gas station had no paper towels. He wiped the stick on his sock, put it in again, and found that it was about a quart low. "Let's see some of that oil." He unscrewed the cap on the engine where the oil went, unscrewed the oil, poured it in, screwed the cap back on, and closed the hood. "I don't know how much of that trannie fluid I got in without a funnel."

"Thanks for trying."

He cocked his head like a curious pooch. "I didn't get your name."

"Liz." She offered her hand.

He took her cool fingers in his grimy paw. "James T. Crack, at your service. Hey, I wonder if you wouldn't mind giving us a ride up the road about a mile or two."

"No problem." She never stopped smiling. "If my car will go."

"Can we fill these with gas first?"

"Sure," Liz said and went to the window to tell the old woman something in Spanish.

"What's with these gas stations stripped down to nothing but taking your money?" Jim muttered one more time, scanning the station one more time for a bathroom.

"I've got five bucks on pump six," Larisa said.

"Lemme have another quart of that oil," said Jim. She handed it to him. "I'll be right back." He walked around to the rear of the cashier's booth and pulled his Beam from his pants, unscrewed the cap, and took a big swig. He shivered and unscrewed the oil. "No regard for your average motorist's needs. Put your money in the drawer and fuck

73

you. It's like the crack house of gasoline. Preying on addictions like pushers," he mumbled, as he poured the oil on the concrete outside the door of the kiosk. Then he undid his fly and pissed in the spreading puddle of oil. A woman pumping gas spotted him and he lifted his chin to her, toasted her with the empty oil bottle, and she turned away. When he was done, he tapped, zipped and walked back around the corner of the kiosk.

Back at pump six, Larisa was trying to pump gas into the plastic quart containers, but the mouths were too small for the nozzles, and she spilled as much gas on the pavement as she got into the container, and she kept having to stop to let the bubbles recede, then pour in a little more and stop and pour a little more.

The five dollars on the pump ran out before the fourth quart was full. Liz was waiting by the open door of the Mustang to let them into the back seat. They got in reeking of gasoline, and Liz started the Mustang. She put it in gear and it revved like it was in neutral for several seconds before it jerked forward with a screech of tires onto the street. The inside of the car smelled like the first floor of Nordstrom and a NASCAR pit.

"This is my mom," Liz announced. The old woman said something in Spanish. "She says God bless you for helping us."

Jim's eye twitched like a sneeze was coming. A little statue of the Virgin Mary prayed on the dashboard. Jim's mother kneeled beside his bed. He had already been taught Now I lay me down to sleep I pray the Lord my soul to keep if I should die before I wake I pray the Lord my soul to take.

"Why do we want the Lord to take my soul, Mommy?"

"Because you want your soul to go to Heaven."

"What's a soul?"

"It's the spirit that lives in your body and lives on in Heaven after your body dies."

"What's Heaven?"

PART 1: INTERNAL COMBUSTION

"Heaven is a wonderful place where you get to be with all the people you love and who love you, and you never feel bad, or sick, or scared." She smiled, but she looked sad.

"Why can't we go there now?"

Her eyes darted back and forth. "We have to prove that we belong there first. Only good people can go there."

"What happens to your body?"

"It turns back into dust."

"Dust?"

"The Bible says God made people from dust."

"But Mommy, we're made from skin."

She didn't say anything.

"Momma, where do the people go that aren't good?"

"The bad people go to a place of fire, and they burn forever and ever because they were bad."

"Does it hurt a lot?"

"Yes. But you can ask God to help you be good, so you won't go there. Clasp your hands like this and say, 'Our father,'" she waited for him to repeat, "'who art in Heaven hallowed be thy name thy kingdom come, thy will be done on Earth as it is in Heaven give us this day our daily bread and forgive us our trespusses as we forgive those who trespuss against us lead us not into temptation but deliver us from evil as thine is kingdom and the power and the glory forever and ever. Amen. God bless Mommy and Daddy and Grandmas and Grandpas and everyone I love and help me to be a good boy. Amen.'"

They practiced it for a few nights until he could do it without any help, and then he added a little request not to have any scary dreams, but rather something more along the lines of a Road Runner cartoon. It had become something he recited silently, unconscious of any meaning to the words, a rhythmic chant to dispel his discordant thoughts in times of dread.

"I'm sorry, what?" Larisa said.

"I didn't say anything."

"I thought you did."

"No."

"Oh." She turned away, looking out the window so that all Jim could see of her was her soft brown hair. At least it looked soft. Like his mother's had been. Those weeks before he saw her last, streaks of white hair had grown down from over her temples, and she haunted the house at night in her flowing night gown, sleepless, he knew because he would hear the clanking in the kitchen and he would see her pass back and forth in front of his door, and she would come in to kiss him sometimes.

"We have to make a left up here," said Larisa. Liz waited for a lull in the oncoming traffic to turn, blinker blink blink blinking blink blink blink. Jim fought screams over the sizable gaps Liz let go by without turning. A Sleestack sound escaped his post-nasal cavity.

"I'm sorry," Liz said. "I'm afraid the transmission will slip, and we won't get through."

"That's okay," Larisa said amidst the shaking of Jim's head and a Donald Duck quacking from the back of his throat before a demonic belching sound erupted from his chest, and Liz punched the gas, but the car only rolled forward a few feet into the path of traffic, engine revving violently, the next wave of traffic a hundred feet away and closing fast. Horns blared, tires screeched, and the Mustang shot across the intersection and onto the boulevard.

When they arrived back at the Datsun, Adam was lying on the hood, and Jeffrey was in the car with the dome light on. Adam sat up as Jim and Larisa got out of the car. "What took you guys," he said.

"You gotta ask? Life, baby. You know me. Life takes me," said Jim.

Jeffrey got out of the car. "What took you?"

"We got gas," said Larisa. "I can't believe you left the lights on inside. You know the battery is weak. And I can hear the radio. I hope you didn't drain it." She walked to the gas cap flap on the side of the

PART 1: INTERNAL COMBUSTION

car. Jeffrey walked close enough for her to push him away. "Go turn off the lights and the radio, and pull the handle on the floor to open this gas door thing." She unscrewed a quart of gas. Then she unscrewed the gas cap.

Jim noticed how everything had to be unscrewed all the time. "Should we just walk the rest of the way?" he asked Adam.

"What if they're having a problem with their battery? Shouldn't we try to help them?"

Jim said nothing. He felt like his life was a boring movie, but there wasn't anything else to do, so he kept watching.

"Try to start it now," Larisa said. The car went wuuwuu wuu wuuu wuuwuu wuuuuuuu wu w-click. Click. Click. "I knew it. You drained the battery. First you run out of gas, then you drain the battery." Jeffrey's head receded deeper into his ribcage.

"I think we've got some jumper cables in our car," said Adam.

"Fuckadoodledoo." Jim thought how often he had had to be jumped. Had had dead batteries, burned out alternators, faulty regulators, worn-down starters, and shitty ignitions. All in about three years of driving. "It's not a stick, is it? If it's a stick, we can push start it." Getting it rolling was the hard part. If you were by yourself, you had to push on the frame at the open door with a hand on the wheel. Push with both legs at first, until it's moving, then push with one leg and then the other, taking straining steps, and with that little momentum, you build speed up to walk, and then a jog, and a run, and then you jump in, and pop the bastard into gear, and a lot of times it'll start, your heart thudding in your chest.

How many times had he had to push-start a car? How many cars? The square back, the Z, the Baja bug, the Fiat. Probably some more he didn't remember. And those were just the sticks. None of the automatics he'd burned through—the Olds, the Buick, Gramma's Chrysler—could be push-started. How many times had he push-started a car in sandals? Barefoot? In the rain? He had to push-start the Fiat one entire year. Push-start it to go to work in the morning, push-start it to go home. Push-start it to the store, and hope no one stole it while he left it running. He got to where he didn't even mind. "I got the Flintstones car," he would tell people. He was always looking for parking places pointing downhill.

One time the Fiat stalled in the rain, and he pushed it to where the road dipped under a Santa Ana Freeway overpass. He rolled down under the freeway and got it started briefly before it stalled again in the foot of water that had pooled in the nadir of the underpass. Forward or backward, no matter which way he went, it was too steep to push. "I've hit a real low point," he said to the walls of the underpass, and laughed maniacally. "It's all uphill from here." He crawled into the back seat of the little Fiat and fell asleep on a bed of parking tickets to the sound of rainwater cascading all around him, and the smell of almost-empty beer cans in his nostrils.

"If we can get a ride to our car, we can come back with some jumper cables," Jim heard Adam say. He shook his head, but his memory clouded his senses.

"Uhm." Liz made a noise like she'd rather not and edged toward her car. "I'm just worried that I'll kill us all at the next left turn I make in traffic with the transmission acting up."

The water must be rising. He was too tired to look. In his half-asleep dream stupor, he imagined it was beer rising all around him. At first it was wonderful, cold beer climbing over his body, but the beer turned old and rotten and stunk. A panicky paralysis gripped him. He heard a tapping on the glass. "You okay in there, buddy?"

Jim did not stir. He hoped the voice would go away and let him drown in peace.

Rap rap rap. "You can't park here." Rap rap rap.

He opened one eye. His vision was blurred and the window was fogged. He made out the round outline of a helmet. Shit. It had to be a motorcycle cop. Or a spaceman. That would be better. Maybe he was

PART 1: INTERNAL COMBUSTION

going to be abducted by an alien.

"Sir, please step out of the vehicle."

Jim wondered what would happen if he ignored the cop. He heard him try the door. It would open only a few inches. Jim had tried to make a tight turn at a gas station around a pole too short to see, and it rumpled his door at the hinge so that he had to go in and out the window when the top was up, like the Dukes of Hazzard.

He heard footsteps walking on water around to the other side of the car. Maybe it was Jesus. *Maybe I'm saved*, he thought. Then he heard another car drive up. "What you got?" A woman's voice.

"He isn't responding. Looks like a DUI."

Jim sat up. *Am I drunk?* He clambered over the seat and ended up awkwardly with his back up against the windshield and his knees in his face and the stick shift poking him in the ass. His legs were numb and unresponsive. He jiggled the passenger door handle, and it opened and poured him out into the puddle of water around his car. He used the open door to pull himself, muddy water trickling though the hair on his forearms. A billion pins and needles pricked his calves and feet.

"You deaf or something?" the cop asked, kind of dickishly. He must have been about ten years older than Jim. His nameplate said HAND. Officer Hand?

"I'm sorry, I was like paralyzed or something." Jim was shivering and sweaty. He lifted a foot from the water and tried shaking some blood into it, and spattered little drops on Hand's pants and boots.

"You have your license and registration?"

Jim pulled his wallet from his back pocket, and handed over his license. Hand handed it to the lady cop, who took it up to a black and white patrol car idling at the top of the underpass, red and blue lights swirling. Another cop sat behind the windshield. Three of them. Somewhere a little old lady was being robbed. "I think the registration is in the glove box."

Hand stayed close behind him while Jim shuffled through the glove box. "Smells like alcohol. You been drinking?"

That was a good question. He tried to think. He didn't know anything. For all he knew, he'd been cryogenically frozen and had awakened three thousand years later, but the world was still the same shitty place. Let's see. Last he could remember, it had been Friday. That's right. He'd been on his way home from the petroleum products shipping yard where he worked. It had been a slow day from the rain; a lot of the trucks were hung up in snow on the Grapevine, and the walk-in business had been dead. Uh-oh. Craig, the other yardman, had taken twenty bucks from the register and sent Jim to the liquor store for a case of beer. Jim had been drinking. Like ten or so beers. How long ago was that? The time of day beneath the freeway was inscrutable. The rain had slackened to a drizzle, but what little sky could be sign was incalculably gray. It could have been dawn or dusk or noon. Could he have slept through the night? He checked the white strip in the tan around his wrist where his watch had been before the leather band had finally rotted apart in the rotten weather outside at the yard a day earlier.

"No, sir." He found the registration and handed it to Hand, who put in in his breast pocket and took from the same pocket a pen light.

Hand said, "I want you to follow this light with your eyes without moving your head. You understand?"

Jim nodded.

"Don't move your head."

"Okay."

He stared into the penlight and tried to follow it back and forth and up and down with his eyes, but his teeth were chattering and he was sniffling.

"It's not looking too good for you, guy. You sure you haven't been drinking?"

"I wish I had been, officer. The open road, an open beer against your balls. One of the great feelings of freedom, don't you think?—or

PART 1: INTERNAL COMBUSTION

I guess you wouldn't know anything about that."

The Sam Brown belt, with its holstered gun, and bullets, billy club, and handcuffs, creaked. "I'm going to administer a field sobriety test. Put your feet together, point your toe up, and lift your heel about two inches off the ground. Lean your head back, put your arms out from your side, and touch your nose."

"Dude! We're standing in two inches of water."

"Listen, amigo. I am an officer of the law. You don't call me 'dude,' okay?"

"I'm a citizen of the U.S. Don't call me 'amigo,' okay?"

"Maybe you'd prefer punk."

"Maybe you'd prefer pri—"

"He checks out," the woman cop returned from the patrol car. "Your shift is about over, isn't it, Jerry? You want me and Gonzalez to handle this? It looks like it's about to start raining again soon."

"No, I—" Officer Hand started to say when Jim's breath caught, hitched, hitched, and hitched again, his eyelids fluttered, his nose screwed up, and he sneezed, and then another, and another, and for the grand finale, a massive, heaving blast of pathogens that left his fingers draped in snot and his upper lip glistening. He wiped his nose with his wrist and wiped his hands on his pants. "I did promise the wife I'd read to the kids before they went to bed tonight. I'll let you guys handle the American citizen here." Hand strode over to his bike and mounted it with all the majesty of John Wayne upon a faithful steed. He kicked the bike to a rumble and rode through the puddle, parting the waters like he was Charleton Heston.

The lady cop had a worn, handsome face. BEAVER was etched on her nameplate. A surge of pragmatism checked Jim's juvenile impulses, enabling him to suppress the Ferris wheel of snickery comments that leapt to his tongue. She walked him out from under the overpass to where the street flattened out. A cool breeze chilled his damp skin. He searched the ashen sky for some clue to the hour, and the clouds broke open revealing a sly Cheshire Cat grin of crescent moon in the darkening sky. Like a clipped fingernail. His mind cleared.

"Officer, I want to apologize." He sniffled. My car stalled down there, and it wouldn't start, and I was waiting for the rain to die down before I went for help, but I fell asleep." He sniffled.

"Okey," she said, and she put him through the field sobriety test, had him say the alphabet, walk a straight line, heel, toe, heel, toe.

"You seem pretty lucid."

Lucid? Did she say 'lucid'?" Maybe she said 'stupid'. How many other of Jim's run-ins with the law were revealed by the that Orwellian credit card strip they were putting on the backs of licenses now? His previous violations, infractions, detainments, misdemeanors and arrests swirled around his brain. 'Lucid'? Maybe she was one of those cops who was still in it to help people. Maybe she didn't just get off on having a gun and imposing the will of bourgeois bureaucrats on the people. Maybe she wasn't on a power trip. Maybe she believed the Highway Patrol could help motorists, rather than rob them to put more money in state coffers to pay more bureaucrats.

"I could write you a ticket for being stopped illegally, but I'm not going to." Her lips tightened into a flat, barely discernible smile. "I used to have a Fiat when I was your age."

"What are you tripping about?" Adam asked.

"Nothing. Dude, let's go." Jim made for Liz's Mustang. She tilted the seat forward and let him in back.

"Uh, okay, so then we'll get those jumper cables and be right back," Adam called and got in next to Jim.

Adam looked at his watch. "Guess what time it is."

Jim heard, but he couldn't respond. He wondered if this was how stroke victims felt. His will had been so subverted. To what? To the automobile. He felt undead. If he wasn't the master of his own destiny, or at least of his own direction and propulsion, then what was the point of living at all? The car revved, and the transmission balked. It

PART 1: INTERNAL COMBUSTION

would be a dicey proposition pulling out into traffic again. He hoped they got hit and hit hard. Hoped they got flipped by a hard-charging, fuel-carrying semi. Hoped the Jaws of Life could not save them.

"Can you jump me?" he asked Officer Beaver.

"Hey, Gonzo," she called back to the patrol car. "Should we give this guy a jump?"

"Is that safe to do in that puddle? Maybe we should just call him a tow truck."

"Let's push him out." She turned to Jim. "Make sure the car is in neutral and the brake is off."

Jim climbed into the Fiat, and Gonzo brought the front of the patrol car against the Fiat's back bumper and pushed it out from under the freeway. "Pop the hood," said Officer Gonzo. Jim did, then crawled out of the car. The hood of the CHP car was up; it looked like it was about to swallow the little Fiat. Gonzalez brought jumper cables from the trunk and hooked them between the batteries. "See if it'll start," he said to Jim.

It started right up. Jim climbed out the window again as Gonzalez disconnected the cables. The clamps tapped together, and a sprinkle of sparks fell hissing to the damp pavement. "Wow," said Jim. "You guys are great. Thank you so much."

"Don't shut it off until you get to a garage. Could be the generator's dead, or you might need a new alternator, or anyone of a number of things that could be wrong with that car."

He thanked them again, revved her up, shifted into gear, let off the clutch, and stalled it. Patrolpersons Beaver and Gonzalez pulled alongside him, shaking their heads. "We'll radio you a tow truck," she said, and they drove away.

An ambulance came screeching down the boulevard, and even though the transmission hitched, Liz was easily able to turn into its wake as the other cars had pulled to the side to let it by. The ambulance slowed into the gas station where Jim and Larisa and Liz had just been.

As Liz guided the Mustang around the corner, Jim saw a few people tending to a man lying on the concrete behind the cashier's kiosk. He wondered again why he did the things he did.

He leaned against the fender and waited. Didn't notice that the car was wet, duh, until his cheeks were cold and damp, and then he reckoned it was too late to do differently, so he stayed there, jaw ping-pong-ing from side to side, waiting. He hated waiting. Waiting in lines, waiting in traffic jams, waiting for red lights, waiting at court, waiting to hear his name called to wait in another room to get his name called in hospitals, office buildings, and human resources waiting rooms. He was a well-fed white American, and waiting was the scourge of his existence. He hated it worse than poverty, worse than homelessness, worse than war, worse than man's inhumanity to man. It was torture equivalent to having his fingernails pulled out one by one. If somehow torching some village in Mongolia was the difference in his not waiting thirty minutes for something, there were times he would have seriously considered the torching.

And he waited. The misshapen moon appeared in the window of an office building up the road, and he watched it move without its seeming to move from one window to the next. Waiting, the seconds drained away; mortality rushed at him, and with it, the torturous recall and assessment of his life to that point. All the missteps, blow-its, fuckups, and bad breaks in his memory would engulf him in a madness, and he would become possessed with an implacable need to move on. Fight or flee. Move or die. Like a shark. It was not merely impatience, but the need to prevent his own decay. He'd walked out of potential jobs waiting to be interviewed, walked out of pharmacies without his pills, and walked out of courtrooms letting traffic tickets turn to warrants for arrest. When the last tip of the moon disappeared off the building—suddenly for its clock-hand slowness—bolts of energy coursed through Jim's legs, and he was gone.

He was a mile away before he wondered where he was going, and

PART 1: INTERNAL COMBUSTION

still he kept walking, not knowing the answer. He passed boxy, windowless buildings, one after the other, in an area devoid of life, as if in some *Twilight Zone* episode where all the people had disappeared, soundless but for the steady breeze blowing across his ears. "Hello," he called.

"Hell-hell-hello," his voice echoed off buildings as the sky flickered brightly in the distance. Jim counted twelve paces before detecting the low rumble of thunder. Still he walked. He passed the chain link fence of some body shop where a smell of ozone hung in the air and clung to his tongue. He mused that ozone would replace brimstone as the odor of Hell when a terrible snarling of fangs and claws, a three-headed dog, Cerberus, lunged for his throat, and crashed against the fence, generating a force of fear that nearly knocked Jim into the gutter. Pitbulls. He kicked against the fence at them and barked, heart pounding erratically. Fuckers. He had to urinate and was glad to do so, directing the stream at the heads of the dogs. They backed away and sniffed at the steaming splash. The splattering seemed to grow all around Jim; he thought that the acoustics that had produced the echo were amplifying the sound of his piss hitting the pavement, when a cool drop hit his arm. Drops plopped on the concrete all around him. He looked up and they hit him on the face and ran down his cheeks. He remembered in like second grade when kids would say it was the angels crying. By fifth grade, it was God pissing down on the world.

"Here it is on the right."

Liz pulled up alongside the ruins of Jim's soup can tower. He and Adam got out of the car and thanked Liz and her mom. The wheels spun in the dirt when the transmission caught, then catapulted the car into the street. Adam went to open the door, and finding it locked, patted his pockets. "Dude, you have the keys, right?"

"Yeah, I grabbed them before we left." Jim frisked himself. "No."

They hung from the ignition.

Jim leaned against the car and took a swig of his bourbon while

Adam checked to see if any of the doors were unlocked. Jim wasn't surprised to find that none were.

"You idiot."

"I swear to God I grabbed them before we left." He looked through the glass at the keys gleaming like precious metal. There always seemed to be some invisible barrier between where he was and what he wanted.

"Obviously, you didn't."

"Whatever."

He stopped and turned unsure of where he was. He walked back the way he had come; the dogs' barking subsided behind him, the patter of raindrops became more insistent. He came to a three-way intersection. Nothing looked familiar. He read the sign of the street he had come to. Rampart. He looked for the name of the street he was on, but there was no sign. This profoundly disturbed him. In twentieth-century America, every street had its sign, but here was one of those strange omissions, a typo of civilization, a street with no sign in the middle of the bustling modernity of Orange County. Had vandals removed it? Had some worker neglected to install it? These conjectures seemed unlikely to Jim. He knew it was the multiversal fuckaround. He turned right on Rampart. It didn't seem right. The car was on Orangewood, by Angel Stadium. He looked for the Big A. Where the hell was he? The street curved around to another three-way intersection with only the Rampart sign and not the cross-street's. The top of the Crystal Cathedral came into view between two warehouses. The Reverend Doctor Schooler's multi-million-dollar palace of worship and TV studio. Jim remembered one morning when his mother said she wanted him to go to Sunday school for his Mother's Day present to her. There weren't any cartoons on Sunday morning, anyway, so he consented to go. She walked him to the corner, and a big green bus arrived, and he got in. At the church, they started in a big room where a man talked a while. Jim couldn't understand him. Then all the kids got

PART 1: INTERNAL COMBUSTION

sent to different rooms, depending on how old they were. Jim got sent to a room where a woman with a chalkboard told a story about when she had locked her keys in her house, and accidentally broke a window trying to get in, and how that made her angry, and she wanted to get mad, but she didn't. And you know why boys and girls? Because when you get mad, that's The Devil getting in you.

And then they sent everybody back to the big room, and a white-haired man in robes came out and told them something, and Jim saw everyone put their heads down and close their eyes, so Jim put his head down and closed his eyes, too. And the old man was saying things Jim didn't understand, and he went on and on for a really long time, and Jim didn't know when you were allowed to open your eyes again, but all he could hear was that old voice going on and on, saying more words he didn't understand, and Jim didn't want to get in trouble for opening his eyes, and he kind of fell asleep—until he felt a tap on his shoulder and looked up, and a man was looking down at Jim, and he looked angry. It was one of the Sunday school teachers, and he scolded Jim in a fast whisper for not heeding the word of the Lord.

When Jim got home his mom asked if he would go back the next week, and Jim said, "No."

He came to the end of the street. Towne and Rampart. At least the new street had a name. He turned down Towne.

Later he asked his neighbor, Ron, what The Devil was, and Ron said The Devil was the boss of Hell.

"Hell?"

Ron looked around. "Yeah. It's underground and there's a lot of fire, and they burn people there and stick 'em with forks."

The fiery place where the bad people go. "What's The Devil look like?" I'll run away from him.

"He's got horns comin' out of his head, and..." Ron took one of the white stones that lined the planter along the walkway to the front door of his house, and on the concrete he drew a circle with two smaller circles inside, and slanted lines over the small circles to make angry eyebrows, and he scribbled a triangle that was a beard, and drew a mouth full of triangle teeth, drew triangle ears, and triangle horns, and a body with stick arms and legs, and a tail with a triangle on the end of it.

Jim looked at it and nodded.

Towne wound around and he came to another street. Rampart. Rampart? Rampart! Unfuckingbelievable. How do you come to the street you just left behind? "What the hell is this?" he asked himself. "The goddamned Devil's Triangle?" He scanned the horizon above the rooftops of the deserted buildings for some sign of the big A with the halo around it at Angel Stadium. If he got to that, he could find State College and Orangewood and get back to the car. But all he could see was the top of the Crystal Cathedral. Rainwater running down its sides made it look like it was melting. He felt he would go mad. He wanted to punch something, to break glass, to create a jagged, bloody hole. He put the cathedral to his back and sprang over a chain-link fence, ready to put his fingers in the eyes of any dogs that came at him. Fuck the streets. He would just keep that glass cathedral at his back and climb or destroy whatever blocked his way to the Big A. Like King Kong making for the World Trade Center. He came to a big van and stepped onto its bumper onto its hood onto the top of it and strode across it to the roof of the building it was backed up to, pulled himself up and walked across the roof. There was the Big A. He was headed right for it. He hung from the roof by his fingers and dropped to the ground. Clambered over another fence and onto a new street. A signal blinked from red to green at the end of the street. He focused his vision like the Bionic Man and scoped the name of the street. State College. He felt something like triumph, ha ha, as if he had outwitted some cosmic antagonist, yes yes, he had beaten The Devil. Two steps later, he snorted sardonically, knowing it would never last.

Adam slumped against the door until he was sitting on the ground

PART 1: INTERNAL COMBUSTION

and began to gently bang his head against the car. Jim swirled the last of the bourbon around the bottom of the bottle. He felt like smashing it, would have enjoyed the musical splash of the glass shattering.

"Dude, we need to call a tow truck and get one of those guys here with one of those slim- jims to open the door," said Adam.

Jim held up the bottle to a street lamp and stared at the light through the swirling amber. Like the flashing yellow hazard lights on the top of the tow truck when he got back to the Fiat. The bed of the truck was already inclined, and Meatloaf was hooking a cable under Jim's car. Jim broke into a jog. "Whoa! Whoa! Wait up!" The truck was idling, and the air was thick with diesel exhaust.

Meatloaf pulled a lever on the back of the truck and a winch began to pull the car up onto the inclined flatbed.

"Whoa! Hey, man, I don't want this thing towed! I just want to get a jump!" he shouted over the noise of the winch. Meatloaf released the lever and pulled another one, which lowered the flatbed to a horizontal position, and he proceeded to set blocks under the Fiat's tires. The rain became more insistent. Jim stood right in front of Meatloaf. "Dude, I don't want my car towed." The guy walked around Jim and hooked a chain to the bumper. "I don't want my car towed," Jim said again, but the guy walked around him a second time and began tightening a chain on the other side of the truck. Jim walked to the first chain and began loosening it.

"What the fuck are you doing?" Meatloaf asked.

"Dude, I don't want my car fucking towed. I only want a jump."

"This your car?" He continued tightening the chain.

"Yeah, and I don't want it towed."

"I already got it up. I gotta take it in."

"You can just put it down again. It's my car, and I don't want it towed. It only needs a jump."

Meatloaf came around and replaced the chain Jim had removed. "I'm taking it to the yard." He pulled off one of his gloves.

"The yard? You can't do that." Jim stepped toward him. "Get my car down, asshole." A long, low peal of thunder snarled across the sky.

Meatloaf smirked and put the glove back on. He reached into the cab and took out a heavy wrench. "You can call the cops to find out where to pick it up." He slapped the wrench in his hand a few times. Jim took two more steps before stopping. He wasn't afraid of Meatloaf and his wrench, but he knew the result would be him sitting in court again.

"That's what I thought," said Meatloaf. He got into the cab. "Bring cash." The engine revved, and the tow truck rumbled forward. Jim immediately regretted not going after the fucker. He searched for a rock or something to throw at the truck. A Coke bottle came rolling along in the current in the gutter; he grabbed it and heaved it, where it struck against the bumper of the Fiat and smashed as the truck drove away.

Jim got up and tossed the bottle of Jim Beam out into the street. "Let's break the fucking window," he said to Adam.

"No."

"Just tell them some starving homeless guy broke in to steal some soup. I'm sure they got insurance. It's a company car, for shit sake. It won't even affect you at all."

"We should call a locksmith or a tow truck or something."

"Call a-! A tow truck! Call-! Are you high? You want to go for another five-mile walk to a phone booth so you can call someone to come out and screw you over? They're just going to screw you, dude. They'll screw you one way or another. THEY WILL SCREW YOU!"

"Who's 'they'?"

"THEY, man, THEY! Everybody. The cops, the locksmith, the insurance company, your boss, the tow truck drivers, anybody who's got you under them's going to want to keep it that way, but if we bust this fucking window, we can dodge all that! Then we're gone in sixty seconds instead of two hours. Save the night, dude. Save the night and

PART 1: INTERNAL COMBUSTION

just let me bust this fucking window."

Jim shivered. The rain ran icy down his hot back. He was stuck. He was stuck. He was stuck. For a time immeasurable, he couldn't summon the presence of mind to take a dozen steps under the bridge out of the rain. He wished the tow truck driver would hydroplane, flip, and be pinned under the tow truck with rainwater running up his nose. Justice. The rain ran down Jim's face and mixed with the snot on his lips. Snot plagued him. It always had. He had been allergic to everything since the third grade. He woke up mornings congested with mucous the consistency of a mollusk, but by the time he got to school, clear, watery, fluid ran perpetually from his eyes and nose. He blew his nose in Kleenex until the box was empty, and then toilet paper until the roll was gone, and then sandpapery sink towels, and then his shirt, and when that was soaked, he blew his nose into his fingers and wiped them on his pants until everything he wore was drenched.

His second stepmother took him to see an allergist. They wheeled in a gleaming stainless-steel cart with a few gleaming instruments of medieval torture. They dipped hooks into vials of essence of ragweed, Chinese elm, cat dander, molds, mildews, grasses, dust, dust motes, dust mites, dairy products, shellfish, bee venom, air, people, life—he didn't know what all—and they crocheted his back full of allergens, a hundred and twenty of them. The dozens that swelled the skin and became itchy, were those to which he was allergic. Every week thereafter his stepmother drove him to the Kaiser in Bellflower where he received injections of those substances to which he was allergic, so, the doctors said, to build up his immunities. His stepbrother would have to come, too. Every Wednesday, a trip up the freeway in stop-and-go traffic to wait in a waiting room for years. His allergies never improved. "Industrial particulates," one doctor said. "I'm afraid there's no immunity for that."

Jim stood transfixed by the mystery of the purpose of human suffering. If he had to suffer, why did it have to be something so irritating as constant snot flow and dickhead tow truck drivers? Why couldn't it be something epic and noble? Why couldn't he be a prisoner of war or a man stranded on a desert island? Does evil cause suffering? Did God create evil? Or does He just allow it? Or is He struggling against evil, too? Or is there no God? Or no evil? The storm raged Lear-like around the overpass. The thunder became awesome, and the rain came down furiously. The lightning was no longer flashing in the distance but crackling in the sky right around him. Zeus, the mighty Thor, the Navajo Thunderbird, Yahweh—myths? Atmospheric conditions? Nonsense words made up to answer unanswerable questions—CRACK! A thought-executing thunderbolt tore the sky and struck the transformer atop a telephone pole, throwing the night into a flash of light and shadow; the transformer exploded in a shower of green fire, a spasm of fear rushed through Jim and knocked him to the street, as if from the force of the blast.

The street lights went out up and down the street, casting Jim into utter darkness but for the jagged streaks and garish flowers of light splashed across his vision by the imprint of the fulmination upon his retinas. His molars ached hot, and his heart beat a syncopated free-form improvisation. Many seconds later, he could still hear the blast rumbling away from him before fading into the sound of the rain. An acrid smell filled the air, and even in the downpour, he thought he could hear the hiss of livewires in water. He scrambled up the sloped concrete embankment beneath the overpass to where he felt a ledge tucked up just under the bottom of the freeway. An array of unpleasant odors jostled through the snot running out of his nose. He groped around the ledge and felt cloth. He stuffed his hand into the pocket of his wet jeans and extracted a lighter. It clicked and sparked twice before the flame caught. Its shimmering halo revealed an old blanket and some clothes, a few beer cans, a Kentucky Fried Chicken cup, and the bones of Colonel Sanders. The light blew out. A homeless home.

He realized he was shivering and thirsty. The sound of the rain

PART I: INTERNAL COMBUSTION

reverberated through the underpass. Water, water everywhere, but not a drop to drink. He wished there were some slithery creatures to bless. He considered filling the KFC cup with rainwater, but what if there were *germs* in it? Maybe they were the slimy creatures for him to bless. He took the cup and felt his way over to the curtain of rainwater that fell across the entrance to the underpass. He filled the cup, but as he brought it to his lips, a wave of revulsion came over him, imagining the lips of the bum that had touched the cup before him, and he tossed it aside. He cupped his own filthy hands and slurped water to his mouth. It went down cold gritty. He stood on the edge of the shelter of the bridge and wondered if he should be unstoppable and just march through the rain, daring the elements to strike him down, when another blast of lightning rattled the bones in his ear, and the sound of the rain changed to a clatter, and he realized it had begun to hail.

He returned to the ledge and sat with his back against the wall, teeth chattering. Wouldn't life be pleasant and dull without conflict? Would lack of conflict be so dull as to become hellish? He wondered if homelessness—real, sleep-on-the-streets homelessness—would bother him. Or would he welcome it? To step outside the system and be free. His stomach growled. He shuddered. He felt for the old blanket and scooted closer to it. It was dry. He peeled off his cold, wet shirt and wrapped the blanket around himself, fighting disgust, as he imagined the blanket infested with rat turds, and cockroaches, and cockroach turds, and whatever ate cockroach turds, and worst of all that it had touched some bum's skin. Some nasty-ass bum with running sores, and pustules, and piss-stained pants, and an unwiped ass. *Why does God hate me?* he wondered. *Is it because I curse and constantly lust for flesh?* Another nearby crash of thunder seemed to confirm his suspicion. *Fuck*, he thought. Another wave of sneezes racked his body and left him coughing convulsively for a full minute. He rested his head against the concrete. Soon the utter darkness blotted out even the voices in his head.

He awoke blindly, gasping like when you break the surface after diving deeper than you had meant. He'd had a horrible dream. His father was standing outside an apartment on a sidewalk lined with cigarette butts. A TV detective came out with some Polaroids. A dough-white body lay in the Polaroids on a linoleum floor, a knife beside the body, and a scrap of paper on which was written bluntly in pencil: KILL. And then he was in the Earth. Underground. A beast slithered over him, the flesh of its pulsating belly glistening as if coated in sweat or mucous. It took a man into its powerful hands, pulled him from his skin, and pushed the femur into the orifice in its demonic face. Jim sought to flee, but came to a cliff, and peered over the edge. A river of blood and flesh flowed below. The beast pounced on him, and Jim fell back, down into the gore. That was when he awoke, gasping and panicky, cold and burning. He could see only blackness and guessed that he was awake from the chill on his burning skin and the sound of water running and dripping all around. His body was wracked with spasms of coughing in which he took grim comfort in its indication that he was in reality. He felt the concrete beneath him with his hand to assure himself that he remembered correctly that he was under a bridge.

The storm had reduced to a steady rain. He stood up, crouching in the space beneath the bridge, and felt his way along the ledge for a place to urinate. New fears always supplanted conquered ones. No boogiemen lurked in the dark. Nothing tingled the back of his neck. Nothing inhabited the edge of his peripheral vision. He was a grown man, but despair and insanity were like vapors that might leak in through one's defenses.

He unbuttoned his fly, fished out his dick, and crouching, had begun to piss, when a shriek pierced the darkness, and a cold hand closed over his wrist, and he almost fell down the embankment as he yanked away. He knew it wasn't the demon, but that was his first thought. He nearly fumbled the lighter out of his pocket and flicked it. A head

PART 1: INTERNAL COMBUSTION

floated in the dim circle of light the flame provided. The flame blew out and Jim studied the residual image. It had bloodshot, red-rimmed eyes, and its hair was steaming. Maybe it was the demon.

A light shone on Jim. "What do you pissing to me?" croaked a voice behind the light, half Ricky Ricardo, half Mai Lai massacre, a staccato of pitch, rising and falling, echoing off the walls where deformed shadows jerked all around. Jim squinted past the light. A man sat in a sleeping bag gesturing at Jim with a flashlight. "Pong jew pito, mang. I ang no hoto." He pointed the beam where Jim's shriveled penis protruded from his fly, still pissing.

Jim turned and pissed down the slope, then shoved his dick back into his pants trying to pinch off before he was totally done. The guy's hair was steaming because that was where Jim had pissed. "Sorry, dude," Jim said. A relieved breath escaped him, almost a laugh. He buttoned up. "I didn't see you." The fog of his breath and the shadows cast upon his face from the flashlight gave the man the appearance of a Chinatown dragon. Jim saw that he had a knife and backed away. He shuddered an exhalation. "I'm super sorry, bro."

The dragon held the fierceness of his expression a little longer before folding his knife. He rummaged around in his bag and pulled out a paint-spattered flannel shirt. He rubbed his hair a few brisk strokes and tossed it to Jim. "Mang, jew gonna fleeze to deaf."

Jim caught the shirt. His head shook. The man waved the backs of his hands at Jim. "Take it."

The man put the flashlight in his mouth and moved to a bundle wrapped in a plastic tarp behind him. He undid the bundle and removed a metal bucket, a half-used bag of charcoal, and a tin of paint thinner from among a collection of tools and paintbrushes, then tied the bundle back again. "Es pinche cold tonight, eh mang? Pon tha schirt."

Jim deliberated a few seconds and put it on. "Gracias." Grassy ass. "Sit."

CAR TROUBLE

Jim's pants were even more uncomfortable now as the warm urine seemed abrasive in the cold dampness. He went to get the blanket and settled back onto the ledge with his back against the wall and his legs down the embankment so that his stiff, wet pants wouldn't pinch. The man clicked off the flashlight and the dark rushed over them. Jim tensed a moment, listening for what the man would do. The wind blew steadily through the underpass. Jim's teeth chattered uncontrollably, and the cold forced a groan from his throat that might have been the prayer of a Himalayan monk. As the groan died down, he heard paper tearing, and the noise of a few briquettes being dumped into the bucket, and the chunka chunka sound of the paint thinner tin being squeezed. A long time seemed to pass before the strike and flare of the match poofed to fire in the bucket. Jim watched the shadows dancing and stretching on the wall a minute before he scooched closer. The man produced a bottle of Kamchatka from his sleeping bag and Jim pictured Felix the Cat, who whenever he gets in a fix reaches into his bag of tricks. Jim had one breath of a laugh before he coughed so much his sides did ache, his heart went pitter-pat. The man unscrewed the bottle and took a short swig and handed it to Jim. "Drink," he said. "It make jew inside warm."

Jim studied the wetness on the man's lips and eyeballed the mouth of the bottle before grabbing it around the neck. "To your health," he said and tipped three good gulps down his throat, inducing another series of wrenching coughs.

"Notsu mush." The guy's voice rode a rollercoaster.

Jim handed the bottle back and wiped tears from his eyes with the back of his wrist. "Grassyass. Now all I need is a cigarette."

"Jew shoo not to smoke. Shit is bad to you." He had another pull of vodka, winced, and handed the bottle back across the flaming bucket.

Smoke blew in Jim's face and he slumped lower trying to find some air. "Right." He drank some, and then drank a little more. His teeth stopped chattering. He handed the bottle back to the man. "Why

PART 1: INTERNAL COMBUSTION

are you here?"

"Why I am here?" He spread his palms apart, and his inflection said, "Why not here? Where else?" As if there were many bridges he could be under, but this was the one he was under, and by extension there were also many lands where he might be, and even other worlds, but he was in this place only and not anywhere else, so wasn't the question moot?

"Where are you from?" Jim asked.

The man nodded. "I ang from China. My father he's from Tibet. But I live in Cambodia when I ang boy. Mang, it was bad. They kill to my father. We beeleeb de Buddha. We beleeb de Dalai Lama. Dey say kill to de soldiers. But I not. I not to kill. Not one person. Not one soldier. Not one bird. Dey say to kill to me! Dey kill my father. Dey say to me to kill soldiers o dey kill to me. I go. I go in de night. I no tell. I ang painter. I ang no soldier. I ang no to killing. I go in boat to Peru. I ang working, working, working to making clothes. I not like it to make it the clothes. I like to paint. I wish to see America. I go to Colombia, Panama, Costa Rica, Nicaragua, Meshico. I ang painting. I learn the Spanish. I learn also the English. I ang painting and walking. I go to America. Now I ang here."

Jim nodded. The man took another drink. "Why you are here?" he asked Jim.

Jim blew through his lips. "I don't know. Because I attract evil."

"Evil?" The man sounded taken aback.

"Yeah. Evil and assholes and chaos."

"What is attrack?"

"Attract? That means it comes to me. It's always around me. You know, like flies are attracted to shit. Evil comes to me."

"You are evil?"

Now Jim was taken aback. *Is that the problem? Am I evil?* Suddenly he had no idea what evil was. It was as if inconveniences and minor misfortunes were evil. But no. Evil is murder and rape and greed and

97

malicious intent. But there was something more pervasive, something about everyday life that went against nature. Like the world had been created a certain way, and men had been opposing the way of the world's creation since—since men became men. *That's the fucking problem*, he thought. *Cars and clocks and bullshit. As if murder and rape were actually part of the natural order of things. Predator and prey. Wolves killing deer. A gangbang of ducks. Man eating hamburger.*

"I don't know." Jim drew his knees up and dropped his head on them. "I hope not."

He looked at Adam. "Fuck, dude, do you think I'm evil?"

"For wanting to break the window?"

Jim tugged an eyebrow. "Na, man, because like, I don't know. Because of this shit. Does this shit happen because I'm a bad person, like is God punishing me because my Karma is bad or whatever? Like maybe because I skipped work to get high, and beat off, and smoked out, maybe this is the way you've got to pay for it."

"I never see you pay for anything," Adam said. "If that's your way of paying for things, no wonder you owe everybody. I don't know why you can't just pay money like everyone else."

"That doesn't answer my question. You're just getting bitchy now. I'm not the one who locked the keys in the car."

"How could you be? I'm the one who always drives—Wait a sec—Yes, you did."

"No, you don't. Did I?"

"Yes."

"So, you're saying I AM evil because what? I take advantage of people and never do anything in return?"

"Whatever. I'm just ticked off. You're not evil. Evil is whatever makes people leave babies in trashcans and causes guys like Dahmer to do their thing. You're not evil. I don't even know why you're talking like that. You're just drunk."

"What I mean is," Jim said to the man under the bridge, "I'm here

PART 1: INTERNAL COMBUSTION

because a man took my car when he shouldn't have. I told him not to do it, but he did it anyway. A lot of things happened to put me in that position. He left me out here on a freezing-cold, stormy night. He was evil to do that. He fucked me over. You know what 'fucked over' means? When people get fucked over, it's evil. So, I'll just let you draw your own conclusions about me. I guess I'm just stupid, but I suppose stupidity is just another kind of evil."

The man took deep breaths as if trying to inhale the meaning of Jim's words. Jim thought the man had fallen asleep, but then he said, "I think you no evil. You think that the good and the happy is when you have car. You have house. America is like dis. But I think if you life is simple, you happy. Simple impo'tant to happy. Happy to have food, drink, warm, shelter. America have many wonderful, but no is simple. I have shelter." He used his upturned palms to indicate the bridge over their heads. "Warm to de fire. Drink. I eat food today. I ang happy. Jew in same place like me, but you no happy. Jew see?"

Jim closed his eyes and tried to see. He tried to see wisdom in the man. Tried to see him as some philosopher oracle placed in front of him though divine intervention to deliver a special message in time of great need, but he thought maybe the man was miserable and just didn't know it, that he was not quite speaking gibberish. "No, I don't see," Jim said, but he was nodding.

Nodding. He concentrated on breathing. Nodding off. The man's babbling faded out of Jim's head, and Jim fell asleep, a sleep of smoke and heat and cold and darkness. Darkness in which he could see. See that he was wrong. Wrong about everything.

Rumbling. Voices. Pain. Cold. His eyelids fluttered open. Even the pale, pre-dawn light was daggers to his eyeballs. He felt his head for bullet holes. His breath fogged and vanished, fogged and vanished. It might have been smoke the way his throat burned. He closed his mouth and found he could breathe though only one nostril, but the burning was less intense. The man was gone. Jim wondered if the man had ever been there, but Jim was still wearing the flannel shirt, and the bottle was still there, half empty. He sat a while before doing a slow inventory on his body parts. He wiggled his toes, flexed his hands, straightened and bent his arms and legs, clenched and unclenched his gluteus maximi, rubbed his face, and sat a while longer, waiting for the thought that would get him going.

Men in yellow hardhats had blocked off the underpass with candy-striped sawhorses and were maneuvering a cherry-picker into place at the blown-out transformer. A woman manning an orange and black MEN AT WORK sign spotted Jim. He swallowed reflexively and gagged, wincing. Water. The thought came. Water. He slid slowly down the concrete, squatting on his haunches, skiing on his sneakers, duck-walking when he stalled. A lake of rainwater lapped at the top of the curb. He tried not to swallow and did, spasm of pain wracking his entire body. Butts and fast food wrappers eddied over the clogged storm drain. The water would be cold.

The woman watching him said something to one of the men and he watched Jim, too. His eyes burned. Fuck them. He knelt and scooped a handful of water into his mouth. His shoulders tensed as the water pulled in the glue of his closed throat and came coughing out his mouth and nostril. He wondered what mortar shrapnel would feel like tearing through his neck. His throat hurt out to his ears. His fingers contorted in anger and agony. He tried to compose himself. He had not just stepped on a land mine. He had not just lost a child to a pedophile torturer. He just had a sore throat. He steeled his will and hocked as much shit up out of his throat as he could, doubling over with the effort to withstand the pain. His eyes darted to the workers and saw that they had turned their backs on him. Good. Fuck them. He spat and even just forcing the air through his throat to do that was epic pain. He had to have some moisture in his throat. No spit to swallow. He scooped another handful of water into his mouth and

PART 1: INTERNAL COMBUSTION

swallowed what felt like bits of broken glass. Fuck it. He turned and walked out from under the bridge.

Dawn had appeared in the east like a Vegas hooker after a night's work, rouge and lipstick smeared, lit up with neon. The sky broke and rippled in the puddles through which he walked, puddles like loopholes through which you might fall into Heaven, but cement blocked the way. His feet squished in his wet shoes and socks, and he could feel the rub of a blister developing. He stopped and pulled of his shoes, peeled off his socks and wrung the water from them, but left the socks in the gutter. He squashed down the heels of his shoes and walked in them like that, socklessly, laces flitting about. A phone. He needed to find a phone. When he found a phone he would call—who? He'd cross that bridge when he came to it. Figure out where his car was. Find that motherfucking tow truck driver and kill him. Kill him, and Jim would gladly take his lethal injection, and God would gladly take him into Heaven where all the all-knowing sainted souls would know Jim was justified, and would exalt in him for having banished the evil of that fucking tow truck driver to Hell where he belonged—

Wondering whether he had change for the pay phone interrupted his musing. Jim had to stop to summon the memory of how to reach into his pocket, to summon the will, the strength, the coordination. His pants were cold and stiff still. He had to work his fingers into his pocket, wiggle them down, shove his hand in up to his wrist. He felt blindly, a book of matches, a coin, some paper. He pulled the pocket out and emptied the contents into his hand, fumbling the matches to the sidewalk. He didn't stop to pick them up. They were in the past now. In his hand, he had a dime and a penny and a couple of wadded up ones. He pulled out the other pocket. Lint.

He continued walking with his pockets hanging out like he was playing the old kiss the bunny game. He struggled through the air like it was quicksand. Air wheezed in his lungs and throat and sinuses. The clouds became ice cream and whipped cream, if only he could get a bowlful for his aching throat. The light tore at his eyes, snakes' tongues of color flicked before him, he could hardly see the intersection in all the light. He jaywalked across the street squinting and made out the sign for a Denny's a few blocks farther. The parking lot was jammed. The entrance was stacked with people. He pushed through them, realizing how bad he smelled, and made his way to the bathrooms in the back. He hardly recognized the man in the mirror. His eyes seemed to sag down onto his cheeks, his jaw hung open, and his face utterly lacked expression. He placed the coins on the counter and turned on the hot water in one sink and the cold water in the other and rubbed cold water onto his stubbly face and into his eyes and bent down to the faucet and slurped the cool water, swallowing painfully.

He turned off the cold water and then splashed the hot water from the other sink onto his face, and washed his hands and splashed some water onto his head and tried to compose his hair, before collecting his eleven cents and stepping out of the bathroom where he found a pay phone. He looked under F for Fuckaround Tow, but it wasn't listed. He opened the phonebook to the first page. A number for the Anaheim Police Department was listed there.

He went to the front of the restaurant and approached the cashier. "Could I get some change for the pay phone, please?" His raw throat whispered like some ham actor uttering his dying last words. He tried to smooth out one of the ones before holding it out.

"I'm sorry. We do not have enough change. Perhaps if you order something." His nameplate said KENT MANAGER.

Jim spotted a phone on the counter. "May I use that one? It's a local call," he said, wincing.

"I'm sorry. That is not a public phone. There is a public phone near the restrooms."

Jim sighed heavily, hoping to breathe streptococcus into Kent's mucous membranes. He walked past a row of butt cracks peeking above the jeans of truckers and others perched upon stools, eating

PART 1: INTERNAL COMBUSTION

Grand Slams. At the bathroom again, he picked up the phone and tried to call the cops collect.

"Whom shall I say is calling, sir?"

"Lieutenant Crack."

"I'm sorry, sir. They do not accept the charges."

Jim dialed 911. "My car has been stolen." The words were a cheese grater on his vocal cords.

"Sir, this line is for emergencies only. You'll need to call your local department's watch desk. They'll take a report."

He hung up and walked back to the front counter. KENT was gone. Jim picked up the telephone, called information for the Anaheim Police Department, and wrote the number on his hand with a pen he found near the register. The phone was ringing on the other end when KENT returned and disconnected the call. "Sir, this is not a public telephone. Since you persist in violating policy, I shall have to ask you to leave. I will call the police if necessary."

Jim tried to say, "That's what I'm trying to do, you little prick hole!" However, the sound that escaped Jim's throat was that of twisting metal, of Godzilla attacking Tokyo. His hands rose and gnarled into fists, and KENT screamed and dropped to the floor as if struck.

The busy clatter, the forks scraping plates, the breakfast conversation, the chewing, sipping, ordering, complaining, scratching, picking, and wiping all stopped, and the patrons and employees turned their attention to the commotion. "I didn't touch him," Jim tried to say to a waitress with a coffee pot who had frozen near him, but all that came out was a phantasmagoric whisper that left him grimacing and clutching his throat. The waitress backed away. Jim tried to move past her and out the door, but he brushed the pot, spilling hot coffee down her wrist, and she shouted, "Shit!" as it crashed to the floor.

Jim went through the parking lot and sat on the curb. He lay back with his feet in the gutter and his knees bent. He was thus twenty minutes later, when a shadow fell over his closed eyes. He opened them and smiled thinly. The cop offered the same smile and said, "Why don't you get up?"

Jim stood. He felt like Taylor in *Planet of the Apes*. He pointed to his throat and opened and closed his hand like a talking mouth and shrugged and shook his head. The cop looked at his partner. "Is he deaf?"

"Or retarded."

Jim pointed to a pen in the cop's breast pocket and nodded and scribbled with his fingers on an invisible notepad, smiling like a mime. The cop handed him the pen and a small notepad. "My car was stolen," Jim wrote. He wiggled his fingers around like he was doing sign language.

KENT emerged from the restaurant. "Officers! Thank God you got here so quickly this time. This man has been terrorizing my staff and customers. He assaulted me and one of my servers."

Jim shook his head vigorously, pointing at himself.

"Now, Mr. Peters-"

"Peter. It's Mr. Peter."

"Mr. Peter, are you sure you've been assaulted? I don't see a mark on you. You've called us at least six times in the last month or so and…"

"And you never do anything about all the riffraff we get in here. I don't know why I bother." KENT stomped back into the restaurant.

Officer McCord called in Jim's description of the Fiat. Blue. '73. Convertible. License plate SNH287. How had Jim remembered that? It wasn't the first time he had been towed. He'd been towed from apartment complexes that didn't have adequate parking and got kickbacks for every car towed. He'd been towed from in front of red curbs, fire hydrants, blocked alleys, and beach supermarkets. Once the Fiat broke down on Back Bay Road and had been towed before Jim got back to it with a tow truck.

McCord called it on the radio. "Can he hear, or what?" asked McCord's partner, Malloy.

PART 1: INTERNAL COMBUSTION

A voice crackled over the radio. "The vehicle was not stolen. It was picked up by Fuck-A-Round Tow last night. It's at their impound lot on Harbor."

"Can he read lips, or do you think we should write it down for him?"

McCord looked at Jim and said very loudly and slowly that Jim's car had not been stolen. Jim affected a look of puzzlement. The cop wrote the address on a slip of paper and handed it to Jim.

"He looks like he's about to cry," said Malloy. He scratched his flattop. "You think we ought to give him a ride?"

"Maybe if we do, KUNT will think we arrested him, and he'll quit bitching to the watch commander."

"Or maybe we'll just encourage him to call every time somebody walks into his Denny's without a tie and shave."

The backseat of the cruiser was stained with spots of blood and smelled faintly of vomit. Jim fidgeted thinking of the other times he'd been in that position under less favorable circumstances, when his mouth was running off without him, cursing the guys in the front seat, telling them the only reason they were cops was because they weren't smart enough to get some job where they wouldn't have to be assholes for a living.

Human heads impaled upon spikes protruded from the razor wire atop the walls of the tow yard where the cops dropped Jim. He scanned the battlements for vats of boiling oil as he approached the gate. An intercom was mounted to the wall alongside the gate where the impassive eye of a camera stared down on him, unblinking, like HAL. Jim depressed the button on the intercom and heard a tone pulse, but nothing happened. He tried again, but still nothing. One more time. Nothing. He turned and slumped against the wall. Somewhere there was a world of lakes and rivers and forests. He'd seen it on TV.

A high-pitched squeal sounded in the gate, and it creaked open automatically as a truck rumbled up. A drawbridge was lowered across the moat, and the truck rolled through the gate hauling a mangled Japanese import. Jim stepped through the gate just before it closed.

A vast elephant's graveyard of car carcasses and mechanized death stretched to the horizon. Jim walked between mud puddles across the hard-packed dirt to a small office he spotted in a valley between mountains of cars. The windows were covered by bars, but the door was unlocked, and he went in.

Glass of a thickness the Incredible Hulk could not shatter separated Jim from a large black woman admiring her hot pink and silver, three-inch fingernails as she talked on a phone. She looked up briefly at Jim before returning her attention to her nails. Jim rapped on the glass, but it seemed to absorb the energy without producing a sound. He watched her fingernails grow another inch before she hung up the phone and wheeled her chair to the window. "Uhm-hum," she said through an intercom.

Jim tried to work up enough spit to lube his vocal cords, swallowing painfully. "I need to get my car out," came the gravelly whisper.

"ID."

"It's in the car."

"I cannot release any vehicle without proper identification," she said and wheeled back to examine her fingernails.

"Can I get the ID out of the car then, please?" he rasped.

"I cannot allow access to any vehicle without seeing proper identification. And if they brought it in before midnight, it will be one hundred and twenty dollars cash up front. And it's sixty dollars for every twenty-four hours after that."

A tirade most profane exploded form Crack's chest and became trapped in his ailing throat. He felt like his chest would burst and he reared back and unleashed an elephant sneeze that splattered the window with thick clots of brown and yellow glop which began to sizzle corrosively on the glass. A noxious smoke rose. Perhaps he could burn through the shield and slay the demon on the other side. But no. It had been a trick. His mucous did not burn through the glass. It slid slowly down, slug-like. The woman shrank in horror, distorted by the smear of bacteria on the glass, wriggling like an insect.

Jim exited the office. Her voice came over a loudspeaker. "Butch and Tony to the office. Code red."

Jim wandered the maze of glass and steel and rusted chrome. Money to get the car, ID to get the money, ID in the car. Was the bank even open? What day was it? Would he even be able to get his money without ID? Money to get the car, ID to get the money, ID in the car. It became like a mantra as he staggered between the columns of automobiles. A friction rash had begun to grate his thighs behind his balls. He noted it dimly, grimly. It didn't matter. They would be coming soon.

He stopped. There it was. The Spider. His Fiat. He climbed through the convertible window that he'd unzipped and never zipped again because you couldn't see shit through it anyway. When he had finished the necessary contortions and was sitting in the driver's seat, he gripped the wheel. A choir of angels sang as the keys winked at him where they hung from the ignition. It wouldn't start of course, but—

He put her in neutral and undid the brake, then undid the top and lowered the roof. He climbed over the door and eased her forward. She rolled easily. He got out and pushed, as he turned the wheel. Pushed her to a jog. Pushed long strides. Pushed to a sprint, hopped in, popped her into first, and yabba dabba doo! She fired up and lurched forward as two men in coveralls came around the row of cars and began running after him. He stomped on the gas pedal, and slid around the corner, nearly running into a tow truck that had just come in through the open gate.

He turned the wheel hard and spun out, and the back of the Fiat slammed into the rusted fins of an old Cadillac and stalled. The tow truck driver stopped and got out as Jim did the same. He walked at Jim, yelling and cursing, as Jim started pushing the little Fiat forward again. The driver was a hundred feet away. Jim pushed as hard as he could, pumping his legs. The two men in coveralls came running around the corner to block Jim's path as he jumped in, afraid he hadn't enough speed. He jammed in the clutch and shoved the stick into first and she revved to life when he let out the clutch. The gate shuddered and began to close. The men dived out of the way as Jim threw her into second gear two hundred feet from the gate. He swerved around the truck, kicking up dust, and was determined to get through the gate or ram it head on. With no seatbelt. Fuck it. The driver stood between Jim and the half-closed gate, and Jim hurled the car into third, gunning for him. They made eye contact. It was Meatloaf. Jim pushed the gas pedal down as far as it would go. Meatloaf held his ground. Jim smiled and hunched over the wheel, grinning madly through the windshield, and Meatloaf turned and ran through the nearly closed gate. A crunching bang jarred the car as the gate clipped the side-view mirror, and Jim launched her into fourth gear and shot out into the street, just missing Meatloaf. Tires shrieked and horns blared, as he turned the wheel hard and fishtailed between to oncoming cars and on down the road free! Free! Free!

Ten minutes later he was handcuffed and face-down on the asphalt, close to suffocation, as a burly, buzz-cut cop dug a knee into Jim's back while frisking him. It wasn't until he heard the whoop of the siren that he'd noticed the red and blue lights in the remaining side-view mirror. "Put both hands out the window and keep them there!" a voice boomed over a loudspeaker. In the mirror, Jim watched the car door open and a huge black shoe hit the earth and the head of a bull emerged from the vehicle and shut the door, one beefy hand atop the butt of his gun, holster unbuttoned. "Open the door from the outside and lay flat on the ground," the minotaur bellowed.

"I climb out. The door doesn't open."

"This car was reported stolen," Officer Minotaur said, once Jim lay prone before him.

"It's my car," Jim tried to say and started to turn over.

PART 1: INTERNAL COMBUSTION

"Stay flat on the ground!"

Bits of gravel bit into Jim's cheek. "It's my car," he wheezed. He was really not feeling well now.

"Got any weapons I should know about? Any drugs?" The minotaur patted Jim as a pair of boots walked to the other side of the Fiat and opened the door.

"No," Jim gasped.

He heard the boots rummaging around in his car. "You Jim Cr—Crack?"

Jim tried to say "yes," but his throat would no longer cooperate. He nodded, grinding bits of road into his face. He tried to gather the air to say that he needed his inhaler, but the air didn't seem to be there. He reached down to his pocket for it.

"Freeze!" The boots hurried around from the other side of the car. From the corner of his eye, Jim saw the barrel of the gun pointed at him before the minotaur dropped its knee heavily onto Jim's back and twisted his arms back, cuffed him, and patted him down.

He felt Jim's inhaler in his pocket. "What's this?"

Jim could only wheeze.

"Won't talk, eh?"

Jim was pulled to his feet by the cuffs. Crack hardly noticed the pain in his shoulders. Even the pain in his throat seemed gone. He was yanked around to the squad car and shoved down in the back. It was very comfortable other, than he couldn't breathe and snot ran down his face. With his hands cuffed, he had no choice but to let it drool over his lips. He laid his head down and closed his eyes.

"WHERE'S MY FUCKING VICODIN!"

He awoke in a bed. Light filled the room. A hospital bed. The sheets were stamped ORANGE COUNTY MENS JAIL SANTA ANA. An IV fed into his inner elbow. The raw burning of his throat seemed to have diminished but was still sore. His chest rattled with phlegm. His skin felt cool, but sweaty.

He remembered being moved from the car. "I don't think he's breathing," someone had said.

"Better give him mouth-to-mouth."

"I ain't doing it."

"Let's get him to the infirmary, pronto. If he dies, we're fucked with paperwork and hearings. Let's hurry the fuck up."

In the bed next to Jim, a man whose head was bandaged with blood-stained gauze was handcuffed to the metal railing around his bed. A spiderweb was tattooed over his elbow, and the bottom of a swastika peeked out from the sleeve of his hospital gown. "WHERE'S MY FUCKING VICODIN!" he yelled, straining against the cuffs.

A door opened and a woman in a light blue hospital-looking shirt came in with a guard. She sat on the edge of Jim's bed and unpeeled a plastic thermometer and stuck it between Jim's lips. "Under the tongue," she said. She put a stethoscope to her ears and listened to the busted Model-T radiator in Jim's chest, frowning. She took his pulse and blood pressure and took out the thermometer and checked it. She held a tongue depressor to his mouth. "Open." She shined a pen light in his mouth. When she was done, she wrote on a clipboard and said, "You've got strep and probably pneumonia, too, but we're not going to do X-rays for you here. Your fever is starting to come down, though; that's what's important."

"When can I leave?" Jim croaked.

"You'll leave here in a day or two when your fever has gone. As far as getting out of jail, I don't know anything about that."

She went to the guy whose head was bandaged and shined the pen light in his eyes. "Where's my fucking Vicodin?"

She clicked off the light and left the room.

The room had neither windows nor clocks, and the days and nights were distinguishable only by the fact that the lights were sometimes

PART I: INTERNAL COMBUSTION

off and sometimes on. He had fitful, feverish dreams of a white cockroach, an albino mutant never exposed to sunlight, crawling among the usual darker ones over the unidentifiable grime on the walls of a closet-sized cell with no door. Surely, he had lost his job by now, and his car would be amassing impound fees. People would be wondering where he was—actually, he couldn't think of a single person who would find his absence unusual. As his voice came slowly rasping back, his coughing increased, but he was at least able to try to extract information from doctors and nurses as to why he was there and when he could leave. None of them had any answers.

Sometime later—it may have been three days, it may have been a week—a couple of guards came in. "Crack!" one shouted. "Which one of you assholes is Crack?" Jim sat up. He guessed it was the middle of the night, because the lights were off. They checked his wristband. "What kind of name is that?" one of the guards asked. Jim said nothing. A nurse removed his IV. "Let's go," said the guard. They uncuffed him.

"Where?"

No answer.

"Where?" he repeated.

"You hear something?" one guard said to the other.

"No, but I smell something."

He was ordered to remove his hospital gown, and they led him through a maze of corridors in his underwear and socks to a small room where he had to put on a blue jumpsuit before they handcuffed him to a bench.

The room was not much bigger than a phone booth. A bare light bulb hung out of reach. The wooden door had no knob. There had once been a cage window opposite the door, but it had been boarded over. He studied his hands and the hair on his arms. Ice ages came and went. Seconds stretched into eons. Big bangs sputtered in and out of the void. Then, the door in the side of the universe opened, and a girl wearing a mini-skirt, tube top, and stiletto heels was ushered in. A girl with a five o'clock shadow. The guard threw a blue prison jump suit at her. She turned her back to Jim and wriggled out of her tube top. Mascara ran down her face. She donned the jumpsuit, and the deputy handcuffed her to the bench and walked out and shut the door. The room was not big enough for the two of them. The transvestite curled up on what bench there was unoccupied by Jim and whimpered quietly. Jim moved as far away as the cuffs would allow, partly out of revulsion and partly out of some kind of chivalry; he felt bad for the poor bastard, and wanted to allow her space to be comfortable, but she cuddled up close to Jim and rested her head on Jim's thigh.

Fuck it. Jim leaned his head back and banged the top of it against the wall over and over. It was something he often did. The jarring of his skull had a relaxing effect, dislodging more disturbing thoughts; the vibration traveled down his spine, against the flow of most of his other impulses, creating a kind of balanced meditative state, which for Jim was something like serenity.

He heard a squiggly sound at some slight change in atmospheric pressure that precipitated the drain of fluid from one sinus cavity to another. He laid his head to one side and let the fluid pool behind that side of his face, clogging that nostril. Then he tilted his head the other way for an hour or so, and it was the other nostril that was clogged. Then he held his head forward so as to load both barrels, and he sucked into his mouth the largest loogy he could muster. He suctioned off the saliva and swallowed, leaving on his tongue a slug the consistency of the garden variety. Taking the deepest breath he'd taken in days, he circled his lips to about a .38 and shot the slug up onto the ceiling where it stuck with a wet slap.

As a kid, he had taken pride in the heft of the loogies he could launch, knowing that his were particularly gross. He'd spit them at the roof overhang in front of his classroom doors, hoping that at some later time they might land on the teacher or someone else he didn't like. The thickest ones crystallized and hung like stalactites to be marveled

PART 1: INTERNAL COMBUSTION

at by him and the other kids during the dry months.

Clank. The door opened. A deputy stepped in. He looked like a munchkin on steroids. "Josie," he said. "I can't say this last name. Which one of you faggots is Josie?" The untransvestite did not respond. "Josie!" The deputy shouted, as if he had spotted the leader of the Pussycats, or the outlaw Wales.

"Jose," the kid whispered between little sobs.

The deputy leaned down toward Jose's face. "Josie, this is America, and we speako English, and your name is Josie. Got it?"

The splotch of phlegm hung down six inches from the ceiling, a few feet above the head of the deputy.

"Or maybe," the deputy chuckled through his nose, "you prefer to be known as Josephina?"

Jim's eyes narrowed over the deputy's head, trying to determine whether the mass of the globule would overcome the strength of it adhesion to the ceiling before the deputy moved out from underneath it. The bottom grew rounder as its midsection thinned. It stretched down at least six inches.

"Don't you look at me!" The deputy leaned into Jim's face and barked. "You look straight ahead at the wall or you get your head slammed!"

Jim lowered his head and stared at the floor.

"Come on, Josephina." From the corner of his eye Jim saw her jerked to her feet. Then:

"WHAT THE FUCK!"

Jim looked up at the grimacing deputy as he frantically wiped at the glob of mucous that had fallen onto his forehead and was running into his eye. He looked at his fingers, squealed, and flung his hand away trying to throw the gunk off, and then he wiped his hands on the shirt of his uniform.

"YOU LITTLE MOTHERFUCKING BITCH FAGGOT!" he roared and spun Jose around, twisting her arm up behind her back.

113

She cried out, and the deputy slammed her against the wall, twisting the arm up even higher. Jim feared it would snap.

"Dude," he heard his voice rasping. "You're going to break her arm, man—his arm. It's not his fault. It was an accident. I did it."

The deputy gave Jose a short blow to the head with his elbow and let her fall to the floor. He shot a hand out and closed it over Jim's face with a finger dug into his ear and his thumb clamped across the bridge of Jim's nose, and he slammed Jim's head against the cement wall. Crack felt his brain wobble on its stem, a gong upon his medulla oblongata, a dark curtain closed over his eyes. Two images of the deputy's face appeared in the photographic negative. They vibrated apart and back together again. The curtain slowly lifted, and Jim was staring into the teeth of the seething deputy.

"…suburban punks like you. You're a fucking disgrace to your race and a drain on this country!" Jim had been jerked to his feet, but the way his wrists were cuffed to the bench, he was hunched over to keep his shoulders from being wrenched any further. The deputy gave Jim an uppercut to the solar plexus and pushed his head against the wall. Jim's knees buckled, and the deputy released him. He slumped onto the bench, gasping and retching.

The deputy whirled, caught Jose around her miniscule bicep, dragged her out, and slammed the door. Crack's mouth tasted salty and metallic. He leaned forward, drooling blood on the floor. He had bitten his tongue. *If only I had done so sooner*, he thought. *But then the little guy would've gotten beat up because of me. So? So, that isn't right. Oh, yeah. You're the paragon of doing the right thing. Whatever.*

He had a long white beard with birds' nests and squirrels in it that disappeared when the door opened again. Two deputies came in and unlocked him from the bench. They said nothing as they guided him through the halls, and neither did he. They reached a big room with about a hundred other prisoners in it, sitting on the concrete floors and leaning against concrete walls. The deputies took off the handcuffs

PART 1: INTERNAL COMBUSTION

and the chain around his waist and went back out the way they had come. At irregular intervals, a guard would come through a door on the other side of the room and read names off a clipboard and those prisoners who had been summoned would shuffle through the door to what fate Jim could only speculate. For a while he would look up when a guard came in and hope that his name would be called, but after the first few hours, his molecules dissolved into the air and dissipated around the room. Bits of him bumped against the cement walls and ceiling, slipped through vent covers, leaked under doors, out the building, evaporated into the sky, became caught in air currents and circled the globe, encompassing the world. He became nothing but hunger and lust and thirst and cold, and then just nothing.

Nothing. And then through the nothing, the name, the sound, that was him. "…Crack…." An atom joined another and another and another. "…Crack…." The sound echoed across the universe. Some central energy that was him began to reassemble his matter. He sprouted legs and arms, and stood. A line of men shambled through a door. He shambled after them.

The prisoners stripped off their blues and threw them into laundry carts, while two more deputies behind a counter checked the prisoners' wristbands and brought out plastic bags with their clothes.

They gave Jim a silky pair of lavender Dolphin shorts and a mesh tank top.

"These aren't mine," he lisped with his swollen tongue.

"You Jim—Crack?" Slight snicker.

"Yeah."

"Well, according to our paper work, this here's your shit."

"I was wearing Levi's and a T-shirt."

"You want me to book you back into the system while we try to find you your knee-highs and fishnets?" His eyes gleamed.

Jim put on the Dolphin shorts. The tank top was cut in such a way that no matter how he arranged it, one nipple was exposed.

"Personal items, valuables, watches, keys, wallets, and money can be picked up during business hours, beginning at nine tomorrow morning." They gave him some paperwork for a court date.

A door buzzed open and the prisoners were released onto the dark street. Jim felt surprised to find himself in the cool open air, felt an exhilarating freedom at the sight of the sky, the few bright stars; felt possibility in the relatively sweeping vista of a space that did not end in a wall a few feet away. Ah, but it was short-lived. As soon as he tried to figure out where to go, the black air closed around him and became cold. He wasn't really any freer. Moving on seemed pointless, but finally not as pointless as standing there, and after a few minutes he took steps away from the jail.

Taxis lined the street outside the jail. A couple of cabbies played cards on the hood of a car. "Hey, you fairy, you don't ride in my car," said some Iranian-looking guy. Jim had the urge to lunge at him and commit violence upon his person, and the other cabbies looked hopeful of a little excitement, but Jim felt weak and out of breath. He moved on wordlessly, arms folded tightly to his chest, trying to preserve a vestige of warmth.

He judged it to be about 3:12 in the morning. A minute later a clock through the window of a bail bond office showed 3:13. He looked through the window of a newspaper vending machine and checked the date. Tuesday, April 15. What day had he been picked up? Worked Friday. His car was stolen Friday night. Spent Friday night under the bridge. Abducted Saturday. Been in there since Saturday then. April 15? He hadn't filed his taxes.

This is not my life, he thought. His soul had been mistakenly thrust into some foreign body in some foreign place. He tried to remember who he was, imagine what he looked like or where he lived, and nothing came to him. Maybe he wasn't Jim at all. Maybe he was a gay prostitute like Jose who had only invented the persona of some white guy to live in while he was in jail. Maybe he had a nice, fat Mexican mama

PART 1: INTERNAL COMBUSTION

who cooked for him and missed him and would welcome him back home and take him to church. He tried to remember where she lived, what was her phone number. Surely she would come and get him.

He came to a twenty-four-hour laundromat, was drawn to its warmth, and there she was doing a load of laundry. His heart leapt. Maybe she would have some warm clothes for him, and he would help her fold the laundry, and she would take him home and make him some quesadillas and beans. She looked up for a moment and returned to her laundry. Did she not recognize him? Her own son? He stood there waiting for her to look again, and when she did, she cast a withering glance, and he knew that she was ashamed of him.

"No tengo dinero," she said.

"I'm sorry." He held his hands up, beseeching her forgiveness, and Jim saw his reflection in the glass drier, clothes tumbling behind it, and he saw that it was him, Jim, and he knew that it had been him all along and that he was acting like a dipshit.

"I'm sorry," he said again. The buzzer went off on the dryer. She stuffed a last few items of clothing into an already heavy canvas bag. Then she took some change from a pocket in her dress and put it in his hand. "You go now," she said.

He wanted to hug her and took a step forward, and before he knew it, she pulled a can from her purse and shot him in the face. "Aaagh!" He wiped at his eyes. Shit!" She swung the heavy bag at him, knocking him sideways, and he felt her brush past and out the door. "God damn it!" The burning in his eyes seeped into his sinuses. "Idiot!" Through his tears, he spotted a sink in the back of the laundromat. He splashed water on his face and rubbed at his eyes with it, but the stinging hardly seemed to abate. Staggering outside, he hoped the cool night air might soothe the pain. A pay phone stood out front. Through his tears, he dialed Pete and Adam. The phone rang and rang, but he hung up when the answering machine came on so he wouldn't lose his quarter. Who could he call at three in the morning; who would actually answer the phone?

    A dark glass ashtray sat atop the pay phone, and he picked it up. It reminded him of his father in it its smell and hardness and opaqueness. Jim stared into it trying to picture his father's face. At first, he couldn't remember it, but then his fierce blue eyes blazed from out of his shrapnel-scarred face. Was calling him a bad but necessary idea, or just a plain old bad idea? He strained the muscles in his scalp trying to make himself think harder. His father. His father. His father had grown up on the outskirts of St. Louis. Jim had often surmised that the overriding difference between his father and him was that his father was a product of the fifties Midwest and Jim had grown up surrounded by Southern California in the seventies. He had often heard his dad rail against his mother's decision to live in California, and Jim thought the only reason he didn't go back to the Midwest was because his dad wanted to keep a healthy distance between himself and his own father. Maybe that was why he had joined the army as soon as he had been old enough. Got married the night before he shipped out and was fighting in the jungles of Vietnam when Jim was born. Jim was nearly two, before he and his father met for the first time.

    His father. His father. His father had taught Jim, through myriad lectures, tests, and hands-on activities, that life was a trial, that the world was full of people who would cheat you, and that the only way you might not—MIGHT NOT—get fucked was if you stuck to a very narrow path. Go to work. Go home. Go to sleep. Go to work. Save your money. Wash. Rinse. Repeat. If you strayed from this path, you would only invite misery into your life. Jim knew his father saw him as having strayed from the path, as having rejected the formula, as having created all his own problems. His father may have loved him, may even have helped him, but he had ultimately rejected Jim, because, though Jim had always worked, he had ignored the parts of the formula about going home, going to sleep, and saving his money.

    He went back into the laundromat and sat on a chair in front of

PART 1: INTERNAL COMBUSTION

a dryer. Leaning his forehead onto the glass, he stared at the close-up of his reflection, and a third eye appeared between the first two. "Remember when your stepmom told him you and your stepbrother were fighting, and he grabbed you both by the hair and banged you heads together?"

"That was like the Three Stooges. I saw stars circling my head on that one for real," said Jim.

"And 'member that time he balled the chest of your shirt in his fist and lifted you off the ground and slammed you into the stucco outside the house? What was he so pissed about?"

'I don't remember," Jim said. "It was Christmastime, though. He loved Christmas. I always got lots of presents at Christmas."

Three-eyed Jim sighed. He heard the tinsel tinkling in the breeze on the tree lying out at the curb, the wooden cross that was its base, fallen to the side like an X, where he sat, sniffling, the shouts of his mother and father reaching out to the street.

He remembered another time, later, when his dad wouldn't let him leave the table until Jim had given his dad's new girlfriend a kiss. "Aw, c'mon, one little peck." Jim studied the soft white hair on her cheek and the multitude and depth of her pores and was revolted. Many long minutes passed. The only way to get away was to do it. He puckered his lips slightly and touched them to the side of her face for an instant. "Ah, go on, now." His father released him disgustedly. Jim scurried out the door and didn't know where to go. He walked on a wall and twirled around a tree.

"Fuck it," said Jim. "He's an asshole, and he doesn't like me, but he'll help me because I'm his son." He got up again and left the laundromat, got out of earshot of the three-eyed one. He found a taxi and got in, stumped for a heartbeat as to which of the houses he'd lived in was the right one to tell the driver to take him.

"Where to?"

The house in Tustin, the house he'd lived in when his parents were still married. He could almost remember a time there when they had been happy. Coming back from the swap meet with Tijuana-velvet Snoopy World War I pilot paintings to hang on the powder-blue walls of his room, over the bed that had not so long ago replaced his crib. "You like your new room, Jimmy?"

"Yeah, Dad! Thanks! Snoopy! Snoopy! Hurray!" *Maybe he'll come into my dreams, yes, yes, and chase away the monster.*

"Good job, Daddy." Jim's mom kissed his dad and they embraced. Jim wanted to tell the cabbie to take him there.

Happiness is a Warm Blanket, said the Linus on Jim's bedspread. It was the first thing he had learned to read, before suddenly having to share the room with his new stepbrother who wasn't too clear on whose stuff belonged to whom. They would have slow-motion Six Million Dollar Man vs. Bigfoot bionic death-matches that would warp into fast-motion nine-year-old hate-filled fist fights, and droplets of his stepbrother's blood had fallen onto Linus's face, staining him.

"That's my Stretch Armstrong!"

"No, it isn't! Yours has a hole in his skin the stuff leaks out of."

"Nuh-uh! That was yours. Mine was in the freezer."

"Yeah-huh, liar."

"You're a dick."

"Oooh, I'm tellin'."

"Better not."

Then he'd hit me and run down the hall and say that I'd hit him, Jim remembered. *My dad would whup me, but he never touched Markie. Except that time he banged our heads together. Mark and his mom moved out soon after that. I bet we'd get along okay now. I bet we'd drink and laugh about it all now. Just regular kids, we were, but under so much pressure in that house.*

They all moved to a bigger house in Westminister where they could have their own bedrooms, but they didn't stay long, because his father wanted to live where the signs were in English, somewhere where there were other white people to go to church with on Christmas Eve.

PART 1: INTERNAL COMBUSTION

"Who knows how many of these gooks are NVA," he'd heard his dad say. So, they moved to Garden Grove. Jim and Mark called it Garbage Grove. *That was where our heads got banged together. Mark and his mom left us there. Years ago. Dad lives in Brea now.*

"Where to?" the cabbie repeated.

"Brea," he mumbled. "Off Imperial Highway. By the mall." As they drove along, old eight-millimeter home movies were showing on the walls of the freeway. A freckly boy waited on the corner of his street for his other mother's car to appear at the bottom of the hill. The boy kept waiting and waiting. He was still waiting when they reached the stop light on the off ramp, and Jim watched him with stinging eyes and heavy breaths. He was still waiting when the light turned green and they drove away leaving the boy behind, and now the sides of the buildings they passed were covered with the same wallpaper as his room in Yorba Linda, a scene of the sun setting through forest trees, a fiery lake seen through the leaves, the silhouettes of which took the shapes of evil beasts. It was where they'd moved when Mark and his mom left. "Anyplace that produced Richard Nixon is good enough for me," Jim had heard his father say.

Sometime after Jim's sixteenth birthday, his father married a fellow security guard from Disneyland. When she left a couple of years later, he and his dad moved to Brea. This was the house he was trying to remember how to get to. He sat in the cab and wondered how much he had contributed to the failures of his father's marriages, and Jim remembered the day that he thought he was leaving for good:

As long as Jim could remember, his father had taken pleasure in twisting Jim's arms. He would twist at the wrist, the elbow, right up to the shoulder, and Jim would grimace but make not a sound. Not a sound. He never wanted to acknowledge that it hurt. His father would twist a little further, trying to elicit some response. Minutes would go by, Jim perfecting silent endurance while his dad amused himself with his little game of sadism.

"I can still kick your ass," he would tell Jim as Jim grew into manhood. He was squat and heavy, and Jim suspected his father felt threatened that his son was becoming taller. Jim would come home from school, step out of the bathroom, walk down the hall, or bring a plate into the kitchen, and run into his father, and his father would take his arm and start twisting. Even as a child, Jim had complied, but he would not cry out, not utter a syllable, and his father would become bored and release him. "You're a masochist," he would say.

Then one day, during his first year in college, Jim went home to his dad's house after playing basketball. His father caught him in the hallway and began to bend his wrist. "Where have you been?"

"Playing basketball at the school."

"Who with?" He torqued it up another notch.

"Whitaker. Smith. Mike. Some of those guys," he answered, keeping the strain of his ligaments and tendons dislocated from his mind.

"How did your shirt get dirty?" Torque.

"I don't know. We were skins. It must have gotten dirty when I took it off."

"Who won?" Another notch.

But that was it. Jim was done. He began to count in his head, one, two, three, trying to keep his cool.

"Who won?" Another notch.

Five, six, seven, he realized that when he got to ten, if his father hadn't let go, he was going to turn around and punch the cartilage of the fucker's nose into his brain. Eight. Jim turned and stared into his father's face and penetrated his eyes. Nine. His father let go.

"Nobody won," Jim said.

That night after work, Jim didn't go home. He went to Whitaker's and passed out on the couch. And the next night. And the next. And for the next Jim-didn't-know-how-many-hundreds of nights in a row, he didn't go home, but passed out instead on some friend's spare bed, someone's couch, anybody's floor, anywhere but there.

PART 1: INTERNAL COMBUSTION

And now here he was, going there, going home. "Right up here," he said.

They turned onto a street of nondescript homes. "The one with the white truck in front." The cab slowed to a stop and Jim opened the door. "Can you wait here a minute? I have to go in and get money."

As he neared the door of the house, he felt nauseous and the skin on his face became heavy and hung from his skull. He stepped onto the dark porch, trying to wonder about the day's sports scores. His father kept the place locked up tight as Fort Knox. As Pelican Bay. San Quentin. Didn't want the decorative collector spoons to get burgled, Jim supposed. His teeth were chattering. The cab's engine idled. He touched the doorknob, and the dog started snarling as if it had just fallen into a pit of rabid swine, and Jim heard it attack the door like a battering ram. He stepped back from the porch and studied the lawn gnome. The cabbie blew the horn, and the dog doubled the intensity of its barking. The porch light came on.

The door opened a crack. A sliver of porch light fell across an ice-blue eye. "That you, boy?" The voice was hoarse and dry as if his throat were full of dead leaves. Jim stepped into the light. He could make out the shadows of his father's features peering out the partially open door, one hand behind the back, uncocking a pistol, Jim knew.

"Thor! Heel!" The barking stopped. The door opened wide and his father stood illumined and shadowed by the porch light in front of him and the light in the entryway behind him. He looked smaller and heavier, had the density of a collapsing dwarf star. Neither of them moved or said anything. The driver blared the horn again. Drinking seemed like such a frivolous waste. "I—I mean they—that is, my… wallet—the car—I don't have it. They—I don't know what happened. They—I don't know—they took my car, and they took me. I don't have any money. My money. On me. They took it. I don't know why." His father looked made of wood. Jim's eyes burned, and his throat lumped up, and he broke down into silent tearless sobs. His father pulled him close by the back of his neck and Jim hyperventilated on his shoulder, noticing that he was a man, flesh and blood and bone; and then it was Jim's turn to turn to wood.

His father rubbed his neck for many minutes, long after Jim had wanted to pull away. The taxi driver turned the engine off. The hyperventilating stopped; Jim wasn't sure he was breathing at all. He looked around, dispassionately embarrassed, clear-headed. It was the setting that was confused. Not him. "How much do you owe?"

"I—They—You know, I don't know. I don't know."

"All right. You're freezing. Get inside. Sit down." His father led him in, shut the door, and sat him on a La-Z-Boy on faux-brick linoleum. He disappeared down the hall and returned with a fistful of dollars, went outside, and soon again returned. "Why don't you get cleaned up? Take a shower and put on some warm clothes. Get some sleep. We'll talk about this tomorrow."

Not even the dread of that conversation would keep him from sleeping. He went down the hall with his fingers on the wall and into his room where he collapsed on his bed. He slept a dead, dreamless sleep of which he remembered nothing more than opening his eyes from blackness.

Still wheezing. His room was how he left it, he guessed. He seemed to remember his childhood room better than this one. This one was mainly bare. Every time he and his dad had moved, they took a little less furniture with them. His father had left nearly every scrap of furniture with his last ex. Jim had a bed and nothing more. No dresser, no pictures, no mirror, no lamp. Just bare white walls and the light from the ceiling. Most of his clothes were in a pile on the floor in the closet. He heard coughing. His father was home. Hadn't he gone to work? Dread. He felt like Gregor Samsa in his bed, like a roach on its back, unable to right itself. Soon his fit of coughing overtook him, and his father looked in. He had a glass of water that he brought to Jim. They talked. Jim tried to explain what had happened. The more he tried

PART 1: INTERNAL COMBUSTION

to explain, the more confused it became, the more it sounded like a lie. Jim could see his father didn't believe him but had decided not to question his story any further.

"Here's what you should do. You can—and should—stay here. But you'll have to stop the drinking and the drugs. We'll get you enrolled in AA. I know a guy that can help you with that. If you do well with it, I'll get you a job at the park. But you can't screw me on this. I can't have you sullying my good name. If I'm going to help you, and if you're going to stay here, you do it my way. If you don't want to do it, or if you think you can't, you leave. And if you leave, don't come back here in the middle of the night after you've pissed away your last dime, got it?"

Silently, Jim hated him. Somehow this offer of help made Jim hate his father even worse than before, but he hated himself even more, and when the time came for Jim to say something, he said, "Okay."

And his father helped him get his things from the jail and they junked the Fiat and got Jim a used Buick. Jim quit his job at the petroleum products yard and started working at Disneyland. He went to weekly AA meetings and his sponsor went with him to his court appearance, and the judge let him off with a fine and community service (for what violation, Jim still wasn't sure, but he pretended to understand.) He was even able to give up drinking and smoking. For a while.

His father had found a new fiancée in Jim's long absence. She was a quiet, heavy, obedient, Germanic-looking woman. Jim kept his thoughts to a minimum and tried to stay out of the way, and no one wanted him to kiss her. He worked in his father's yard as often as possible. Every hedge was thorny. It was like pruning barbed wire. The bougainvillea had two-inch spikes that stabbed him through his gloves as he tried to stuff the branches into garbage bags that shredded. The juniper gave him rashes and pyracantha pricked his palms. You had to be ginger with the holly, too. When he wasn't working, he stayed in his room and read. He read *The Grapes of Wrath* and *Huckleberry Finn* and

CAR TROUBLE

Bukowski and Fante and Whitman and Edward Abbey. He could tell his father was unhappy with him because Jim didn't watch more TV in the living room with him and Frau Blucher, but every time Jim sat out there with them, old memories would bubble up, like how his father would sit on his chest with his knees on Jim's arms and tickle Jim who hated to be tickled.

"No, Dad, don't. Please don't. Don't, Dad, please."

And he would tickle him slowly at first, under the arms or chin or sides or neck and would increase faster and faster against Jim's protestations, and Jim would flinch and grunt and finally submit numbly as if being raped.

"Oh, for Christ's sake, what are you crying for?"

Memories like these came unbidden and replayed themselves in his mind against his will, and he would flee to his bedroom and his books.

He had trouble sleeping. He would lie in bed craving a beer or a smoke or an acid hit or any kind of mistake. He would lock the bathroom door and stand at the open medicine cabinet with a bottle of Robitussin DM for long minutes and returned it each time, but when he bumped into Whitaker at the market and Whitaker offered him a Glad bag, his body went ahead and made the transaction as Jim stood apart, horrified.

He hid the weed under the spare in the trunk of the Buick and tried to go about his routine, raking leaves, playing Goofy, watching ball games with his dad, and conversing mindlessly with his stepmother-to-be, with the siren song of the marijuana playing in the background all the while. At dinner, they would talk about the details of the coming matrimonial ceremony; she wanted her parents to be there, and a few close friends, and his father wanted to invite no one.

"I just think it will look a little strange tomorrow if there's nobody there from your side to witness it," she said to her potatoes.

"Jimmy'll be there, won't you Jimbo?"

PART 1: INTERNAL COMBUSTION

Maybe after they go to sleep tonight.

"James?"

"Huh? Oh, yeah. You bet, Dad." Jim noticed a half-formed scowl on his father's face. "Don't worry. Pop. I'll be there." He smiled.

That night, harps and violins and flutes and an all-women's choir performed arias from the trunk of the Buick. Jim rose from bed, picked his keys from his pants on the floor, and glided down the hall like a specter. In the kitchen, he rolled a piece of aluminum foil around a pencil and removed the pencil so that he had a tube which he fashioned into a crude pipe. He scratched Thor under the ears for several minutes before going to the front door where he turned the bolt millimeter by millimeter, and then the knob, and then clenched his teeth as the hinges squeaked, until there was enough room for him to sidle out.

He opened the trunk and put the bag in his underwear and gently, ever so gently, pushed the trunk closed and returned to the house.

The rhythmic basso profondo of his father's snoring reverberated off the walls with a resonance that suggested to Jim the breathing of the house itself. When he stepped back through the door, its absence was startling.

"What're you doing, boy?" His father's voice came out of the darkness down the hall.

"I couldn't sleep. I was looking for a book in the car, but it wasn't there." The marijuana's pungency rose from Jim's underwear.

"Well, try to get some sleep. It's a big day tomorrow."

"Okay." The old pregnant pause. He sensed that his father was trying to decide if he smelled anything funny. Jim had the ridiculous idea the aroma would set off the smoke alarm. *Ugh. Please go back to bed.*

He heard his father turn and plod back down the hall. Heard him piss and fart and climb back into the creaking bed. Jim got back into his own bed. The music was gone. Smoking weed seemed pointless and stupid and still he wanted it. He wanted to rise and expand. Wanted to tap into his imagination. To see the hidden meanings behind ordinary things. The house started to breathe again. He needed fire. He tiptoed down the hall and located a book of matches and took them into the bathroom. He turned on the light and a fan came on in the ventilation shaft over the toilet. He removed a nugget of bud and placed it in the pipe, put the bag back in his underwear and closed the toilet lid, stood on the toilet, and took a deep breath, lit the match and hit the pipe. *Why am I so stupid?* He blew the smoke up into the ventilation shaft. When he was done, he crumpled the pipe into a little ball and flushed it with the spent matches. He was a long time at the door listening before he turned off the light and opened it. He crept back to his bed. Somewhere in the middle of the ensuing dread, his limbs did disincorporate, and he became a heart in the blackness that surrounded the world.

The next morning, Jim opened his eyes and his father peeked in tying his tie. "C'mon, Bud. This thing starts at ten. We're leaving in an hour."

"Okay. We're going in separate cars, though, right? I mean, you two will be leaving afterward by yourselves, so I'll need to get back home, right?"

He could see the lenses of his father's eyes focusing on him with more acuity. "Yes. Don't be late."

"I'll follow you guys."

His new stepmother-to-be had left a plate of pancakes and sausage for him at his place at the dining room table. He ate, showered, dressed, and they all went out to the driveway together. His father started his car and Jim started his, and his father pulled out of the driveway, and Jim saw the gas gauge and remembered he had been needing to get gas for about two days. He weighed the chances of making it to the chapel without stopping for gas against the magnitude of the fuckup it would be to run out of gas on the way there, and he pulled into a gas station as his father continued to the chapel.

As the gas pumped, he leaned against the Buick and thought it

PART 1: INTERNAL COMBUSTION

smelled funny. He wanted to check the oil, but he didn't want to get his hands dirty and need to wash up, thereby creating two more minutes in which his father would be imagining terrible things about him. By the time he was on the freeway, the smell had worsened and there was a definite rattle coming from under the hood. The rattling turned to more of thump, like sneakers in a clothes dryer. "Just get there," Jim begged the car, when a piston rocketed through the hood of the Buick like a gunshot. The bang sent a spasm of fear through him that jerked his arm and sent him swerving into the next lane, where in avoiding the car there, he turned too sharply to the right and went skidding off the freeway and down an embankment where he crashed into a cinderblock wall.

A couple of concerned motorists had stopped at the side of the road and came skidding down the embankment on foot. "Are you okay?"

"No," Jim said. "I'm doomed."

The front end was rumpled like an old beer can. Foam fizzed out of the radiator, but Jim was unhurt. And that was the fucking problem. If only he had broken his neck, or crushed some internal organs, or even just had a nice gory gash on his temple, there might have been some sympathy for him rather than the suspicion he would be met with. Perhaps if his suit had been covered in blood and oil, or singed; perhaps if it had had to be cut off him by paramedics, everything would have turned out all right. Yeah, right. The official cause of this collision would be drug-related, probably. Irresponsibility at least. Stupidity for sure.

After the Buick had been towed away, Jim walked the last few miles to the chapel. Not a soul remained by the time he got there. He walked the roughly ten miles back to the house, with the usual lava lamp of words and images moving through his mind. Each liquor store he passed whispered to him. The newlyweds would be honeymooning at the Disneyland Hotel, where his father got a discount, for two nights. "Two nights of freedom," the liquor stores would remind him as he passed. Two nights alone. The closer he got to the house, the more apparent became the futility of not drinking, and at the last liquor store before he would have turned in to his father's neighborhood, Jim stopped and went in and bought two twelve-packs, which he lugged the rest of the way to the house.

He was on his third beer in the darkening room when the phone rang. Jim told his father what happened. "How could this happen?" his dad asked. Jim said nothing. "How do you expect to get by without a vehicle, James?" Jim said nothing. "I'll tell you how. You expect me to take care of it. Well, I'll tell you something, pal, I won't do it. I can't do it." When his father was through, Jim drank his beer in the flickering room with the TV on and the sound down.

The next morning, he awoke with a half-finished beer in his hand, surrounded by empties. He felt fine and took another swig and went to the kitchen, where he jerked off with his teeth mouthfuls of French bread from a loaf sitting on the counter. Crumbs clung to his sweater. Some tumbled to the floor. The chewing worked his jaw muscles and he felt able to think.

He could call his one-time stepfather, Josh, but Jim did not want to contaminate him with his problems. He wasn't even sure Josh was technically his stepfather anymore, but they had stayed in touch, linked by shared loss, and made the effort to get together at least a few times a year. Josh had a soothing way of describing life, and Jim needed to hear him now. He didn't want to call him, though. He needed to see him face to face.

He took the keys to his new stepmother's car and decided he would ask around at Mother's and at the yard. On the freeway, he felt the suffix "-less" applied to everything about him: Hopeless, brainless, useless, worthless, mindless.... Whatever. He made his way to Mother's near the Santa Ana and the Fifty-Seven near where Josh worked and parked. He got out of the car and went to the front door. He pulled the

PART 1: INTERNAL COMBUSTION

door open and stepped past the sucking of air into the dim room. The Bloody Mary Crew was having Sunday Services. Jim crossed to the bar and sat on a cracked vinyl stool and twirled back and forth beneath the mounted head of a moose.

"Hey, Mother. How ya been?" Jim said to a scraggly-bearded man with a big belly.

"I been. What brings you in here? You twenty-one yet?"

"That I am, Mother, but I haven't come for a drink. I'm trying to find Josh. Have you seen him?"

Mother called down the bar, "Any a you seen Josh Wesley around?"

"I saw him at the yard when I got in a while ago. He just come in from Denver and was waiting to unload. He might still be unloading, or he might be gone already," said a guy Jim knew everyone called Santa.

"Thanks, Mother. Thanks, Santa," Jim said as he walked out.

The yard was across the freeway from a mortuary and crematory. A dark smoke poured from the chimney at the crematory and carried over the freeway to mix with exhaust and fuel fumes at the yard. Jim found Josh's rig idling a low rumble at the loading rack. Josh was climbing a ladder up the side of the big chrome tank. Jim's reflection warped away from him like in a mirror at a carnival funhouse. Josh disengaged a hose from the top of the tanker and spotted Jim. He smiled and yelled, "Dry balls!" When he was done, he slid down the ladder and pulled off his work gloves. He and Jim shook hands and hugged.

"Haven't seen you in a while."

"I know. What are you doing? You got time?"

"Actually, I thought I'd get some breakfast. You hungry?"

"I'll drive."

They drove to Bob's Big Boy. "Is this your car?" Josh asked as they drove to the restaurant.

"I had a Buick, but I blew a piston yesterday."

Josh blew air out his nose and shook his head. "Nice to know everything's normal."

"Yeah."

They parked and went into the restaurant. "So, whose car is it?"

"Two." Jim held up that many fingers and a hostess led them to a booth near the breakfast bar. They sat down. "Two coffees, please. It's my stepmother's."

Josh sighed against the insides of his cheeks before laughing a soft *ha*. "What's she, number four?"

Jim nodded.

"How is she?"

"She's nice. Quiet. I don't really know her that well. They only got married yesterday."

Josh blew some more air through his nose. "And your car broke down yesterday, too?"

"Yeah. I missed the wedding or whatever it was. My dad called last night all pissed off."

"You really are just surrounded by tornadoes, aren't you?"

A waitress came and took their order. Jim asked about Denver so there would be something to talk about other than what they were thinking, and John told him about Denver for the same reason. The food came. They ate without talking. With nothing left to distract him but the sound of their scraping forks, Jim's thinking entered a compartment of his mind he had been trying to stay out of, and tears spilled down his face into his biscuits and gravy. He tried to pretend like it wasn't happening; he didn't want Josh to notice, but Josh reached across the table and gripped Jim's hand hard. "I miss her, too," Josh said.

Jim sniffled and cleared his throat and shoveled in another bite.

Josh said, "You know, she would have come back. Your mother just wanted—she needed to get away for a little while. She was just trying to put things in perspective. Sometimes you have to get away in order to do that, so you can look back from afar and sort things out. She

PART 1: INTERNAL COMBUSTION

didn't know she was leaving for good."

Jim hardened his voice, and he forced his tears to stop and resolved never to be so weak again. "I know. Fucking cars collide into shit every day. People die in them all the time. I just wish she hadn't been so miserable when it happened. I wish I would have handled everything better so that she wouldn't have felt so guilty about my psychology. I feel like I'm the one who made her leave that day." He stared through the walls of the restaurant and could almost see, hundreds of miles away, years ago, like he'd been there, her crumpled purple Plymouth Duster upside-down out in the desert. Where was she going? What was she going to do? "I feel like it was me she needed to get away from."

"You can't go blaming yourself. It isn't right. I know hearing that probably doesn't make you feel any better, but it's true."

The waitress came with more coffee. Many minutes passed, and neither of them spoke. Then Josh said, "So you're car-less again?"

Jim nodded. Josh reached into his back pocket for his wallet. "I won five hundred dollars in a truck stop Keno game yesterday. It ain't enough for a Corvette or an airplane, so I don't know what I'm going to do with it. Santa's neighbor is selling an old Volkswagen real cheap. What do you say we go out to Costa Mesa and have a look at it?"

They bought the car for $999 after they had dropped Jim's stepmother's car back at his dad's house. When Jim returned later that night, his father's truck was out front and his new stepmother's car was not. He approached the house cautiously, as if the lawn were mined, the doorway booby-trapped. He had a wedding card in a white envelope, a flimsy shield. Smoke poured down the hall from the family room where he found his father, dragging a Marlboro, sitting alone in his spot.

"Hi," said Jim.

"Hi," he answered tonelessly.

"Where's June?"

"She left."

CAR TROUBLE

Jim waited to hear more. No explanation came forth. He dropped one corner of the card and held the other between his thumb and forefinger as if he were holding a dead rat by the tail.

"I got a car."

"How?"

"Josh Wesley helped me."

He blew smoke out his nose. "I didn't know that was his responsibility."

"It isn't. Wasn't. He said I could pay him back when I get a chance."

He snorted smoke through flared nostrils.

Jim said, "I better get to bed. I have to work in the morning."

Over the next few days, Jim's father's silent unhappiness became so palpably oppressive, it seemed to Jim that the air pressure in the house had increased to the point that he had to push through the smoky hall whenever he left his bedroom.

"I'm going to the Home Depot," his father announced.

"I've got laundry to do this morning," said Jim.

He waited two minutes after his father had pulled out of the driveway before dashing to the backyard to breathe in some different feeling, illusory or not. When the hit flitted through the pipe, he held the smoke in as long as he could, crumpled the foil pipe, and tossed it into the neighbor's yard.

He was sorting whites from coloreds, high, applying some Jim Crow to his clothes when his father returned. His father came in and put on a football game and sat on his spot on the couch across from where Jim sat in a rocking chair holding a sock and a pair of underwear, sidetracked by a butterfly of thought.

His father lit a cigarette. "What's the matter with your eye?"

"The matter?"

"Yes. Your right eye. What's the matter with your right eye? It's all red."

The truth will set you free, an Obi Wan voice seemed to whisper in his ear.

PART 1: INTERNAL COMBUSTION

"I don't know." Jim shrugged. "I'm a little high."

The old man's head jerked, his eyes narrowed, hardened. "What does that mean?"

"I smoked a little marijuana."

Jim was surprised and amused at his father's agility as the fat old man sprang over the coffee table and came in with a sharp right cross that caught Jim under his ear. The old man's belly shook as he reared back on one leg and kicked Jim square in the chest with the other. Jim could easily have caught his ankle and thrown him to the ground, but he absorbed the kick as he the rocking chair tipped over backward. His father grabbed Jim around the neck and cocked his fist. He looked to Jim like a minor marvel of nature, yes, like a boiling mud pot. "You brought that shit into my house, asshole! That shit in my house!" He drew his fist back and punched Jim in the side of the face. "You brought that shit into my house!" His voice broke, and he dropped his hands and bent at the waist leaning on his knees, panting.

Jim got up, stepped around him, and picked up his keys and wallet off the counter. When he walked out the door, he knew with perfect clarity that he was leaving forever, for good. He pulled the door closed behind him and resolved never to think of his father again. It would be easy. He was forgetting him already. He was gone, but for the ache in the hinge of his jaw. It felt good. It was a good reminder to forget. He tossed his wallet on the passenger seat of the Volkswagen, got in, started her up and headed toward the Happiest Place on Earth, where he was scheduled to be Goofy, eyes red from exhaust and....

Jim rubbed his eyes and stood up to face himself in the glass. Again. He could see the outline of his head reflected in the window, but the face was darkened, the head faceless. "I don't get it," he said. "All these barriers and then glass seems like the most pernicious of things, a barrier you can see through that will cut you and make you bleed."

Adam said, "You're talking nuts again. Windows are just to keep the wind out and let the view in."

"Don't you see? That's just it. Who are we to say where the wind can and can't blow?"

Adam put his hands over his face and lowered them slowly until he was dragging the skin down under his eyes. "I don't know. I give up. This is stupid. Go ahead and break the window. Let's get going. Pam's going to leave without us.

"I can break the window?" Jim was surprised to find that his window-breaking THEY-rage had submerged. Without any impulse, he stared at the window wondering how to break it. He thought about using his forehead. It might be more memorable for Adam. He tried to summon his rage. He thought about the toad at the auto parts store, and about tow truck drivers, and cops, and Henry Ford, and CalTrans, and CEOs, but unadulterated apathy had set in. "I can't do it."

"Why not?"

"I don't know. I just can't. I don't have the urge now. Why don't you do it?"

"I don't want to get cut."

"What if I get cut?"

"So, what if you do? You never cared before. It would probably do you good. Leech the poison out of you. Bleed the demons out of you."

Jim studied Adam. "Where did you get that shit? Demons. I like that. You're talking like me now, aren't you? Making fun of me, hah?"

"Yeah. Whatever. You been acting like a whacked-out pussy freak, dude. I'm just trying to speak to you in your own language to get you to do something, but I don't really want the window broken anyway, so fuck it, I'm walking to a pay phone."

Jim's fist shot through the glass. It *was* a release of demons, a nearly orgasmic rush, watching the barrier crumble. The pain in his knuckles was sharp and short, but corporeal; it had at least manifested itself physically, like a thorn being removed. His father was right. He was a masochist. He could release his psycho pain in acts of physical pain,

PART 1: INTERNAL COMBUSTION

violence, and destruction. Oh, he felt better. Aggravation vented out of his throat in a triumphant bestial growl. He was panting for some reason, and his skin tingled and he wanted badly to fuck. "Let's pick up the girls."

"Cool," said Adam.

After they had changed the tire, Jim walked around to the passenger side and got in. Adam looked at him incredulously. "I thought that door was locked."

"It was."

"You idiot."

"What? It was locked. I pulled the handle twice to try to open it. Why it isn't locked now, I don't know. Just chalk it up to the Cosmic Fuckaround and let's go."

They got back onto the freeway and were about to take the exit to Pam's house when Adam said, "Dude. We forgot to bring the jumper cables to Lorisa and Jeffrey."

"It's no use arguing with you and your little conscience, so I guess we better just turn around. Might as well forget about this party or ever hooking up with any chicks tonight. We can just drive around and look for people to help."

"That's seriously a cool idea. We should do that sometimes."

"I was being sarcastic."

They exited the 55 and went under it and got back on it going the other way and exited again and came to the road where they had left Jeffrey and Lorisa. As they pulled up behind the Toyota their headlights lit up the inside of it and they saw the scraggly outline of Jeffrey.

Adam got out, walked to the Toyota talked a few seconds and came back. "He doesn't want our help. He says we've helped quite enough."

"What happened to whatsername?" Jim knew her name.

"Sounds like they had a fight. She left him, and it's all our fault."

"Good. Let's go."

In the stop-and-go-and-stop traffic where another massive

construction project was extending the freeway out toward the Pacific, they headed back down the 55, past the glittering South Coast Plaza movie houses with their multi-level, pay-to-park garages, past multi-million- dollar shopping complexes that beckoned with blinking lights for the consumer masses to feed, feed, feed it, lest its profitability wither and bring down the prosperity of the whole country with it.

They traveled past well-kept lawns of upper Newport Bay to where the lights of the homes on the cliffs shimmered in the water below and stopped in front of a Spanish-style mansion, lit up by pink and green ground lights that were masked by banana-less banana trees and elephant-eared philodendrons. The car doors thunked as they shut them, and a thousand impulses squirted around the inside of Jim's head trying to gain purchase. A fountain tinkled. He felt nervous and wrong and out of place. He tried to concentrate on just moving his feet toward the door. He knew he was just going to clam up, and bring the whole party down with the heaviness which suddenly seemed to pull on him. He took another step. Another. He thought he ought not to drink anymore. He felt in his pants for the fifth, but it was gone, and he groaned and stumbled over one of the ground lights along the cement path to the door. The trunks of the philodendron had the eyes of Argus. *Yes, the gods are watching, I must be brave, I must be fearless.* He took three steps more to the door. He would prove what amazing and unbelievable things he could do. Moths rammed the porch light. *That's all we are.* He thought to use his head to knock on the door. He used his knuckles. Adam rang the bell.

Knock ding rap dong knock ding rap dong.

Jim took a deep breath. The moths moved into his stomach. *What the hell is wrong with you?* Six months earlier he'd been sitting on the couch at the birthday party of the girl who was Pocahontas. Adam was excited about meeting Pocahontas. "I want to poke Pocahontas," he said. When they got there, her nose was big, and she didn't have any

PART 1: INTERNAL COMBUSTION

tits. "She doesn't look anything like how she looked in the cartoon," he lamented.

Jim dropped his head on the back of the couch and stared open-mouthed at a polar bear in the cottage cheese on the ceiling, feeling the snot in his sinuses drain into a deeper sinus cavity with a high-pitched gurgle.

"Whoa, who's that?" Adam elbowed him in the ribs.

Jim came down from the ceiling. The fluids in his head bogged forward. He knew who before he'd even looked. His shift at D-land had just ended the first time he had ever seen her. She was coming to the gate of the employee break area as he was going in. She startled him, appearing so suddenly in the limited frame of vision the Goofy mask allowed. She held the gate open for him. He felt a rush of embarrassment and mumbled an unheard apology, and she smiled brightly as her presence mauled his senses, his lungs expanded, and he sucked in a breath of the Goofy mask, rich in carbon dioxide and Lysol.

He pulled off his head. The fresh air that bathed his sweat-soaked face seemed to come from her. She joined some other cast members at a round table, and he stopped on his way to the locker room, transfixed. Her face was inhuman. She was more a creature than a person. An animated sculpture. Her beauty was holy, her skin without pore; the symmetry of her features confirmed intelligent creation, artistic creation, omnipotent creation. Yes, holy, sacred, beauty. Her cheekbones emanated happiness, her forehead was cleansed in the fountain of youth. Her eyebrows arched playfully. Her nose—it was indescribable, a plastic surgeon's nightmare—its perfection could not be copied. Women with perfect noses would be going into offices in Newport clamoring for such a nose, and the surgeons would flee screaming to their yachts to disappear to Easter Island. If they could have reproduced and packaged her earlobes, they'd have sold out off the counters of every Kwik-E-Mart in the land. He wanted to put his tongue in her dimples, wanted to finger the slight cleft in her chin—*No! You evil bastard. How dare you think such profanities about so pure a beauty—!* The eyes. It was the eyes. From out of the purity stared the eyes of the ancient harlot. Jezebel and Salome and Eve herself stared from those eyes—

She moved away. With terror pounding in his chest, he fought the urge to look below the perfect smoothness of her neck, he got as far down as the hollow of her throat and averted his eyes for fear of the inescapable sleeplessness he would find below that. He forced himself to one of the commissary windows and ordered a double bacon cheeseburger with extra mayo. Flesh flesh flesh. He was in the throes of craving. He shoved his fists into his armpits to keep his fingers from clenching, his wrists from snaking, and he tried not to look, he tried, but lasted about three seconds before his eyes again sought her radiance. Augh! She was sitting with *him*. The fucker in the lederhosen, that Matterhorn fucking Wayne guy, operator, that frat dick at Fullerton. "Thirty-seven." Jim felt his chin protruding, his jaw locked itself into an underbite, as he watched her face melt into different beauties with each change of expression. "Number thirty-seven." His hand was on her thigh! Augh! He felt as if he would walk out of his skin and throttle the bastard. He held onto the railing that funneled people to and from the commissary windows.

"NUMBER THIRTY-SEVEN!"

"Oh." He picked up his dead steer and found a table with a good vantage point, and bit into it, staring at her as if through binoculars, feeling the desire to protect and violate her, the instinctual love/lust combo with which she must have filled every man who saw her. Flesh. Flesh. Sins of, cravings for. Lust. Hunger. A trip of Biblical proportions. To crave flesh is to want to live. It clogged his heart and was irresistible, this daily gnawing in him for meat—for flesh. In order to live, you must kill and consume. Whose plan is this? Ah, but there were days he no longer wanted to live, yet the hunger remained. He wondered if his lust for grease and cholesterol wasn't a slow suicide

PART 1: INTERNAL COMBUSTION

attempt after all, and as the contradictions had gobbled each other up, he'd decided his prevailing philosophy would be to eat and drink as his urges dictated and not to think or talk about anything so pointless and unfashionable as his gastronomical moral dilemmas—and it was so much more, this idea of flesh. He ripped into another bite and saw a hint of nipple under her shirt, and he began to lick his tongue around it, his meat stiffening, and a squirt of grease and mayo fell onto the front of the Goofy vest.

A woman in a red blazer approached him. Fuck. Judy Tuna. "Didn't you get the new memorandum?" she asked.

He tried pretending not to hear her.

She stood right in front of him. "It's a reminder to cast not to eat in costume."

He ripped into the flesh with his teeth, ripped into the vision of her flesh with his imagination.

"Excuse me!" The sharpness of her tone penetrated his rapture.

He noticed now that he had gathered the attention of the other breaking employees. He took another bite and stood up. "Sorry, Ms. Tuna," he said with his mouth full of ground beef, cheese, mayo, pickles and saliva. He swallowed. "I'm just going to change now."

She consulted a clipboard. "You're Jim Crack," she registered curtly. "We'll be expecting you in Mr. Flemish's office in twenty minutes."

He took another bite, wiped his mouth with his sleeve, and dumped the rest of his burger into the trashcan.

"Cuh-rackhead!" Wayne called out shrilly and Jim heard laughter from around the table. She wasn't laughing, though.

There were steps on the other side of the door.

"Yeah," he had said to Adam. "I've seen her around. She's Tinkerbell."

"Is she with anybody?"

"I think one of the Matterhorn operators fucks her. That guy she's talking to now. His name's Wayne."

"I've seen that guy at Fullerton."

"He's an asshole."

"Why?"

"Just for being with her when he's so not worthy. He's a total frat dork, too, a TKE. Their whole aim is to get an orgy going at their house. That chick is too beautiful to fuck."

Wayne held a beer bong tube to his lips as chanting supporters poured multiple beers into the funnel. He gulped it all down and stood up and blew a rain of foam over the revelers in the kitchen and then pounded his chest in primate glory.

"Wayne! Damn it! You soaked my new dress!"

"Take it off then," he said and grabbed his crotch and mugged for the onlookers.

"You're such a dick."

He grabbed his crotch again. "You'd know, wouldn't you?"

She threw her beer in his face and walked away.

"Yeah, baby! Lick it off me now!"

She went out to the balcony and closed the sliding glass door behind her.

"I'm going to talk to her." Adam stood up and went out to her. Jim watched their lips moving through the glass. Whatever Adam could have said to her was a mystery to Jim. She smiled.

All the fucking time I agonized over approaching her—all the mumbled hellos, and Adam just walks right up and knows what to say. Jim watched her tilt her head sideways to talk to him, watched them lean on the railing with their elbows touching, and he could feel himself disappearing until he was nothing more than a pair of eyes fixed into the back cushion of the couch. The party went on around him. The guy who was the Mad Hatter made out with girl who was the Alice in Wonderland without ever noticing the two eyeballs on the couch right next to them; the eyes hardly noticed them, focused as they were on the moving lips, glossy-wet, smiling, forming words out there on the other side of the glass.

PART 1: INTERNAL COMBUSTION

But then the lips frowned. Jim's eyes pulled back and found her scowling at Wayne, who smiled at first but then grabbed her arm and snarled into her face. She yanked away, and Adam put his hand on Wayne's shoulder. Wayne turned and grabbed Adam around the neck and Jim's eyes grew arms and fists and legs and they stepped out to the balcony and threw a haymaking overhand right that caught Wayne flush on the cheek, spinning him against the rail where he looked at Jim in disbelief. Jim deliberated a moment and punched him again, straight in the eye. A calm few milliseconds passed in which Jim watched Wayne's eye begin to balloon shut, and then he felt himself being pulled by the collar back into the apartment and turned in time to see one of Wayne's friends swinging a chair at him. He knocked most of the chair away but lost his balance and fell on his back. In an instant Wayne was on him, blood dripping from his face onto Jim's, but Adam bear hugged him long enough for Jim to scramble to his feet.

"Stop it! Stop it!" Pocahontas was in the middle of the room screaming. "Fucking assholes! Get out of here!"

"Come on, bitch," said Wayne to Jim. "Let's take this outside."

Jim was breathing heavily, but he didn't think he'd been hit, except maybe part of the chair had glanced off his side. Wayne was muscular and broad-shouldered to Jim's tall and wiry, but Jim knew he could focus his anger better. Wayne's eye was swollen shut and blood was flowing over his mouth onto his torn shirt. Jim blew air out his nose.

"No. You win," said Jim. "I'm leaving."

He turned his back and started for the door. Tink looped her arm through his. "We're going with you," she said. Her other hand clasped Adam's.

Out the door and down the stairs they went, Wayne coming after them, yelling, "Six feet under, Crack! You're six feet under!" He caught up with them on the landing and lunged at Jim with a wild punch that Jim sidestepped, and catching Wayne by the wrist, he twisted his arm up behind his back and pushed him face first into the stucco wall.

Jim growled low in his ear, "I don't think she likes you. Get used to it. Fuck." He realized he could have been talking to himself. Wayne tried to elbow Jim with his free arm, and Jim twisted his arm higher and slammed him back into the wall. "Get it through your head, or I'll break your fucking arm and throw you down the fucking stairs." He was practically whispering in Wayne's ear, and he felt a surge of endorphins, a giddy sense of power and victory, and he twisted Wayne's arm up a little higher. Wayne whimpered, and Jim saw his own reflection smiling in the glass fire extinguisher case that said IN CASE OF EMERGENCY BREAK GLASS. He saw who he was, who he would always be, recognized the fate laid out for him at conception, and his will vanished. His head ached. He felt feverish. His wheezing sounded like the crackle before a thunderclap. "I got a better idea," he said, and he let go of Wayne, punched the glass, and threw *himself* down the stairs.

There must have been a split second of zero gravity after he had jumped out over the stairwell in which he was no longer on the way up, not yet on the way down. Suspended in space for that instant, he felt also somehow suspended in time, and for a moment he glimpsed infinity. He looked down at the earth below him and all he could see was covered in concrete, none of it any good but for driving. He sighed. A poem he'd read came to mind, a poem a guy in high school had pointed out to him because the author's name was Dickey, about a stewardess who had been sucked from an airplane and fell thirty thousand feet. It was an amazing poem and Jim recalled it as he began his descent, and he thought he might like a little Bailey's and coffee. He fell from there, halfway to the ground, six feet. He felt like shooting some pool, fell another three feet, fell to one and a half feet above the concrete, fell to nine inches, to four and half, two and a quarter, one and an eighth, fell right down nine four thousand ninety-sixths of an inch and then Bam! The steps came rushing up and slammed his body. Down he tumbled and lay in a heap at the bottom of the stairs.

PART 1: INTERNAL COMBUSTION

Tink came rushing up. "Oh, my god! Are you okay?"

Jim sat up. "I don't feel anything." Someone threw an open can of beer and hit Jim in the back of the head. "I felt that."

"You're fucking crazy!" The can of beer rolled around near Jim's thigh, bleeding its contents. He picked it up and took a drink.

"We better get out of here," said Adam, taking Jim by the arm and pulling him to his feet, Jim wincing.

"Where can we shoot some pool and get some coffee and Bailey's?"

As the night had worn on, Tink became cozier and cozier with Adam, and Jim, the odd man out, limped back to the white house alone and went to sleep on the couch. She and Adam woke him when they came in. They wanted him to roll a joint. He rolled it for them, still in his underwear, blanket draped loosely around his waist. After they smoked it, Adam took her back to his room, and Jim could hear her moaning, mounting pulses of volume, a song that drove him insane. He stood up and kicked the screen off the window and pissed to the ground two stories below.

The next morning, he said to her, "You're sure a loud fuck." He had the nerve to talk to her, now that it was too late.

Her giggle seemed to feign embarrassment. She was in the kitchen popping grapes into her mouth. He leaned against the doorjamb and wondered along with everything else how the hell did any grapes show up at Pete and Adam's house, but there they were and so was she.

"Where's Adam?" he asked.

"He said he had to go to work. I'm leaving in a minute."

"It's okay. You don't have to rush."

The wind spirited through the window and the paper towels danced with the grape bag.

"How long have you guys been living here?" she asked.

"Uuuhhm, I don't really live here. Adam and Pete let me stay. I've got a mattress on the floor in Pete's room right now. He's up in Santa Cruz a lot."

"So where do you 'really' live?"

He shrugged. "Nowhere."

"You don't live," she popped another grape into her mouth, "anywhere?"

I'm homeless, he thought. He said, "I'm between homes."

"Or between lives, maybe," she suggested.

He didn't know what she meant, but he said, "Yeah, that's it."

"When's your birthday?"

"Why?"

"I believe you can tell a lot about a person by when they were born."

"How?"

"Because the universe is like a big clock, with all these little springs and gears and stars and people, and they're all interconnected. I think you can tell a lot about the pattern of a person's life by how the heavens were arranged when that person was born."

He stared at her blankly, trying to hide a sense of astonishment. "June twentieth, nineteen seventy," he eventually said.

"No way."

"Is that bad?"

"You've got all kinds of stuff going on. You must have like at least three personalities, right? You're a Gemini/Cancer cusp, and you were born on the Solstice. Do you know what time you were born?"

"'Round midnight."

"Noooooh."

"That's what my mom said."

"I would be very interested in seeing how your life turns out. Trust me, you've got epic struggles in you. I've seen it in other cusps, but it's worse when you're Gemini. My uncle was Taurus/Gemini. He was a big, strong, wild, bull-headed, crazy man, but he could be so sweet, and everyone who ever knew him said he was the funniest guy they had ever known. I loved him so much."

PART 1: INTERNAL COMBUSTION

"Love-D? Why the past tense?"

"He was murdered. My mom told me the story once. He was a big fight fan. He had a bar in LA, and he knew all the fighters and promoters and managers and whatever that fought there. There was a Mexican kid who was supposed to lose, but didn't, and he was killed behind my uncle's bar. My uncle knew the whole story, and he was going to testify in court, but he turned up beaten to death outside his apartment."

She ate another grape. "You've got more going on that, though. You're already tilted toward Sol to begin with. You were born in the northern hemisphere, right? The sun burns right down on you."

He wanted to say, "Hogwash." "Hogwash" was the exact thing he wanted to say, but an imperative came up from below his belt preventing him from so bluntly disagreeing with her *Cosmo* philosophy. Even with her makeup smeared and her hair mussed, her eyes swollen a bit, she was beautiful. She owned his ass.

He said, "I don't think anything is predetermined. It's all luck. Random luck. That's what rules the world."

"Do you believe in karma?" she asked.

"Karma's a Hindu thing from India, right?—or wait, isn't it a Buddhist thing? It's like if you're good, you'll have a better reincarnation, or something, right?" Duh.

"I think it has to do with if you put out good energy, good energy will come back to you, but if you put out negative energy, negative energy will come back to you."

He supposed the physics of all that made sense somehow, even if only because she owned his ass. The barren grape stems sat like some alien skeleton in the bag on the table and she stood up. "I better go. It's Monday, right?"

Jim's heart leapt. Say something. Don't let her go. "Okay," he said.

She took her purse and sidled through the doorway where he was leaning on the jamb. Their faces were inches apart as she passed, and he could feel himself falling out of his eyes into hers and then she looked away to the front door which she opened, looked back and smiled, said, "Bye," and left him staring at the shut door, as he was now, months later. A dead bolt turned, the knob turned, and the door pulled in, and there she was again, not a hair out of place, makeup perfect, the porch light's reflection glistening on her lips; he was afraid to look any farther than her spaghetti straps. She threw her arms around Adam's neck and gave him a kiss on the lips.

She gave Jim a hug and a kiss on the cheek. He smelled the cinnamon of her gum and something he guessed was lavender body wash and something else that had him swallowing tablespoons of spit. *Better only look at her a little bit*, he warned himself.

"You guys want to come in for a little bit?" A shiver ran up Jim's spine from his testes. Her smile had a hint of leer. "Cold, Jim?" She reached down to his wrist and pulled him in.

"Are your parents home?" Adam asked.

"My dad left for EuroDisney," she said, appalled. "I just found out today he's going to be gone two weeks," she said in a much brighter tone. "My mom's in her room tripping." She flipped her hand over her shoulder.

They had stepped into a large Spanish-tiled entryway that was railed off from the lower level of a split-level living room done in wrought iron and leather with hardwood floors. A spiral staircase wound up out of sight.

"Got any beer?" he whispered.

"In the kitchen," she whispered back, mocking him.

She led them toward a hall. In a length of sliding glass doors that went around the room, on the other side of which the last stars of the evening were appearing over the ocean horizon, Jim saw through himself.

She led them along a hall with walls covered by photos, of her in her cap and gown, as a little kid on Mickey Mouse's lap, the little

PART 1: INTERNAL COMBUSTION

family in Aspen or something, in front of the Eiffel Tower, her dad getting an award from some guy in a suit, one of her in her cheerleading outfit, and then the wall ran out and they were in the kitchen. Something was simmering; Jim eyeballed the aroma. Chicken. Wisps of steam did the hula off a crockpot on an island range.

Tink pulled open the door of a big side-by-side refrigerator and handed back a Corona. The size of Jim's hand multiplied in the stainless steel as he reached for it and shrank back as he brought it to his chest. Tink bent further into the fridge. All Jim could see of her were her perfect ass and legs, denim-clad down to the round of her calf, ankles and feet held to a preposterous height of heel by crisscrossing of straps. She straightened and turned holding two beers nipple-high. "Ad?" She extended one to Adam.

"Nah. Ah, all right," he murmured.

"It goes in your mouth." She put it in his hand. "Lime, anyone?"

"Limes are for pussies," Jim said. "How 'bout a freaking bottle opener."

"On the fridge."

Jim took a refrigerator magnet bottle opener to open all the beers and chugged down half his with a couple of gulps. He replaced the magnet next to a picture of Tink in a bikini on a palm-treed beach, held to the refrigerator by a magnet that Jim at first thought depicted Minnie Mouse slapping Mickey. A big red "SMACK!!" was splashed across the top of the otherwise black and white image, but upon closer inspection he saw the "SMACK!!" was actually Minnie kissing an apparently surprised—as evidenced by a cloud of question marks emanating from his perplexed-looking head—Mickey. "You darling —MM-M-M—" said Minnie's bubble, her eyes closed, lashes long, lips leaving red lip prints on Mick's face.

Adam hopped his ass up on an inner corner of the counter and Tink leaned into his crotch, using his thighs for armrests. No one said anything for what seemed to Jim an eternity of minutes. A shroud of silence was lowering upon him, entombing him in the final pointlessness of all speech. Tink had to save him. Say something, Tink.

"So, what should we talk about?" she said.

Whew. The weight lessened for a moment, but now someone had to answer. Answer, Adam. *Answer!* Adam, in a trance, stared into his beer. Tink turned her gaze upon Jim. He searched his soul and came up with this: "I'm hungry."

"That's fascinating," said Tink, mocking him again, as if he had just revealed the secret of the universe. She departed Adam's thighs, opened a cupboard, and removed a bowl. "Don't you ever think with anything other than your stomach, Crack?" she asked.

"I use my head, too," he said and tugged his dick through his jeans, but she didn't see.

"You know, Jim, I can't wait for you to eat my girlfriend tonight."

"You mean like cunnilingus or cannibalism?"

"What?!"

"You want me to eat your girlfriend."

"*Meet*, meathead. I want you to *meet* my girlfriend."

"That's not what I heard."

"Whatever." She had a ladle now and went to the crockpot to fix Crack a bowl. "You're going to love this. My mom's housekeeper Anita is the best cook. She loves me." She handed him the bowl. "Wish I could have some."

"Why don't you?" Jim slurped a spoonful of chicken and broth and carrots and celery and tomato and pepper into his mouth.

"Duh. Calories. You can't be a future diva if you're fat. It's bad enough I'm already having a beer."

"Ahso." He took another slurp. "You got a bigger spoon?"

"Tsh. Ya want the ladle?" She held it up and it dripped on the floor.

"Lemme try it." He held the bowl near his mouth and ladled in the stew.

"You are so goofy."

PART 1: INTERNAL COMBUSTION

"Why did Mickey Mouse slap Minnie Mouse?"

"I've heard this. She kept sitting on Pinocchio's face screaming, 'Lie to me! Lie to me!'"

"No. He slapped her because she was fucking Goofy."

Adam was still staring into his beer. "What's with you?" Tink said to him. "Turn me on, dead man."

Adam shrugged. He pulled her into an embrace and she snuggled her cheek against his neck. Jim felt like puking his stew. "How did it go at work today?" she asked him.

"Crap. My head hurt all day. I had the worst hangover. I was supposed to set up a Campbell's display at a Vons in Tustin, but when I got out to Tustin I realized I'd forgotten the address. I thought if I drove around I might remember the right streets when I saw their names, but I just got lost up in some canyon back there. I had to ask at a gas station for directions. I swore I'd never drink again."

"Then give me that." Tink reached for his beer, but he held it away. "Nuh-uh," he said.

"Why not? That doesn't make any sense."

"Because I'm just going to stand around like a zombie all night if I don't start drinking."

"I hear that!" Jim crowed and put down the bowl and chugged down the rest of his beer. "Let's bail."

"No shit, huh?" Tink slammed down the rest of her beer. "Let's get outta here." Nobody moved. "Okay, guys. This way."

Jim's boxers tightened as he watched her walk down the hall. He went to the fridge and took out two more beers. "For the road," he said and waited for Adam who took a mere swig from his bottle. "Dude. Pound that. Quit pussin' over it and let's get out of here."

Adam unleaned himself from the counter, glugged the rest of his beer, put the bottle down, made a face, and belched.

"That's more like it," said Jim. He put his arm around Adam's shoulders. "Let's go have some fun."

"Lead the way."

"We'll let Tink do that."

They went down the hall to where she was reapplying lipstick in the hall mirror. "I heard that, Crack," she said. "I better not hear you call me Tink anywhere tonight, or I'll mess you up good."

"I believe you."

"You better." She capped her lipstick and blew herself a kiss. "Mom! I'm leaving!" she yelled up the spiral stairs. No sound came down. She opened the front door and they were inhaled into the night. Jim breathed the cool air and felt a lot better than he had in the same spot twenty minutes before. *Life's weird like that*, he thought. "Here, buddy." He put one of the beers in Adam's hand.

"Thanks," said Adam.

"You guys want me to drive?" Pam asked.

"Fuck that," said Jim. "We got the company car right here."

"What happened to the window?"

"It was in the way."

"In the way of what?"

"Everything."

They piled into the front seat, Jim driving, Corona between his thighs, Tink in the middle. It was prime time for parties on the peninsula in Newport Beach. The traffic had ebbed, but the parking was scarce—beyond scarce, not to be had. Jim hadn't minded the first twenty minutes while he still had beer to drink and Tink's thigh was touching his, but twenty minutes later when the tape they were listening to was on its second lap, and his beer was gone, and she had laid her head on Adam's shoulder, he began to get antsy; his leg bounced up and down, and his grip on the steering wheel tightened. Up one street and down another, a party raged on every block, nubile chicks practically pouring out the windows, beer flowing into the gutters. "There's a space!" No. It was a driveway. "There's one!" No. Fire hydrant. Space? Red curb. Space? Not big enough.

PART 1: INTERNAL COMBUSTION

"Omygod. There's Janine. Stop the car," said Tink. Jim stopped. "Get out, Adam." Adam got out. She rushed to greet Janine and they squealed and hugged and exchanged howcuteyoulooks. A car behind honked.

"I'll go park this fucker and meet you guys back here."

"Don't park it where it'll get towed."

"I won't, but hide a few beers for me."

"I'm afraid when he says he won't, he means he won't do what I ask him," Adam said to Janine's very happy-to-see-you titties. She was clearly wearing a G-string beneath her flimsy, clinging skirt. The car behind Jim honked again. That seemed to be all there was to know about her, and so he said, "Seeya in a bit," and drove back onto Balboa and across Pacific Coast Highway and up Superior.

He found a place to park by the hospital, a mile or two from the party. He took some ones and change from a compartment in the dashboard and got his skateboard out of the back seat. He locked the car, even though the window was broken, and put the keys in his pocket. Hoag Hospital: He'd spent a night there, mostly anesthetized, the summer previous. They'd been having a kegger. Some freak no one knew was pissing everybody off, some speeding space invader, and Jim, Jim the action man, Jim, who knew he himself was a freak, was appointed, or self-appointed to force the rival freak's departure. So, Jim puffed up his chest and rolled his shoulders forward and gave the freak a few shoves out the door. The freak soon returned, though, and threw a bottle through the front window of Jim's and his roomies' rental. Jim chased him to a house down the street, into which the freak ran, shutting and locking the door, just as Jim got to it. The freak stuck out his tongue and flipped Jim off and pushed his face against the window, and Jim punched him through the glass. The freak fell backward, as Jim pulled his arm back through the falling panes of broken glass, incognizant of the sudden limpness in his wrist, the profusion of blood. Another guy came out of the house and Jim met him with a left to the eye. They scuffled, until Jim, still not figuring out that his right arm had become useless, slipped in the blood on the concrete patio.

"Dude. Look at your arm," said the guy. A jagged gash the size of a post-partum vagina, hemorrhaging, hung open across his forearm. "You better get to a doctor," said the guy, who had a gash of his own, though smaller, over his eye. He walked Jim back to this place, where the college brain trust used an electric guitar cord to tie off his arm above the cut and had him hold the stricken limb over his head, giving him the appearance, somewhat, of a prom queen bathed in pig's blood.

He had severed three muscles in the arm and the nerve. A surgeon sewed him back together, and he spent the summer in a cast. As he thought back on it, his fingers clenched, and he rubbed his hand over the dead part, from the base of his thumb halfway to the elbow where there was still no feeling, just a maddening phantom sense of something that should be felt and wasn't. Jim tore the gauze off the wound he'd gotten slamming the phone that morning. He peered into his rent flesh and flexed his hand and saw that he had learned nothing from his summer in the cast, nothing from the atrophy and therapy and sunburn after the cast was finally removed.

His memory faded into the present on the hill up Superior. He stood with his skateboard poised, his foot on its tail and its nose in the air, ready to drop down the hill, when the Pacific wind blew over him and the oil derricks off the coast looked beautiful, immortal, almost otherworldly, a testament to man's genius to his industry; Jim felt peace, even in the irony of it, that men were capable of fixing structures into the oceans; and they, the derricks, blinked at him, winked, not unlike a buoy off Howth. A bat flitted against the starlit firmament in which was set the black mass of Catalina, and the present seemed for a while not to become the past at all, nor the future, and Jim felt momentarily immortal, as if he could live forever in such a moment, and unlike the derricks, he had the advantage of not being fixed. He could go wherever he wanted, and he made up his mind that he

PART 1: INTERNAL COMBUSTION

would, and he dropped the nose of the skateboard and gave a howling shriek and plunged down into the time that would come, bearing a grit-toothed smile against all that could go awry, not the least of which was the rough pavement sliding beneath him around ten feet a second, hungry for a little flesh.

The light at the intersection turned green just as he came to the bottom of the hill, and he shot through ahead of the cars, his momentum carrying him several blocks down Balboa without a kick. He hopped it up onto the sidewalk, the seams in the concrete clacking under his wheels. He leaned down Forty-First Street and zigged around a shirtless guy running the other way and zagged around a gal chasing after him, crying. Jim cut down an alley and nearly collided with a surf punk carrying down the stairs of a duplex a surfboard on which was mounted a pair of steer horns. Coasting out the alley and onto Seashore, he saw two cops pull over a guy riding a girl holding a tiki torch on the handlebars of his bike. A throng of revelers was dancing on a patio table when it collapsed, and they all roared joyfully at their folly. Another group of people staggered out into the street, screaming and laughing, duct-taped into a mass of limbs trying to make it down the sidewalk without falling over. Jim zipped out onto the strand that ran along the sand and threaded his way through rollerbladers and bicyclists and pedestrians. He spotted a guy open a longneck and put it on the little wall around a patio, and Jim swiped it as he whizzed past and tipped it up and guzzled as he cruised, but on his second guzzle, he forgot he had a longneck and chipped an incisor.

He kept skating until he arrived at a house where a big party was going on. One dude leaned over a balcony and puked and Jim swerved around the cascade while a couple of other guys were working a beer bong with a thirty-foot tube. One guy upstairs poured beer after beer into the funnel while the guy below chugged it to the chants of the crowd. Jim slowed and turned up the walk to the house. A guy was passed out in the entranceway and partygoers had drawn a chalk outline around his body and covered him in beer cans and stuck a pencil in his mouth. Three guys wearing the cardboard cases of empty twelve-packs on their heads like helmets posed like superheroes, fists on hips, for a photo. Jim picked up his skateboard and walked in. A guy in baseball pants and nothing else was breaking a full beer can open on his forehead before tearing it open with his teeth and gulping it down. A band of guys dressed like the Village People were playing some loud, feedbacky garage grunge and girls were squealing and giving themselves whiplash. The walls of the place were covered with sports pennants, mirrors with liquor logos, and posters of bikini babes advertising beer. Empty booze bottles lined the window sills. A thousand bottle caps had been pushed into the ceiling, some of them arranged in a constellation that spelled TITS N ASS. A TV was perched on a pyramid of empty kegs, a Dodgers game flickering on its screen. A couple dozen keg caps were tacked to the wall like trophies over a table where kids sat bouncing quarters into a schooner. A guy pantsed a girl as Jim walked past. Jim found some people sitting around a coffee table passing a joint around, and he sat with them and took a long drag just as a guy came diving headfirst down the stairs with a girl riding on his back. Another group of guys were fondling a cardboard cutout of Jessica Rabbit, taking turns licking her cartoon boobs near where a couple was making out unaware that a big dude right behind them had dropped his shorts and was bending his hairy ass to their heads less than a foot away. A beagle sat in the middle of it all, wearing sunglasses and a straw hat with an American flag sticking out of it, sedately observing the proceedings, ready to attack, Jim guessed if things got out of hand.

"Crack! Dude! What's up!"

"Kazi man!" They slapped hands in a soul shake. "I'm supposed to be meeting Adam Smith and some girls at a party on Thirty-third. I was skating by when I saw this place raging. What about you?" Kazi was a guy everyone called Kamikaze. Jim had heard that his real name was

PART 1: INTERNAL COMBUSTION

William, but no one ever called him that.

He smiled and his eyes slitted. "Just enjoying the fool's life. Partying. Huhuhu." His head bobbed. "Wilson said he wasn't going to celebrate his birthday anymore. Huhuhu. He says birth is a bloody, painful, traumatic experience. Said he was going to celebrate his conception day. Huhuhuhu. Cause that's the orgasm that created him. Hiumhium. So today is nine months before his birthday and this is his conception day party. Hih."

"Where is he? I want to wish him a happy conception day."

"Actually, he started trippin' that his conception day was—what did he say?—Fraudulent. Yeah. He says his parents hate each other, and he's a mistake and now he's locked himself in the bathroom and won't come out. People are pissing all over the place. You had any punch?" His eyes unslitted a second and Jim saw himself in Kazi's pupils. "It's in the fridge way in the back on the bottom. Don't tell anyone else."

Jim followed him to the kitchen where a couple of guys were kicking their way through a wall into the half of the duplex next door. Kazi opened the fridge and pulled out a pitcher full of red punch on which was taped a note that said DRINK ME. He scooped up a Dixiecupful and gave it to Jim. Plaster and drywall dust settled onto the rippling surface of the punch. One of the guys kicking through the wall was about six five with long hair and about size fifteen shoes. The other guy was the shirtless guy wearing baseball pants. He was going at it with metal cleats. They had made it through the first wall and were working between the studs, taking turns kicking at the wall of the place next door with savage yells and laughter, drinking beer between blows, and then the guy in baseball pants took a running start, cleats scrabbling on the kitchen linoleum, and rammed the wall head first, breaking on through to the other side. Jim downed the punch. Fog started pouring through the hole. The big guy went in behind the guy in baseball pants, and there was a moment of relative silence before they reappeared and stepped back through the hole, fists raised over their heads, howling in victory.

Jim wondered where the fog was coming from. Bits of the wall crumbled around him as he peered into the hole. The room was without form and void. He put his head through the hole and stepped into the room and found his feet submerged in water. He felt air push past him and ripple upon the water and he located a light switch and flipped it and the light was divided from the darkness. He looked up and could just make out the ceiling through the fog and looked down and saw that there was about three inches of water flooding the floor. He stepped farther into the room and found a marijuana plant growing in a pot of earth on a window sill. A fishbowl had been upended and he spotted a couple of goldfish swimming across the floor beneath a parakeet in a cage hung from the ceiling. He came to a couch whereon a cat mewled plaintively. Jim went farther into the fog and came upon a young man, younger than Jim, who was slumped on the couch next to a keg floating in a trash barrel, with the tap in his hand left open, a trickle of beer overflowing his mug, drenching his pants and the couch, the amber mingling with the water on the floor.

Jim was appalled at the waste of beer. He tipped the last few drops of punch from the Dixie cup into his mouth and tossed the cup to the floor where it bobbed slowly in in the current with some empty cans and an apple core. He took the tap and flipped the valve shut. He took the mug from the young man, who stirred. Jim gulped the beer.

"I thought I was gonna get laid tonight. Where did she go?" asked the young man, younger than Jim, as he winced and rubbed his ribcage.

Jim shrugged. "What's going on in here?"

"Wilson gave me an idea with his conception day party. I've heard that a man reaches his sexual peak in terms of arousal at the age of eighteen. You ever heard that?"

Jim said that he supposed that he had somewhere heard such a thing.

"Well, today is the midway point between my being eighteen and

PART 1: INTERNAL COMBUSTION

nineteen, exactly six months into it. I'm neither closer to seventeen nor to nineteen today, so this day is the very height of my eighteenness, see? It's the horniest I'll ever be. From here on out, all I'll get is less and less horny until I'm old and can't get it up anymore." The young man looked deeply saddened. "So, I put out fliers that I'm having a big party, a Sexual Peak Party, and I'm hoping like hell to get laid. Epic, huh?"

"You get any chicks to go along with it."

"A bunch said they'd come. I was trying like hell to get some thirty-year-olds to come because I heard that's when chicks hit their peak."

"What's with all the fog and water?"

"Oh, God. Geon and Jeb—you know those guys?— they went up to the Physical Sciences building and pried the lock off the dry ice refrigerator and brought it all to the party. We put some in the bathtub and some in all the sinks, but it got so foggy in here no one could see or breathe and everyone bailed, but they left the water running and flooded the place and it started leaking through the ceiling downstairs and the lady there called the cops and everyone bailed."

Cops? Jim wanted no part of that. He sloshed through the water, groping walls for an exit, and found a door. It opened to the outside world and he went out into it. The air felt like cool water. He walked to the beach. The waves boomed along the shore. He felt electricity humming through his body. If a blade of grass was an astonishing unit of growth, a journey work of the stars, a miracle as profound as any, wasn't a grain of sand a representation of nature's capacity to pulverize? Do I contradict myself? The words ran through his head. Very well, I contradict myself. I am large. I contain multitudes. Who said that? It was on the tip of his mental tongue.

He wondered until he became aware of the skateboard held in the curl of his fingers, the sandpapery grip-tape rough against the skin of his inner forearm. He examined the skateboard, running his fingers over the wood and spinning the wheels, fascinated again at man's

159

capacity for invention, and at the millennia that had gone by leading up to this skateboard, this simple plank on wheels. Yeah, but concrete had to be invented first, said another voice. Hah, he answered, you couldn't ride it in the sand, and he dropped the board down and put his foot on it. It seemed to be a very long way down, just shy of infinity, between his mind and his feet. That was some punch. I needed a good punch. A good punch in the mouth. He gave an exploratory push and rolled forward along the strand, crunching grains of sand beneath the wheels. He felt a little unsteady with his feet so far away, but he gave another push and picked up speed and another and soon he was gliding down the shoreline, and the membrane of flesh that separated him from everything else seemed to dissolve and he became a spirit moving through the air.

A white dog with a gray beard came around the corner. Jim's mass, with its resultant gravity, suddenly returned to the skateboard, which was on a collision course with the dog. Jim swerved around the dog, skirting the edge of the sidewalk with half of one wheel over the sand, heading straight for a palm tree. The wheel caught in the sand and the skateboard stopped with remarkable abruptness. Jim's body, however, continued onward, and this time there was nothing pseudo-mystical about his flight: he crashed headlong into the trunk of the palm.

When his eyes opened again, his vision stretched across a dunescape that disappeared into a horizon of blackness. Each grain of sand contained universes. Footprints, remnants of humanity's passings on a late-summer day, filled with shadows as meaningful as those cast by the pyramids of Giza. He rolled onto his back and was unsure if the stars he saw were of his own making or the ones normally traversing the heavens. The tree seemed to be trying to pretend that nothing had happened, when the dog came up and started licking Jim's face, and then the tree whistled and looked the other way.

O to be self-balanced for contingencies / To confront night, storms, hunger, ridicule, accidents, rebuffs, as the trees and animals do.

PART 1: INTERNAL COMBUSTION

Jim sat up. He looked into the dog's face. "How you, doggie?"

The dog cocked his head and licked his gray beard. *Hungering, hungering, hungering.*

"Where's your master?"

What do you suppose will satisfy the soul except to walk free and own no superior? What is independence? Freedom from all laws or bonds except those of one's own being.

Jim shook his head and tried to wipe the grit from his eyes, succeeding only in scratching his cornea.

The dog sat.

I exist as I am, that is enough, if no other in the world be aware, I sit content, and if each and all be aware, I sit content.

Whitman? This dog is telepathically quoting me Whitman. Maybe it's Whitman reincarnated. Jim stood up and brushed at the sand on his shirt. He could feel the grains with their universes shifting farther down into the front of his pants. It seemed to have infiltrated every part of him. He tried to wipe it from his ears, to blow it from his nose, to shake it from his hair, and only abraded himself in hard to reach places and wedged universes under his fingernails and in his underwear.

A part of him wanted to scold himself for reveling in such transcendental nonsense and another part of him wanted to scold himself for wanting to deny the wonder of it all. Life *is* full of mystery. Beyond even those opposing thoughts, looming above them, superseding them, were two even higher callings, two ideas which gave him a renewed sense of purpose and vigor: Beer and Pussy. The dog trotted over to the tree and lifted its leg and pissed on it. The tree barely shrugged.

"Beer and pussy," Jim iterated aloud, and then he heard the giggles of a gaggle of girls walking toward him on the sidewalk. Not girls—women. They held glasses and plastic cups and Jim believed the plastic cups had beer, because the world could sometimes be provident to those who would attune themselves to its mysterious ways.

He retrieved his skateboard as the girls approached and the dog ran to them and sniffed their crotches. Jim admired the dog's approach and was weighing the potential results of trying the same when one of the women, laughing, asked if he was a football coach.

"A football coach?"

"Yeah," she said. "You look like a football coach because of your clipboard. Don't football coaches use clipboards a lot?"

Jim looked down for whatever it was she could be talking about. "This is a skateboard," he said.

"Are you thinking up plays?" she asked.

"Yes. Can I have a sip of your beer?"

"Carrie, hurry up," one of the women moaned.

"Weren't we here? I think this is the spot."

"Yeah, I remember wishing I was married to whatever guy owns that big house right there," another of the women answered.

Carrie handed Jim her cup. "Hold this."

They went out to the sand and began groping around on all fours, the dog romping among them. Jim comforted his cock and tried to diagram a play, but the dog beat him to it, mounting one of the women. Jim took a swig of the beer.

"Will you get your fucking dog off me?" she screeched.

"He isn't my dog," Jim said.

She hissed through clenched teeth, "Just get him off me!"

"Uh—here, boy." He went over to the dog and pulled him away by the scruff of the neck. The dog barked a few low syllables. "I know," said Jim to the dog. They watched the women sifting through the sand. "What are you looking for?" Jim asked.

"A diamond ring."

"Don't tell him! He might find it and take it!" one of the girls wailed.

"She had it here when we were lying out today. I remember because she had it on when she was putting tanning oil on my back. I

PART 1: INTERNAL COMBUSTION

think it must have slipped off after that," said Carrie.

The other woman moaned. "I can't believe you're telling him this."

"He's a nice football coach. He won't take it, will you?" She looked at Jim.

He took another swig of the beer and shook his head. "Don't worry," he said. "If I find it, I'll trade it to you for some baseball cards."

"Baseball cards!" she sobbed. "Hell-OOO. It's a *DIAMOND* ring!"

"So?"

"So, it's valuable."

"Why?"

"*WHY?!* You don't understand. It's worth a lot of money. This is an eight-thousand-dollar ring."

"Now you're telling him," said her friend.

"So, you could trade it for a lot of baseball cards?" He eyed a wine glass, the base of its stem in the sand where the owner of the lost ring had placed it.

"God, no!"

"And like a lot of beer and pot and tickets to places."

"No. Look. It's *a symbol*. Do you understand what a *symbol* is? It shows how much my boyfriend really loves me."

"Oh." He finished the beer. "How?"

"Because when I wear it, people know that I'm taken care of by a man of means. It means I'm his."

"Bought and paid for."

"Yes. No. He makes payments on it."

"What does he get out of it?"

"He gets me."

"He gets you." Jim put the cup in the sand and picked up the wine. "You get a ring and he gets you." He took a drink of the wine. "Shouldn't it be enough that you get him? Why do you need an eight-thousand-dollar piece of glitter on your finger?"

"Ucxh. You're an idiot. Why am I even talking to you? Please just

163

go away."

He gulped down the rest of the wine and backed away, releasing the dog. Beer and pussy. It had turned out like some kind of Monkey's Paw wish fulfillment. Revulsion crept into him. Ah, but at least the diamond-seekers knew what they wanted. Their satisfaction was identifiable, while his own wanting of nothing or freedom or whatever it was he wanted was an unreal thing, a wild goose, a chimera. He found himself walking slowly out toward the waves wondering if his life would not be wasted, would be no less an endeavor than it was, no less a meeting of the challenge, if he were to swim out as far and long as he could, until he could keep himself afloat no more.

The ocean lapped at the toes of his sneakers. He watched the breakers explode against the jetty and remembered a year or so earlier when, because of the apogee of the moon's orbit, the lowest tide in twenty years sucked the water out a hundred yards farther than usual. He went out along the jetties and collected ten of the biggest crabs he could find, elated that he might live, for a night at least, off the bounty of the sea. He took them in a bucket to the kitchen sink and tried to wash the sand from the crabs but succeeded only in fouling the garbage disposal. He boiled the crabs and got a few tiny morsels of gritty crab meat. Later the dishwasher ground to a halt because of the sand. He ended up going to the drive-thru and getting cheeseburgers.

Jim heard the porpoises giggling beyond the jetty and he walked out, like Christ on water, he thought; so sure-footed where his steps in the dark on the slippery jumble of rocks it seemed miraculous. At the edge of the jetty he thought he could see the darker forms of the porpoises darting about through the reflections on the dark water. That was life. Weren't they perfect creations? Couldn't they eat, drink, sleep, and shit all in the same comfortable place they were born into? They hadn't gone and fucked up their existence with roads and buildings and guns and clocks. They were content the way they were. Only man had tried to outdo his own creation. And so, hadn't God scattered

PART 1: INTERNAL COMBUSTION

their tongues and allowed chaos to overwhelm all of man's efforts? And men themselves would never let men be. Jim clambered down closer to the water. The salt spray licked his face and smelled of everything in the world. He could just slip into it right there, float or sink, just be the way he was created. Would God reward him for that? Or would his soul be punished? Or would he just become fish food? He lay back on the rocks and asked the heavens aloud, "Why was I made? Why am I here? What should I be doing?" He lay there a long time without hearing any answer.

The ocean rose and fell around him, the horizon nearing and furthering. A long time. A long time still, and still no answer. The idea of the ocean's immensity swallowed him. He drowned and became a barnacle. A long time passed. He had no more significance than a barnacle. And then, in the trough of the noise of a wave came through the air the sound of men laughing.

He scrambled back to North America, sneakers gripping the slime on the rubble of boulders as if it were mortar. He reached the beach and trudged along, acceding to the sand the backslide of each step until he reached the sidewalk where he tailed the laughing men, invisible behind their banter and camaraderie, a shadow in the shadows.

They entered a door from which poured raucous noise, a bar with big windows, Mutt Lynch's. The doorman was talking with a lovely little honey and perfunctorily checked a few ID's before waving in the lot of them, never noticing the shadow, Jim. He moved through the air and bodies and sound, invisible still and able to read people's minds through their faces, able to see their histories and understand their private fears and hopes. Each face that he saw, he had seen somewhere before, had seen that face's archetype; somewhere he had come across them and their mothers and brothers all before.

In the small room in back, the sound seemed less excessive. Some girls were throwing darts at a dart board and mostly hitting the wall around it. "Get closer," one of them told the other.

Jim thought he recognized the girl who'd said that. He knew her from somewhere. Had they gone to kindergarten together? Had she been a neighbor? Maybe she was the great- granddaughter of some silent movie actress waif he'd seen in some TV clip obit. Jim tried to summon his voice from across the time and space since he'd last used it, and it came out of his chest deep and alien. "Mind if I play?" With that, he reappeared, began again to reflect light.

The other girl pulled her darts from the wall and said, "Hey, you're that guy we gave a ride to tonight."

Jim tilted his head to one side and tried looking at her with one eye. She had frizzy black hair and full lips and the skin tone of a Fijian. When she smiled, her braces glinted, and he put it together. "Oh, hey, yeah, wow, right. Where's Lainey?"

The girl with the eyes bigger than her tits looked crestfallen. The Fijian was happy to say that Lainey was out front scamming on the bouncer.

An odd-looking Puck character with preternaturally red hair stood off to one side sipping his beer and watching intently. He looked even more familiar than everybody else. Jim sensed that he wanted to talk to the girls but hadn't the courage, and the girls wouldn't have minded at all, in fact would have enjoyed the addition of a new voice and new thoughts to their own, which were already well-known to each other. Jim met the guy's stare and an odd look came over the odd-looking guy's face. He scurried off through the shoulders of the crowd to the bar where between the movements of patrons Jim glimpsed snatches of him speaking into the ear of a man with a bowling ball for a head sunk into the fat-rolled neck of an immense blob of a torso with a Hawaiian shirt stretched over it, from which thigh-sized arms bent to a pitcher of beer; a stool disappeared into the bowling ball-headed blob's ass.

"Are you any good?" asked the frizzy-headed girl whose name eluded Jim.

PART 1: INTERNAL COMBUSTION

"I'm okay sometimes. Do you know how to play?"

She stood front square to the wall and lobbed a wobbly shot into the outer border of the board.

"Are you right-handed or left-handed?" Jim Crack asked.

"Right-handed."

"Stand sideways to the board with your right foot in front. Hold your arm from the shoulder to the elbow parallel to the ground."

She handed him the darts. "You go."

He lined up in front of the dart board. It seemed so simple. He waited until the moment felt right and then he tossed both darts into the red bull in quick succession, as easily as if he had been pressing an elevator button.

"Wow! Do you play a lot?"

Jim was himself impressed with his precision, and at the same time he felt he had seen ahead of time he would put the darts where he wanted. "Actually, I don't play that much. But it's easy. It's all about knowing when to let go of the dart. Knowing the right moment. Using the power of the moment. The power of the man and the power of the moment." The words emanating from his throat did not seem his own, and he listened to them as curiously as she did. "The man is not enough—or gir—ur, woman, in your case—without the moment."

He crossed the eight feet to the board, removed the darts, and stepped back to the line. "It touches all aspects of our daily lives, really, anything that involves effort, right? Like if you go to start your car, and the battery's not hooked up, it ain't gonna start, see?" He noticed the one girl was scribbling in her notebook. "But in more profound ways, ways that affect our spiritual beings, it's true, too. Let's say you want to write the Great American Screenplay, and you sit down and try to force it out without the Moment, it'll be contrived crap, a starving man trying to take a shit, for shit's sake. You have to be in a moment in which you're spiritually poised to create, see? But the times we live in now, man, it's all MTV and lip gloss right now, you know? You need to live in a current of ideas that nourish the creative power, in a time where society is permeated by fresh thought, intelligent and alive, a time of knowledge, in which you can exercise that creative power—but we don't." He tossed another dart into the bull. We have to settle for the physical moment," he let go another dart into the bull's-eye, "rather than the metaphysical. We live today in a world of images," he hit the mark again, "not of ideas." In a mirror advertising Newcastle, he noticed his words came out smokily, as if some visible evanescence of soul had leaked from his body.

"Oh, my God," said the girl with the notebook.

(Or maybe)

"Are you God?" He heard her ask.

(it was just)

"Bravo," said a voice in a silky commonwealth accent.

(smoke and mirrors).

Jim turned to see who had said "Bravo" and was met with a face that introduced into his psyche the idea that God and the Devil might very well be one and the same.

"Matthew Arnold, I believe." He sounded like Shere Khan, the tiger. The clown-haired dude stood a little to one side and behind him like some henchman awaiting the snap of a finger and some bidding to do.

"Uh, no—my name's Jim."

He smiled at Jim with his lips closed, one-sidedly, ironically, as if Jim were somehow precious, a precocious toddler who had done something cute. "Yes, I know. Jim Crack. My friend here was just telling me about you. I'm called Ben. I see you haven't a drink. Let me buy you a pint. Alonzo, do you mind?" The clown-haired dude went to the bar.

"You Aussie?" Jim asked.

"Kiwi." He wore a rugby jersey and had spiked hair that was blond on the ends and spiked at the root. His smile revealed a jumble of

PART 1: INTERNAL COMBUSTION

crooked teeth where the chisel of his good looks had slipped, one incisor was turned sideways and looked thin and pointy, the other, was just thin and pointy without being turned sideways, while the teeth on the bottom looked to have been arranged by the spirits of the same druids that had erected Stonehenge. He had a golden tan and lines around his eyes that belied his otherwise carefree demeanor.

The girls whispered into each other's ears, eyes peeking over the hands cupped over their mouths.

"What was your friend telling you about me?" Jim asked warily.

"Let's wait for that beer," said Ben. He took the darts and threw three bull's-eyes. "Bulls are cheap tonight. Like throwing them into a funnel tonight, isn't it? The important thing is to keep it effortless, I think. Do it, don't try to do it."

Alonzo brought the beer. The foam on top looked to Jim like spit. He blew off the head and stuck two fingers into it and flung the foam to the ground, looking at Alonzo to see if he reacted, but his jester-like countenance never changed. Jim took a sip, eying him over the glass, and then a gulp, and then chugged about half, more for effect than any great fondness of stout.

"Shall we play?" Ben asked.

Jim shrugged and nodded.

"Cricket?"

Jim shrugged and nodded. He missed and missed badly, again and again. His will seemed to have deserted him. The dart board smiled mockingly and a well-known and profound frustration at his inability to control the slightest things returned. Ben threw two triple twenties and a nineteen on his first turn. Jim's next shot was four inches right and low of his aim, his next four inches left and his third four inches too high. Ben racked up his points on the chalkboard. Jim looked at the precise spot he wanted the dart to penetrate, aimed and threw, but the little missiles had their own inclinations and he began to wonder why they didn't just start doing U-turns and flying into the crowd at the bar. His oneness with the universe had become something sweaty and antsy. He gulped back the rest of his beer. Ben looked at Alonzo and made a little toss with his head at the bar, and Alonzo went over again and soon came back with another beer.

"Cheers," said Ben and clinked his glass against Jim's. "Alonzo tells us you're the bloke that got his brothers locked up."

A second or two passed and then Jim was startled. The wet glass slipped through his fingers and in bringing to bear his other hand to keep it from dropping, he spilled a brown stain down the front of the shirt he had borrowed from Adam.

"Relax," said Ben. "Don't turn into a jumpyroo on us. Al's brothers are blithering idiots—aren't they, Al?"

Alonzo scowled. "You got some fucking balls," he said to Jim.

A few months earlier, Jim had been staying several weeks or so on the couch of some friends nearby. After a party, they had awakened to find the microwave missing. And the VCR. And an expensive camera and some stereo equipment, a bunch of CDs, a computer, and a pair of mounted steer horns that had been hung on the wall. Jim felt personally responsible. His friends had allowed him to live in their place rent-free and had treated him with nothing but brotherly love. He had offered to pay them some rent, and they told him not to worry about it. They left the door unlocked so that he could come and go. He wanted to do something to help them get their stuff back and so repay them. Over the next few days he kept asking people who had been at the party if they remembered anything, and they described a surf punk with dreadlocks and a pierced tongue who no one knew, and who had stayed after most people had left or passed out. The word was that he lived somewhere nearby. Jim began prowling the neighborhood in the evenings and mornings, looking in windows to see if he might spot any of the missing stuff. One night, just across the street and down an alley, he came to a garage from which he heard gunshots and screeching tires. He peeked through the crack along the edge of the garage door

PART 1: INTERNAL COMBUSTION

and saw a group of people sitting around a television under the steer horns watching a video on the stolen VCR.

What came over Jim? Not even he, who prided himself on being crazy, could look back on the matter and believe he was *that* crazy. He went back to the house where he had been staying on the couch and selected from among his meager possessions the Kirk Gibson model Louisville Slugger he'd been carrying around worshipfully since 1988, and he went back to the garage and stepped through a door on the side and said in his best Clint Eastwood, "What the fuck are you doing with our VCR?"

A guy and a girl scrambled out the door. Another girl and a guy with dreadlocks sat frozen on a mattress on the floor. The inside of the garage was covered with graffiti. It had been converted into living quarters. Someone had installed a sink and a toilet, near which a couple of surfboards leaned against the wall. A curtain hung from the rafters. Jim pulled it aside and there was the missing microwave and a guy lying in a sleeping bag on the floor.

"You try to get out of that sleeping bag, and I'll fracture your fucking skull." The guy on the couch started edging toward the door, and Jim stepped back to block his way. "Smile, fuckface. I want to see what your teeth look like before I knock them out." Jim brandished the bat. "I said smile!" He leered at the guy with dreads, who smiled with strained face muscles, revealing crooked yellow teeth. "Shit," Jim said. "I'd be doing you a favor. Sit back." Jim gave him a little jab in the gut with the bat. "You got a phone?"

No one said anything. Charles Bronson menaced hoods on the TV behind Jim.

"YOU GOT A FUCKING PHONE?"

The dude with the dreads shook his head. "No, man, no. We ain't got no phone."

Jim looked at the girl. She was in a bikini and cutoffs and looked supremely bored with the whole situation. He looked her in the eye,

171

but the whole periphery of her seemed to be filled with breasts. "You like this guy?" Jim asked her.

She looked beyond him, out the door. "All right. I don't care if you do or you don't. You can go, but do me a favor and call 911. If the police aren't here in twenty minutes, I'm going to beat this fucker's head to a bloody pulp. Just don't call and see what happens."

He stepped away from the door. "Goodbye." She sat a beat before she got up and ambled away as if without a care in the world.

"You better fucking call!" Dreadlocks yelled after her.

Jim had no watch and there was no clock to check. He wondered what it would be like to bludgeon a man's head in. He guessed if they tried to resist him, he'd probably drop the bat and fight them with his fists. That seemed fair. He hoped, though, that he could remain convincingly murderous until the police arrived. And if they didn't? Maybe he could get the guys to help him bring the stuff back to the house.

"Dude, we didn't steal your shit."

"How'd it get here?"

"I don't know, man. We don't live here."

"Who does?"

"Some dude. We don't even know him. He ain't here."

"Isn't that a stud in your tongue?"

"Yeah."

"Let's see what the cops say."

"Man, don't bring the cops around here. You can take the shit back. We can give you money. We'll—"

"How much?"

"I don't know. A lot, man. Let us go. We can talk to a guy."

"Why would I trust you?"

The police arrived much more quickly than Jim would have guessed possible, four of them, guns drawn. Jim was ordered face-down and handcuffed along with the other two guys. Lucky for Jim this time,

PART 1: INTERNAL COMBUSTION

the officer who had taken the report the morning after they'd been burgled recognized Jim and had him uncuffed. The cops discovered several grams of various contraband and a trapdoor in the ceiling leading up to the roof where they had a nice little marijuana garden going. And so, thanks to Jim, the stolen property was recovered, several ounces of dangerous marijuana never hit the streets, and the violators of trust in a civil society were put behind bars.

"Do you want to be a bobby when you grow up?" Ben asked.

"A what?"

"A constable, a cop, a police*man*?"

"Hell, no."

"Me brother's a policeman back in New Zealand. He's less interested in justice than you are, though. He just likes to harass Maori. We get along okay him and me, but Oi get along with the Maori, too."

"Anywhy," Ben went on, "Me friends an Oi were really impressed with the way you handled yourself, having your swag ripped off and all, and we'd like to offer you a job. It pays well, and you won't have to do much." He handed Jim a folded slip of paper. "Call this number tomorrow between five and six. Ask for Benny. There's a grand in it for you for starters. We'd need your help for about an hour. You don't have to do anything criminal, really. We just need a stranger with balls."

Jim wondered if he had blundered into a nice cold plate of vengeance. He wasn't so worried about Ben or Alonzo—he felt sure he could break both their noses—but the big Samoan at the bar could break Jim's neck. Just then someone threw an arm around Jim's neck from behind. Jim flinched and dropped under the arm, whirling with his fist cocked, and in so doing he sucked in a whiff of vodka and a flowery body lotion, and Jim arrested his roundhouse mid-swing, knowing it was Lainey a nanosecond before he saw her jiggling in front of him.

She let out a whoop and shuddered her hips. "I knew we'd find you," she slurred. "Why weren' you at the parry? We saw your cute

173

friend Adam. He was fighting with his grilfrien." She smiled a close-lipped, wasted smile.

Adam and Tink were fighting? He turned to Ben, but he had gone to the bar and was talking to the big Samoan. "Let's go to the party," he said.

Lainey, Lisa, Tamara, and Jim snaked single-file through the crowd to the door. Jim heard the F-word all around him and he involuntarily pictured faceless, naked bodies writhing sweatily in the darkness, genitals morphing into one another. He closed his eyes and in the darkness of his mind the images remained, penises plunging into orifices, labia apart and throbbing. The hallucination's continuing absoluteness disturbed Jim and filled him with dreaded soulless disconnection. He opened his eyes and this ball of Fuck went on humping itself in his skull. He could see around it but not through it; the whole of the physical world seemed to have to be negotiated along perimeters of this vision of Fuck. Doggy-style close-ups dissolved into shaved-pussy reverse cowgirls which warped into three-on-one gangbangs, hands grasping, erections spurting, and all over again. He shook his head and rubbed his eyes and stumbled a little. Lainey reached back and took his hand and pulled him along behind her. Her hand made him feel full of warm beer, and for a few seconds he had the same rising sensation he'd had back in the schoolyard when the red-haired girl tied his shoe for him, and he almost felt he could rise above the Fuck with her, that he could peer over the top of it with her lifting him.

They stepped out onto the sidewalk and Jim gave a backward glance through the door, through the Fuck, and Ben was there on a stool, a girl on his lap, another kissing him, his eyes followed Jim through the window, and he made a gun with his fingers and pointed it at Jim and winked before Lainey pulled Jim away.

The party was a short walk from the bar. Lainey babbled happily as they strolled past the pier. Adam's name kept coming up, and she let go of Jim's hand and did a wobbly cartwheel in the sand, skirt falling

PART 1: INTERNAL COMBUSTION

up, cheeks quivering. Suddenly Jim was tackled into a patch of crabgrass. Alonzo or Ben? he wondered, driving his elbow into the side of the head of his assailant. "Fuck! Ow! That fucking hurt." Adam slurred.

Jim bucked and rolled Adam onto his back and pinned him. He made a point with the knuckle of his middle finger and knocked on Adam's forehead. "I'm tired of that word. Don't use that word around me anymore. It's meaningless and it degrades love and everything else in the world. You're supposed to be Mormon. You should know better." Jim listened to himself in dumbfounded curiosity.

"What the fuck are you talking about?" Adam asked.

There were traces of cock ramming a cunt. Jim dug his knuckle into Adam's skull. "Quit profaning the world, you— you— bad... person." Jim got off Adam. "That's why we feel like shi— why we feel so bad all the time. The words we use shape the world we live in."

"Who feels bad?" Adam asked. "I feel great." He sounded like Tony the Tiger.

Lainey cartwheeled over and sat down. "Yeah, who feels bad? I feel great!"

Tammy and Lisa stood on the sidewalk smoking. "Come on, you guys," Tammy called. Lisa groped in her purse and took out her notepad and pen.

"Where's Tink?" Jim asked.

"Fuck if I know. Fucking bitch is all fucked up."

Jim lunged for Adam, and Adam bolted away before Jim tackled him and grabbed him by his pec and administered a vicious titty-twist.

"Owowowowow—She's at the party still. She and that other chick are all hammered. Dude, let go."

Jim released him. Lainey was wriggling out of her top. "Let's go skinny-dipping!" She tried to unzip her skirt as she ran to the surf and fell laughing. Adam got up and chased after her.

"Aren't you going skinny-dipping, too?" Tamara asked.

Jim sat on his knees and peered down the beach, where he could just about see Lainey's nipples stiffening through her bra at contact with the cold surf, her panties becoming transparent as she got wet. Adam tackled her clumsily, and she screamed and laughed. *That should be me*, Jim thought, *but*—he turned his attention up the street in the direction of the party. "No. I'm going to look for my friend."

"Who's your friend?" asked Lisa.

He thought for a second. "Beer," he answered. "I'll come back in a while to see if they're drowned or not. If Lainey needs mouth-to-mouth, I'm on it, but if Adam does, you're going to have to cover that." Jim got up and walked to the street.

"Can I come?" Lisa asked.

"I won't stop you."

"I'm going to stay out here," Tamara announced.

As they walked up the sidewalk Lisa said, "You know we're not really twenty-one."

"No shit."

"I'm eighteen, but Lainey and Tammy are seventeen and sixteen. Tammy's cousin is that big Pacific Islander guy at Mutt's. He knows the owner or something and they let us in, but we have to stay back by the dart boards so we can go out the kitchen door if the police come in to check ID's."

Bass thumped as they neared the house. Jim felt nothing. He felt not the least bit buzzed, high, drunk, or stoned, though he knew a police blood test might have gotten him locked up on a number of charges. He felt merely and matter-of-factly alive and nothing more.

Some dude stood by the open gate smoking a clove cigarette. "Two bucks," he said.

"Beat me up," Jim said, walking past him. Lisa came cautiously behind him. A couple made out on the stairs, and Lisa and Jim had to press against the rail to get around them.

Through the window in the front door, Jim saw a vast metropolis of cans and bottles. He turned the knob, gripping it tightly before

PART 1: INTERNAL COMBUSTION

his fingers found purchase in its greasiness. They went in and were greeted by an odor which suggested that someone had poured nacho cheese into an ashtray filled with Meister Brau barf. The loudness of the music kept rising and abruptly falling, and they overheard snippets of an argument. The couches and floors were reminiscent of some cult suicide, littered with passed-out bodies. Jim scanned the room for Tink. He identified Janine by her ass, sprawled face down on a couch, one leg akimbo, her skirt hiked halfway. Someone had drawn a big happy face across her buttocks with a red Magic Marker.

Jim crossed the kitchen, soles momentarily sticking to the linoleum, each footfall screeching mutedly at its separation from the floor. A long hallway of closed doors loomed before him. He picked up from a table a warm, unopened Lucky Lager, cracked it open, and took a swig. "Want some?" Lisa made a face like she didn't, but nodded and took the beer and drank. Jim looked at the underside of the cap. The rebus showed the word NO + 1 + a picture of a nose + 4 + a shoe + R. "That's the truest thing ever," he said, and then he snapped the cap across the room, knocking over the beer can next to the one he was aiming at.

He padded down the hall. The first door was shut. Light leaked through from the space between the door and the floor. Jim put his ear to it and listened. A horrible scarfing, scrunching sound could be heard, as if the Blob were ingesting a pride of lions feasting on a zebra. Jim pushed the door in, and a circle of primordial savages looked up briefly from their burritos, hot sauce running down their chins and wrists. One of them snarled ravenously at Jim and he, having ascertained that Tink was not among them, pulled the door shut.

The next door was ajar, spilling a narrow parallelogram of light into the hall. It was the room from which emitted the roar and ebb of music. Jim peeked in and observed two jumbo-sized jocks, nose to nose.

"Dude, I'm tellin' ya for the last time, it's too fucking LOUD."

"Shut up, ya little bitch. This party would still be ragin' if you weren't such a little anal-retentive little bitch about noise and cleaning and shit."

"Fuck you. You're the MORON who keeps getting the cops called over here. If it wasn't for me, they'd have come here tonight."

"No. You know what, dude? I'm sick of your shit. Why don't we step outside and settle this once and for all?"

A fierce little denim-clad blonde girl stepped in and shoved jumbo-jock A in in the chest. "Fuck you, Randall!" Her voice ranged somewhere between soprano and cats rutting. "Get out of here!"

"Bitch, I live here. YOU get the fuck out." She shoved him in the chest again. "Dude, you better fucking get a grip on your bitch. She shoves me one more time—"

"Who you calling a bitch?" She shoved him again, and he shoved her back. She tumbled over the corner of the bed and folded in half against the wall, legs in the air, crotch on her chin, and then it was on: a Roman-Greco-Sumo-kickboxing match in which the first casualty was a lava lamp which fell to the floor, bleeding.

Jim withdrew. "The three F's of post-partying," he whispered to Lisa. "Food, fighting, and fuc—" He suddenly felt nauseous, as he considered the final door. He pressed his ear to it. Breaths, breathing inhalations, exhalations, movement, creaking, a low, sighing moan. "Go away now," his self told his self in his head, while another self wondered if he should clear his throat, rap gently on the door, call her name. He tried the knob, but it was locked.

"I'm going to wait out front," Lisa said.

The hallway ended in one last door that opened onto a small deck with stairs that went down to the driveway in the alley behind the house. Jim heard muffled groans from the window of the bedroom with the locked door. He turned to go back into the house and then turned again and went back onto the landing. Grasping the wooden railing with both hands, he shook it. It wasn't very sturdy, but he slung

PART 1: INTERNAL COMBUSTION

a leg over the rail, and then the other, and holding the rail with one hand, leaned out, a story above trashcans full of broken beer bottles, trying to see into the room. He could see a crack of soft red light where the blinds did not quite come down to the window sill. The railing creaked as he tried to maneuver into an angle at which he could see through the crack into the room. Some guy was fucking a girl on her back on the bed across the room. It was Wayne. Fucking Wayne. Fucking Wayne fucking fucking a fucking chick on the fucking bed. He couldn't see her face. Jim loosened his grip on the railing enough to allow himself the length between knuckles to lean farther out. His fingers were sweaty and he felt the need to pull himself back and wipe his hands, give up this madness, but he waited a little longer. Her knees were splayed, and her fists pounded the squeaking mattress. Wayne supported himself with his palms on either side of her head—only she didn't have a head.

Jim leaned out to the last of his fingertips and Wayne pulled the pillow from over Tink's face. She gasped a moment for air and then he put the pillow over her face again.

A bolt shot through Jim and his foot slipped from the landing as he tried to pull himself in. He hung for a moment by one hand, before scrambling over the rail and back into the house again. He was through the door as if it were made of cardboard, the lock fitting splintering out of the door jamb. Jim crooked his arm around Wayne's sweaty neck and pulled him off Tink. Wayne arched his back and bucked, and they fell to the floor, Wayne's hard, slimy cock erect. Jim rolled on top of him and could feel it poking against his leg.

Tink shrank screaming in the corner as Jim drew back his fist. Then, "Jim? Jim! Stop it! Oh, my god! What are you doing?" She held a blanket to her breasts and stepped from the bed to pull Jim off. "Oh, my god. Get out of here."

"I thought—he was—I thought—I thought you needed help! He was raping you! He was going to kill you! The pillow! I—"

"Oh, my god! Jim, no. He wasn't—He wasn't raping me. He—I wanted him to."

A confusion, like static on a TV garbled Jim's mind. Tink pulled him away from Wayne, and Jim fell sitting on the end of the bed breathing heavily. A dreamy exhaustion fell over him. He hardly noticed that Wayne had closed his hands over his throat. Hardly noticed Tink slapping at Wayne with the bottoms of her fists.

Jim didn't care that Wayne was choking him, but he did think a breath of fresh air might do him good. It occurred to him that he might step out for a breath of fresh air and come back and let Wayne finish choking him. He tried to walk past Wayne, but Wayne choked him back down to a sitting position, his now-flaccid dick flopping around less than a couple of feet from Jim's face. A few seconds went by during which Jim sighed resignedly, as well as one can sigh while being strangled, and then stood and rammed his knee into Wayne's testicles. Wayne doubled over on the floor, and Jim stepped over him and walked out of the room, down the hall and out the front door.

He found Lisa out front, smoking. "I had to get out of there," she said. "That place was freaking me out."

"Me, too."

She took his hand. "I'm sorry," she said.

"About what?"

"Your friend."

"I don't know what you mean."

She let it drop.

They walked to the beach in silence. Jim scanned the sand for some sign of Adam, Lainey, or Tamara. The surf broke, drawing a line of phosphorescent foam along the shore. A sea monster had washed up. A dark, writhing, three-headed thing, conjoined mer-triplets in the desperate, mindless throes of a full moon, springtime grunion run.

Jim was staggered by a series of sharp, burning hiccups. He bent forward and retched violently, three lava bursts of noxious toxins that

PART 1: INTERNAL COMBUSTION

splattered his shoes and left snot and drool hanging from his tearing face.

He felt Lisa's fingers cool and dry on his brow and in his hair. She took a moist towelette from her purse and wiped his face. He kicked sand over the puke, and she pulled him over to a bench under a streetlight. "Here," she said and she took the foil wrapper off a stick of gum and put it in his mouth. "Better take two." She stroked the back of his hanging head and tears continued to fall from his eyes even after the effects of his heaving had subsided. His breathing hitched and she pulled his head onto her shoulder.

A shudder of gratitude fell over him and he hugged her tightly, and then she was kissing him, with open lips, her tongue in his mouth, and he kissed her back wondering detachedly, *Why? Why are we kissing? I just barfed. Does she like me?* Angela retied his shoes. *Or is it just that everybody else is getting busy, let's not be the dorks that didn't get any?* She repositioned herself so that she was sitting on his lap facing him with her legs on either side, and he wondered if he liked her and pulled away from her mouth a minute and held her face in his hands and studied it. She was pretty. It felt good. Her soft smoothness was so placating and her kissing him, his arms around her, hers around him, seemed to wipe away the whole world which was his terrible loneliness. She began to massage through denim his budding erection, which grew with each beat of his heart, and he caressed a thumb over a small soft breast.

"Where can we go?' she whispered.

To hump? he wondered silently, and cinnamon spiders ran up and down his esophagus. He guessed she lived at home with her parents and that her place was not an option. He looked around. The lamps on the pier had halos in the light fog. "Want to walk to the pier?" Maybe they could go under it somewhere. He needed a couple of blankets.

"Mmhhmm," she said and kissed his neck.

"Where's your car?" he asked her. Maybe she had blankets in her car.

She pulled back and looked at him with her eyes closed. "Mmmhhmm," she said, and her head lolled back. "It's over there," she said and laid her head on his chest.

"Let's go," he said. He stood up with her legs wrapped around his waist.

"Give me a piggy back," she said.

He put her down on the bench, looped her purse over his forearm, and turned around so that she could climb onto his back. He felt lighter with her on him. "Do you have any blankets in your car?"

"Mmhhmm," she answered. "I'm house-sitting for my sister. Do you want to come?"

All he said was a toneless, "Okay," but it masked something more like a big ten-four, roger that, ching ching ching ching ching, ching ching ching ching ching.

"Which way is your car? What street is it on?"

"What about my friends? I'm supposed to give Lainey and Tammy a ride back."

"Adam will give them a ride," Jim lied.

"Go up here." She wrapped her arms tightly around Jim's throbbing Adam's apple, and she settled her chin on his shoulder. He felt the cool of her cheek against his burning ear, and heard little over the sound of her breath. Newport had become quiet as if someone had flipped a switch turning it from a loud, rowdy beach town to a sleepy seaside community. They saw nobody. Quiet as a boy hiding under his bed. All quiet on the western front. Quiet as Balboa himself must have been when he espied the Pacific from atop that lofty peak in Darien.

"Which way?"

"I don't remember. Right or left, I think."

"That narrows it down."

They spent forty-five minutes going up and down the Thirties trying to locate her sister's blue Nissan with, for him, an increasing need to urinate. Soon her breaths became longer and deeper, and Jim felt

PART 1: INTERNAL COMBUSTION

a trickle of drool down under his collar and realized she had fallen asleep. The need to piss became insistent, and he turned into an alley and stepped behind a family of trashcans, with frenzied thoughts of unbuttoning his pants and relieving himself where he stood. He wondered where he could put Lisa down. Not seeing any likely place, he undertook the delicate task of undoing his jeans and peeing with one hand while holding her to her perch with the other. He observed some scientific formula of inverse proportions at work, whereby the less appropriate the pissing circumstances, the longer the piss would take. This was a three-minute job, and his grip on Lisa's ass became more and more tenuous. "Lisa," he whispered loudly, eliciting from her a short snoring snort. He hunched and hitched her up higher on his back. She whined a little and turned her head so her hair tickled Jim's nose. He soon discovered that unbuttoning with one hand was a simple thing, but buttoning one-handed was nearly impossible. After several minutes of trying to get it done while blowing hair from his mouth, and the strain on the ass-holding arm approaching unendurable, he gave up buttoning his pants and proceeded with the search, fly undone. He didn't get far up the next block before his pants began to creep down his hips, and by the time he'd reached the corner, he was walking along Balboa Boulevard, reduced to baby steps with his drawers at his ankles. He tried squatting down to pull them up, but he was afraid Lisa might fall. He tried waking her by calling her name, but she did not respond.

"Dude, just lay her down, button up, and pick her up again."

"I don't want to just put her on the sidewalk."

"Who cares?"

"I don't know."

"You're an idiot."

"I know."

He decided to step out of his pants altogether, and got about ninety percent through the process before his shoe became stuck in the leg of his pants. Even the most violent and frenzied shaking would not dislodge it.

A savage, guttural scream echoed through the empty streets.

Jim continued along, nodding and mumbling to himself. He couldn't have told anyone how much time had passed before he realized he was shuffling past a blue Nissan. It was half blocking an alley and half parked in a red zone, in front of a fire hydrant with a ticket on the windshield. "Lisa." He shook back and forth. "Lisa."

She made no answer. He gave her ass a pinch. She was out cold. He turned his back to the car and let her slide onto the hood of the car and fished through her purse for the keys. Suddenly a blast of light froze him. "Put your hands on your head," the light ordered through a loudspeaker. Jim's head sagged, and he did as he was told, feeling checkmated by an oversight thirty moves ago.

Creaking and jangling approached with a pair of silhouettes that appeared in the light like black ghosts. One of them was pulling on a pair of rubber gloves. "Turn around." Jim sensed an officer stoop and go through his pants. "ID."

"I don't have it. My wallet was in my car when it caught on fire this morning."

Jim thought he heard a little laugh. "It's a misdemeanor to be in public with no ID in Newport Beach," said one of the cops. Another bit of snickering, like a laugh track on very low volume.

"What's your name?"

"Jim Crack." Again, the sound of canned laughter, like a sitcom punch line going off in another room.

"Crack?" Hahahaha.

He spelled it.

"What's going on here, Mr. Crack?"

What does it look like? Shit. I'm fuc—screwed. Can I say "screwed"? Can I think "screwed"? I got a drunk minor on the hood of a car with my pants around my ankles; I'm going through her purse, and my brain is sizzling. A guffaw

PART 1: INTERNAL COMBUSTION

rang out in the distance. *Use the truth, Luke.* "I'm just, uhm, helping the girl to her car." Chortle chortle chortle.

"What's wrong with her?" Tee hee.

Go away. "I think she may have had too much to drink." Hohohoho. They didn't go away.

"She doesn't look old enough to drink. What's her name?"

"Lisa." *Shit.* "I don't know her last name." Titter. "I didn't furnish any alcohol." *Shoot, I mean.* Giggles.

The other cop took the purse and found a wallet which he opened. "Lisa Brown," he said. "Seventeen."

"She was already drunk when you met her?"

"Yes. No. I met her way earlier when she was sober, then I didn't see her for a few hours. Then when I saw her again she was drunk." Hahahaha. *Is someone's TV on in a nearby house? Or is it my head?*

"Who's driving?"

"Uhm. I don't know. We were going to her place, and I thought she was going to drive. I was giving her a piggyback and she passed out."

This time the cop really did sniff out a short laugh. "Um-hum." One of them was scribbling in a notebook. "And why, pray tell, are your pants around your ankles?"

"Uh, my pants fell down because my button came undone while I was giving her a piggyback, and she fell asleep, and I didn't know what to do with her. I couldn't button up again without putting her down, and I didn't know where, so I kept going like that, and my pants fell down." Jim listened. No laughter. Uh-oh. Jim summoned every milliliter of sobriety he could muster, reached deep inside of himself, right down into the quarks of his recessive DNA, and pulled out an honest and good-natured young man just trying to do the right thing. "Officers, I'm just trying to get this girl home safely. I was thinking she was going to drive, but I'm glad you're here, because I now realize the wise thing for me to do is to find a pay phone and call a cab."

Crickets chirped.

"Make sure you do. We'll be around. Smile." A flash of light within the light went off. A Polaroid. He heard them walk back and then it was dark, and they were gone.

Jim didn't take his hands off his head for many seconds after the police car had disappeared into the alley. He sort of patted himself to make sure that had all really just happened. He'd just been let free. He rubbed his eyes and slapped himself a few times before opening the car door and smacked Lisa's head against the roof trying to get her into the back seat. The muscles under his jaw clenched in the universal oops sign. He stood a moment. Something was missing. *Shit—ver me timbers. My skateboard*. He'd left in in a wormhole somewhere, back on the beach; the talking dog was probably hanging twenty.

He looked down at Lisa. The street light irradiated her cantaloupe-colored hair. She was beautiful. He bent down to kiss her goodbye. Gave her an innocent peck on the cheek. How would he find her again? He stared into the bliss of her face and decided to kiss her on the lips as if to break Maleficent's spell. He was no prince. He tried again and slipped his tongue between her teeth. Nothing. He got in next to her and pulled the door shut. He cracked the windows so that they would not become fogged and slumped down, peeking an eye over the bottom of the window a long time before a car turned around the corner and he ducked down. He heard it go slowly by, and waited a long time before peeking again. He watched a long time before his gaze returned to Lisa. He ran his fingers through her hair. It was cool to the touch and he leaned down to her and stroked his cheek with a handful of hair. He glided his fingers back and forth over the inside of her forearm. She stirred not. Damn. She hadn't seemed that drunk. He rubbed his hand back and forth over the thigh of her jeans and each time he brought his thumb up closer to the seam in her crotch. He imagined he was doing it unconsciously, but he knew he wasn't; soon he was consciously unconsciously running his thumb up and down the denim over her vulva.

PART 1: INTERNAL COMBUSTION

Back and forth, up and down, round and round, his fingers wrote passionate love letters on her pudendum while snake tongues flicked his intestines and his breaths grew shorter, until his conscience fled to the ceiling of the car and watched from above as he undid the buttons of her jeans and his hands crawled down into her panties.

Her pussy was like a cleft lump of floured cookie dough. No, no, no. The walls of it were dried together. No, no, no.

He yanked his arm back, punched himself hard in the temple, then opened the car door, and shoved himself out onto the sidewalk. "What is wrong with you!" he bellowed. Then he hissed at himself. "She's only seventeen. And she's passed out. You sicko."

"I just need to touch somebody," he whined. "I need to feel and be felt. Is that so wrong?"

A light came on in the house next to the car. He tossed the keys into Lisa's unbuttoned lap, locked the door and forced himself to shut it.

Muttering bitterly, he walked away. "What is wrong with you?" He was sane enough to wonder who was asking whom.

"It's like there's two of me," he said aloud. "Everybody must be like this, right? We're all split down the middle. We all straddle the split down the middle of us between doing what we want and doing what's— What? Right? Socially responsible?" His volume rose and fell. He shook his head, frantically trying to dislodge the demon in him, or the good guy, either one, so long as there would just be one, once and for all.

His heart had begun to beat more slowly as the adrenaline from his external/internal struggle subsided. He abruptly became very tired. Too tired to think. Sleep became a number-one survival priority. The beach was a field of poppies. In among the million-dollar glass homes was a white wooden cottage with a clothesline in its yard, from which hung a few towels. He lifted his leg over the white picket fence, stalking the towels, when a light on the side of the house came on. He froze and ducked, tense, ready to run, but there was no one there. The light must have had a motion sensor. He crept to the towels. They hadn't exactly dried in the misty evening air, but he helped himself to two of them, before stepping back over the fence and somnambulating zombie-like down the beach. He placed a towel under a lifeguard tower and lay on it, curling fetally under the other towel, and in two breaths oblivion closed around him.

PART 2

EXTERNAL COMBUSTION

Oblivion grayed from black to white, and his eyes opened to a corpse-colored horizon where transparent corneal worms floated, and behind which the sun existed, unseen, like God. The damp air muffled the sound of the surf. A multitude of seagulls dozed on the beach in a long row, beaks tucked under wings, a few preening before the day of screeching bustle that lay ahead. He became aware of a powerful tension in his penis. Lainey, Lisa, and Tink kneeled around him. As much as he wanted to rut with them, to lick and suck and finger their breasts, their vaginas, to palm their buttocks, he dispelled them. Things, he decided, were not going to get any better, a real girl was not going to come to him, until he gave up jerking off, gave up the instant fantasy of self-gratification, until he spurned his onanistic ways. He was, he resolved, going to embark on a new life, a new era, resistant to sin, and free of vice. First, though, he needed some coffee.

He gathered the towels, stood up, and cracked his head against the bottom edge of the lifeguard tower. The resulting savagery of his jumping scattered the seagulls to the sky as heinous curses fought violently to his lips, and he beat them back into his spleen, wondering if they would simmer resentfully and become twice as hateful. He gritted his teeth at the gulls, who shook their fists at him and voiced their own shrill curses sans adulteration.

Jim turned away, trying to leave the pain in the past, but it tailed him to the cottage, where he hung the towels over the white fence. He walked to Balboa Boulevard and went into a 7-Eleven. He found enough change in his pocket to buy a coffee and a Slim Jim. He tore open the latter with his teeth and ate it in front of the store, but having a little food in his belly only made him hungrier. He searched his mind for a plan of action. He needed to walk to the car and drive up to the park and pick up his paycheck. But first....

He walked to the street where he had left Lisa and found that she and the car were gone. He endured torturous pangs of regret and love lost as he walked up the hill to the Campbell's Soup sedan. He patted his pockets warily as he approached it. The keys were there. He opened the door and got in. The car started right up! Already God was rewarding him for his new attitude. Up the freeway, he went inland, the marine layer lifting with each mile. Traffic was light. The Disneyland "Casting Office" (Jim called it the "Castigating Office"), which other companies called Personnel or Human Resources, was not normally open on Saturday, but he knew they had issued an open call that Saturday for the holiday program, and the offices would be staffed to hire new cast members. He was afraid he had been fired, but he was going to go in there and tell Fleming that he had become devoted to service and workmanship. He just wanted to pay his dues and move up the management ladder. In fact, he was going to study hard in school and learn business administration. He'd enter the corporate end of things. Yes. He would engineer mergers and acquisitions, would develop popular family motion pictures, design a theme park in Bombay. Yes yes. He would give up drinking and fu—ooling around and acting like a- a- a goof. Yep. He'd donate money to churches and charities and he'd serve turkey to the homeless on Thanksgiving. Life was going to be good.

He stepped through the blackened glass doors of the office. The temperature was many degrees lower. An animatronic receptionist sat at a desk in front of a huge portrait of Walt. She looked like she wore long-sleeved nightgowns to bed and had a cocker spaniel at home named Lady. She was the same android they'd had in there the day he went in for his interview, and the day they'd hired him, and the days he'd had to go in to sign his write-ups for eating in costume and for insubordination. What a word. He'd failed to play his part as a lower

PART 2: EXTERNAL COMBUSTION

order. That was his problem. He was out of order.

"Would it be possible to see Mr. Fleming today?"

She looked up. She had on a headset. A distasteful flash of recognition stole across her face before it resumed its air of professional indifference. "You need to sign in, please."

With unsteady hands, he signed in on a paper clamped to a plastic clipboard.

"What is this regarding?"

"I'd just like to talk to Mr. Fleming about—about my future."

"Mr. Fleming is very busy today. If you would like, I can make an appointment for you during the week."

Jim's crest fell. He somehow knew that it was now or never. A universe existed between now and an appointment during the week. All manner of derailments might occur. He rubbed grit out of his eyes and scratched sand from his hair. A flicker of humanity crossed over the animatron's face. "I can try to find out if he will see you today," she said.

"Thanks." Jim smiled. She pressed a button and spoke into the headset. "Mr. Fleming, there's a Jim Crack here to see you."

Brica braca firecracker sis boom bah Bugs Bunny Bugs Bunny rah rah rah.

"Mr. Fleming will see you now." She sounded impressed. Though Jim knew the way, she led him to Fleming's office. *His orifice. Quit thinking like that*, he thought. Fleming was pulling a manila folder from a filing cabinet and wheeled back to his desk in a dwarfing leather chair. He had thinning gray curls and the crisp way his tie fit in his collar broadcast impeccability. Perched over his downward-turned nose, round, brass-framed eyeglasses reflected pictures of his family and various Disney knickknacks on his large, dark, wood desk. "Mr. Crack." He smirked.

193

CAR TROUBLE

Jim needed a shower. His hair was a mess. He burped vomit. He needed to go for a jog. He wondered why he felt so much hatred so often. He led an easier life than ninety-seven percent of the world's population, but he was sure he was in the bottom three percent of happiness-feelers. *Hatred of life is just a brain chemical*, he tried to convince himself. Jim saw through the false respect of calling him "Mister" and ignored it. He would remain steadfastly polite from now on. Fleming folded his hands on his desk.

"Mr. Fleming, sir, I've had a revelation."

Again the smirk. He leaned back. "A revelation?" he asked stentoriously.

"Well, sir, it's like this:" He coughed. "I want to pay my dues. I've always believed up until a few hours ago that all men are created equal, but obviously, sir, that isn't entirely true. Some are born luckier than others. Some are bigger or stronger or smarter. Some are born richer. There are clearly hierarchies. I believe now that I need to work within the system to earn my way up. No one owes me forty acres and a mule. Sir, I see now that the pursuit of happiness is a wild goose chase, sir, a fool's game. A sucker bet. Sir, all I'm saying is that I want to work. I want to work in the system. I want to work hard and be respectful, and I only want whatever rewards I earn. Sir, I want to impress you with my newfound work ethic. I want to show up early and stay late. I'll accept any job, and you watch and see. I'll ride buses to work every day until I can afford a car again, and I'll maintain that car in top working order, and I'll keep it clean and polished. I'll eat right and take vitamins and get plenty of rest. I'll never be late or miss a day. I'll be the best employee this company has ever known, and I want to do it not just for my own gain but for the collective gain of the company and all of us who are working hard to make it…uh, work."

Fleming had listened patiently. He sat forward. An amused look played across his face and he rotated a pen back and forth between his fingers. It looked to Jim like he was trying to decide what to say.

PART 2: EXTERNAL COMBUSTION

Something had struck Fleming as funny, and he was weighing whether to say it or remain professionally dispassionate. "Crack," he said. "That's good. You'll go far with an attitude like that. Maintain that outlook, I encourage you. But you're through here." He picked the file up off his desk. "We maintain very thorough personnel records. I didn't need to look at yours, but it's all there. And in such a short time. I know you've had car trouble and health issues, but it's company policy. It comes from above. You've been kept on longer than we ever should have allowed out of respect for your father, but your employment here is ended. But trust me, son, if you continue to believe what you're saying today, you will find success and happiness. The decision here has been made, however. In fact, your final paycheck has already been sent to your home with your termination notice."

Home. Dad's. Fu-ugh. Again Jim floated away, bumped the ceiling, could have floated through, but watched curiously his corporeal form below, which, he noted from above seemed to be taking this news complacently. He descended into his body again. His pulse was slow. His blood pressure felt normal. The idea of overturning Fleming's desk and punching his glasses into his face seemed appealing for drama's sake, but ultimately futile. Jim stood and extended his hand to Fleming. "Well then, sir," he said good-naturedly, "I shall devote my energies elsewhere. Thank you and good day."

He walked down the hall. It seemed a place he had never been. Implications started sinking in. A first furious bubble percolated up from—was that his spleen where it was all housed? Or was it a germinal factor originating in his father's testes, something he had been born with? He brushed past a fern-topped water cooler and a bubble glugged angrily from its depths and burst on the surface. He pushed through the doors and outside. The sun glinted off the cross atop the Crystal Cathedral. "God, forgive me for being the way You made me," he muttered.

Home? His paycheck was at his father's house? He might have been

CAR TROUBLE

able to sneak in while his father was at work, but his keys were fused to the ignition of the Volkswagen. He had a few hundred dollars in the bank, but it would be useless to try to withdraw it without his ID. He went to the Campbell's Soup sedan and sat a long time in the parking lot of the Disney Casting Office. An armed security guard appeared at the front doors of the building and stared at Jim as Jim stared at some ultra-dense ball of nothing a few trillion light years away, a ball that might explode into everything.

He turned the key in the ignition and fired up the old internal combustion. The engine idled. His stomach grumbled, all the usual hungers consuming him. He thought he might have a few bucks in his locker at the park. Then what? Look for a new job? Mug an old lady? What were his options? He needed clothes, but he wasn't, under any circumstances, going back to his father's house. Maybe he could sell the Campbell's Soup sedan. Sell it and report it stolen. No. Or rent it. Be a rogue taxicab driver and ferry passengers from their hotels to the park. Right.

The idling car stalled and shuddered to a halt. Jim tried to start it again, but the key wouldn't turn in the ignition. He kept jiggling and pushing and pulling, to no avail. His facial muscles tightened. A minute passed—two, three. The security guard started toward Jim. The key wouldn't turn. The dick came closer, the key ring bit into Jim's fingers, and then—BAM! He punched the windshield before he knew it. A spiderweb of cracks extended in all directions. He could feel it coming on. He felt for his pills, knowing the bottle was empty. A panic was coming on. The freak show was about to begin. He fought to remain peaceful. A frog buried in the mud. But if he had to talk to that—that fucker, he was gonna blow. He knew it. He opened the door and got out. He turned his back on the advancing guard and walked.

"Sir. You need to remove yourself and your vehicle from the premises. Sir!"

Jim kept walking. He had once loved to read books while he walked

PART 2: EXTERNAL COMBUSTION

to school or work. The light of the world would go down around him as he read, and the words on the page became a shroud of imagination within which some uncanny, built-in radar alerted him to the presence of curbs, cars, and other pedestrians in the darkness of the outer world. This was the real world he walked in now, though, was a world of unformed images, riddled with wrongs and oppositions evincing a litany of bitter abstract mumblings.

He found himself at the employee entrance to the park, and he detected Jerry, the security guard, out there and he waved to him before entering the labyrinth of catacombs beneath the Happiest Place on Earth. He made his way through throbbing electric tunnels to the men's dressing room. He had been away a long time, it seemed, but two seconds after he walked in, he smelled something familiar. Wayne. It was his fucking cologne or hair gel or something. It was Wayne.

Judy Tuna did not seem to be around. Jim went to the costume window and checked out the Goofy suit. The girl wasn't supposed to give it to him if he wasn't scheduled, but she hadn't checked the schedule, bored and resentful, underground all day. Her mouth said things, and Jim's mouth said things back. Jim took the Goofy suit and sat a long time at a lighted mirror. The Seven Dwarfs where all set to go trooping out together. Prince Charming was applying rouge to his cheeks. Jim searched his mind trying to figure out what was on it. Nothing. An immense nothingness. His mind didn't seem to belong to him. He probed it and learned nothing. A guy across from Jim with tousled hair said nothing, and neither did Jim. *I'm so hungry, I don't think I can take it anymore, and I'm so lonely, I just don't know what to do, I'm so lonely, feel like I'm gonna crawl away and die, and I'm so hungry feel like I'm gonna hack it apart, I'm gonna hack hack hack it apart, I'm gonna hack hack hack hack it apart I'm gonna hack hack hack hack it—seems like there oughta be a good reason to be lonely lonely lonely,* he sang in his head, picking at a wart on his finger until it bled. Ugh. Stymied. Maybe he would just go out and have fun being Goofy one more time.

Adjacent to the dressing room, a row of showers was kept perpetually drip-less by an army of Disney plumbers. Jim thought he might shower, and it seemed to him like the first real, normal, practical thought he had had in a long time. He went to his locker and waited a minute for the combination and opened it. He pushed his shoes off with his toes. He sat a while. He peeled off a sock and sat blankly a while before peeling of the other sock. His feet were unnaturally white, and his big toes had big calluses. He stood up and pulled off his shirt and dropped it to the floor of his locker, and undid and stepped out of his pants.

He felt a bowel movement coming on and decided to eliminate prior to showering. He selected the first of a row of stalls. He placed a seat liner, dropped his drawers, and took a seat. Sitting on the shitter beneath the Happiest Place on Earth. Sitting on the Happer beneath the Shittiest Place on Earth. *Stop it*, he told himself. Then he heard the chimpanzee laugh he knew belonged to Wayne. It grew closer. Wayne was at the urinal talking in a low voice with someone and giggling. Jim could see through the crack of space along the edge of the door Wayne's head sticking up from the hairy body of the Beast. Jim felt skinny and vulnerable with his underwear stretched across his thighs. He did not want to get caught with his pants down and the remains of a dead steer protruding from his butt-hole.

"I was working working working that pussy, dude, BANGING away, when that fucking tripper fucking Crack busts in like he's the fucking cavalry or Superman, and I hopped up and beat his ass fucking butt-naked." He laughed again, hyena-like it was now.

"Isn't he the one that beat you up at Claire's party?" asked the other guy.

"What, dude? He fucking sucker-punched me. If we square off face to face, he knows he gets his ass wasted."

Who was Wayne with? Jim strained to find an angle to see. "Dude, I'm gonna be late," said the voice. He moved into Jim's sight. It was

PART 2: EXTERNAL COMBUSTION

what's-his-name, Luis, who played the White Rabbit. "I'm supposed to do character greeting with Tweedle Dum and Tweedle Dummer. Ever work with those guys? I think they like each other. I've gotta go change."

"I'll be right behind you," said Wayne. "I'm going to be with that hot new chick who plays Belle up by King Arthur's Carousel, but I'm going to try to work my way over to New Orleans. I got my eye on a betty there too, that works the line at the paddle wheel."

Jim peered through the crack. Wayne was examining his face in the mirror, trying different smiles. A crucifix hung from a gold chain around his neck, and he lifted it to his lips and gave it a kiss. Then he winked at himself and walked out.

Jim wiped his ass, wondering about the sanctity of the mind that created a creature of such functions, and the abruptly flushing vortex of shit was a counterpoint to the lack of finality in any answer. He tried to flush the thought from his mind, though it kept swirling and swirling. Cautiously, he walked to the showers and turned one on. He wasn't sure the steam wasn't coming out of his ears. He should have jumped the jerk right then and there. He had nothing to lose. He was going to find that bastard and beat him again in front of everybody. Squared off face to face.

He got out of the shower. He did feel refreshed. He used his shirt, or rather Adam's shirt, to dry off. It was torn and dirty. He turned his underwear inside out and put them on. He pulled on the Goofy brown trousers, the long-sleeve orange pullover, attached the suspenders, donned the green vest. He unrolled his damp socks and pulled them over his feet again and then put on the big Goofy shoes, then the white gloves. He took the paper and small change from his jeans and his inhaler and the lighter, put them in the pocket of Goofy's pants, and closed his locker door.

The joints in this thumbs ached. Jim pulled on the head of Goofy. His breathing was shallow in the mask. The air was close and hot and helping his nose run. He couldn't wipe it. He looked out through a dark screen in Goofy's mouth. He was about to pull open the door and go out when the White Rabbit pushed in. "I'm late," came the muffled voice. He grabbed his large pocket watch off a bench and rushed out again. Jim followed him down the hallway, the taps on the bottom of the Goofy shoes clacking on the concrete. He opened a door and came out under the tall, multi-colored mushrooms across from the base of the faux alpine mountain Matterhorn.

Ten paces toward the spinning cups of the Mad Tea Party, he was tapped on the back and turned to meet a beautiful, beaming teenage girl. He slapped his gloved hands to his Goofy cheeks and bent his knees in a pantomime of elation. He posed for a snapshot and was soon swarmed by adoring fans, clamoring for autographs and hugs. He grabbed the hands of a little girl and danced around with her, kicking his heels out and lifting his knees up high before waving goodbye and skipping happily under the flying, wing-eared elephants to high five the line of people waiting for a jaunt on Mr. Toad's Wild Ride. Even as the first trickle of sweat tickled down his agonizingly unscratchable nose, Jim had what for him was the strange and wonderful sensation of feeling loved. If he had to submerge his true identity behind a mask to be loved, so be it. He frolicked around Fantasyland, feeling loved.

Then he spotted the Beast.

It was holding hands with Belle, greeting guests as they exited Peter Pan's flight. The air pressed hot against Jim's forehead and settled leadenly in his lungs. His underwear felt full of damp beef jerky. He took a candied apple from a candied apple cart manned by a girl with candied apple cheeks. The girl gave a nonplussed tilt of the head but did not protest, perhaps out of deference to Goofy. Jim struggled in his gloves to unwrap the apple from its plastic case, but eventually succeeded. He then went into an exaggerated cartoon baseball pitcher's wind up and fired away with all he had, beaning the Beast between the horns with about a seventy-mile-per-hour fastapple. The

PART 2: EXTERNAL COMBUSTION

crowd roared its approval. The Beast crouched, turning this way and that, seeking the author of the missile.

Jim took another apple from the cart and pretended to pull the stick out of it with his Goofy teeth as if it were the pin of a grenade and threw it as hard as he could, striking the Beast in the chest. Beast spotted Goofy, stamped a hoof, and charged. Goofy assumed the role of matador, shaking an invisible red cape. He sidestepped the Beast's clumsy charge and applied a kick of his big shoe to the back end of the Beast as it stampeded past. The crowd applauded and a circle of people formed around the combatants as the Beast turned to charge again. Goofy juked to the left and stuck out his long leg and tripped the Beast, who went down in a tumbling heap. A security guard stood on the fringes of the crowd, unsure whether or not this was all part of the show, until Goofy put the Beast in a headlock and the Beast elbowed Goofy in the stomach, and Goofy ripped off the Beast's head.

A gasping hush fell over the crowd and a little girl broke into terrified wailing. Goofy delivered a half dozen unanswered uppercuts to Wayne's face like Nolan Ryan on Robin Ventura. The security guard advanced and Goofy released the Wayne/Beast and took off in a gawky, loping run. He attempted to hurdle the rail around the carousel, but the toe of his big Goofy shoe did not quite clear the top of the rail, and Jim went down, sprawling face first, calliope music enhancing the pratfall-ishness of the collapse. He reached up and grabbed a passing brass pole of the merry-go-round, using the hindquarters of a hydraulically galloping fiberglass unicorn to pull himself up, perne in gyre. He turned to see the security guard attending to the headless Wayne/Beast, escorting him offstage before scanning the crowd for those guards that would materialize out of the woodwork to subdue Jim.

A tourist-looking undercover guard with an earpiece approached the carousel. Jim knew that park security was trained to carry out their duties causing minimal disturbance to the illusion. The guard hesitated. After one revolution, Goofy/Jim saw the guard waiting by the exit and another guard circling around the other side. Goofy/Jim stepped off the infernal machine, wobbled to the rail, and climbed over. He walked brusquely toward Frontierland, brushing off admiring Goofy fans debarking the Casey Junior Circus Train. The guards kept pace behind him as he wended his way around Big Thunder Mountain. Two more undercovers advanced toward him out of New Orleans Square and he turned to the dock at the big white Mississippi sternwheeler, *Mark Twain*.

She was about to leave port, *Mark Twain* was, and the attendant had drawn the chain across the guide-rail to the gangplank. Jim tickled his way to the front of the line and stepped over the chain. The riverboat had just pulled away and Goofy/Jim leaped six feet over the water, wrapped his arms over the gunwale, and pulled himself aboard. He turned and waved enthusiastically at the line of people behind him, who clapped and whistled and waved back.

Goofy/Jim posed for a few more photos and signed some more autographs. He wrote silly offhand stuff. On one kid's paper he wrote, "You can blow your nose in toilet paper and still wipe your keister with it, but not the other way around." On another he wrote, "I," and he started to draw a valentine heart, but scribbled it out and started over with an approximation of the anatomically correct organ complete with atria and ventricles, an aorta and vena cava, so that it said, "I (heart) trans-fatty acids." On another he wrote, "Plato laid sod in in Aristotle's backyard."

Around the backside of Tom Sawyer's Island, he went aft and, after waving to the crowd, did a clumsy swan dive off the port stern into the Rivers of America. His neck bent awkwardly as the big mask struck the surface. An unexpected panic seized him as he feared the big shoes would fill with water and sink him like a mafia turncoat. It was the head, though, that filled with water. It ran up his nose and dragged him down with surprising rapidity. The Goofy shoes, rather than weigh him down, actually worked like swim fins. He gave a couple of strong

PART 2: EXTERNAL COMBUSTION

kicks but could not tell which way was up or down. He fumbled with the mask, trying to remove it, breath running out. Who cared if Jim drowned—but Goofy? He couldn't let that happen. Maybe if he could push the mask up to the surface, he could empty it, and it would float there, and the kids would think Goofy was treading water. He succeeded in removing his head, but his oxygen had run out. Jim saw a white light. How peaceful it might be to just relax there. His father had once taken him to swim in the pond on the ranch of a war buddy. Yeah. Swimming in a *pond*, pretty exotic for a suburb kid. Just as they were walking out to the door, War Buddy, said, "Look out for cottonmouths. I get 'em down there sometimes." As his father rowed them out to the middle of the shadowy pond, Jim risked asking for the third time what a cottonmouth was. This time his father answered him. "It's a kind of snake." He looked Jim in the eye. "Don't you be afraid, though. They hear you and they just go the other way." He stopped rowing and took out a cigarette. "Well," he said to Jim expectantly.

"I don't want to go in, Dad."

His father burned his eyes into Jim's. "Just get in."

"I don't want to, Dad. I'm afraid."

"Don't be a coward, son. Get in, or I'll throw you in."

Jim was crying as he slid over the side of the rowboat into the writhing water.

"Swim," his father ordered.

"No, Dad, no." He clung to the side, crying, seeing disgust in his father's eyes.

"Let go, son."

Jim let go. He could feel himself sinking. The white light hovered over him. *Just let go,* he thought.

The white light drew him. If he just went to it, everything would be better. He would never feel hunger or anger or hatred again.... But no! That is life! Pain is life! Painlessness is death! Life is better a precious, painful, short while to feel agony and suffering, without which pleasure and beauty would be rendered meaningless!

"Kick, Jimmy, kick. Swim, son. Don't be afraid."

Jim kicked. He kicked toward the white light, which was really just the sun shining down through the water. It wasn't so much his decision as it was the cells of his body demanding air. Air! They dragged his soul with them. He broke the surface, sputtering in the churning white wake of the *Mark Twain's* paddlewheel. The passengers on the boat craned to see him. Jim took a deep breath and dived. The Goofy shoes propelled him along the mucky bottom. He held his breath like he'd taken a bong hit. When he came up again, the boat had gone around the bend. Jim frog-kicked along the surface to the bank opposite Tom Sawyer Island where he slithered through the mud and hid in the brush as the Sailing Ship Columbia motored by, firing its cannon. He pulled off the Goofy shoes. Across the river a log cabin burned. White settlers had been attacked by redskin savages. Ha. They'd just wanted a little more West to go.

He skirted the brush along the track of the Disneyland railroad. He crossed the tracks and tiptoed through the trees, up the berm, to the high barbed-wire fence. He studied the razor wire, wondering how he might escape Disneyland, soaking wet, with no shoes, in a bright orange sweater with a green vest. The steam whistle blew announcing the train's arrival in Critter Country. Jim ducked as the engine chugged past, then sprang from the bushes and ran alongside an open-air passenger car. "Look, Mom! Is that Huck Finn?"

Jim fell back and waited for the last car. A ladder bolted to the back of the caboose provided a handhold, and Jim had to run not quite as fast as he could to keep pace and pull himself up. He climbed on to the roof and lay flat, hoping to remain unseen. A jolly warmth inflated in him like he was Kerouac the hobo running free across the land, before everything went all wrong. The train slowed into the Fantasyland Station. People on the skyway were pointing at him. His cover was blown. He had to keep moving. He belly-crawled back to

PART 2: EXTERNAL COMBUSTION

the ladder, slid down, and jumped to the soft, well-watered soil in a grove of pine trees between the warped angles of Toon Town and the tent over the dance floor of Videopolis. Peering from the shadows, he observed a line of guests waiting to ride the Skyway to Tomorrowland. Jim stepped out onto the pavement and hotfooted it to the shade of the covered Skyway line, where he found himself the object of much interest among a group of tourists whom he presumed were Japanese. He posed for a few more photos, throwing his damp arms over their shoulders, smiling halfway around the world and scanning the thickening horde of people in the park for signs that he would be apprehended.

"Sir, where are your shoes?" asked one of the Skyway operators, a pretty girl in lederhosen. "And you're all wet! What happened?"

"I know, miss," said Jim, hooking his thumbs through his suspenders. "I was nearly drownded. I may as well be drownded for real once my Aunt Polly sees what I done to my clothes and that I lost muh shoes."

She looked puzzled a moment before smiling. "Tom Sawyer! Is that you? I didn't know we had a Tom Sawyer."

Another gondola swung around on its cable, and she helped a party of tourists into it. "But Tom, what are you doing here in the Alps?"

A phone rang in the control booth and Jim watched closely the face of the guy who answered it. "I know," said Tom. "Everyone thinks I'm drowned. I 'spect they're dragging the river for me now. Hain't you heard the cannons?"

Another gondola swung around and the guy in the booth stepped out to get a look at Jim before returning to the booth. Jim could see him affirm something into the phone. He'd been spotted. The minions of Disney would soon surround him, subdue him, and take him to the Disney jail. They'd handcuff him and sit him in a metal folding chair in a concrete room beneath Main Street. They'd probably call his father. But no. They would never take him alive.

As one of the gondolas began its ascent up the cable, Jim made a break for it. He leaped up and caught the door of the gondola and hung there, while the tourists who had just photographed him screamed in the swinging bucket of the car. It was thirty feet high before the operator stopped it and Jim pulled himself up into it. He smiled—reassuringly, he hoped—at the tourists. Soon a contingent of Disney security appeared, including several of the more serious uniformed variety. He watched them confer at the operator's booth. Soon the Skyway resumed its climb over the park. They would undoubtedly wait for him on the other end.

The tourists conversed nervously in Japanese. Across the park, a wobbling, smiley-faced clock began to bong the hour, and the tourists turned their attention and cameras to it as a small army of dolls paraded around the tower. Jim's eyes fixed on the peak of the Matterhorn, where Skyway passed through a tunnel in the mountain. As they drew nearer, Jim slid the bolt back, opened the door, and stood up. One of the Japanese men threw his arms around Jim, but Jim shook him off, and, holding the bars on either side of the door, he leaned out chest first. The gondola pitched wildly with the weight shift and the scrambling of the tourists to find safety. Jim ignored them. He closed his eyes and felt the wind on his face. When he opened them again, the mountain looked to be about fifteen feet or so below. He closed his eyes again, bent at the knees, and jumped out.

With the air, fear and elation blew through his armpits and crotch, over his ears, and up his nose. He seemed to fall longer than he should have. He threw his arms and feet out, as if to assume the position of a cat-like landing, and hit the side of the mountain like a bug hitting a windshield. He slid down several feet and came to a halt, the wind knocked out of him. It sounded like a gong had been struck. Bare-chested eunuchs clutching cushioned mallets tumbled and somersaulted across the hall of some echoing palace. The ringing was replaced by the beating of war drums that was the pounding of his pulse, until only the muffled trumpet of the wind blew over his ears. He

PART 2: EXTERNAL COMBUSTION

opened his eyes. The horizon sloped between blue sky and bird-guano-white mountain. Somewhere up there was a door in the side of the mountain that led to a maintenance stairwell. He edged over, bolts of pain running jagged through his body. If he was quick, he might get away before they figured out what had happened. With each movement, new pains jostled for transportation on his nervous system. He was sure he had broken a rib or two. His left wrist was swelling, and his right knee was stiffening by the second. A rivulet of blood ran down the mountain from his elbow, and looking down, he'd lost most of one big toenail.

Halfway around the mountain, he spotted the well-camouflaged catwalk and small cave leading to the door. He worked his way gingerly over to it and stood grimacing on the catwalk. He opened the door with the hand attached to the unhurt wrist and limped into the mountain. He waited for his pupils to adjust, wondering how soon it would be until word spread that some psycho had jumped from the Skyway. Soft light bulbs lit a stairway going down. He dragged himself down as quickly as possible. After a few flights, he came to another door and heard shouting behind it. He put his ear to it and listened. Thumping, running, yelling, squeaking. He depressed the thumb knob, pushed the door open a crack, and peeped through. The basketball court, of course. There was a basketball court inside the Matterhorn, an employee rec area. A little five on five going on. Jim tried to act naturally as he crossed the court struggling not to limp. The guys were too absorbed in their game to pay him much notice. Skins versus shirts. His wrist throbbed. He scooped up a gym bag and passed through another door into a small break room lined with vending machines and lockers and a couple of doors marked MEN and WOMEN. He pushed open the women's door and looked in to see that it was unoccupied. He locked the door behind him and put the bag on the sink. His toe was bleeding profusely. He sat on the toilet. The nail was half torn off and sticking up at a right angle like the dorsal fin of a shark. Jim bent to it, and pinching the nail between his thumb and forefinger, he gritted his teeth and tore off the rest of the broken nail with a guttural growling scream.

Quickly, he pulled off a yard of toilet paper and pressed it against the ragged digit with one hand. He unzipped the bag and found hula girls among the palm trees at sunset on a hibiscus-covered Hawaiian shirt cavorting with a pair of sandals, a Gilligan-type floppy hat, clean socks, shorts, and underwear, some loose change, and a wallet. In the wallet were credit cards, ID's, and cash. He took out the guy's employee ID. William Elias Coyte. It looked enough like him. He put it in his teeth and counted the money. Sixty-seven bucks. Precious seconds passed before he tossed the wallet back into the bag, money intact. He pulled on the Hawaiian shirt, clapped the hat onto his head, donned the sunglasses and put the ID in the breast pocket. As he unrolled the socks, he spotted a sanitary napkin dispenser bolted to the wall, and fished out a quarter from the bag to buy one. He positioned the pad over his bloody toe and gingerly pulled on one sock then the other. He slipped his feet into the sandals, pushing the socks between his toes to accommodate the thongs of the sandals, stood up, and listened at the door. Hearing nothing, he pushed it open a crack, and after ascertaining that no one was there, he crossed the break room, leaving the bag on the table, and forced himself down the stairs hurriedly to another corridor.

A uniformed security guard rushed past. He bit down hard on his tongue as a way to focus on pain that had nothing to do with walking, and strode as naturally as possible, nodding nonchalantly. Past halls and doors, he kept moving through the Magic Kingdom's subterranean netherworld, expecting to be seized at every turn. When he emerged into the sunlight and crossed the parking lot, he felt like a political prisoner escaping through some DMZ. He walked past the guard at the gate without looking back.

He stepped onto the sidewalk wondering if the corporation owned

PART 2: EXTERNAL COMBUSTION

that, too. Surely, the city government and the local PD did its bidding. He feared he would never be beyond its retribution, that Disney officials might bust into whatever room he might make it to, and haul him back to the Main Street jail. *If they don't own the very air*, he thought, *they're in cahoots with the lobbies and lawmakers who control its contamination.* Mumbling down Harbor, he dragged his feet through a glaucomic tunnel filled with frightened faces, concrete, and cars. Déjà vu all over again, again. He came to the street with the crumbling sidewalk, turned down it without deciding to, and by the time he came to the white house, he believed that Adam was his sole ally, the one person who saw Jim not as a psychological freak, but created in the same image, and of the same dust, as himself.

One step at a time, he climbed the stairs to the door, each inhalation stabbing his side. It was unlocked and he went in.

Pete's eyes were swollen slits fixed above a never-ending close-lipped smile. "Dude," he said to Jim. "Adam's gone. He just caught a plane and bailed back to Utah, like right now, just like that. He wanted you to do something about his car. He left you a note on the counter. Want a bong rip?"

The letter said, "If I stay here any longer, I'm going to end up pushing my belongings around in a shopping cart for the rest of my life. I'm going back to Utah and get my—" -the word shit was scribbled out- "—life straightened out. You should do the same. Maybe our paths will cross again sometime. Leave the keys and the car here at the house, and I'll figure out what to do. PLEASE DON'T DRIVE IT. Good luck."

Jim staggered to the sofa and dropped. Everything hurt; the throbbing of the pain intensified each second he sat. "I gotta go," said Pete. He walked out, and Jim heard his motorcycle drive away. The bong smoldered on the coffee table. Ghostly fingers beckoned. Jim reached out, wincing, and took a lemon-drop-sized piece of marijuana bud from a Glad baggie on the table. *Kill the pain. No, no, no. Smoking pot is wrong. It's illegal. I'll be a bad person if I do. I'm going to be good from now on.*

Ahh, what's the point? He tamped the bud into the bong's bowl. *What's the point of trying not to smoke? It's my nature.* He took up the lighter. *Isn't my nature God's will?* He flicked the lighter and touched it to the bud and smoked it through, staring into the flame. *Blasphemy. God's will is that you resist temptation. He gives you free will to make such choices or not, you dummy.* Jim blew out the smoke. He leaned back on the couch. The pain in his body did subside somewhat, but now the escapees of Pandora's box hovered in the smoke all around his head, tormenting him as he fell into a restless sleep.

He awoke in gloom. The pain was dull and constant until he moved, and then it coursed through him like an electrical current. He dumped the weed bag onto the coffee table and limped into the kitchen. There was no ice in the freezer, but he was able to chip enough frost from the walls and ceiling with a butter knife to fill the bag. Deciding what to ice was a toss-up, but he went with his ankle. He returned to the couch and stared at the wall. Somewhere in his brain, decisions were being made, and he waited, staring at the wall, until they made themselves known to him. He stared at the wall a long time before he fished a wet and tattered piece of paper out of the Goofy pants. The ink was running, but he could still make out the phone number Ben had given him. There was a clock on the wall. Its face was a background of stars around which a comet went on the minutes hand. Jim studied the hours hand for signs of movement. He picked up the phone and dialed. As it rang, he removed the bandage from the base of his thumb and picked sand from the gash.

"What?" demanded a voice.

"You tell me," said Jim. "I was told to call this number about a job."

He heard muffled voices, as if a hand were over the phone. Then, "The job pays one thousand dollars...five hundred at the start and five hundred when it's done. You'll get a car...it's an old car...but you'll be able to do whatever you want with it when the job is done." The

PART 2: EXTERNAL COMBUSTION

voice seemed to be repeating these instructions. "You might have to break the law a little bit...do you want to know more?"

A voodoo master instructed the zombie Jim to say, "Yes."

"Once we tell you the rest, you're in on it. If you fuck with us in any way, we fuck back. Got it?"

"Yeah."

"Where are you?"

Jim gave them directions and was told someone would be over with more details in an hour or two. He went out the front door to the landing and sat on the top step, battling his thoughts. He decided he would not acknowledge pain; he would pretend it didn't exist. As the sun fell to the rooftops, the world around him took on the glow of molten lava. Under those roofs, innumerable stories played out innumerable conflicts multiplied exponentially around the world. Somewhere on the edge of a Bangladeshi dump, a one-legged boy ate triumphantly the meat of a dying seagull he had caught, while in some Newport Beach mansion a woman wept in misery because liposuction had left loose skin around her waist. Happiness and misery were apportioned equally to all, no matter the setting nor circumstances. The sun took a dive, the light went out. *Maybe*, he thought. Or maybe there were a lot of rich happy scions running around without conscience nor compunction, having a great time sipping champagne and eating caviar on their yachts, who had state-of the art health care, who never got canker sores nor runny noses, who had the money to be installed into the offices of power where they enforced the lack of freedom of Jim and his ilk, and prosecuted wars and corporate raids, further amassing power and fortune, turning common men, simple men, into slaves, and they laughed a lot.

"Whatever," he muttered. He was hungry, and he pulled himself up and went into the house to forage. He found a pizza box with uneaten crusts that caused his jaw to make cracking sounds while he chewed, and he sucked water straight from the kitchen faucet for lack of a clean cup. He spent the next hour or so wanting a cigarette, never smoking one, but never not wanting it. Eventually, a pair of headlights came knocking and pinging down the street, and sputtered to a stop in front of the house. It was a white convertible with its top down, and stopping behind it was a brand-new black SUV with tinted windows and dealer placards in the license plate frames. A guy with the physique to be wrestling on Saturday morning TV extracted himself from between the seat and steering wheel of the convertible and climbed out, cursing the fucking busted door. His chin came straight out of the comic books, and he turned his droopy-lidded eyes to Jim and said, "You Crack?"

It was the voice from the phone. Jim went down the steps, trying his best not to grimace. A backseat window on the SUV came down with an electric whir. "Hello, Jim. And how are you this evening? Everything okay?" It was Ben. A hulking Samoan or something sat next to him.

"I'm fine," said Jim.

"You don't seem to be walking so well. Stay there, I'll come out." He stepped from the SUV with a brown paper bag. "Do you live here?"

Jim shrugged and shook his head and nodded. "C'mon up."

"Is it all right if Kenny comes as well?"

Jim shrugged again and went upstairs. He cleared a table of junk mail and they sat down around it. Ben produced a couple of bottles of Steinlager from the bag and opened one with a church-key on his keychain and put it front of Jim, then opened one for himself. "Kenny?"

Kenny shook his head and tipped back in his chair, arms folded, biceps bulging. "Okay, then," said Ben and took a big draught off his Steinlager. "Let's get down to it." He took out an envelope and put a pink slip on the table and counted out two stacks of five hundred-dollar bills. "I know this fellow, mate o' mine, really, we shared a place at the beach. Good guy. An American. Big black dood. He's also a bit of a gun enthusiast. Daft about the military, and he's got all these guns.

PART 2: EXTERNAL COMBUSTION

Twenty or more. All kinds. Hand guns, assault rifles, serious shit. But it's funny, he just goes out into the bush once in a while to shoot at cans and bunny rabbits, and that's all."

"Now like I say, we're friends. But he owes me money. Rent money, a few lost wagers, no big thing, but he hasn't paid. Where you come in is, we'd like you to take that car out there—and you can have the car—take the car, get the guns, put them in the trunk, and keep them until such time as we get our money. If he doesn't pay in thirty days, we're going to sell the guns. It's all legitimate and fair, really, if you think about it. The only thing is, someone's got to get into the house and get the guns. If Kenny or I do it, he'll know it was us. You get five hundred now and five hundred more when we get paid or sell the guns. Plus, the car. That car belonged to Kenny's grandmum. She's just died. The ownership paper's yours if you want the job."

Guns? Somewhere in Jim, Robbie the Robot went, "Danger! Danger, Will Robinson! Danger!" Somewhere else, another voice was thinking, "Cool. Guns. I knew I was a tough customer, and other people get it now, too." On top of all that, was no voice at all, just a reason. He needed money and a car and here they were.

"Okay," he said. "*Are you out your fucking mind?*" screamed the loudest voice of all. He strangled it to silence.

Ben took a swig of his beer. Jim only looked at his. Kenny was staring at Jim. Ben handed Jim a slip of paper. "This is the address. The guns are in a closet in the back room, just sitting there. He has a couple of flat mates. They're all partiers. Half the time you can just walk right in."

Jim took the paper. "Why you dress like such a fucking goofball?" Kenny wanted to know. In a fraction of a second, Jim's mind turned a few computations. He noticed that some certain thing that he had lived with his whole life and that had factored into everything he had ever done was suddenly gone: fear. Even though Kenny could surely have broken Jim's neck if he so chose, he wouldn't harm Jim until Jim had finished this job. Ben and Kenny were working for someone else. Someone who would be upset if a new sucker had to be found to do this job. Jim took up an unopened bottle of beer. Then he stood and kicked Kenny's tilted chair out from under him. Pain shot through his leg, and he screamed from his guts and bent over Kenny, ready to smash the bottle into his face. Panic filled Kenny's eyes.

Jim smiled and backed away. "This is my uniform, Holmes," he said. "I'm a professional goof. A major league fuck-up." His voice was laughing and growling. Kenny popped up and shoved his chest into Jim's face. Jim leered up at him. "I'm a stooge for you and everyone else. See? When I wake up in the morning, I'm already dressed. Get it? I'm already dressed."

"You're fucking crazy." Kenny shoved Jim into the wall and backed off.

"Very dramatic," said Ben. "Is that what you Americans call 'getting the drop on someone'? None of this is like that, so please leave your Hollywood action fantasies out of this. Kenny, wait downstairs." Kenny left, smirking and nodding at Jim until he was out the door. "He's a dangerous bloke, and he's not even in the top five of this thing. Understand what you're in now. If you play it right, you can make some money. You play it wrong and you end up fucked. Do I need to elaborate on the meaning of 'fucked'?"

"I'll get you what you want," said Jim.

Ben studied him a long moment before pushing the pink slip and one of the piles of hundreds across to Jim. "Get it done in the next twenty-four hours." He finished his beer and stood up, handing Jim a piece of paper with a phone number on it. "Call when you've finished. The keys are in the car. The guy with the guns is called Derb, by the way. He almost always wears combat fatigues. He's big, but he's harmless. When you have the guns, call. The sooner the better." Ben took the other five hundred. "You'll get this when it's done." He left.

Jim sat on the chair, absent of thought, until the final traces of

PART 2: EXTERNAL COMBUSTION

twilight deserted the windows, and he went down the stairs. The car was an early-'80s Chrysler LeBaron. He circled it, noting a missing hood ornament and a tail light with a perfectly circular hole in it. In his imagination, wearing a mask and a beltful of gadgets, he leaped over the trunk into the front seat, cape trailing behind, and sped away to crusade against injustice. Gingerly, however, he lifted his aching ankle over the door that wouldn't open and slipped into the driver's seat, knocking from the center console a cup which spat into his lap what his fingers learned with revulsion was tobacco drool. Kenny's Revenge. Jim blew a one syllable laugh through his open nostril and turned the key. The car cleared its throat and coughed to a wheezing idle. From a broken speaker clacked heavy metal and static. The needle on the gas gauge was a little above E. He turned on the headlights, adjusted the seat, threw the cup onto the passenger's side floor, and backed out of the driveway.

On the freeway, his hair danced like a fire in the rearview mirror, lit up by the taillights in front of him and the headlights behind. His essence swirled around. He was nothing more than a collection of experiences contained in corporeal being. Circumstances without him dictated his actions. He might have been a probe sent from outer space to collect data.

The address Ben had given him was down on the peninsula, a number near the Balboa pier. He took the freeway to Jamboree to Balboa Island and rode the ferry across the harbor. The Balboa Pavilion shimmered on the water. All those sailboats and waterfront mansions—some people did have—what? They did have life, liberty, and the pursuit of happiness. Or were they just as tormented as he was, but with mansions and sailboats? The ferry operator came to collect the toll.

"Oh, uh, crud, you know, I forgot I only have a hundred."

The guy wasn't looking at Jim. A quartet of freshly tanned women in their summer evening tanks and shorts, about his and Jim's age, was leaning over the rail, the ocean breeze sending tendrils of hair in the direction of him and Jim. "All right, Bud. Don't worry about it this time. I got you." He flashed Jim a smile and made his way over to the girls, keeping a banter with them going as he circled the boat collecting the fares. By the time he'd completed his circuit, he'd extracted their destination and invited himself along after his shift ended. *I could never talk like that*, Jim thought. *Not without about six beers in me. You can't be loved if you can't express something beautiful.* The words went around a corner of his mind like a Times Square stock ticker. *So, I need beer to be loved.*

The ferry pulled into the dock at the Fun Zone. All around guys were holding hands with girls, smooching while they waited for the Ferris wheel, sharing cotton candy, touching ice cream to each other's noses. He felt like he was viewing some strange alternate universe through a telescope the wrong way. When his turn to disembark came, he drove up onto the street. He had a job to do. He turned onto the boulevard and located the address Ben had given him. A few guys were standing out on a balcony, tending a barbecue and drinking from plastic cups in front of an open sliding glass door. He was afraid he was going to need to have a few drinks to pull this off. Not for the courage, but for the lack of judgment necessary to follow through on the plan. The first twinges of reality were beginning to poke through his fog of deliberate ignorance, and he began to have sensible thoughts of self-preservation which he quickly brushed away. This *was* self-preservation. He tried to focus on the next five hundred dollars and on the fact that he had a car. It wasn't enough, especially if he got caught, but there didn't seem to be any other options. He would *definitely not* get drunk, though. He couldn't afford to bungle this. Cool and sober. He had to stay cool and sober.

He parked in an unnecessarily red zone, a perfectly good parking spot along a curb painted red only to extort more money from persons desperate to park, so as to pay the city bureaucrats more. Kenny's dead

PART 2: EXTERNAL COMBUSTION

grandmother wasn't going to care too much about the ticket, though. Jim climbed clumsily out of the car and crossed the street to a pizza joint. He'd been there once before. Yeah, one glorious day, he and his friend Marcus rented kayaks and paddled past herons and egrets, out of the wetlands of Back Bay, into the busy harbor, dazzling, sparkling like—what else could you say?—like it was composed of sapphires and diamonds. They tied their kayaks to a dock right there and ate pizza and drank a pitcher of beer. Kayaking back, Jim felt grateful to be breathing, to have the sun burning down on his neck, to feel the ache in the muscles of his chest, the cool droplets on his arm.

Ol' Marcus got married and moved to Carlsbad. Oh, the hemming and hawing Marcus put in the phone when Jim suggested he come down for a visit and meet the wife and kid. Jim got it. He understood the stammering and the reason for it, couldn't hold it against ol' Marcus, wife and kid to take care of.

The heat of the oven was pouring out the door of the pizza place as Jim went in. *Maybe I can kayak with a friend again someday*, he thought. *Maybe on the Great Salt Lake. Maybe Adam knows some girls from his church who we could go kayaking with us on the Great Salt Lake.*

He was smiling when the quartet of cuties from the ferry came in. One smiled at him, and he opened his mouth to say something beautiful, and nothing came out. Again, he wanted a drink. Even just a beer—if he fucked up tonight, though, it might be the last beer, the last pretty girl, for a long time. *Throw yourself one last little going-away party.* No! He had to do it right. Cool and sober. Party when the job is done.

He ordered a large pizza with everything and plate of pasta Alfredo with garlic bread and salad. "Anything to drink?" asked the cashier in his floured apron. Jim froze in the middle of scratching his temple. His hand slid down his face dragging his cheek and one eye with it. Tap handles batted his eyes.

"Yeah." He could've sworn he'd intended ordering a glass of water.

CAR TROUBLE

"Pitcher of Bud," came out of his mouth.

"ID," said the pizza man. Jim showed him the ID of William Coyne.

The cashier shrugged and drew him a pitcher. "How many mugs?"

Jim thought of parties where he'd drunk from pitchers as if it were his personal tankard, for the spectacle of it; finish them off in a couple trips to the lips. "Just one." The cashier poured a frosty mug until foam ran down the side and rang Jim up. Jim handed him one of the hundred-dollar bills. The pizza man counted back the change. Jim pocketed it, took the pitcher and the mug, and turned to survey the seating. The tables inside were all occupied, though a chair sat unused at the table where the four pretty girls sat. Out on the sidewalk, at a table with several chairs, an old guy in a seaman's cap sat with a glass of red wine and a cigarette between his dusty-looking fingers.

Jim moved. "Alright if I sit here?" he asked.

The old man nodded and held some kind of kazoo up to a hole in his throat and, sounding like a robot, said, "I'm alone."

Jim sat. He stared a long time into the amber bubbles, the neon in the windows giving it the sickly glow of a witch's potion. "You gonna drink that beer or stare at it all night?" the man kazooed.

Jim said nothing.

"I tried to quit drinking once," the man said. "It wadn't no fun. But what else are guys like you and me to do with money in our pockets?" The man's voice was like a Cylon Warrior's.

Jim said nothing.

"I didn't drink when I was your age, much. Times was tough then. But we didn't care, much. Everyone was in the same boat. We made gin in a bathtub in our basement. Had a piano down there. We used to sing and dance. They was tough times, but they could be good times." The man kept pausing for Jim to say something, and Jim kept on not saying anything, and the man would go on. "You could always find a way to make a buck or two. Sell a few fish, swab a deck, do some painting. It's hard to work like that anymore. A white man's got to be

PART 2: EXTERNAL COMBUSTION

on a payroll now and pay taxes just to survive and keep from being locked up anymore."

Jim was thirsty. The salad came out, and Jim asked the waiter's back for a glass of water. He wasn't sure the waiter heard him. He picked up his fork and pushed a stabbing of lettuces into his mouth. The cool, crisp, wetness was godsend with which his body might repair itself.

"I know how it is. I see the little devil and angel on your shoulders, whispering in your ears." A tricked-out Nissan, lowered, bass booming, rippling the surface of Jim's beer passed slowly as the driver checked out the girls through the window, leaving behind an urban Amazon of twittering car alarms. Jim wondered if he shouldn't become a kind of superhero and devote his life to tracking down cars with obscenely loud basses and destroying them.

"I tried to give up drinking once. 'For brethren, ye have been called unto liberty.'" He hiccupped and took another drink. "Only use not liberty for an occasion to the flesh, but by love serve one another." He put down his wine and hung his head a moment and went on, hiccupping. "But if ye bite and consume one another, take heed that ye be not consumed of one another. Walk in the Spirit, and ye shall not fulfill the lust of the flesh. For flesh lusteth against the Spirit, and the Spirit lusteth against the flesh: And these are contrary to one another so that you cannot do the things that ye would." He burped. "Now the works of the flesh are manifest, which are these: Adultery, fornication, lasciviousness, hiccup, idolatry, witchcraft, hatred, variance, emulations, wrath, strife, seditions, heresies, belch, envying, murders, drunkenness," he held up his glass and smiled with slitted eyes, "revelings, and such like: of which, hic, shall not inherit the Kingdom of God."

Jim stared at him.

"I was married once," the man continued. "My wife made me learn that. I read the Bible from cover to cover. And I tried to live it.

Didn't drink. Turned away from beautiful women. Celebrated not. I was meek. Turned the other cheek. Let people walk all over me. I was bored to fucking death!" He slapped the table and widened his eyes, staring into Jim. "Wasn't any happier. So, I decided to listen to my body. I figured, if you can count on your body to let you know when you've got to shit, then you can count on it to let you know when to eat and drink and fuck and smoke and so on. And you know what? Turned out I wasn't any less miserable, but at least I wasn't bored all the time! And now that I'm old, I look back fondly on my days of drinking and whoring, more fondly than I do on days of being sober, chaste, and married."

The pizza came out and the waiter left before Jim could swallow his salad and ask for water. The salad had primed his hunger, and he was ravenous now for something more substantial than lettuce. He pulled off a slice of pizza and bit off a piece and swallowed nearly without chewing, before he realized he'd scalded the roof of his mouth and the top of his tongue. The volcanic cheese sat in his esophagus where, in a panic, Jim thought it would burn through his ribcage and fall back onto the plate. He reached for the nearest liquid, the beer, took a big draught straight from the pitcher and felt it splash over his cheeks and down his gullet and extinguish the inferno in his chest.

And that was it. Beer was in him. Might as well finish the pitcher. He could quit after that.

"Much better," said the old man.

The roof of Jim's mouth hung down in shreds and his uvula hung raw and swollen down the back of his throat, gagging him. He threw the pizza onto the table disgustedly and poured himself a pint and drained it. The old man cackled and coughed.

"So," Jim growled, "you're a higher authority than the word of God?"

"If God is the creator of all the universe, then all words are God's words, including mine. I didn't make myself. Nobody says that I

PART 2: EXTERNAL COMBUSTION

created the world. I did not create my impulses, nor my nature, nor my weaknesses."

"Are you saying we have no choice as to who we are, no no no free will?"

"Aye."

Jim was stunned. He felt the man was making the speech he himself should have been making, but in hearing it, he saw another side. We do choose our fates. Temptation gives us freedom. He suddenly felt more helpless than ever. *If God and Satan were talking to me, I wouldn't know which was which. You don't know when you're being deceived. We've got it all wrong.*

The quartet of girls exited the restaurant and paraded past, giggling and jiggling. *I can't help that I want to have sex with them, but I can control my effort.* Maybe the devil had been whispering in the ears of the men who wrote the Bible. Maybe that was why pleasure was wrong. Maybe fleshly pleasure and appetites are gifts from a benign creator, and an evil force had twisted it all around so that we go through life confused and unhappy, believing we are to subvert our desires. Maybe that's the choice. To see through the deception of those claiming to know what good is, and instead listening to your own soul. The girls went into the Balboa Saloon next door. Jim drank down the beer. He wanted to get drunk enough to talk to them.

"Hallelujah!" The old man threw up his arms and fell out of his chair. Jim looked at him and poured another beer before going over to help him up. The old man was on his back, wriggling to right himself like an upended cockroach. Jim bent to assist him. The hole in his neck looked perfectly natural, just another bodily orifice, but hot air pushed out of it, reeking of toxicity and decay. "I've read too much," the old man hissed nearly soundlessly through the hole, frisking the table for his kazoo. He made noises. He might have mentioned Nietzsche and Sartre and existentialism, or he might just have been gasping for air. His eyes were red and yellow. Jim lifted him into his chair like a bundle of kindling and he grabbed his kazoo. "Books mess with your mind," came the air out of the hole in his throat. "The laws of God are words in a book written by men!" The Ferris wheel in the Fun Zone started again, filling the air with hurdy-gurdy music. "Never read anything. Never listen to anybody, then your mind would be pure."

These words bounced around the walls of Jim's mind for a while before coming to a rest not far from his hypothalamus. "You want any of this pizza?" he said eventually.

"And ruin this buzz? No, thanks. You want a smoke?" He shook the end of a Pall Mall out and Jim regarded it a moment before putting it between his lips. He had an idea that smoking it would be breathing Earth. The old man leaned across the table and flicked a Zippo, and Jim puffed up the smoke. Jim remembered going to an AA meeting with his father at the Veterans' Hall. A girl there with a pierced nose (apparently the meetings were not limited to vets) told how she and her friends would not eat when they went out so they could get more buzzeder.

Jim downed the last of his pitcher and held it up over his head so that the guy at the counter could see him through the window. "And whatever he's having," Jim mouthed, pointing at the old-timer. Waiting for his next drink, Jim's fingers drummed and his legs bounced around. The old man kept babbling, and Jim had stopped hearing him. Fantasies of befriending the pretty girls wrestled with ideas for planning the job. He thought of calling Tink and quickly dismissed it. He thought of calling Adam for a second, before it hit him that Adam was gone. And this time it hit him like Tyson body shot.

Adam was gone? Back to Utah? Adam, who knows what a freak I am and still offers friendship? He'd left without saying goodbye or leaving Jim any way to find him. *Because I'm such a dick all the time*, Jim thought. *I've got to make it up to him. When I finish this job and get the money, I'll go out there to Utah. Shit.* Jim's shoulders slumped. *I'd be the last thing he'd want to see out there. Augh.* He shook his head. These were not the things to be thinking of with a big arms heist to plan. Where was that pitcher? He

PART 2: EXTERNAL COMBUSTION

wished the dude would hurry up. He took long sighing drags off the cigarette and then placed it butt up on the edge of the ashtray, thinking to hasten its demise, when the beer finally arrived. He poured himself a glass and pushed the wine in front of the old man, who snored gently, head slumped on chest.

Jim didn't want his beer much anymore, but he drank it because it would have been uncomely to leave it there, like he was some lightweight pussy. He forced down gulp after gulp. His swollen uvula hung down the back of his throat, and he gagged on it with each swallow of beer. He sat drinking and thinking, wondering if he should go wait in front of the house until the time was right to go in, or if he should go to the saloon and try to talk to some girls, but because his uvula was lolling around on the back of his tongue, he kept having to scrape air along his palate to get it out of his throat, making a ghacking noise each time. He tried another bite of the now-cold pizza, nearly swallowing his uvula along with it, before it snapped back like a bungee jumper. Cghack.

Another couple of pretty girls walked by, and Jim called out, "Hey, how ya doin'? Ghack. You guys want to drink some beer with me?" The girls looked at him and looked at each other saying "Oh my God" with their faces and kept on going. "Okay," called Jim. "I'll just go fuck myself." He laughed. That was more like it. He downed his beer purposely and immediately reloaded.

And downed and reloaded until the beer was gone and he had to make a decision. He drank the old guy's wine and stood up, more than a mite wobbly. *Fugh it.* He pulled out his money and dropped a twenty on the table. He put the four hundred-dollar bills in his sock and the other about fifty or so in his pocket. *Bitches didn't know I got hundreds on me, or they'd-a been all over that.* He had a plan. He'd spend the fifty in the saloon, and then he'd go to work.

He felt the first beginnings of having to piss. But he resisted going to the toilet, because once that started, there was no stopping it, every fifteen minutes he would have to piss, like clockwork. Better to hold it in and take one really long piss every hour. He walked down the sidewalk like a man walking in a canoe on a lake, cghacking every half minute, and the canoe tilted him right through the door of the Balboa Saloon. He crossed to the bar and inserted himself between two people on stools with their backs to each other, in different conversations. Mounted fish frozen in poses swam nowhere, everywhere on the walls. Were they plastic? Or had they once been living? "What'll it be?" asked the bartender.

"Uhm…" A chasm of uncertainty yawned before Jim. He had no idea. What *will* it be? It seemed to be asking so much. He had to think fast. He had to say something. "Jack and Coke," he said firmly, trying to make like it was what he wanted all along, and he put a twenty on the bar. He didn't even like Coke, but you couldn't stand there wavering in front of a bartender, indecisive, like some kind of amateur. Jim noticed flagrant distaste in the bartender's face before he turned away to make the drink.

Jim tried to imagine being a better person. How would that be done? *Let's see. Maybe if I'd have bathed with soap this morning. And if I wasn't dressed so shabbily. I'd be wearing a watch, probably. I'd donate money to church charities. Help little old ladies across the street—Oh my God! Is kindness a cliché? I should be working to become a doctor. I should be committed to vaccinating villagers in third-world countries. I should be working to wipe out malaria. No. Then the world would become overpopulated. The oceans wouldn't be able to handle it. The Earth either. But wait. Doesn't E= MC squared? So, it doesn't make any difference. Shit.*

The bartender brought his drink and Jim raised his glass and toasted everyone in the bar. "E equals M C squared," he announced and tipped the glass to his lips. For some reason, he thought he was doing a shot, though, and the Jack and Coke got wrapped around his uvula, and he ended up spitting most of it down the front of his shirt—or well, let's be accurate, the front of William Coyte's shirt.

PART 2: EXTERNAL COMBUSTION

"Gimme cghack another one," he said. The bartender unfolded his big hairy arms and twisted one end of his mustache, regarding Jim with a cold eye before taking a five from Jim's pile of change on the bar. When his new Jack and Coke came, Jim was careful to cghack before taking a manageable sip, and this time the whiskey stayed on his tongue long enough that he struggled to keep his face in check. He shivered and turned to survey the room. He was noticed by no one, and he turned back around with his elbows on the sticky bar and a foot on the brass rail, feeling a little like a cowboy as he studied the soda gun. A TV over the bar was showing a shootout. It looked like the O.K. Corral. On another TV, another shootout was taking place; bank robbers in bullet proof vests fired assault rifles at police. Jim wasn't sure if it was a movie or the news. A third TV showed ballplayers standing at attention for the Star-Spangled Banner, the gunfire mixed with the melody.

After the bombs bursting in air, but before the land of the free, a guy down the bar called to the bartender, "Baseball's fucking boring. Change the channel."

The bartender took the remote and began flipping through the channels. "Say when," he said.

There went John Wayne storming the beach, Jimmy Cagney with tommy guns blazing, Butch and Sundance charging the Bolivian army, Dirty Harry making his day, bullets bouncing off Superman's chest, Rambo mowing down scores of Vietnamese, bi-planes strafing King Kong, the Death Star blowing planets to pieces—Where were the beer commercials? Why couldn't life be like a beer commercial? That was what Jim truly wanted, from the bottom of his soul, and wasn't that the same as wanting world peace, really? He wanted to be dancing between two hotties in bikinis. Click. The TV shut off. "There isn't anything but garbage on," said the bartender. A disk of white light stared out accusingly from the otherwise dark screen. "It's all crap," said a woman near Jim. She wore spinsterish, square-framed glasses atop a smart, sharp nose and high cheekbones. A raven had been walking around the corners of her eyes croaking, "Nevermore," but the only trace of it now was its footprints, magnified slightly by the lenses of her glasses.

"They pipe into family rooms all across the country make-believe people who are all good-looking and witty and whose lives have plots and themes which by comparison our own lives are rendered meaningless," said a guy with a ponytail and an intellectual growth of hair on his chin.

Gesturing with an unlit cigarette, he went on, "I have a theory that television destroyed true love. Before television, you lived in a town and you went to school and there were just a handful of boys or girls to whom you were attracted. And other than the thrill of being attracted to this person, there wasn't a lot to do except maybe go for a soda at the drug store and neck in the back seat of a Ford or something. And so, you did whatever job you knew, and you got married and raised sturdy families and stayed together 'til you were dead.

"But now, we all sit there while this endless parade of impossibly good-looking, interesting characters with nice apartments strolls through our homes, and our expectations are unrealistically raised, and suddenly hubby Hank's beer gut ain't looking so good, and you start wondering what else is out there. Thus, the seeds of the break-up of the traditional nuclear family are sown. That's why no one our age is getting married. Why settle for one wholesome, reliable girl when there are bevies of *Baywatch* babes to pursue?"

Jim wondered if TV split his parents up, but flames and an acrid stench infiltrated this question. After his mother's aunt had died, his mom had wanted to use her inheritance to get new wall-to-wall shag carpeting for the family room. Jim's father was opposed. He thought day-to-day expenses were tight enough, and with a kid spilling juice and tracking mud all the time, carpet wasn't practical. But Jim's mom decided it was *her* inheritance, and she was going to do with it what

PART 2: EXTERNAL COMBUSTION

she thought best. It wasn't as if she were spending it on herself. She was investing in the value of the home. Or so Jim had pieced together from fragments of speech he had overheard.

He remembered plainly the day the carpet had been installed, and the way his mother had busied herself preparing a dinner for his father, complete with candlelight. She was boiling hotdogs to feed Jim, so she could put him to bed. The houselights were dimmed and mom rushed around in breathless anxiety as the hour of her husband's arrival loomed closer. Jim kneeled on a seat at the table staring into the flame.

He could see it clearly even now. Streaks of light, individual and specific, emanated from the fire, and little Jim could follow the beams of light straight from their source right to the point where they entered his eyeball. If he squinted a certain way, he could push the beams back into the candle. He padded over to the table in his footed pajamas and climbed onto a chair studying the aura around the flame. He was tempted to pass his hand through it, but he knew fire could burn, so he took what passed for a formal napkin on his father's budget in those days, a folded paper towel, and he passed it through the glowing halo around the flame, through the rippling light, sending a thin line of black smoke undulating to the ceiling. Hypnotic. He did it again, more slowly. The flame waved and bent as if trained to follow his command, as if he were some wizard with elements at his whim, like Mickey commanding the stars and comets. The flame snaked up the side of the paper towel. Jim tried to blow it out and it threatened to slither up his wrist. The spell broke; his powers deserted him, and he threw the burning paper to the floor, where in a widening circle, the flame burned the new carpet, leaving a bubbling blackness. In horror and fear Jim watched in paralyzed silence until his mom, apparently smelling the burning of polyester and Dacron came ohmygodohmygodomgod with a pot of boiling hot dog water and doused the fire, the sweaty weenies arranged in the cancerous hole with all the aplomb of two turds on the floor.

Steam rose to Jim's face where tears rolled and fell to the scarred carpet. "God damn it," seethed his mother. He'd never heard her say that before. She had always counseled Jim not to take the Lord's name in vain, like Daddy did, because the Lord would punish you. They heard the door being undeadbolted. "Jimmy, go to your room now. Now. Don't come out until I say it's okay," she said with an urgency that frightened him.

Jim hid under the bed and cringed against the wall as the house shook with bangs and slams and shouting. "YOU DON'T LISTEN TO A GOD DAMN WORD I TELL YOU!" his father roared. "No, James, don't. Please don't do this," he heard his mother's sobbing pleas. After a while he heard the front door open and shut and the car started up and drove away.

It was quiet a long time before he slid out from under the bed and tiptoed to the door where he pressed his ear. Hearing nothing was as scary as hearing their shouting. The door whined as he pulled it open. He crept along the hall past a fist-sized hole in the drywall. The den door was splintered and hanging awkwardly from one hinge. Who would be out there? He prayed that it would be his mother. He peeked around the corner where his father sat smoking. "Come here, son."

Jim did as he was told, stopping about five feet in front of his father. His father squinted in the smoke. "What happened?"

"I don't know."

"How did the carpet get burned?"

"I had a paper towel by the fire and it caught on fire and I dropped it."

"Were you playing with fire?"

Jim nodded.

"You could have burned the whole house down." Flecks of ash from his cigarette fell to the upholstery of the Lay-Z-Boy and to the carpet. "Don't you know better? Haven't I told you not to play with fire?"

PART 2: EXTERNAL COMBUSTION

Jim couldn't recall that he had, but he nodded again.

"I'm going to have to punish you, you know." He took off his shoe and stood up. "Come here." Jim took a step forward, and his father took him by the arm and struck him three swift, stinging blows to his buttocks. "Now go back to your room and think about doing what I tell you."

Hyperventilating, Jim crossed the room and stopped, afraid to speak, but needing to know. "Where's Mommy?"

"She's gone. Now do what I tell you."

"You got a light?" The guy with the ponytail was looking at Jim.

"Fuck off ghack," Jim said and turned his back to him and drained his drink. "Ghack. Gimme another Jack and Coke," he said to the bartender, "no Coke."

"What?" the bartender asked, irritated.

Jim squeezed the empty tumbler in his fist, thought of firing it through the mirror behind the bar. He thought of the money in his pocket. Thought of some vigilante group of bar-going regulars holding him until the cops arrived. He dumped back a mouthful of ice and ground it between his teeth before putting the glass down on its coaster. "Nothing. I'm sorry. I don't know what's wrong with me. I'm going to leave now. Ghack." He left over ten dollars in change on the bar and walked in a canoe out the door and onto the sidewalk. He tried asking himself what he wanted. The beer commercials were all fake. What was the next best thing? To be left in peace. To wake up when you feel like it. He imagined a cabin in the woods, plenty of game around, clean water, clean air. Or a cave in the desert. He could eat roast horny toad and kangaroo rats and elf owl eggs. And peyote. And Jimson weed. No. He would do the job and leave for Utah. It was becoming more and more attractive and foreseeable. He would become Mormon and prosper and live happily ever after.

But first the guns. He made his way to the house. The balcony extended almost over the edge of the sidewalk. Below it was a patio

229

where a three-legged Weber grill kept company with a pair of plastic chairs. The patio was separated from the sidewalk by a brick planter sprouting yucca blades and littered with plastic cups and cigarette butts. He pushed through the creaking iron gate and padded along a narrow walkway between a wall and the duplex with a strange sense of déjà vu—no, not déjà vu; he'd been there before, at a party maybe a year earlier, he'd sucked whippets of nitrous oxide, right where he stood now; the walls throbbed around him, his heart floated in his head before it wore off.

A light flickered in a window upstairs, someone watching television in the dark. Jim went back to the car. A parking ticket had been placed under the windshield wiper. The seats were dewy with condensation from the coastal night air. He found fast food napkins on the floor and wiped the seat before starting the car and pressed a button to close the roof. The motor whined, but the roof wouldn't close. He turned the car off, let his skull fall back onto the headrest, and studied the coronas of what stars showed through the light fog, gagging on his uvula, wondering if it wouldn't suffocate him in his sleep—

He awoke to the white sky, damp clothes, a runny nose and an ache in his neck that was slightly relieved by tilting his head to one side. He judged it to be shortly after seven in the morning and a meter maid was writing another ticket.

"Good morning," sniffled Jim, head tilted, the world not all that more askew than usual from that angle.

"You're parked in a red zone."

"I already got a ticket for that."

"That was for yesterday. This," he placed another envelope under the wiper, "is for today. And it's street-sweeping day, but if you move your car right now, I won't give you that one."

"That's okay." He sniffled. "Go ahead and write it, but think about what you do for a living. Are you making the world a better place or a

PART 2: EXTERNAL COMBUSTION

worse place, ghack?"

The meter maid didn't respond, but began writing again in his ticket book. Jim climbed out of the car and limped to a liquor store/bait shop on the corner where he bought from a bearded deadhead clerk in a tie-dyed shirt a gallon of water, a packet of vitamins, a bottle of aspirin, some beef jerky, Nyquil, and a couple of Rice Krispie bars. From the stands of free publications in front of the store he selected a Guide to Motels of the Southwest. The clerk tilted his head so that his eyes were on the same plane as Jim's and rang him up. Jim returned to his car as the meter maid was driving up the street, and had Jim's fingers not been occupied in tearing open the vitamin packet with his teeth, he might have saluted the fiend with the long one in the middle. He tossed the bag with his purchases onto the passenger seat and climbed into the car. As he unscrewed the bottle of water and winced down the vitamins one at a time, he thought he should try to move the car to where he could keep an eye on the house, but first he needed something to sop up the acid in his stomach. He then realized the Krispie treats were going to scrape the shit out of his uvula—the jerky, too. He thought of going back for some bananas or baby food or something. Or maybe a fifth of something or at least a can of beer in a little paper bag so he could be hard-boiled. But no, it was time to quit fucking around. He had to find a parking spot where he could surveil the duplex where the guns were. He alternated Krispie bites with sips of Nyquil, thinking a cup of coffee would've been good, too.

When he'd finished his breakfast, he turned the key and pumped the gas, and the engine in the old car sputtered reluctantly to life. He backed her up, turning the wheel until he'd kissed the bumper of the car behind him, then turned the other way going forward until he'd kissed the front car, trying to wriggle out of the spot he'd been left in, when he heard something snap, and the wheel became hard to turn as if a power steering hose had burst. It became an arm wrestling match against the cars and the curb and perhaps the devil himself, or some lesser demon, and his grip was less than usual with the wound on his thumb and his wrist sending bolts of pain through him, but he succeeded in working the car out into the street. He rolled up Balboa and parked in front of a donut shop near the liquor store. He would buy some flowers or something to make a phony delivery at the house to find out if anyone was home. If no one answered, he could try busting in. Get up on that balcony and see if the sliding glass door was locked.

He waited in line behind a guy with a bucket of tackle buying a six-pack of Coors and package of squid from the deadhead. Jim stared at into the deadhead's T-shirt. What was up with tie-dye? Had they, through some chemical engineering breakthrough, reached a new level of consciousness in which staring into the swirl of colors revealed miraculous visions? The deadhead again tilted his head like Jim's, approximating the same plane of vision. "You know anywhere nearby where I can buy some flowers?" Jim asked.

"I don't know about flowers, but I know where you can score some weed."

"Oh, yeah?" went Jim's eyebrows. "How much?"

"You can get an eighth of Montebello Dirt weed that tastes like Mexico City smog for twenty—it's mellow, but it's a little bit of a downer; or you can get a gram bag of Humboldt Skunk that'll leave you feeling good and high for twenty-five."

"Yeah, dude. Set me up with the Skunk," said Jim's mouth. "And how about a good bottle of scotch, like what's good, like that Glenfiddich or something." Jim had to break another hundred. The deadhead gave him his change and the little gram bag of green weed, and Jim put it in his sock while the clerk put the scotch in a brown bag.

"You got a gift box or something? And a little card?"

At the car, Jim put the boxed scotch and a newspaper on the passenger's seat and again climbed into the convertible. Not far down Balboa, he found a parking spot along the median with an excellent vantage point for casing the house. He wrestled with parallel parking

PART 2: EXTERNAL COMBUSTION

and shut off the engine. All seemed still. He flipped through his Guide to Motels of the Southwest, looking for something in Utah that advertised a good weekly rate. Nothing. He read the sports page. The Phillies had beaten a sorry-ass Dodger team. He read the funnies. *Calvin and Hobbes* was the best. He worked on a crossword, did the Jumble, read This Date in History. By 9:15, he had read every word of the paper and still not detected any signs of occupation at the house. He took the box of scotch and headed for the front door. He wished he had an invoice or a clipboard or something.

He rang the bell. No answer. He knocked on the door. He waited a while and tried the knob. Locked. He turned away to circle the house when the door opened, and a mop of wet hair squinted out, attached to a bare torso, a tanned arm clutching a towel around the dude's waist.

"I have a delivery for this address. It's a bottle of scotch ghack."

"We didn't order any scotch," the guy said groggily and began to shut the door.

"It was sent as a gift. You don't have to pay anything. You just have to take it."

"Okay, man. Thanks." He took the bottle and was about to shut the door.

"You'll make sure he gets it? It's for Derb. What time will he be home? I work for Hi-Time Wine Cellars."

"He went to work. He might be back around five."

"You think you might be able to give it to him? Make sure he gets it? I don't want to get in trouble if he doesn't get it."

"Yeah, man. I gotta go to work. I won't be home until way later, man, but I can just leave it on the table for him."

"Is anyone here who can give it to him?"

"Not 'til tonight. I'm running late. Why don't you come back later?" He gave Jim the scotch back.

Bingo. You bet I will. "Okay," said Jim.

233

Ten minutes later the guy came out, hopped on a scooter, and left. Jim uncapped the scotch and took a swig. *That guy's going to know it was me*, thought Jim. *Whatever*. He took another swig and put the bottle under the seat and got out of the car and crossed the street. He strolled past the house and spotted a woman through the sliding glass doors of the downstairs half of the duplex. She was reading a magazine. Ever so stealthily, Jim wheeled the barbecue next to the wood planter to a spot just below the overhang of the balcony—if not out of earshot, at least of out eyeshot of the woman on the couch. He stepped, grimacing, onto the planter, reached his hands up to the edge of the balcony, and using the barbecue for a foothold, hoisted himself up onto the balcony as different pains jostled for primacy. He swung his leg over the rail and kicked the lid of a hibachi, but he guessed a lot of banging around wouldn't arouse the suspicion of a woman living below three young bachelors. The door was locked. Jim pressed his palms to the smudged glass, pushing upward, and easily lifted the door from its track. He stepped into the house, froze, and stepped back out. He didn't think anyone would call the police to report a bunch of illegally owned guns missing, but he wiped his prints from the glass with his shirt. William Coyte's shirt. No, it wouldn't be the police he should worry about, but maybe more personal forms of justice. *I'll have to watch my back now*, he thought. *Maybe not in Utah, though.*

Flies buzzed over the remains of a card game littering a table. A First Cavalry banner hung on the otherwise bare walls. He went quickly through the place and discovered the guns in a closet in a back bedroom with nothing more than a mattress and some blankets on the floor, and scattered issues of *Soldier of Fortune*. The guns were dark metal, cold to the touch. Jim was amazed at their number and variety. He spread a blanket out on the floor and placed the guns in the middle. A few were pistols of various caliber, but there were about fifteen different machine guns, Uzis, AK-47's, and M-16's that he recognized from movies, and some he didn't recognize at all.

PART 2: EXTERNAL COMBUSTION

Houseflies buzzed his head. Horseflies buzzed his head. Flying elephants dive-bombed his head as the enormity of what he had gotten himself into dawned on him. *I seen a house fly. I seen a horse fly. I done seen 'bout everything when I see.... This is insane.* He wondered how many years he would get if he were arrested with so many guns. He wondered what horrific crimes would be committed with these very guns. Gangbangers shooting at each other? Drug dealers protecting their shipments? *What if some church-going kid gets caught in the crossfire of guns I'm supplying?* There was no way of knowing. *Maybe I'll be taking them somewhere where they'll be less likely to kill. If I don't move them, someone else will. And shit;iIs a thousand dollars enough money? There's gotta be five thousand dollars' worth of guns here, at least.* He would ask for more. And if they wanted the fucking guns, they had better pay. *What am I getting into? How do I know they'll pay me at all?* "Fuck this," he said aloud. He'd give them the car and the money back. He went to the door, turned the knob, stopped. *Just get the money and go to Utah.* He went back to the room, threw the corners of the blanket together and flung the bundle over his shoulder like some sick Santa's sack, his aching wrist straining against the weight. Down the stairs he went, gun muzzles bristling from the blanket. The woman downstairs was watering her plants.

He tried to go quickly and quietly past her.

"You guys were pretty noisy again last night," she said.

"Uh, sorry about that." He wondered if he should offer her a gun. "No one's going to be home all day. It should be nice and quiet." He turned away.

"I don't sleep during the day."

"You should," he called over his shoulder.

He crossed the street, fiddling in his pocket for his keys, when a corner of the blanket slipped from his grip, spilling assault rifles onto the middle of Balboa Boulevard. He winced at the clatter and wondered for the first time if any of the guns were loaded. As he squatted to rearrange the bundle, a shiny, winged angel, nude, atop the gleaming grill of a Rolls, floated to a stop in front of Jim. A horn blew. Gabriel, maybe. Through the windshield an old woman motioned him to hurry up.

"Sorry," Jim mouthed, and scrambled to repack.

When he got to the Chrysler, he opened the trunk and laid in the guns. He drove back up the peninsula without any idea where to go. He didn't think he should go to Pete and Adam's. Better to go somewhere he could think things through without being found. *Maybe I ought to take the car to Earl Scheib. Doctor the license plate and disappear. Holy shit! How much could all those guns be worth?* He was going to have to renegotiate.

Preoccupied as he was, he didn't notice the rollerblader come shooting out into the crosswalk, and Jim nearly ran him down. "Asshole," the rollerblader called, and thumped the trunk of the Chrysler, which popped open.

Jim threw the car into park and jumped out. "What the fuck, motherfucker!" He went around back and slammed the trunk, but it popped open again. "You're the dumbass flying out into the street without looking."

The blader circled back. "It's a crosswalk, asshole."

"Yeah, it ain't a force field, you dumbshit. If a rollerblading faggot plays chicken with a moving vehicle, rollerblading faggot loses, see. It ain't the laws of the road we're talking about; it's the laws of physics." Jim slammed the trunk again with vicious force, and again it popped open.

The blader rolled over and got in Jim's face. "You want some, dick?"

"Do I want some dick? See, I knew you were some kind of queer." The voices in Jim competed for control. *Just get in car and leave*, said one, but another, the one that came out of his mouth, said, "You know what, shithead? Lemme explain to you again the laws of physics. See

PART 2: EXTERNAL COMBUSTION

you're on rollerblades *and* you're wearing that faggoty-ass spandex, and so when you try to hit me, you won't be able to get any leverage, and you're just going to flail around while I'm landing solid blows to your shit head, and when you go down and scramble to get up, you're going to have your wheels slipping out from under you while I'm kicking your head in—"

Bweep Bweep Seven Mary Eight. A motorcycle cop flashed his lights and pulled up. *Oh, shit*, Jim thought, *I've got that weed in my sock. And an open bottle of scotch under the seat. Oh, yeah, and a fucking terrorist arsenal. Wow. I'm incredibly stupid. And screwed.* He pushed down gently on the trunk, and it stayed closed.

The cop got off his bike. "Officer, I'm glad you're here," Jim said wondering what would happen if the cop asked him for license and registration. *I am a freaking cop magnet.*

"What seems to be the problem here?"

"This guy blew through the crosswalk," the rollerblader reported.

"No, sir. He shot out into the street and punched my car as I was driving by." Cold sweat scurried down from his armpit like a cockroach. "My trunk popped open and I had to get out and shut it, and now he's accosting me and on the verge of assaulting me, as if I were to blame for his poor judgment cghack." Jim could tell by the way the officer's nostrils flared as he studied the rollerblader that the cop found the blader's spandex as distasteful, unmanly, and indicative of a larger cultural problem, as Jim did. Whoa—waitasec—Jim knew this face. The nameplate confirmed it. It was Officer Hand from under the bridge. Jim sniffled, and the cop turned his attention to Jim, eyes narrowing. Slowly, he looked from Jim to the car, and Jim noticed how dirty it was, and Hand seemed to be having a difficult time trying to decide who was the bigger asshole here, and he ordered them both to sit on the curb.

Jim thought about trying to plant the weed in his sock on the blader. He didn't want to waste it if he didn't have to, though, and

237

decided he'd only do it as a last resort. He hung his head, hoping Hand wouldn't remember his face. *At least if I go to jail, all my decisions will be made for me now. Prison won't be that much different. Except that I'll have even less freedom than I have now.* This thought chilled him, and he felt a sudden condensation on his eyeballs when, "Aw, shit," said Officer Hand. He had stepped in a wad of gum. As he scuffed the heel of his boot on the asphalt, he turned his face and the palm of one hand to the sky as if questioning the heavens as to the reason for gum when a miraculous thing happened: A seagull, a lost descendant, perhaps, of the flock that saved the Mormons from the locusts at the Great Salt Lake, shat, and the prevailing wind currents, and the seagull's direction and velocity, and the pull of gravity, all came together so that a white and green glob of digested fish heads and French fries plopped into Hand's open hand. "Goddamnit!" he ejaculated. "I hate working the beach." He shook his hand, trying to fling off the guano.

"Officer," said Jim, pointing at the blader, "he spit out the gum you just stepped in."

"That's a lie."

"No, it isn't. I saw him."

Hand seemed to be looking around for a place to wipe his hand. His eyes settled on the blader's spandex a moment before he said, "Both of you get out of here. If I see either one of you again today, I'll figure out a way to bring you in. Now beat it."

Jim walked as nonchalantly as possible back to the car, got in, and drove up Newport Boulevard. His mouth had dried up with the cop's appearance, and his lips were like the scales of a molting cottonmouth. He was too nervous to even risk reaching for his bottle of water to uncap and drink while driving. He scanned the boulevard for a driveway to pull into and spotted The Grant Boys. A little cartoon boy on the sign had a hay straw in his mouth, a hat with a bullet hole in it, and arms full of arms—guns, that is—and camping gear. Jim pulled into the parking lot. The building had the look of an Old West storefront, with

PART 2: EXTERNAL COMBUSTION

wooden sidewalks out front. He gulped down half a gallon of water and went inside where he found glass cases full of pistols and ammo, and racks of rifles and shotguns on the walls. Men, women, and children busied the salesclerks and Jim edged between them to get a look at the little white price tags tied with strings to the guns. Many of the prices were in the thousands. *I might have more than ten thousand dollars' worth of guns,* Jim thought. A rattlesnake flicked its forked tongue from a flag warning "Don't Tread on Me," above a bumper sticker that asked "Without the Right to Bear Arms, How Will We Protect Ourselves?" Jim overheard an old man wearing a tank top emblazoned with "The Right to Bare Arms" ask about a gun for his grandson.

"What kind of gun?" asked the salesman.

"Just to shoot cans," he said.

They looked at Jim, and mumbled in unison the punch line, Jim guessed, to an old joke, "Afri-CANS, Mexi-CANS, Puerto Ri-CANS..." They stopped laughing when they saw that Jim didn't.

"You sell those snake flags?" Jim asked. "I want one."

The salesman turned to a shelf and brought a folded yellow flag to the counter while Jim went up an aisle filling his arms with random boxes of ammo. He wasn't sure what kind to get, but he didn't think he ought to be asking too many questions about Uzis and AK-47's, lest the salesman call the FBI to report a humorless, non-white-supremacist inquiring about machine gun ammo. He hoped if he bought enough varieties of ammo, he might have a few matches to the guns, if the time came that he needed them for anything. "Great plan," he muttered. "If you need them?!" Jim laid the boxes on the counter and the clerk eyed him a moment before he rang them up.

With bags of boxes of bullets slung through each fist and the "Don't Tread on Me" flag draped over his shoulder, Jim crossed the parking lot and dropped the bullets onto the front seat of the car and laid the flag over them before strolling the street in search of a pay phone. A few doors down, he came to a restaurant called El Matador. The

CAR TROUBLE

Killer. Beneath piñatas, past serape-festooned booths, he folded open the door of an old phone booth, stepped in, and closed it. He fished the phone number out of his pocket, breathless for a heartbeat that it wouldn't be there. His finger hovered a long time before the buttons until he finally dialed the number.

Ben answered.

"I got 'em," said Jim.

"Already?"

Jim didn't say anything. He heard muffled exclamations, then, "Where are you?"

"Not so fast," said Jim. He felt like an actor in a B-noir potboiler. His stomach knew better, though. It had forgone the butterflies and gone straight to Chuck-Yeager-piloted stunt planes. "I want more money."

"We had a deal."

"It's not enough."

"You're getting the car."

"The car's a piece of shit. It ain't gonna last six weeks. I should be getting a fucking Porsche for all these guns. I want—" he didn't know how much to say, but said,

"two thousand. More. On top of what we've already agreed to. That'd still be less than half of what they're worth. Shit, I bet those machine guns are worth a thousand bucks each, at least. Some of the pistols are probably worth that much. I should be asking for five or ten or more."

An awkward silence, like a fizzling phone call to a girl who didn't want to date you, fell over the conversation. Finally, Ben said, "Well, you're both smarter and dumber than I thought."

"You've got 'til dark tonight to decide. I'll call back. And don't try any shit. I'll be ready for that Kenny asshole. I bought a few magazines, you know what I mean? Go ahead and send that big fucker and see what happens. I've got nothing to lose." So, liberating, nothing to lose.

PART 2: EXTERNAL COMBUSTION

"You don't know who you're dealing with," said Ben. "I don't really even know. Mexican Mafia, Colombian drug lords, I think it's some fucking Golden Triangle syndicate, to tell you the fucking truth." Ben's voice had changed entirely. His suaveness, even his accent seemed to have gone. "Now you're putting me on the spot."

"Then I guess you better come up with some more money." Jim hung up. He couldn't believe the words that had come out of his mouth. Nervous adrenaline. A slight giddiness. He went into the bathroom and stared into the eyes of the person in the mirror, disgusted. He hated everything he had ever said or done. A joyous, manic, rage filled him and Wham! He head-butted himself in the mirror. A red spider web draped itself over his faces. He peered into the split skin in his forehead. He pulled the cut open with his fingertips, could see the white of skull there, and the giddiness increased. It was the happiest he could remember feeling in a long time. The Happiest Place on Earth was the shitter at El Matador, the killer. He was relieved. A great weight had been lifted; he would forever forth abandon all pretense of sanity and society. No more would civilized standards of right and wrong weigh in his decision-making. He would do whatever was in his heart.

He walked out of the bathroom and sat in a booth under a glittering sombrero, sat down, and held a napkin to his forehead. Applied pressure. On the wall, within a dirty frame, under smudged glass, a drawing of the temples of Tenochtitlan rose in geometric splendor from the middle of the great lake in a valley ringed by volcanoes. Figures thronged the plaza; a priest outstretched his arms from atop the pyramid, about to tear out some poor bastard's heart. Whoa. It spoke volumes. It was as big in its world as Manhattan, D.C., or Christendom. Wiped out by guns. Guns, wheels, armor, horses, and microbes. Guns. *Those people were as fervent in their religious beliefs as Aztecs as Americans are in theirs*, thought Jim. The waitress came.

"Sir, your head!"

Guns rule. Guns decide right and wrong. "Tequila," he said, without taking his eyes off the picture.

"You're bleeding! I don't think I can serve you," she said.

He looked at her. "I was in an accident," he said. "It's not as bad as it looks. I'm going down to Hoag to have it looked it, but you know how hospitals are. It might take hours." He put a couple of twenties on the table. "Hospitals make me nervous. Can I get a Cuervo, please?"

The waitress brought his tequila. He shot it and got up to look at the other framed pictures at each booth. Slaves hauled the multi-ton head of some God or emperor up an earthen ramp to the top of a pyramid under construction. *That's what we do*, Jim thought. In another frame, an observatory, judging from its dome, crumbled in the jungle. Jim stared at it a long time, holding the napkin to his head.

"Anything else, sir?"

Nightfall was hours off still. "Another tequila. And some fish tacos? I haven't eaten all day. And a bottle of, I don't know, Corona, I guess."

"I'm sorry, sir. Your face is covered in blood. I think you should go now."

He walked down the street to the Goat Hill Tavern, but the bartender, who seemed to believe that only the coolest people in the world got hired to work the bar at the Goat Hill Tavern, would not serve him, so he went next door to into the dimly lit Helm. A grizzled old salt with faded forearm tattoos of hula girls poured his drink without a word. Jim sat at the bar, pressing napkins against his forehead, and watched the TV, seeing nothing but the skyline of Tenochtitlan. When he walked out again, dusk was coming down.

He stepped to a phone booth on the sidewalk and dialed the number. Ben answered on the first ring.

"Listen, I can get you more money, if you're willing to do an extra job."

Clearly some bend had been gone around. "Make it another twenty-five hundred, up front, and I'll deliver all the guns. Then we can talk

PART 2: EXTERNAL COMBUSTION

about other jobs."

"You know the restaurant El Ranchito?" Ben asked.

"Yeah."

"I'll meet you there in one hour."

Jim felt another tough-guy-running-the-show "Not so fast," ready to blurt itself out, but caution had dissipated like so much gun smoke. Where didn't matter to him. "O.K. Corral," he said

"What?"

"Okay. I'll be there."

He wanted to get there first, and he wanted to be ready. Trepidation visited him until he saw that the convertible was still in the parking lot of Grant Boys, untowed, the ammo still sitting on the front seat. He drove down Newport Boulevard and parked at a bank where he could see the entrance of El Ranchito. A steady flow of customers entered and exited a nearby liquor store, intent on their purchases, oblivious to him. He opened the trunk and selected a small pistol, then returned to the front seat. He held the gun in his lap in fear of shooting his dick off. The gun was cold and heavy in his hand. How to figure out if it was loaded or not? It had a cock. He cocked it and uncocked it. He pushed on what he thought might be called the chamber, and it opened and he spun it slowly, discerning under the streetlight that it was not loaded. A little lever on its side was the safety. He flipped it back and forth, and pulled the trigger and felt that it was locked. Then he opened the boxes of bullets one after another, trying to find the kind that fit. A box that said .38 caliber did the trick. He loaded it and again pulled on the trigger with his nuts in his throat until he felt that the safety was on. He tried putting the gun in his pocket; it didn't fit, so he put it down the back of his pants, the barrel like ice running down his crack. *Don't sit at the bar, dumbass*, he whispered, and crossed the street and went in. It was busy, but not crowded. He found a corner near a window where he could sit with his back to the wall, see the whole restaurant before him, and the car parked across the street.

The place was covered in what looked to Jim like bathroom tile. Streamers with beer logos hung from the ceilings where speakers blared Mexican polka music. A coven of nubile young women whooped it up, celebrating with tequila shots their own beauty and its power to make men do their bidding. Jim's mind, though, kept turning over his situation. Would Ben come alone? Or would he bring that thug, Kenny? Or some other thugs? Would they jump him in the parking lot? Not until they knew where the guns were. Would they kidnap him, torture him, to find out? No. That was preposterous. Wasn't it?

He ordered coffee from a guy who called him Señor. He was on his second cup when a big Pacific-Islander-looking dude came in and stood at the bar. Coffee drummed through Jim's fingers and toes, the gun pressed uncomfortably against his spine. In a minute Ben came in wearing a white cowboy hat and a Hawaiian shirt that rivaled Jim's in loudness. He sat down and slid an envelope across the table. "There's a thousand."

"I said twenty-five."

"You'll get that, and more," Jim noticed a trace of weary regret in Ben's formerly suave mien, "if you take them to Las Vegas."

"How much more?"

"Three, total."

Jim tried to disguise his enthusiasm. Three thousand dollars! That would set him up with food and rent in Utah for at least a couple of months while he looked for a job and a pretty Mormon wife to save his life and soul, and Vegas was on the way. He would never drink, smoke, or curse again, and good things would happen for him because of the purity of his heart and his escape from the sinful temptations of California. Wow. If he found work quickly, he'd have enough left over for a decent down payment on a reliable car. Shit, maybe there was a ranch or something out there where he could work and not even ever have to get another fu-lipping car. If he could just make it to the vernal mountainsides of Utah with a few grand in his pocket—

PART 2: EXTERNAL COMBUSTION

"How do I get them there?"

"That's up to you. If you want the job, you'll figure it out. Use the car."

"It's about fifty-fifty that thing'll make it to Vegas."

Ben leaned forward. "Listen—I'm telling you so you don't do anything stupid—I don't want to be mixed up in anything stupid. You don't have a lot of choice in this. At this point, you have to do it. Just drive the speed limit and get there with the cargo, and you're home free with three thousand dollars to get a suite and some hookers in Vegas or whatever the fuck you want to do, but if you fuck it up you're dead. Literally dead. Do I make myself clear?"

Dead. Jim felt himself flinch and it angered him. "When do I go?"

"Go tonight. You know how to get there, right? When you cross the state line, you call me, and I'll tell you what to do. You'll meet a bloke named Ollie. He'll pay you, and then it will be all over." All over.

"Why me? Why not Kenny or someone?"

"Kenny's a two-time loser. He's not particularly bright." Ben leaned back. "You're the one who can get it done. You da man." Ben smiled without a hint of humor. He took a cigarette from a pack in his breast pocket. "Kenny won't be too far behind, though, just in case."

"In case what?"

Ben lit the cigarette and let the question linger in the air with the smoke. Jim wished there were some friend at the table he could turn to and laugh about how crazy this all was, some friend who would laugh along with him, and then would say, "but seriously," and talk him out of what he was about to do. But there was no one. Had he burned them all? "Give me a minute. I'll be right back."

He pushed through a door marked HOMBRES. Among flecks of dry blood, the scarlet mark on his forehead glared at him from the mirrors, and he fought the urge to put his head through the white tile above the urinal. How long was it to Vegas? Five hours? In five hours, he could have three grand in his pocket and be on his way to starting a new life in some little Utah town that time forgot, in some little cabin far off the road, with a pretty little Mormon wife or two. He zipped up, walked out of the baño, and sat across from Ben again. Jim took the envelope and put it in his breast pocket, resisting the urge to tell Ben that if things didn't work out, if they tried to screw him in any way, that *he*, Jim, would come after Ben personally. Jim felt a wave of unstoppableness. "So, I just drive out to Vegas and call you?"

"Call me at Stateline. It's that simple."

"Awright." Jim stood and put out his hand.

Ben shook it smirking. "Good luck."

Jim stepped out the door and scanned the world in front of him, waiting for the attack. Nothing. He shrugged. Fate would be his master. He limped across the street with the idea that they would jump him, take the car and the guns and the money, and leave him lying bloody on the asphalt. He got to the car door, and as he pulled out the keys, the vulnerability of his back encompassed him and he spun quickly, hand on the gun in his pants. No one. Maybe they were as afraid of him as he was of them, he thought, amazed. Maybe they thought that he *was* the man for the job. He put the pistol in the glove box.

Or maybe they were just waiting until he'd gotten across the state line to take him out.

He gassed up, topped off the radiator, checked the oil, and put air in the tires. When he got in the car and started it up, the gas gauge stayed at E. *Swell. How will I know when I'm running out of gas?* He considered renting a car, but decided he would need this jalopy once he got to Utah. Until he had enough scratch for something better, he would just see how far the old Chrysler would take him. He readied himself for a nice leisurely drive under the stars through the vast lonely desert, but the 91 was bumper-to-bumper all the way out to the Fifteen, and after an hour he'd made no more than twenty miles and his whole body ached and his joints felt locked. When he reached Cajon Pass, a road crew was doing shoulder work, and a lane was closed, bottlenecking

PART 2: EXTERNAL COMBUSTION

traffic. The radio started coming in mostly static and satanic voices. Jim turned it off and listened to the drone of combustion all around, fumes rattling his lungs, and the voices in his head deliberating the outcome of his trip.

The highway through the vast lonely desert was actually miles and miles of eighteen-wheeled semis leapfrogging each other while death-defying sports cars zigged in and out between, punctuated by the long strip mall towns of Victorville and Barstow. Overhead, past the towns, more stars than he had ever seen lit up the sky, among which an orange one Jim took to be Mars glared down on him, and his thoughts turned to the instruments of war and mayhem in the trunk, and he began to think of taking the evil machines and burying them in the wastelands somewhere out beyond Yermo. He pulled off the road at Zzyzyx and pissed on ground sparkling in the starlight; the vast lonely desert was salted with broken glass. Unseen critters buzzed warnings all around. Up and down the off ramp, big rigs had pulled over for the night, while several teenagers were draped over an old Cadillac, drinking beer in each other's arms. As Jim zipped up, he spotted a new SUV with tinted windows idling a hundred yards behind his car and wondered if it was Kenny.

He got back on the Fifteen and soon hit Baker. The world's tallest thermometer showed ninety-five not long after midnight. Jim pulled into a gas station, gassed up, and moved on again into the dark Mojave, pitch-black silhouettes of geological formations jutting up into the Milky Way. He wondered if he would sense a chill, a rush of wind, some glowing figure on the side of the road that would tell him the place where his mother had passed into the eternity of never coming back.

The stars faded over a hill out the side window, like the sun might be coming up. Around a bend, the reason revealed itself: a lake of lights on the dark desert floor. It took much longer to reach it than it seemed it should have; like a mirage, the glowing lake seemed always to keep its distance.

"It's a wicked place." His father broke a long silence. Jim was with his dad the only other time he'd come this way, about ten years old, half-asleep. "I hope you never get into drugs, or alcohol, or gambling, boy. They ruin lives." He took a long drag of his Marlboro. "Your uncle Johnny never was any good at resisting temptation. I ought to just leave him in jail, but he's family, son. You've got to do right by your family, no matter what." Jim thought they were there, but it was only Stateline. It was a long time yet, before they got out of the car in Vegas at AAAA Bail Bonds. Two red aces, two black.

"Never give an addict money directly," his father said, writing a check. "Even family. You give them food. You try to get them help. We can get Uncle Johnny checked into a rehab program if we post bail."

They brought the bond to a drawer in a glass and steel mesh cage at the jail a few blocks away. A woman deputy instructed them through a microphone to sit down among rows of fiberglass seats bolted to the concrete floor among the concrete pillars. Among the dozen or so other people, there was little talking, least of all between Jim and his dad, and Jimmy began to imagine all the coughing he heard was conversation in another language. Hours passed. Occasionally persons were discharged from a metal door in the concrete and would exit with whoever, if anyone, had been waiting for them. New arrivals continuously replaced departed waiters, and soon outpaced them. By sun-up, the room was nearly full, and Jim saw his dad look worriedly into his box of cigarettes and shake it. Jim was hungry, but he dared not say so. At first his father had paced the room and looked up whenever the steel door opened, but now he was half-slumped in a chair and his gaze did not shift at the sound of the door opening, until finally, "Crack. James Crack." Jim's father stood and crossed to two uniformed deputies. "Mr. Crack, will you come with us please, sir."

"Should my son come?"

"That's up to you, sir."

PART 2: EXTERNAL COMBUSTION

"What's this about?"

"It's about your brother."

"Is he okay?"

She shook her head. "No, sir, he isn't."

He was dead. Loud, laughing, lunatic-happy Uncle Johnny hung himself in jail. They spent the rest of the day filling out forms and waiting at counters. Jim waited outside the morgue. Years later, he would marvel that his dad and uncle were brothers, they were such opposites. "My brother didn't come back from Vietnam right," Jim had overheard his father say from time to time when the subject came up. He had also picked up snippets of conversation about bruises on the body, and an autopsy report that did not agree with what his father had seen in the morgue that day. On the way back from Vegas that night, his father's expression was grimly set, the oncoming lights etched the lines even deeper into his face. Looking back on it, Jim thought, his expression hadn't changed since.

At Primm, Nevada, Jim pulled off the highway. He stopped in front of Whiskey Pete's and scanned the parking lot. A sea of cars stretched to the darkness beyond the lighting. Very few people seemed to be coming or going. He saw no sign of the SUV with the tinted windows. He didn't know how much it would cost to call back to Newport Beach, but he was pretty sure he was going to need more quarters than what he had. Not wanting to risk leaving the car unguarded long enough to enter the casino to get quarters and make the call, he drove to a gas station on the outskirts of the parking lot. The gas station was lit up, but no one was there. He turned off the engine and waited. A cement mixer stopped at the diesel pump, and the driver put a card into a slot and gassed up.

"What, is the whole station automated?" Jim called to him.

"Yeah, this guy leaves around midnight and doesn't come back 'til about six."

"I need change."

The driver chuckled. "Yonder casino will have plenty o' that."

Jim was afraid that if he parked the car, Kenny would be able to drive right up to it after Jim had gone in, open the trunk, and take the guns without Jim getting paid for the job. He drove to the valet. "I'm just going in to make a phone call, and I'll be right out."

The valet appraised the car. "We can't park you here." With a wave of his arm he seemed to indicate the Porsches and Benzes parked up front and that Jim's piece-of-crap Chrysler did not belong among them. "We'll have to take it to the garage." Then the car would be just as unattended as if he parked it himself, but farther away, Jim concluded. He would take his chances on the parking lot.

Jim found a space as close to the front of Whiskey Pete's as he could, and went in through the first set of glass doors. He stopped and looked out at the car for many long minutes to see if anyone approached it. Maybe Kenny wasn't following him at all. Maybe they just told him that so he wouldn't try anything funny. Still, he'd get change and make the phone call as quickly as possible. A blast of cigarette smoke hit him in the face as he went through the second bank of doors into the sonic overload of ching-ching-chinging slot machines and intermittent electronic bugling, like cavalry charging to slaughter a village of Utes. Through a maze of twirling cherries and insomniac old ladies, Jim wandered in search of change for a pay phone, and soon came across a prune-faced, androgynous creature with the name plate of NGUYEN WESTMINISTER, CA who turned a five-dollar bill into quarters and nickels. He asked her about a pay phone and he or she jabbered something and pointed. The rows of slot machines angled him in another direction, and he soon came out to a long island of card tables. A smatter of cheers rose from one of the tables when Jim finally found a pay phone near a cashier's cage where little old ladies waited in line with big plastic cups full of coins. He dialed the number and dropped the coins right into the slot. No answer. What time was it? The casino was conspicuously absent clocks. He dialed again; still

PART 2: EXTERNAL COMBUSTION

no answer. *This is insane. Bury the guns and go to Utah. Find some honest way to get set up there. Yeah, right. Get a job at McDonald's and live in a car with no roof.*

He went back to the car and sat. He checked the glove box. The pistol was still there. He leaned forward and hugged the steering wheel. His wrist and side ached. He swigged some more Nyquil past his still raw uvula. He closed his eyes. There were bloodied bodies everywhere. He felt condemned. Clunk. He opened his eyes. A scraggly-haired head moved furtively among the cars. Some tweaking speed freak on a blackjack cold streak, trying to scrounge up enough stake for another gram or two seemed to be checking for unlocked doors. Jim tried to keep an eye on him, but his eyelids were heavy, and his chin could not withstand the gravity of his chest.

They were after him. He was on the run and dying of thirst. He came to puddles, pools, lakes—they all evaporated, turned to sand—click-

—a faraway click—no, not so far away—a nearby squeak: The tweaker!

—the gun! Jim rushed back into himself, shot out his hand and slammed the glove box door on the speed freak's fingers. BANG! The gun went off and so did the tweaker, darting between cars until he had disappeared into the parking lot.

Jim's body tingled, as if all his limbs were asleep. For a split second, he thought he'd been hit, and he checked his shirt for blood. *Shit.* There was nothing, but still.... *Shit.* The gun smoked cordite. A hole went out the back corner of the glove box. Jim stuck his finger in it. *Shit.* Security would be coming. Gunshots fired. Cops. *Where did that bullet go? Was it in the engine? Did it ricochet around? Shit.* He turned the key and the car started. A golf cart with a flashing orange light was coming through the parking lot. Jim backed out, trying not to screech the wheels. *Shit.* He followed the exit signs out of the parking lot. *Shit.* He needed to look under the hood. He couldn't risk getting stranded

251

CAR TROUBLE

with all those guns. He needed to get away, though. Shit. He pulled onto the Fifteen North, toward Vegas. *Shit. Rattlers. Hissing. Vipers. Is that hissing I hear? Asps. What is that hissing? Serpents. Or just my imagination? Running away with me. I need some clean, well-lighted place to look under the hood. No, no, no. It doesn't need to be clean. Just well-lighted. And hidden, preferably.*

He pulled off at some pulsating neon riverboat out in the desert and parked beneath a light in the parking lot. Under the hood, he could make out nothing of the bullet's whereabouts in the weird gallery of shadows cast by the seething glow of the riverboat. Even with the engine off, he thought he detected a faint hissing and a burning acrid smell. He slammed the hood down and stomped into the glimmering, throbbing boat. And came straight back out to see if anyone approached the car. Then went in, and came out, and went in and waited a half a minute and came out and went in and waited a minute and came out and went in. The chiming of the machines seemed muted in air so heavy with smoke and sullen desultoriness. After a U-turning and U-turning time of navigating the psychedelic Sargasso of carpet, he eventually located a pay phone. This time, Ben picked up.

"I'm here," Jim said.

"Where?"

"Jean."

He heard a sound like fingers rubbing a stubbly chin. "You need to get to Vegas."

Jim didn't argue that the deal had been to just get over state line. He didn't feel like sharing his fears about the condition of the car, that someone had shot the engine, that there might be a bullet lodged in the engine block, or a punctured radiator or something. "Then what?" he said.

"Go to the Glass Pool Motel. Get off at Tropicana, and it's right there on Las Vegas Boulevard. Get a room and call me in the morning. Ollie will come to you there."

PART 2: EXTERNAL COMBUSTION

Jim wondered if he would remember all that. "Where's Kenny?" he said.

"I don't know. He might have turned back at the state line. He might be watching you right now. I've got to tell you, chum, I'm pretty far down the chain of command now. Just get to Vegas and call me." He hung up.

There was nothing to do but press on. Like a Lee nail. Onward. Onward Christian soldier. Onward agnostic soldier. Heretic soldier. From summit to summit he coaxed the old Chrylser through the night, watching the needle on the temperature gauge creep into the red zone as a burning odor wafted into his nostrils and skittered up his olfactory nerve like a pair of ragged claws.

The adrenaline surge from the gun struggle was draining away, leaving his blood heavy with exhaustion. The buffeting wind became like a blanket, the headrest a pillow, and Jim's mind began to play movies on the road; the dashed white lines flickered by like the frames of a film. His mother shuffled to him in her ghostly nightgown, leaned over the bed, and kissed him, but when she pulled away, her eyes were gone black, the red of her hair was dark and wet and plastered against her face; it began to run down her neck in bloody rivulets; her skin grayed and peeled, and Jim screamed silently and tried still to hold her to him before she rotted and turned to dust, and then the bed was shaking, shaking, and he awoke with the car thumping along the rough shoulder, and he yanked the wheel hard back onto the road, sweaty with sad terror.

He shook his head and cranked up the radio. "Are you disillusioned and confused by your life? Do you find that you are beset by troubles? Do you feel that there is nowhere to turn? Then you need Jesus Christ, my friend. For the solutions to all your troubles are in the scriptures, the word of God. When you accept Jesus into your heart as your personal savior, then you will find success. Then you will find prosperity. Then you will find joy."

Jim let go of the steering wheel and held his arms out, palms up. "Awright. Have at me, Jesus. Come on in, Jesus. Enter my heart." He closed his eyes and put his head back. "Save me, Jesus," he murmured and stole a glance at the passenger's seat. Nothing. No one. The car had drifted into the oncoming lane, and he steered back across the double yellow line with the roar of a semi's horn doppling past. "I guess because I haven't studied the word of God," he said to the wind. "How are you supposed to know it's the word of God?" he asked the man on the radio. "Men wrote it, right? How do we know they were telling the truth? I wish Jesus would appear to me and do some miracles like He did for Matthew, Mark, Luke, and those other guys. They had it easy; the guy was right in front of them turning water into wine. All we get is the frickin' radio and some two-thousand-year-old book, and a world of people who can't agree on any of it."

"Reason is worldly and demonic," the radio said.

"Whatever," Jim muttered and snapped the radio off. He was tired. His eyes felt dry. He saw, or thought he saw, vaporous phantoms creeping out from under the hood as he ascended the final grade, he hoped, before Las Vegas. He shook his head violently. The car slowed, and his injured ankle protested its agony as he pushed the gas pedal to the floor. The engine groaned and cut out completely as he crested the summit and saw against the dawn the glitter of Vegas sprawled out on the floor of the valley below. It was bigger than he had remembered. The edge of the city was like a shore of lights along the ocean of darkness beyond. He put the car in neutral and coasted a long while at sixty miles per hour, then fifty, forty, and on down as the highway leveled out. He was schlepping along at about twenty miles an hour as he reached Tropicana and coasted off onto Las Vegas Boulevard, the casino lights raging all down the strip. He might have coasted right into The Glass Pool Motel, except that he had to stop at a red light and ended up pushing the Chrysler into the parking lot, ankle, wrist, and knee screaming.

PART 2: EXTERNAL COMBUSTION

Rooms were twenty-nine bucks, the clerk explained, "but we own the Hotel Malaga right next door, and those rooms are nineteen dollars." Jim took a room at the Malaga. He drove over and parked and was so tired he didn't care if Kenny or anyone broke into the trunk and took the guns without paying him. He almost hoped they would, but he took the pistol from the glove box. He opened the door, went in, put the pistol in the nightstand and the keys on top of that, and fell onto the bed like a chopped-down tree. Exhausted as he was, sleep would not come. Jets at the nearby airport seemed to be using the roof of the motel for a landing strip. The air conditioning in the room was ineffective at best, and he pulled off his clothes and kicked off the sheets. An intensifying laser of white light stabbed into the room through the window; no matter how he arranged the curtains, it always found a way in. He sat on the edge of the bed, dug the number out of his pants on the floor, and called Ben.

"Are you at the motel?"

"I'm at the Malaga, next to the Glass Pool. Number nine."

"Don't go anywhere. Ollie will come to you." Ben hung up.

He sat there wishing he was more of a tobacco smoker. He lay back on the bed and tried jamming pillows into his eyes and ears and fell in and out of a sweaty, claustrophobic sleep. There came the pounding of nails being hammered, of him being sealed alive in a coffin. He was paralyzed with exhaustion and too tired to save himself. He would just lie there, and soon it would be all over. He wondered if he would see his mother. No. No. He pushed against the lid and sat up. Someone was knocking on the motel door.

Jim pulled on his grimy jeans and opened the door. A short dark guy in dark glasses said, "You Crack?" He walked in. "Nice place. What happened to your head? Butterfly kick ya?" He had a slight accent of some kind. "So, where they at?" He had a short beard and dark, curly hair, and was wearing a polo shirt tucked into pleated slacks and a light sport coat with the sleeves pushed up showing a gold watch on his hairy wrist. He snapped his fingers. "Hey, hey— rise and shine. Wake the fuck up. Where they at?"

"Are you Ollie?" Jim asked.

"Yeah. Whaddaya fucking think? I'm selling fucking Bibles? Where the fuck my guns?" He chewed gum relentlessly, and his head never stopped bobbing.

"In the trunk. Outside."

"These the keys?" He picked them up from the nightstand.

"Yeah." He had a perfumey smell. Cologne or aftershave—Jim never knew the difference; he'd never worn any himself.

Suddenly he got it. Not Ollie, *Ali*.

"Lead the way."

Jim walked out to the car barefoot. The parking lot burned his soles. He thought of Muslim firewalkers, and thought if they could do it, so could he. Ah, but they had a faith he did not. He balanced first on one foot, then on the other, before retreating to the shade of the overhanging roof of the motel, squinting and blinking. Across the parking lot, someone was leaning against an SUV. It was Alonzo, his flaming red hair dull in the brilliant sunshine.

Ali came out to the Chrysler. "This thing ain't booby-trapped, is it?"

"Yeah," Jim said. "I was a demolitions expert in the Green Berets." He began to feel that the most satisfying thing in the world would be to punch the shit out of Ali.

"You open it." Ali threw him the keys.

"Let me get my shoes."

"Yeah, good idea. Fucking nitz."

Jim pulled on his shoes, feeling as if he'd downed a pot of coffee. He went back out to the car where Ali was drumming his fingers on the hood. Jim turned the key, but the trunk wouldn't open.

"Motherfucker." Ali spat, and Jim punched the trunk and it popped open. Ali let out a long whistle and pulled out one of the machine

PART 2: EXTERNAL COMBUSTION

guns. "Ya done good there, Fonzie," he said to Jim. He cocked the gun and sighted down it as a maid came around the corner pushing her cart.

"Shit, dude, the maid," said Jim.

"I don't give a shit about no fucking maid." He flashed Jim a menacing scowl and pointed the gun at the maid, who quickly ducked into one of the rooms. "She won't say anything," he yelled. "Will you, bitch!" Jim wondered about his exact ethnic origin; he was Arab, but he was like a third-generation Sicilian straight out of a Scorsese pic, and maybe some whitey as well—a pale dark man, or a dark pale man, as if he were the offspring of some Irish moll showgirl raped by a lower-echelon Lebanese wise guy. Jim hated him.

"I gotta make a phone call," said Ali. Jim followed him into the room. Ali tossed the AK on the bed, picked up the phone, and dialed. "Hey. It's me. The fucker got 'em...yeah...Just like they said...I know." A long pause ensued in which Ali said nothing. Jim imagined it was the longest Ali had ever listened without saying anything. Finally, he said, "Kay," and hung up. "Let's go."

"Where?"

"We gotta take these babies to another location." He patted the gun and picked it up from the bed.

"When do I get my money?" Jim asked.

"What money?"

Jim felt anger contorting his face.

"Yeah, I'm just bustin' your balls. You'll get it the next place we go."

"I have to take a piss," said Jim.

"Why'n't ya take a bath while you're at it. You stink."

Jim closed the bathroom door behind him feeling more fucked than he had ever felt in a lifetime littered with feelings of fucked. *Just back out now. Tell them they can have the money. No. No. The pistol—get the pistol from the nightstand.*

257

When he went back into the room, Ali was looking in the nightstand drawer. *Shit.* "No Bible," he said to Jim. "Ready, Annie Oakley?"

"Let's go."

"After you."

Jim stepped outside. "What's the plan? Something's wrong with my car, so I mean, I don't know what we're doing exactly."

"What the fuck. You mean you can't make the delivery?"

Anger overtook Jim's fear. "I just did make the fucking delivery. Why don't you just give me my fucking money and put them in your fucking car and be on your way."

Ali's face took on a dangerous edge before breaking into a smile. "So, you do have a nut or two. I heard you did." His voice became flat, indifferent. "Listen. You're nothing. I'll shoot you dead right here and nothing will come of it. Unsolved. They'll say a pimp killed you. Or you can do what you're told. Unnerstand?"

Jim put his hands up. "All right. All right. I'm sorry. I'm just tired."

"Get my guns out of that piece of shit car and put them in the back of mine."

Jim did as he was told. As he loaded the bundle of guns into the back of the SUV, he noticed a shovel on the floor and someone large sitting in the driver's seat. His stomach dropped. When he was done, Ali said, "Now get in the front seat."

"Hold on," said Jim. "I forgot something."

"If you're talking about that .38 you left in the drawer, don't worry about it. I got that for you." He patted a lump under his coat. "Get in." Then he said to Alonzo, "Think you can follow us without fucking anything up?" Alonzo nodded and got into a green sedan.

Jim opened the door of the SUV. Kenny was sitting behind the steering wheel. Jim pulled himself in. Kenny said, "What's up, dumbfuck?"

Jim felt the magnitude of his own stupidity twist a wry smile onto his lips. "I thought you couldn't cross state lines."

"You thought wrong." Kenny crushed his big white fist hard into

PART 2: EXTERNAL COMBUSTION

the side of Jim's head. Jim saw stars and darkness, and the last of his energy drained away.

Ali got in the backseat. "Let's go." The automatic locks snapped shut on the doors as they pulled out onto Las Vegas Boulevard. "We better get a few bottles of water before we get out there. Stop at that gas station." They pulled into a Texaco. "Get four big bottles of Evian." In the reflection of a windshield, Jim saw Ali pull an envelope from his coat pocket and hand a hundred-dollar bill over the seat to Kenny. "Keep the change." They both laughed. Kenny looked at Jim and took the key from the ignition. "Hey, moron! Leave the fucking air on." Ali said. Kenny started the engine again and strolled into the mini-mart.

Jim tried to figure out what to do. Were they going to take him out into the desert to shoot and bury him? Or were they just going somewhere to drop off the guns and pay him his money? Alonzo sat in the idling green sedan off to one side. Jim's Spidey sense was tingling. He was about to open the door and make a run for it when Kenny came out with the water. "Hey," said Ali, "whyn't you go in and get us some candy bars. Get a few Mars bars or something." Kenny muttered and went back into the mini-mart. Jim saw Ali in the reflection in the window unscrew one of the water bottles and tilt it to his mouth. He glugged the water down, tilting the bottle higher and higher. Jim sighed, twisted at the torso, and punched Ali in the Adam's apple as hard as he could.

Ali sputtered, gagging and coughing, and Jim climbed over the seat and punched him hard in the face and then again in the testicles. He took the envelope and the .38 from Ali's coat, opened the door, pushed him out, and pulled it shut.

Kenny came out of the mini-mart unwrapping a Snickers bar, and took a big bite before noticing that Ali was writhing on the ground alongside the SUV. Jim raced Kenny to the driver's door. Lunging back over the seat, he hit the lock button just as Kenny pulled the handle. Jim worked himself into the driver's seat, threw the car into drive, and peeled out of the gas station. Kenny sprinted after him in the side mirror, as Alonzo started the sedan. The street was crawling with pedestrians and clogged with idling cabs advertising various titty shows. Jim drove two wheels up the curb, hitting the horn, revving and braking, to clear the sidewalk of wide-eyed tourists. Kenny caught up, slid across the hood, and pulled on the locked door handle again. He screamed at Jim the profanities of a man versed in jailhouse rage; flecks of spit splattered the window, and Kenny drew back his big fist and punched. Glass showered Jim as he stomped the gas pedal and swung out into the cross traffic, horns blaring and rubber screeching. Kenny, clutching Jim's ripped shirt, fell tumbling into the street.

In the rearview mirror, Alonzo followed onto the sidewalk; at the same time, Kenny got to his feet and sprinted after Jim. Honking madly, Jim took out a stand of sex newspapers along the curb as he pushed by the standing traffic and turned the corner from Las Vegas Boulevard onto Flamingo. Alonzo sped around the corner, fishtailed, and slammed into a taxi, while Kenny came blitzing after Jim on foot. The light up ahead turned green, and Kenny had nearly reached Jim again before the car ahead moved forward and Jim pulled away. In the rearview, Kenny kept coming long after Jim thought he would give up, but finally he slowed to a stop and bent at the waist, panting. Farther back, steam was rising from the crumpled hood of the green sedan, and Jim turned onto the freeway.

He was doing near ninety before his adrenaline subsided enough for him to slow down to the flow of the traffic. Where would he go? If he stayed on the interstate, he could go straight on to Utah. He had the guns, and—the envelope had fallen on the floor between his legs. He picked it up and looked in. Hundred-dollar bills. At least fifty of them. He tried to think. They might call the police and report the car stolen. Would they risk losing the guns? More likely they were calling some other thugs and telling them to get on the freeway and get after the SUV. Even if they got on the freeway five minutes after him,

PART 2: EXTERNAL COMBUSTION

finding him would be nearly impossible. Wouldn't it? A motorcycle in the rearview mirror sent his pulse racing again. Was it a cop? He was approaching a freeway junction and took the 95 north. He couldn't think straight. He knew that the thing to do was to just get off the freeway, stop somewhere, take the money, and leave the car and guns on the side of the road somewhere, and yet he kept driving.

Fifteen minutes later, the freeway crept out of the sprawling suburbs, past vast housing tracts under construction, into tall red hills. He tuned in a news station. The weatherman said to expect unseasonably cool temperatures as a cold front pushed south, but Jim heard nothing about being on the lookout for a stolen forest-green SUV full of machine guns. For long stretches, he was the only vehicle on the highway. Only occasionally a dusty vehicle would come past the other way while Jim held his breath, but the mirrors remained devoid of anything but road and desert. His mind began to leave behind the fact of the arsenal he was carrying, and the trouble he must be in, and he would become full of the enormity of the land around him, but after an hour or more, once then twice, when the road straightened out, he spotted a gleam of metal and glass in the mirror before he rounded a bend or the road dipped, and it would be gone. He tried to assign percentages to the probabilities that it was a cop, cohorts of Ali, or a random vehicle, and he could not determine that any one possibility was more likely than any other. He thought of slowing down to see, but that ultimately made no sense.

It was too late to abandon the car. It was wise, he decided, to stay as far ahead of whoever it was as possible without getting pulled over for speeding by any cop ahead. *Like fleeing Sodom*, he thought, *what's behind me will be my eternal doom if I pause to consider it.* He was doing better than eighty. The needle on the gas gauge was about three-quarters. The highway straightened out again and dropped into a valley so wide, Jim was sure it once had been the floor of an ancient sea. The gleam in the mirror appeared on the ridge and fell steadily into the valley behind him. Was it closer? It had to be at least three or four miles back. He could feel decisions solidifying in him without his participation. No matter what happened, Ali was not getting those guns. If it came to it, Jim knew, like a hundred percent chance of rain, that he would kill and/or be killed before he let that fucker have the guns. He was slightly less clear in his head about what he would do if it were the police who got to him first. Would they confiscate the guns and melt them down? He put a little more pressure on the gas pedal.

Maybe he could get off the road. He remembered Adam telling him once about all the strange lines he saw on the desert floor whenever he flew between SoCal and Salt Lake. "Even in the raggedest country, where the roads are all contorted by geography, there are these impossibly straight lines cut from horizon to horizon. And in other places, in the middle of all this pure nothingness, there's these trails that curl from nowhere to nowhere. Dude, it's a trip." Jim wondered if he could find one of these. He would ditch his pursuers and dump the guns where they would never be found. Dump the god-damned instruments of evil. God-damned guns. That's how they do it. Guns. Guns had enforced man's desecration of himself and the world. Cortez's guns. The cavalry's guns. The National Guard's guns. The mafia's guns. The CIA's guns. The gang-bangers' guns. The cops' guns. All the fucking guns. Weapons to wipeout entire populations, enslave masses, incarcerate or murder anybody opposed to the manifest destiny of concrete and clocks, anyone who opposed the enslavement of humanity to greed.

Oh, shut the hell up, Jimbo. Was it any better when we were killing each other with sticks and stones? Rending each other's flesh with our teeth? How do you fight Nazi'\s with no guns? How do you fight the pro-slavery South without guns? The Romans had no guns and plenty of slaves.

I don't care. No one's getting these guns.

He looked for turn-offs. The road now climbed steadily upward, multi-hued mountains rising on either side. A dirt road zoomed past.

PART 2: EXTERNAL COMBUSTION

He slowed and u-turned., scattering dirt and jackrabbits where the tires met the unpaved shoulder. He worried the cloud of dust would give away his position to whoever it was in the car behind him. He bumped along the hardscrabble road, down and up washes, between tumbleweeds, locusts flitting away ahead of him. A few times the road forked, and he went right or left at random. In places, the way seemed to disappear altogether, and he picked his way through scrub, around boulders, and then the faint outline of a trail would seem to appear again and he would follow that. The shadows began to lean in the direction he was heading. He came to a tall fence topped with razor wire, and it occurred to him that this must be the military installation where they tested atomic bombs. He drove on alongside it. Eventually, the fence turned off in another direction and Jim left it behind, maneuvering the car toward a pass between two mountains. He was crawling along about ten miles an hour, and there was no sign of a road at all anymore. The needle on the gas gauge had fallen to just below half full. No turning back now. Ha ha. He was gripped by wonder and fear. The possibility of his death seemed more real than ever, and with it was a feeling of largeness, as if the sky were filling him and stretching him across the world. Up between the mountains he went farther and farther, unsure of what he was doing except putting his life behind him.

Hours later, the needle had fallen to EMPTY. Still he went farther. It was very late in the afternoon when the car shuddered to a stop, out of gas. A strange euphoria ran through Jim. He opened the car door. The wind blew, stopped, reversed itself, hot and cold back and forth, a cold front moving in, a high-pressure zone falling apart. His ears popped. His sweat chilled. He stepped out of the car and stood and stretched. The dust and locusts were settling down behind him. He turned and stared a long time back the way he had come. The protrusion of the mountain flanks prevented him from seeing very far. He stood watching a while, fifteen minutes perhaps, for a police helicopter. No one was coming.

CAR TROUBLE

He returned to the car and found one of Ali's water bottles and took a swig. Where was he? Some path for hunting bighorn? Some old prospector's trail? He hiked up the side of a hill to try to get a better look if anyone was coming. The way he'd come was not straight enough, nor level enough, to see very far back. The red hues of the land had deepened and darkened as the sun lowered. Something caught his eye. A sun glowing in the rock. A human figure. Jim walked closer. There were also deer, and a spiral, and wavy lines. A traced hand. A petroglyph, it was.

Just beyond it, a hole, about the diameter of a beach ball, had been eroded into an outcropping wall of rock. The reddish sky showed through the hole like some eye in the mountainside. Sunlight fell through the hole onto the rock, imbuing it with a molten glow. He picked through boulders up the slope and knelt in front of it, his breath expanding in his lungs. All around, the wind blew through crevices and brush, a prolonged, moaning chant. Jim pressed his hand to the outline of the hand on the rock, warming his palm even as the chilly wind blew over him. It blew across his eyes, wetting them, and it blew into his open mouth and hitched in his chest. He leaned his forehead against the rock, and a buzz of pain entered through the wound there. He closed his eyes. *This life. This world. I was just born. I am a creation. What else can I have done?* He hugged the rock, sniffling, and turned his cheek to its warmth, feeling blood run down the bridge of his nose. He leaned back, and again had the sensation of the sky filling him. Soon the gleeful, manic fury returned: He knew what he would do. It wasn't his world, but maybe he could pass its test. Maybe he could make his own little difference.

He scrambled down the slope to the car, fumbling for the keys, and opened the trunk. His eyes moved over the guns. He tittered a little and grabbed the shotgun and a box of shells. He'd seen a documentary about Hemingway on TV once, saw him hunting ducks up in Idaho, saw him lay his shotgun over one arm and crack it open. Jim placed

PART 2: EXTERNAL COMBUSTION

the gun in the crook of his elbow and pulled down on the barrels, and it also cracked open. He tore the top off the box of shells. They looked like the right ones. He fitted two of them into the shotgun and snapped it gently shut. The power in the shotgun flowed into his forearms. He felt it in his muscles. A gun could control you. He retreated a few steps and leaned the gun against a boulder. He breathed the sky in and out and searched himself. Ridiculous. The gun couldn't control him. *Get it together, Jimmy boy*. He picked it up again—yes, yes, he felt a surge of euphoric surety about what to do next; he felt release, liberation. He stood and cocked both barrels. It was too funny. He laughed under his breath, and pulled the triggers. Jim staggered back, tripped over a rock and fell to the ground.

He'd never before fired anything more than a BB gun. He'd started shooting cans, until that got old, and one day he took a shot at a dove on a wire in his backyard in Stanton. Heard the BB piff into its feathers. The dove flew out of sight. That night Jim lay awake wondering if he'd killed it and why. Why?

The shotgun's kick had pushed him off balance. Before he had even hit the ground, the passenger's window had imploded in a burst of glass reflecting the sun in a thousand points of light.

The sound of the blast echoed off the mountain walls. He loaded the shotgun again and blasted a couple more rounds into the car's grill. The hood came unlatched and a geyser of steamy water erupted from the radiator. Jim went about reloading and blowing out all the glass. He shot the tires, and the SUV seemed to sink into the earth. He pumped the doors full of jagged holes, whooping and giggling. He'd never felt happier. When the last of the shells had been blasted into the car, he took the shotgun up to the rock with the prehistoric art and limped around to the back of it. He gripped the barrels in both hands and took a Ruthian swing into the boulder. Pain zigzagged through his sore wrist, but the stock of the gun splintered, and he took another swing and it broke clean off. With one more swing, the trigger mechanism shattered, and he dropped the gun into the dust. A lizard did pushups on a nearby rock, and the wind continued to chant. Jim returned to the car. The holes in the metal whistled. He took the M-16 up to the rock and swung it like an ax down onto the rock, bending its muzzle beyond ever firing another shot. The Uzi proved more difficult, but he eventually busted a plate off the firing chamber from which spilled metal coils, pins and tiny fly wheels.

The pistols were more problematic. He threw them against the rocks with little appreciable damage. He wondered if there were enough fumes left in the gas tank to start the car on fire. He hobbled around the area, collecting tumbleweeds and drought-stricken mesquite, and stuffed it through the broken windows into the car. He pulled the Zippo from his pocket. It seemed very long ago that he had found it. He took one of the hundred-dollar bills from the envelope, flicked a flame, and touched a corner of the bill to it. A thin line of smoke came up from the bill. He blew on it slightly, trying to get a flame. Ben Franklin's face browned and bubbled slightly as the bill caught fire.

Jim pushed it into the dried tumbleweed inside the car and pulled out another bill and stuffed it in next to the first, so that it caught fire, and another and another. The fire started to crackle as he fed it hundred after hundred, and a fragrant white smoke began to collect under the roof and flow out the windows. He scurried around the car, collecting more dried brush and dumping it through the windows. The smoke turned thick and foul-smelling as the upholstery caught fire. He went back to the trunk and gathered an armload of pistols and threw them into the blaze one and two at a time. He tried to see if they would melt, or what, but the smoke and the heat became too intense. He backed away. Outside of the ring of heat that the fire provided, he realized with a chill how cold it had become. The smoke stood out darkly against the last band of lavender light where the sun had fallen between the hills. Jim sat on the edge of the fire's warmth.

PART 2: EXTERNAL COMBUSTION

A whooshing and crackle were all that could be heard, and a profound and buoyant serenity filled him, when BLAM! A gunshot. He rolled away, and squatted, searching the dark hills for Ali and Kenny, his skin tingling. BLAM! A firework of sparks shot from the car. *The bullets. Ha. The bullets are blowing up. Ha ha.* The bullets in the car were blowing up. He laughed and inhaled a lungful of smoke and coughed, coughing turning into fits of laughter, then coughing, and laughter again, back and forth.

The next morning, he awoke shivering and wheezing. He tried to shake another puff out of his inhaler, but it was dead gone empty. He tossed it into the smoldering remains of the car. A rosy-gray band of light glowed wanly between the hills in the east. Jim stood and faced it, turned his back to the car, turned his back on everything he knew, and began walking, walking into the wilderness, walking off into the dawn, singing, "Oh give me a home…".

CPSIA information can be obtained
at www.ICGtesting.com
Printed in the USA
FSHW02n2257280618
49839FS